REELING

&

WRITHING

REELING

&

WRITHING

CANDIDA LAWRENCE

MacMurray & Beck
Aspen, Colorado

Printed and bound in the United States of America
Library of Congress Catalog Card Number: 93-080395

All chapter page quotations are from Lewis Carroll, *Through the Looking-Glass, and What Alice Found There*, Macmillan, 1871.

Publisher's Cataloging in Publication
(Prepared by Quality Books Inc.)

Lawrence, Candida.
    Reeling & writing / by Candida Lawrence
    p. cm.
    ISBN 1-878448-60-9

    I. Lawrence, Candida.   2. Women—United States—Biography.   I.
Title.   II. Title: Reeling and writing.

CT274.L38L38 1994
                                                               305.4'092
                                                               QBI93-22178

Reeling & Writing designed by Susan Wasinger

FOR THE CHILDREN, OLIVIA AND TONY

"I only took the regular course."

"What course was that?" inquired Alice.

"Reeling and Writhing, of course,

to begin with,"

the Mock Turtle replied.

"You aren't on any mercy mission this time.

You passed directly through a restricted system,

ignoring numerous warnings and

completely disregarding orders to turn about —

until it no longer mattered."

Darth Vader to Princess Leia

1

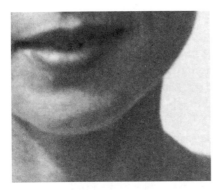

"Once," said the

Mock Turtle at last,

with a deep sigh,

"I was a real turtle."

F OR ME, World War II began in a train station nine months before Pearl Harbor. My Santa Clara cousin Nate, the only son of my mother's "dear sister," had joined the Air Force, a decision prompted by his suspension from San Jose State for brandishing a hammer at the head of his woodshop instructor. He was stiff in his new uniform and looked surprisingly tall and serious. He let me hug him and pulled from behind his back his prized shiny brass bugle. Holding it above his head, he bent down to my ear and said: "You may keep it for me, but see that you polish it, and don't leave it out in the rain."

"But Nate, I don't know how to . . ."

Nate picked up my hand and curled my fingers around the slim middle section of brass. In the dim light of the station, I could see a smudge on the gold where his fingers had been. He kissed my sister Elizabeth on the lips and I remembered the time I had peeked through a crack into Nate's barn and had seen them together in the hay. Why did he kiss Elizabeth when I knew he loved me more? Didn't he always give me a huge flashlight on my birthday? Hadn't we both shaved all the hair off our arms and legs because we wanted to be smooth, and then had to wear long sleeves for a month while it grew back? I'd never told anyone that he used to take bites out of apricots when he worked in the cannery, or that he covered his hand with gasoline and then struck a match in order to find out what combustible meant—*really* meant.

I stood to one side, hugging his bugle, while Nate moved down the line of family. After Elizabeth, he kissed his fiancée, who blubbered and clung, then his mother, with pale, crumpled face. He tipped his hat to his father and stepped onto the train. It was then that I noticed the black windows, and felt an odd sensation of drowsiness pass into me. But there was nothing to worry about. The United States was not at war, and Nate already knew how to fly little planes, upside down, even landing twice (right side up) with a stalled engine, and he told me it was "nothing."

On April 22, I was sitting in my high school geometry room and looked up to see my father (I called him Harry) crossing in front of the class. Harry had never come to my school—it was understood that it was my territory.

"Giershe," Mrs. White said, "pick up your books and go with your father."

Heat climbed up my neck as I stumbled across feet, down the long aisle to the door. The students stared at me. In the empty, high-ceilinged hallway, lined with metal lockers, Harry put his arm around my shoulders.

"Nate is dead. He was killed in a training accident. Nothing left. All burned."

Again I felt that down-pushing sleepiness, as though I were dreaming his words, and waking up was taking a long time.

There was a funeral with guns going off, and an American flag draping a heavy casket (what was in it if he had burned up?), flowers, and Portuguese families sobbing (had they known him, or did they go to all the funerals in Santa Clara?). My uncle cried and acted as though his son had liked him, and then everyone went back to the house where my mother was born and ate a lot of food and recalled the day of Nate's birth. I sat under the walnut tree where Nate had set his hand on fire, the blossom scent so heavy I could not breathe except in short, gaspy intakes.

Harry went to press with a story titled "An American Boy Comes Home."

> The preacher read the burial service. A young sergeant called his squad to attention. They fired the last salute to the young soldier. Behind the trees a bugler played taps. Then the sergeant came forward, slowly lifted the flag from the coffin, folded it carefully and laid the dead boy's cap on it and placed it, oh so gently, on that grieving mother's lap. She bent her head and touched the cap softly and the line of her back and the movement of her arm were heart-breakingly beautiful—as though she were saying, "This is all I have left of my son!" Yes, all she had left, except a forever-enduring pride in the strength and courage of the man she had given to her country. The mothers, too, are brave. And their sons, at last, come home to them.

Everyone said it was the most beautiful thing he'd ever written, but I remembered his blunt bulletin in the school hallway, and began to sniff corruption in all his words.

>>>>>>

After Pearl Harbor, death ceased to be an individual matter and took on the quality of a predator introduced into a tank of minnows. Everyone in the nation suddenly quickened to life. They knit socks, built planes and ships, moved their belongings across mountain ranges, danced with the "boys," wrote letters, learned how to spot planes, blacked out their windows, rationed their sugar and gasoline, read newspapers, dropped German acquaintances, learned the difference between Chinese and Japanese faces, listened to their radios, sent relief packages, planted Victory Gardens, and reelected FDR—again.

Giershe tried to awaken. She went to business school and enrolled in the university. She took classes in the morning, sold war bonds afternoons in a bank, studied at night, and so on, day after day. She knew she was somehow outside the tank, viewing both Death and Life from far away.

A blond fraternity boy named Johnny said to her, his blue eyes mocking: "We have to do it *now*. There isn't time to wait." He wrote from the South Pacific and said he missed most the smell of fresh cotton dresses and the sound of sandals flapping along the pavements between classes. His destroyer went down and his name appeared in a list of "Missing—Presumed Dead" in the *Berkeley Bulletin*.

She stopped dating sailors, and without telling Molly and Harry, vowed to read only religious literature and to turn down all invitations for one year. She fancied the idea of a remote contemplation, a silent vigil over the aquarium. She recited begats and memorized proverbs which rose to the surface of an emptying mind.

In her house with polished hardwood stairs to her bedroom, she taught herself to skip the stairs which creaked, to go down or up soundlessly, to open or close doors as though stealing space were her profession. One night she heard Harry say to Molly:

"How can we worry about someone who is going to school, working, studying at night, and not missing a day? She seems well."

"She's not. She has terrible headaches and doesn't sleep. She reads and reads and sometimes I hear her chanting in the bathroom. She's so silent. She won't go on dates anymore."

"I knew she would get bored with sailors, and she has always been silent. It's nothing new. This morning I got up early and tried to have breakfast with her. I said 'Good morning, Giershe,' and she didn't answer. I said 'Shall I squeeze some orange juice for you?' and she didn't answer. I said 'Do you want an egg?' and she screamed at me, *mimicked* me. And stamped out the back door without eating. I went after her and she turned on me and said 'I do *not* want to talk in the morning. I especially do *not* want to talk to *you* in the morning! If you're going to have breakfast at the same time, then I'll get up earlier and leave earlier, in the dark!' So the hell with her. It was an outrageous outburst!"

"Yes, Harry. I'll try to talk with her."

"Don't try on my account. She will have to apologize to me. That's all there is to it. She cannot live in this house and behave in that manner!"

"Oh Harry—no—I don't want her to move out, and she would, you know. She won't apologize, you know that."

"*Never* in her life has she apologized! Don't I know it!"

Giershe heard the snap of his briefcase.

"Have *you*, Harry? Have you?"
She heard the door slam.

>———>———>

In March 1945, Giershe married an extractor of plutonium. In August—
Hiroshima, Nagasaki. He wept. Even before the marriage ceremony, she had
nightmares about sitting on a porch with him in their old age in identical
rocking chairs, he with his muffler on (he got colds easily) and one of them
saying: "Strange, isn't it, that it's warm so late in September . . . but there *is* a
nip in the air. . . ."

She convinced herself and her nice, hardworking husband that she should
return to college and "finish." The veterans of World War II had returned and
were consumed by the moral conflict engendered by having bombed women,
children and historical monuments. They wore their paratrooper jackets like
hair shirts and were finishing their war experience in the most benign atmosphere they could find. School had never been so exciting! They shouted at
professors, sneered at academic pretensions to moral literacy, day after day
dumped guilt in their tweed laps. The U.S. government paid.

One year turned into two and still Giershe did not finish. Every morning
she prepared breakfast for her husband and every evening she returned home
to fix dinner, alternating hamburger with lamb and pork chops. She tried to
tell him of the discussions she had heard, the books she was reading, and the
excitement she was trying to feel. He stopped using a condom and they
hoped for a baby. He always wore pajamas to bed and she wore a pretty
nightie, usually baby blue or pink with frills. She became a graduate student
and began to daydream about Professor F. She signed up in all the courses he
offered and did "brilliantly." He was an older man (by about ten years), very
handsome though small, and his words spilled out of him like notes on an
alto recorder. Once a week she met with him to discuss her readings and during these very proper sessions her heart tried to attack her as she searched for
words to convey her understanding of delicate, wavering abstractions.

One Monday morning, when all the dogs on campus seemed to be in
heat, the grass new-mown and fragrant, the plane trees trimmed, and every
female in cotton and sandals, Giershe ended her conference with these
words: "Could we go make love in your apartment?"

He answered slowly: "We can go to my apartment and lie next to each
other to see if we want to make love. Let me cancel my afternoon appointments."

That springtime in college she learned about being naked in a sunny
apartment, squeezing, wrapping, writhing and sliding until the room had a

new odor and there was no beginning or end. They drank port wine and cooked vile stuff—brains and cottage-cheese pancakes. She could lie on her stomach in the bed and see her parents' house across the canyon. She could watch her tiny mother clean windows or water the garden.

Just before he left for summer vacation, Giershe said: "I'm leaving my husband," and he said: "But I thought you were happily married!"

>——>>——>——>

When Giershe's husband left for a two-month trip to Europe, they cried. She supposed he cried because he wanted to stay with her forever and sit on a porch with her in their old age. She cried because there was nothing she could do about another's pain and pain seemed always to be unevenly distributed.

There were no reasons. Birds leave nests when it's time to fly. They fly when they're ready, when the wings want to flap and the creature needs to glide and soar and seek food alone.

When her father asked her why and she said she didn't know, he called her "lawless." He felt that man was a rational animal and thought women should be included in the definition.

She drifted through the fall of that year. Professor F. returned to the campus with a wife. Sometimes he and Giershe drove to the hills, took walks together, looked for places to lie down where they wouldn't be seen by others on the same quest. She let him do whatever he wanted to do with her on sharp oak leaves which cut into her flesh, and both of them got poison oak in openings where it was not considered polite to scratch. Their meetings were not pleasant but the pain was not acute enough to avoid. And at what point could she say no? At the invitation to lunch, at the suggested drive, on the walk, sitting down, lying down, when? It would pass. Endure it.

She lived in a tiny apartment and had two part-time jobs. She was hostess in a cozy luncheon spot frequented by faculty and their wives. She smiled and led the way to vacant tables, remembered names of regulars, and tried to match the customers with their favorite waitresses. She watched herself behaving like a hostess and felt like a mind hovering over a windup toy.

The second job was grading examination papers for a doleful, good-hearted English professor. He loved Literature so much that sometimes, when he lectured, he wept with the Beauty and Truth of it. Students who could convey a similar fervor in their examination booklets received A's even if their analyses were irrelevant. He didn't care what she did about all the other students who failed even to unite subject with predicate in any predictable fashion. She held office hours during which she discussed with scared students how they might, next time, improve their compositions. The most frequent complaint she heard was the one about how boring the old fool's lectures were, almost as boring as the readings. She felt no sympathy with their snivelings, and took her job seriously. She enjoyed the power and thought it might be pleasant to have a daily captive audience and everyone too frightened to rebel.

Each evening she locked the door of her room and let the procession of ultimately meaningless words march in front of her eyes. She forced herself to read, learn, memorize, and wrote essays which were an artful rearrangement of the words she had read. She had a recurring happy dream of placing cool bare feet in cold sand, dodging the waves, sprinting into the surf and letting it cascade over her, green loops of falling water, like arms, embracing her.

>>>>——————

Giershe sat on the davenport (that's what Molly and Harry called it) with her binders and books clutched tightly to her chest. The curtains were closed to keep out the late afternoon sun, and all around her she saw beautiful reminders of Taste, eclectic and satisfying—Oriental rugs, early Chinese bowls, brass fireplace implements, van Gogh and Rivera prints richly framed in silver, cut flowers from her mother's garden placed on mahogany end tables, golds and oranges, blue and turquoise, with a deep orangy red introduced here and there. Books on the bookshelves. Magazines (*House Beautiful, Sunset, Partisan Review, Architectural Forum, New Yorker, New Masses, New Republic, Natural History*) resting neatly on the round oak coffee table, forming a mandala of current thought.

Molly sat down tiredly on the opposite end of the davenport. Giershe could not remember a time when her mother was not tired, and had grown so accustomed to seeing her in this state of body and mind, and to discussing it as though there were a more healthful condition with which to compare it, which there didn't seem to be, that she moved smoothly into the routine, hoping today to get it over with quickly.

"Why don't you put down your books? You look weary. You're staying to dinner, aren't you? We haven't seen you for about ten days, isn't it? I waxed all the floors today, but I think I can put together a simple meal if you'll help."

"No—I'm not staying to dinner. I have to get back. . . . Molly, you remember David Kinnard . . . the student I brought here a few months ago. . . . I'm living with him. I want you to tell Harry, and after he simmers down I'll come talk to both of you together."

"Oh Giershe, no!" Her weary face cracked down the middle, the huge brown eyes filling up with tears.

"Molly—it's hard for me, too— I don't enjoy it but I can't seem to help myself. He's after me all the time, he can't stand it at home, wonders what I'm doing when I'm not with him— It's a mess and the only way we can figure to get our work done is to live together and be honest about it. We love each other so much . . ." Giershe hugged her books and began to rock back and forth.

"Oh dear! I don't think I can tell your father this news. He doesn't like David. *I* don't like him—he's too clever, not honest, he's . . . he's going to hurt you . . . you'll see. . . . He'll just do what he wants with you. . . ."

"Oh Molly, that's so old-fashioned. I can dish it out too, you know. I'm selfish and stubborn, as Harry so often tells me. But we know each other's faults, we want to try to love and be happy together. I don't need your Cassandra talk right now. I need your understanding . . . especially you!"

"Giershe," her mother began, more firmly, "I don't think you know what you're doing. Three months ago you were so glad to be alone and now . . . "

"That was before David. Everything is changed now. Everything! Don't you understand? We love each other!"

Didn't her mother know anything about love? There she sat, so tired and joyless that of course she couldn't know a body's passion. She and Harry probably didn't even make love anymore. Had they ever? The way she and David did—at it for hours and hours, groaning and moaning and out of their heads, till they were too weak to sit up, waiting in half-stupor until they could do it again?

She felt faint and was surprised by a sudden wish to spend the night with her parents, not go back to the apartment where she knew David was waiting for her, not phoning, letting her handle it. It would be so peaceful in the bed upstairs, sweet-smelling sheets, no one feeling her, pushing in and pulling out, triumphing when she came as though it were all his own effort, holding her eyes with his, demanding to know every thought.

"I'm going now. I'll call you tomorrow. Don't worry. . . . It's our life."

"I can't explain myself,

I'm afraid, Sir,"

said Alice,

"because I'm not myself,

you see."

AVID AND GIERSHE were a handsome couple, as they say. He was taut, dark, and compelling. He called her "fey" and beautiful, and caught people in a net of words and energy. She seemed content to be his scenery and grew ever more silent and watchful. She fed all the people trapped in his net, waited for them to go home, tidied up, made love with him afterwards, his heavy limbs pressing into her flesh till she thought she'd slip through the mattress, mashed by springs beneath, her absence not noticed until he felt a need for a cup of coffee in the morning.

Each morning she would awaken on an edge, a view of neutral floor below her, David's arm and leaden leg stapling her securely, a sour, overripe, fishy odor rising from sheets and bodies. The best way to get out of bed was to wiggle a half-inch over the edge, descend to the floor on all fours and then scoot into the shower. Even there, she might have company, if he could rouse himself in time. If she hurried through the shower, she would have an hour to herself sitting on the fire escape in the sun, drying the hair which had to be washed every day now because of the smells. It was growing ("All women should have long hair") and its honeyed sheen gave her fresh pleasure each morning.

Every day, David and Giershe talked about how unhappy and how happy they were with each other. He insisted that she find the words to express every twitch in her head and if she failed, or balked, which she often did, he was ever ready with a word pattern of his own to fill the void. Events slid out of existence and into word storage so swiftly that déjà vu was a daily occurrence.

They were seldom apart, and quarreled much of their time together. They quarreled about the following subjects:

1. Her family—were their motives pure?
2. His family—were they uniquely evil, splendidly good, or both?
3. Should he get a divorce immediately or wait until tempers had cooled?
4. Should he sleep with his ex-wife-to-be to make her feel better?
5. Was Giershe's wish to spend an afternoon walking alone in the hills actually an excuse to meet with someone?
6. If she really did wish to spend time by herself, wasn't that a sign that she didn't really love him after all?
7. Was it a woman's duty to serve her husband three meals a day,

plus a midnight snack, clean the house, do all the laundry at a Laundromat, go to school, and work part-time?

8. Was a preference for silence, occasionally, a withdrawal of love, or a flight into thought of another, or the sign of a poetic sensibility?

9. Money—his and hers and theirs: how to spend what little they had, and who should make the decisions. If he insisted on eating expensive gourmet stuff every day, should she have to pay for it? If she wanted a guitar instead of a new tire, who was right and why?

10. In decorating their apartment, what was beautiful and what was kitsch?

They knew they weren't doing too well at this living-and-loving task, but no one they knew in Berkeley was doing any better. They were the elite, they told each other, and you had to expect a certain amount of mess when you had all those fevered brains jockeying for favor, for power, for love, for perfect orgasms.

In her spare time, Giershe was reading every word of Freud's *Clinical Papers*, David was racing through Wilhelm Reich, and they sometimes stood on a street corner near the campus to observe character armor, or watched in grocery stores to see how people handled bananas. They weren't, after all, responsible for Berkeley civilization and its discontents. It was their duty to climb out of bad marriages and into an enduring union, flying the flag of Fidelity and mutual multiple satisfactions. A man had to be a "good lover" or take himself to an analyst to get reconstructed; a woman aimed at being "good in bed," which meant the daily (at the very least) achievement of bliss. Failing bliss, it was imperative to search out the cause or causes lurking somewhere in the twenty years preceding her condition. This might take her ten years or the rest of her life, but meanwhile she could practice and hope for improvement.

Some of the time at home they worked. David was studying to become a scholar, that most arduous of professions, much misunderstood by laymen (or laywomen). Very few people on earth know how much wit, intelligence, sweat, endurance, and cash it requires to take one's place amongst the select community of scholars. One has to have a Calling or one cannot possibly survive the rigors of training. David knew he had a Calling. How he knew this Giershe could never discern, though she tried to find out. Timidly, humbly, she would ask: "David honey, how do you *know* that you want to become a scholar?"

"Giershe honey, you are a very intelligent woman, but you cannot expect to know about these things by standing outside and looking in. You have to be engaged in scholarship before you can understand how important it is for the world that some few qualified people devote their lives to it."

"But David honey, *how* is it important to the world? I remember that you told me that scholars were like ferrets, that they steal from other scholars throughout the world, and base their reputations on the quality of the thievery. They have to be very clever to steal just the right piece from another scholar so that it will fit into their own construction, but—of what importance is this to me?"

"That was a joke! Isn't it amazing how women take everything personally and cast aside the most momentous of Man's undertakings because they cannot see their reflections there?"

He was smiling, but Giershe could tell that he wasn't happy with her memory of ferrets.

"David honey, what about poems, and bridges, and paintings, and novels and airplanes and— Surely Man has done greater things than scholaring?"

She'd gone too far. In a deep, sorrowful voice, he said: "Giershe—if you love me, you will help me in my work. If you try to thwart me, I shall not be able to accomplish what I must. I will not be able to fulfill my obligations to other scholars who believe in me, and I shall be a ruined man. Do you want that?"

"David honey, I was just wondering, just asking. Go back to work."

>>>>>

"David, please, I don't want you to go! You don't have to go! The divorce can be arranged by lawyers—*why* are you going? I don't think I can stand it if you go!"

Giershe was sitting on their rumpled king-size bed, hugging her knees. She was naked. Drying tears stained her face. Her hair was a tangle. Semen was caking on one leg, puckering her skin; the sheet was crusted beneath her.

David was spiffy-clean from a shower, calmly selecting clothes from the closet, laying them neatly in a suitcase. He always handled his own possessions with loving precision. The undershorts he was wearing were smooth with ironed creases exactly in front and rear, like short trousers.

"Giershe, we've gone over this many times. We agreed that I should go north to see her and my parents and the baby. I have to tell her in person that I'm taking you east with me. I can't let a lawyer tell her. And I have to convince my parents that I know what I'm doing." David put his arms around her, but his eyes were on the closet, and he was still thinking about his trip. She pulled away.

"Are you going to sleep with her? Is that part of your plan to get free of Nancy? If you do, maybe she'll get pregnant again like the first time, and you won't know if the baby is yours again, and then what?"

Giershe knew that this attack was like turning an eggbeater in a stomach wound, but she didn't care. He bit his lip, but didn't answer.

"Well, are you? Answer me!"

"I don't know what the sleeping arrangements will be. I don't *intend* to sleep with her, or even if she would want to. I'm not going to cause a ruckus about something that doesn't matter. It's going to be hard enough as it is."

He put four pairs of carefully rolled socks, hand knit by Nancy, into the suitcase.

"David, what about me? What am I supposed to do while you're gone? Thinking about you in bed with her, making love to her, eating her food, all one big happy reunion with your family! I don't know if I can live through it!"

"Giershe honey, I *know* how miserable you're going to be. I wish I didn't have to do this, but that part of my life is ending and I want to do what I can to make it a less . . . agonizing . . . experience for—Nancy. I'm only going to be gone four days. You have your Lit. paper to finish. If you don't finish it, you'll flunk and even though you won't be going to school in the east, there's no point in flunking a course into which you've already put such good work. The last draft of my seminar paper is ready for typing and you said you'd type it for me. We have to start packing—you can get boxes and begin that nasty job. You can visit your family—you're always wanting to and complaining that we never see them. I'll call you every night and say good night."

"I won't answer the phone. You'll have to wonder where I am, and I hope you suffer!"

David resumed his packing. Giershe pulled the sheet over her body and buried her face in a pillow. She did not move when David kissed her head good-bye. She heard the apartment door open and close. She heard the motor start up. He always ran the car three minutes before engaging the gears. She sprang from the bed, grabbed her bathrobe, and ran out to the driveway, screaming "David! David! Come back!" but he had not waited three minutes. The driveway was a sunny desert, and the woman next door was staring at her from an open window.

>>>———

On the first day of David's absence, Giershe slept. On the second day, she woke up feeling better. She showered, got dressed, and changed the bed. She ate toast, a soft-boiled egg, and drank a glass of fresh orange juice. She took her coffee out onto the fire escape. The sun felt delicious, the coffee smelled better than any coffee had ever smelled. She stretched and flexed her right leg, then her left, coaxed a stray Siamese cat to her side and hugged him until he struggled to free himself. She felt ashamed. She'd lost self-respect some-where in the last year, and the best place to find it was right there on the fire escape in the sunshine. The cat had it. He wasn't going to let himself be squeezed to death.

She walked back into the apartment. David's possessions were precisely placed wherever she looked. His typewriter (where was hers?) sat front-center on his desk. His books filled the bookshelves (her books were in boxes in the closet). His desk was covered with his work (she had no desk, and used the kitchen table when she had to have a workspace). His ugly square-shaped yellow crockery, place settings for six, filled the kitchen cabinets (her Mexican dishes were stored with her parents). His Piranesi prints were on the walls (her Murillo and Rivera were wrapped in sheets under the bed).

David was forever telling her she should act out her anger, that she was damaging her stomach with her migraines, and instead of turning fury against herself, she should cry, scream, throw something. In the year she had lived with him, she had been trying to learn how to be angry. His analysis made sense. She recalled a Sturgeon story in which the weapon that could kill an enemy was the contents of one's own stomach. She ought to try vomiting on him instead of down the toilet. She could now cry easily. She could scream, but it hurt her throat and disturbed the neighbors. She had thrown all of his Schoenwald china cups and saucers, full or empty, either at him, or at the windows, open or closed.

She opened the deep drawer of his desk where he kept all his secret letters in a folder marked "Petrine Supremacy" (oh—he was so funny!). She ripped up all the devoted, current letters from Nancy, letters from a former girlfriend, pictures of Nancy and others, some of them nude, and the loving letters from his ghastly mother. She allowed the moral lectures from his father to remain whole. She let the shreds rain down over all the other folders. She closed the drawer.

With eager hands, she mixed and crumpled all the papers on top of his desk, especially the pile she was supposed to type for him. She didn't tear anything. No sense forcing him to do slow work all over again—he was already enough of a Penelope. Every page was numbered. David never typed a page without first putting a number at the top.

She felt better with each rip, each crumple. She eyed his precious eleventh edition of the *Encyclopaedia Britannica* with red-leather binding and pages of tissue-thin india paper. The only way to separate the pages so that you could read them was very carefully to insert a needle point in the middle of a page, and gently pull. He would never allow her to do this because she got so impatient. Whenever she had to look up something, she had to ask him to do his needlework. She chose the F volume, for "fuck," opened it at random, pulled out a page on "fungus," and left it lying on top of the set.

She buried the telephone beneath three pillows.

On the third day, Giershe worked all day on her term paper "The Political Novel." She rewrote all the parts David had helped her with, restoring her own simplicities to the prose. She was typing at the kitchen table when David unlocked the front door, a day early. She had not heard his car, or his footsteps on the stairs. He stood in the doorway looking confused, but soon recovered his poise and rushed to her, saying "Giershe! Honey! How I have missed you!"

>>————>>————>>

And thus they wrestled by day and by night. Should they travel on together, or go their different ways? David had to go across the broad land to a better climate for apprentice workers. Giershe could be his helpmate in that distant place, or she could remain in Hometown in the state of California.

She looked and looked for her misplaced sense of direction, knew she'd put it somewhere, but where? She accused David of hiding it from her. They looked beneath every possession, hers, his, and theirs, but found nothing. She asked her parents, but Molly wouldn't say, and Harry insisted she'd never had one. David argued that she'd be more likely to find it if she looked in more places. There were too many people in Hometown who had lost the same thing, and if they chanced upon hers, they might take it as their own, and, in fact, it was thus that there had come to be a shortage.

This made sense to her. She would go with him, and surely she would find it along the way.

3

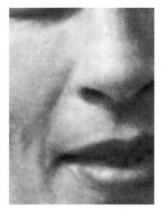

"Who in the

world am I?

That's *the*

great puzzle!"

PRESTIGE UNIVERSITY was in the state of New Jersey. It was very far from the state of California and offered Gothic buildings, dogwood, sycamore, magnolia, much grass, red and yellow leaves in fall, green leaves in spring. Natives of the town had no word for picnic because there had never been a day in its history when the weather had allowed time enough to decide, pack up, get there, lay it out, eat, pack up again, and go home. The annual rainfall was up there with rain forests. The town had a natural outdoor ice rink usable January through March, and during the summer, if you went barefoot, orchids could grow in the environment between your toes.

Still, the place was ideal for both master and apprentice scholars. In fact, it was planned for their pleasure and industry, but shared with other rational communities (prisons, hospitals, the armed forces and insane asylums) an indifference to the baggage the inmates might want to bring with them. Wives, for instance. The scholar who was lucky enough to belong to Prestige's community of scholars was not expected to live the life of an ordinary citizen. He would not have time for a job, for dalliance, for setting up housekeeping, for writing his mother, scarcely even time for eating, sleeping, bathing, toileting. The race was to the dogged. He had to keep his knives sharp, for his first duty was to seek out and injure other, less worthy apprentices. There was talk that a young man who was paying alimony to a former wife and had a second wife in tow lacked the requisite detachment from the world necessary to succeed in his chosen profession. Community criticism was withdrawn, however, when it became apparent that an apprentice scholar with a wife could put her to work at a tedious, low-paying job and set her to cooking, housekeeping, laundering, painting digs, running errands, and relieving tensions at night.

Giershe had been east about a year when Rebecca invited her to drive to a nearby city. There had been a little trouble with David in getting free on a Saturday morning. He didn't have anything special planned for them to do together, and he couldn't explain why he thought it "unwise" to have an outing with Rebecca. It wasn't as if she did this kind of thing often, or ever. She had no friends at Prestige and was far too busy with job and house and husband to seek company. There was too much company in her life as it was, she felt, and another scholar's wife was not her idea of fun. She couldn't for the life of her remember what it was that had given her pleasure in the past, so far away and long ago did it seem that she had walked through hills in benign sunshine or danced a jig in innocent joy. She told herself that she loved David and that they were preparing a future together, but it all seemed quite sad. If love was a sharing of pain, then they surely loved each other.

Rebecca claimed Giershe at the door of the Kinnards' barracks house and turned away David's questions about their outing with the mysterious smile she used whenever David tried to pry into areas she'd staked out as "purely feminine matters." Giershe never knew what she meant. They drove away with David posed in the doorway, looking suspicious and gloomy.

Rebecca was the princess of Prestige. She had the largest breasts, the slopingest white shoulders, the tiniest waist, the broadest hips, the stringiest black hair, the thinnest mouth, and the most devious eyes Giershe had ever seen. She glided into a room on the highest heels and all the clothes she draped on this body were hopeless, together or separately. Her breasts were always flopping almost out of her sweater, her hips bulged the seams of ill-fitting skirts, her hair escaped barrettes and clung to a cheek in listless disarray. Her lipstick outlined lips that weren't there, her mascara was apparently applied with a spoon, and her stockings were usually crooked, mismatched, and snagged. Everyone agreed she was beautiful. It was those breasts. Just being in the same room with her made Giershe feel that her own boyish body should be sent away for reupholstering.

"Where are we going?" Giershe asked as soon as they'd left town and were picking up speed on the turnpike.

"I have an appointment with a psychiatrist and that's where we're going," Rebecca answered promptly. This was the shortest and straightest answer she'd ever given to a direct question.

"For you or for me? Aren't there any psychiatrists around Prestige?"

"I don't want anyone to know that I have an appointment. It's better this way. It must be secret . . . It would hurt him so much. I love him so much."

"Who? The psychiatrist? I wish you would speak more plainly to me. I don't have your *summa cum* and you have to spell it out for me."

"Oh Giershe, you don't need a *summa*. You have everything—David, love, a brilliant future ahead of you."

"And you have Irving, love, a brilliant future ahead of you. We both should be happy forever with so many riches and in that case why are we headed for a psychiatrist?" Giershe reminded herself to go easy on the sarcasm. She didn't trust Rebecca with any hard information about her life with David.

"Why did you hurt me so much last weekend? You know how much I love you. Why did you hurt David and Irving?" Rebecca reached across the seat to pat Giershe's hand, which Giershe withdrew, pretending to adjust a bobby pin.

That word "love," thought Giershe, is beginning to make me ill. Almost as bad were the words "hurt" and "need." She knew Rebecca was talking about having been a guest with husband Irving at the Kinnards'. While Giershe was fixing the super-gourmet dinner she had noticed that Rebecca, half-clad as usual, was leaning against David on the couch, her thigh pressed against his, while the two of them ogled an art book. Irving was pacing the floor giving a speech about Napoleon, not noticing the obvious. Giershe had taken a highball from the tray she was passing and had poured it over Rebecca's head, into her lap, all over the Skira art book. She had said: "Rebecca, if you want any of this very troublesome dinner, please move your thigh away from David," and had marched back into the kitchen.

It had been so quiet afterwards. Irving stopped pacing, Rebecca moved over, David got a towel from the bathroom and handed it to her. She mopped herself, the book, the floor. And somehow they had trudged through the evening, which included hugs all around as they were leaving, in the usual demonstration of how much they all loved one another.

In the mammoth scold which followed, David had used the word "childish" several hundred times, followed by "outrageous lack of trust," "rupture of the fragile fabric of friendship," "extreme rudeness," "breach of manners," and "breaking code of hospitality" approximately fifty times each. And every time he said "childish," Giershe would start to laugh again, spluttering "If you could have seen your face—and hers—and Irving's— Oh my . . ."

Rebecca, who was a novice driver and couldn't risk one-handed steering, bent her long neck over the Kleenex wrapped around her right hand. Bewildering, Giershe thought, what some people take seriously. "It was an impulse, rude, and I'm sorry so many people were injured by it. I'd rather forget it. It's too nice just riding along with you. Let's not talk about it. I've heard rather too much about it from David."

"David doesn't understand you the way I do. He'll never understand," Rebecca said, her chin high in the air. "Understand" was another word Giershe wanted to cast into a huge word-wastebasket. What on earth could she mean? Giershe slumped down in the seat, slipped off her sandals, put her feet on the dashboard, and watched the telephone poles zip by. She'd be damned if she'd encourage Rebecca. This whole day had been planned by Rebecca for some purpose she wasn't ready to reveal, and it would be quite useless to urge her to get to the point. In Rebecca's mind, getting to the point would be like splattering holy water on your face on a hot day, a tampering with sacred mystery.

Rebecca parked the car on a side street. Giershe had been so busy with the telephone poles she hadn't noticed their exit from the turnpike into a quiet residential neighborhood, interspersed with doctors' offices clustered together around small gardens and lawns.

"Are we here? Do you want me to go in with you?"

"Wait, Giershe." Rebecca took Giershe's hand again, and this time, although her touch was usually gentle and caressing, she was squeezing hard. Her nails were digging into Giershe's palm. "You must never tell anyone what I'm about to say to you. Not David. Especially not David. You must promise!" She was crying, hiccupy sobs knocking her breasts against the steering wheel. Giershe inexpertly stroked her limp hair, waiting for her to continue. "Do you promise?"

"Rebecca—what *is* it? Calm yourself—it can't be so terrible. I can't promise not to tell David. I tell him everything. If I don't tell him he doesn't leave me alone until he knows. It's much too difficult to hide something." She felt chilled.

"Irving . . . He and I . . . Irving has never . . . He and I don't . . . We NEVER DO IT!"

The words were out and she slumped into Giershe's arms. Could she believe it? While she hugged the damp head, face streaked with mascara and yellowish tears, she flipped through Rebecca's history as she knew it. Adoring father, brilliant college performance, Irving's childhood sweetheart, wedding attended by thousands of chattering Jews, wedding trip abroad, interpreters of Freud, wedded bliss at Prestige University, and now this sack in her arms who had to say "do it," couldn't say "make love" or "fuck" or even "sleep with." After a night in bed with David, four or five hours of which had been given over to marital obligations, she had escaped a morning in bed with David in order to sit in a parked car comforting a woman who had been married for four years and had never "done it" with her husband! This was truly rich! Giershe hovered over the car, watching the two female human beings draw apart, search through purses for combs and lipsticks, straighten their skirts, stare blankly ahead.

"Rebecca," she said softly, with sudden unexpected sympathy for the creature beside her, "I'm finding it hard to realize what you're saying to me. May I ask you some questions?"

"I want you to, I need you to ask questions, dear friend."

"You have a big double bed in your house and I know that you and Irving sleep in it. How . . ." Giershe wanted to be sure that she wasn't a victim of a metaphoring mind. Perhaps Rebecca meant "It is *as if* we don't do it." She was capable of that.

"We both lie in bed, he in his pajamas and I in my nightie. We talk about our day. Then he kisses me and tells me how beautiful I am. I kiss him and move closer—and then, you know how he signals me to leave the room, or fix the dinner, or be quiet when he wants to talk . . . well, he signals me to turn over and go to sleep. On our wedding night it was the same."

"SIGNALS? What kind of signal does he give in the dark, or is the light on?" Giershe was urgently curious. She felt she was an anthropologist who had discovered a new, living race of human beings.

"He . . . He pats me on top of my head and kisses my nose . . . Sometimes the signal is kissing my breasts and the second part of the signal is when he turns to the wall and goes to sleep."

"Have you ever discussed with him . . ."

"OH NO! I couldn't hurt him by asking him if . . . I'm afraid of him. But I can't go on. I can't sleep. It shouldn't really matter so much, but I can't help it. I think sometimes of other men and once, in Europe, I betrayed Irving."

"Stop, stop, STOP!" Giershe growled. She grabbed both of Rebecca's hands, gripping them tightly. Her words jumped out of her mouth as fast as she could form them. "You and I, WHAT are we doing? Do you ever ask yourself that? You have brains, I have a few, but you'd never know it to look at us. We slave at crummy office jobs to support David and Irving in their careers and they call it love. We call it love too. We ought to call it slavery. They tell us what to wear, how to behave in public, who we can or cannot see, what we can do on our days off, and how we can help them in our spare time. This they call 'loving' and the worst of it is that I think they really believe it. And what's in it for us? Someday—ye gods, when?—we'll be draped over their arms, the adoring wives of Superscholars, all the life sucked out of us by SLAVERY!" She was pounding Rebecca's knee with her fist.

"Giershe, stop, hush! I've an idea. Let's take all the psychiatrist money I've saved for this visit, go find a great restaurant and eat." Rebecca loved to eat.

"I've a better idea. Let's just head for California and when we run out of money we'll work as hostesses. Or let's go buy some clothes. Let's spend the money on subscriptions to *True Confessions* and send them to all the scholars we know. Let's go to the police station and tell them we're lost, can't remember where we live."

"It's no use, Giershe. I want to go home."

>———>———>

Giershe accused herself of every sort of character disorder. Sometimes she made lists:

1. I am unloving.
2. I am a lousy housekeeper.
3. I am a lousy cook.
4. I am not "good in bed," because no matter how well I perform, I usually wish I were somewhere else.

5. I do not value David's work.
6. I do not believe I am beautiful.
7. I'm too much of a coward to leave David.
8. Sometimes I don't wear the diaphragm and don't tell David.
9. I'm a fake.
    a. Sometimes I fake orgasms, even multiple ones.
    b. I hate sucking his penis, and I pretend to submit and be overcome with the thrill of it. Actually I'm ready to vomit.
    c. I create my migraines during which I need not make love, cook dinner, work, or entertain company, and David turns tender and loving in the crisis. Once the migraine comes, it's real enough, but I pretend that I don't want a migraine when in fact I've invited it to replace my life for a while.

It was difficult to find a place to write a list and even more risky to keep it once it was written. Her favorite place for writing was in a graveyard on the outskirts of town. She could drive alongside the quiet plots and hide the car behind a grove of cottonwood. In winter she would sit in the car until her fingers were too cold to bend, and in warmer weather she could sit on a tombstone and feel wonderfully decadent. She wanted to tell David that the blacks were buried separately from the whites, but did not wish to reveal her hiding place.

Sometimes, if she worked it just right, she could start off on a Saturday to shop for food, race through the market, then slip into the Presbyterian chapel on her way home, with paper and pencil hidden in her purse. Someone was usually playing Bach on the organ and David, with his catastrophic Catholic-Jewish background, would never think to look for her there. Religion was another quarrel. David maintained that no matter how bad it was before the Reformation, most of civilization's present evils could be traced to Luther. Giershe liked reformers of anything and thought that if people had to believe in a supreme deity, it was a very cozy arrangement to be able to speak to Him directly rather than through intermediaries. Neither went to church except to examine the architecture.

Inside the chapel she sometimes forgot the hour until the light through the stained-glass windows abruptly flickered out, and she had to find her way to the exit by feeling the backs of the pews.

The most unexpected hideaway for writing lists and other secret thoughts came to her in the third and last year David was at Prestige. Rebecca and Irving began going into New York for a weekend once a month. On their way out of town, they would stop to say good-bye and leave perishables, like cooked duck or cold blintzes. The first time they did this, Rebecca glided through the living room and on into the kitchen with the box of food. While she chattered and pushed food around on the counter, she watched Giershe, and when she knew she had her attention she slipped a house key into Giershe's purse and floated out the front door. Giershe always felt compromised and guilty when the key was in her possession. She had never discussed with Rebecca her lists or her wish for a space of her own; she never told Rebecca on Monday whether she had used the key, and Rebecca didn't ask. The one time she entered the house in their absence, she was prompted by an idle desire to snoop. She wandered through the rooms, all of which were messy except the bedroom, opened a few drawers, tried on one of Rebecca's bras and was convulsed by the effect, tried to glide around on spiky heels, succeeded in twisting an ankle, sat on the couch with paper and pencil, but could not write. Her host and hostess were everywhere in the house—their smells, gestures, ghostly imprints in the air.

Was the key a sisterly act, or a trap? If sisterly act, fine. If trap, was she already in it? How was she to know? Damn Rebecca! Always mysterious, and the mystery serving only the purpose of decorating her own existence. She would not use the key again.

She loved those little scraps of paper, "bile bits" she called them, but there was no place to hide them. Molly kept a diary and Harry did not read it. David talked about trust, how important it was that they trust each other, but this meant that she was to tell him every thought in her head, and he would pretend to give her his secrets. He told her about other ladies in his life, always in the past of course, of ways he had defeated opponents in love or career, fairly or crookedly, of misgivings that he had the brains to make it to the top, of infidelities he knew about at Prestige, of his fear that she would leave him for another man.

The secrets she gave him were never the same as the bile bits. She wrote and destroyed, until speaking her mind on paper began to seem synonymous with destruction of self. David searched her purse, her books, her bureau drawers, her shoes, her side of the mattress—looking for a treasonous thought. She never saw him do this, but could feel that he'd been there looking.

Giershe was David's possession and he proudly displayed her when they were in company. He wanted her to wear black, which made her look alluringly tubercular (he said), to stand straight, hold her shoulders back, never frown, wear high heels with smooth stockings. He liked to remark to the person beside him, interrupting everyone's chatter: "Isn't she beautiful?" and then everyone would stop talking and agree with him, with varying degrees of sincerity.

In the diary she could not write, she would have confessed that she liked being possessed, displayed, devoured by this handsome, flamboyant, charming, not-ordinary man; and she would have written a promise to herself that if it took the rest of her life, she would pull out by the roots and expose to killing light that parasitical part of herself which fed on a more powerful human being.

>>>>>

In their fourth year together, they journeyed across the ocean to Germany. It was necessary for all aspiring American scholars to rub elbow patches with foreign scholars whose sophistication and knowledge, everyone agreed, were far superior to their own. David had received a generous stipend, more than enough to pay their heating bills for a year; they had sold their car and household goods for Giershe's passage, and with a little extra money extracted from Molly and Harry, they were assured they could survive comfortably until Giershe found a job.

During the six months preceding departure for foreign shores, Giershe had been playing Russian roulette with David's sperm. She left her diaphragm in the medicine cabinet every other time, and in the natural course of events, she missed a period, began to vomit, put on weight, and grew a mound across her belly.

In their pension room, she sat tentatively on her suitcase. Even with her body stuffed into mittens, stadium boots, three sweaters, maternity skirt sent by Molly, wool socks, tights, and earmuffs, she was cold. The spilled urine around the toilet in the hallway was frozen. There was no defense except the obvious one she'd used so many times:

"I want a child. I knew you would never agree as long as we were having troubles and as long as you were studying. Time is running out. I am almost thirty. I did it. It's done. There will be a baby." She hugged her knees, feeling the mound tucked tightly in against her backbone. How safe it was, inside her, warm and protected!

"How do I know it is my child? I want to *know* when *I* am conceiving a child. It should be *our* decision, it shouldn't be a unilateral trick! Is it my child?"

She felt so tired. It was morning but already she wanted to sleep again. She wished she could drink warm milk, six or seven glasses, and then sleep.

"Answer me! Is it mine?"

"You know it is. How could it be—"

"You had a key to Rebecca's house! Why? What did you do when you went there?"

"I only went there once, for fifteen minutes. I went there to write."

"You mean you plotted with Rebecca to use their house on their weekends out of town, and you *say* you went there to write!"

"I didn't plot with Rebecca. If you'll just calm down, I'll tell you about it. Rebecca gave me a key—I don't know why she did—I didn't ask her for it. Maybe she thought—"

"Are you asking me to believe that Rebecca just slipped a key into your purse and you knew it was the key to her house and that she was inviting you to use it for whatever purposes you had in mind?"

"I went there to write. I only went once. It's not a good place to write."

"You had a perfectly good place to write in your own home. Are you asking me to believe that you needed another place *for writing?*"

"Believe it or not. It's so."

"If you're telling the truth, where is the *writing?*"

"I destroyed it. I didn't want you to read it, and you would have. You don't trust me, and I couldn't tell you that I wanted a place where I could be alone . . . a place to think, not talk, write the troubles . . . and the pleasures . . ." She was feeling weepy. Suddenly David began to hug her. She rested her head on his chest and one hand stroked her head. Her hair was grimy and she wished she could use all the hot water to wash it.

"If you had told me, if you had been honest with me, I would have found a place for you to write. I could have helped you with the style. We could have set up a desk for you in the bedroom. It was foolish of you to conspire with Rebecca against me. I love you and want you to be happy."

>>>>

After the event, if it was an event, she couldn't be sure that she had not dreamed it. Unlike a dream, it was filled with homely detail, like slipping on the icy street and fingers in her vagina; like a dream, it drifted above her and could not be caught and held.

They had started out together on a cold, blustery day in November, with snow and ice on the ground. They did not speak, but David was gentle and kept a firm grip on her arm to keep her from falling—or was it to keep her from running away? They sat side by side in a bus until the end of the line. They walked, pushing against the knife-wind, past rubble, bombed homes, vacant lots, until they came to a small house. The house stood alone, piles of cracked stone on either side of it.

They walked up the path, Giershe slipped, and David helped her go forward (pushing?). He rapped on the door. Nothing. Sound of wind in trees, but there were no trees. It was late afternoon, and already almost dark. He rapped again. The door opened a crack—an old woman's face, kerchief, earmuffs. David said something in German. The old woman led them to a small room in the back of the house, then left them. The room was very cold. There was a white marble table in the center. A gray sheet covered part of the marble, spattered brownish stains on the sheet. They waited a long time and did not speak to each other.

A dirty old man entered, earmuffs, three or four sweaters, eyes with Mongolian fold, pants with frayed cuffs, filthy bedroom slippers over thick wool socks. Words between the men in a language she almost understood. They helped her lie down on top of the dirty sheet. They pulled up her skirt, pulled down her black cotton tights. The old man's dirty head pressed down on her belly, pushed down. He put fingers into her vagina, pushed, poked, searched until she cried out. He did not look at her.

With hand still in place, he looked at David. David bent down. They whispered. She could not understand the words. The words pushed at her, insistent.

> OLD MAN: *Too late. Four or five months.*
> DAVID: *Not too late.*
> OLD MAN: *Risk her life.*
> DAVID: *She is healthy.*

Giershe sat up, crimping the old man's hand against the sheet. He yanked his hand from inside her. He scowled. She put her feet on the floor, pulled up her tights, wrapped her coat around her, and walked slowly through the cold house and out the door. David caught up with her, held her arm, tried to pull her back. She twisted her arm out of his hand and fell. She got up. They went back home the way they had come. They did not speak.

>>>>>

Their first baby, a girl, was stillborn in the spring. That's what the midwife and David and the doctor said. They said they knew it would be dead, and she wouldn't want to see a dead baby, so they put her to sleep for the birth. They were being kind. And Giershe had a dream, the same dream many times that beautiful spring, that they had stolen her baby and sold it to a childless couple.

Everyone was very kind to her, especially David. He couldn't do enough to fill up her emptiness. He even climbed into the hospital bed and made love to her.

Her grief, for a time, consumed her whole life, and yet, perversely, the loss was full payment for all past misdeeds and guilt, and left her a bit of credit to draw on for any misbehavior to come. She felt absurdly light and happy for months afterwards, yielding wholeheartedly to every blooming tulip, every lilting melody, cherishing each friendship offered to her, giving her all to the whole cocksure universe. She was glad to be alive.

Those around her, believing that what goes up must come down, walked on eggs. She knew this and didn't care, couldn't explain her happiness. She got another office job, bicycled to work and home again. They found a pleasant apartment overlooking a river and settled into a life not too different from their life in New Jersey.

While David was ferreting the livelong day, her radiance attracted a young man where she worked. David had to travel to another city for a few days, and while he was gone, she and the young man stayed in a castle in high mountains, and had croissants and coffee served in bed after a sweet night of loving. David returned, and said:

"You have betrayed me! Why?"

"I don't know why. I just did it. No reason. It means nothing."

>>>——

TELEGRAM TO GIERSHE KINNARD:
I LOVE YOU I LOVE YOU I LOVE YOU STOP DON'T CUT HAIR STOP PLEASE PLEASE STOP WRITE DAILY STOP DAVID

New York City
1.XII.1955

DEAREST GIERSHE:

On shipboard I met a French Jewess from Strasbourg, a lush, vital, overbosomed redheaded creature, who seemed to be trying to make half a dozen men simultaneously. I spoke to her a few times—I flashed my wedding ring and maintained a friendly but definite distance. She confessed to me a passion for Napoleon. She had just read a biography of Josephine, she continued, "and don't you seenk eet's terreeble zat a grreat man like Napoleon was so drreadfully eenfluenced by a verry ordinarry woman?" I couldn't answer for a few minutes, for I had just been seized by an epiphany. I had just realized deeply how passionate is the female desire—and how nearly universal—to find a man who cannot be influenced by any woman. It seems almost the prerequisite for total respect.

This madness is missing in men, for while a man may want his woman uninfluenced by other men, he wants a woman susceptible to masculine influence—as personified by himself. I don't intend to minimize the far more important drive—that is, a woman's wish to leave her own indelible mark on a masculine heart. Undoubtedly many women have done outrageous things merely in order to get a reaction—any reaction—from some cool, lumpish or unresponsive male. Which is simply to say: there's a tension, a competition, a conflict between two impulses and two values.

Strangely enough, this rather irrelevant story has a point. When an egoist tells a story, you should always suspect that the first person singular is hidden somewhere. The obvious point is: I AM NAPOLEON. You might be happier, and you would certainly respect me more, if you could not wound me. Unfortunately, I'll never be imperturbable with you. I've poured everything I have, everything I am, into our marriage and into the constant old attempt to bind you completely to me in every possible way. From the very beginning it hasn't worked very well. Like a general who commits his reserves to combat without a thought for tomorrow's battle, I've spent everything. I'm bankrupt. Had I won, I would have been a great lover and a happy husband. But I lost. I'm electrified with pain and at the same time mortally tired from the fact that I've never possessed you as I've wanted and that I never shall. That we've never become one, become the UNIT. It's now clear that I've failed to hold the outposts of your heart, your body, and your mind.

You are literally and absolutely the only woman—away from you I have no sexuality whatsoever. Still, it is intolerable, inconceivable, and impossible to continue as before. I would simply grow smaller and weaker and less, until eventually I would disappear completely—a wasted life, a blasted mind, a spent intelligence, that might have been the wonder of the world. Where are now the conditions for peace, love, and perfect trust? How can you train your imagination, your nerves, and your body, till you have learned to love me constantly, peacefully, and passionately, when I am with you and when I am not?

I love you utterly, my dearest. Write me every day.

Your
David

Giershe idly plucked from his prose eight sets of triplets. She wondered why this habit of David's bothered her so much.

Berkeley
January 1956

DEAR DAUGHTER:

I have just gone out to stand on the roof of the garage and smoke a cigarette and look at the night. Do you remember the beauty of Berkeley seen from our hills? Our road is like a country lane with the hills at our back and the redwood grove to the right and the glittering beauty beneath us spreading out to the water beyond. It was glorious and I never get enough of it. There's a full moon high behind us and it is difficult to remember it is the same moon that is shining over Germany and you. I wonder and wonder what your Christmas was like without David and if there were friends there to make it comfortable for you. Tell us about it. Forgive my delinquencies. I am shamefully neglectful of all I love.

Harry

>>>>>>

When David became a professor, they set up housekeeping in the small town of Centerville in the state of Connecticut. David was employed by Whitfield College and received a paycheck each month. He was very proud to be part of an institution which would allow him to teach the young all the different kinds of scholarship which they could learn to do. They were good children and listened breathlessly, never interrupted, and wrote their parents that he was the most brilliant man they'd ever known.

Giershe had lots of time to polish furniture with Lemon-Glo, cook exotic casseroles, mix highballs for guests, watch wild geese flying south as the leaves fell to brittle ground, and remember to forget to put in her diaphragm half the time, and take it out too soon the other half. This was a much better system than the one she'd previously used, and before the snow began to fall, that first year in Centerville, she was again pregnant.

David was not happy about her new condition. The perfect moment of Fresh Start had not come to them, and he felt cheated. There was a woman in his house who cooked his meals, washed his clothes, made love with him, listened to his words, agreed with him that she was his and his alone, yet slipped away whenever he tried to define her.

"I want to know that there is no one else, that you never even *think* of anyone else." He stared into her eyes.

"I've told you so many times, must I say it again?"

"I don't believe you when you say it. You must find a way to show me that you are not hiding anything from me."

"I can't show you a negative. You have to take one of those 'leaps of faith' you mention so often. After you've taken a leap of faith, you may still be deluded, but you've agreed not to know or worry any longer, and you feel much better. You want to feel better, don't you?" She was trying, not too successfully, to lighten his burden.

"Your levity is unbecoming. It is very clear to me, from your sarcasm, that you cannot answer me honestly, *can* you?"

"It makes me feel stupid to have to answer the same dumb question several times a day, when my answer doesn't satisfy you, and I have no other way to give you what you want. What if I grilled you this way, day after day?"

"I am faithful to you and have always been faithful. You *know* that!"

"Tosh! I know nothing. For all I know you have a bevy of beauties in every town you visit, and a multitude in your imagination."

David picked up his briefcase and left the room.

>>>>>>

The next day, David came home early. He sat down with his briefcase in his lap. He watched her. She was lying on the couch, her hands resting on the tight mound below her waist. She turned her head, smiled at him, and waited for him to smile. He didn't. She gazed lazily at her shoeless feet in thick wool socks. Every morning the skin across her belly felt a little tighter, her breasts heavier, and this afternoon she thought she felt—almost—perhaps—a tiny scurrying deep inside her, a quiver of intention. She wished she could speak to the invisible creature and assure it that it was safe to wake up.

David snapped open his briefcase, ran his fingers precisely over the tops of file folders, found what he was seeking, and slowly brought out two sheets of gleaming white paper, purple carbon between.

"I want you to read this. Tomorrow we'll take it to a bank. You'll sign it there and we'll have it notarized." He handed her the top piece of paper. She read:

I, GIERSHE KINNARD, agree that, in the event of divorce or separation between myself and my husband, DAVID KINNARD, I shall deliver over to his sole custody, until his, her, or their majority, any issue of our Marriage, and further, I, GIERSHE KINNARD, do agree, that from that day forward, until the aforementioned majority, I will not see or communicate with said issue.

Signed: _____ this day _____ in
February, 19__

Witnessed:_____ this day _____ in
February, 19__

She read it twice and then again. She looked down at his polished shoes. She carefully noted the creases in his gabardine officer pants and gazed solemnly at the lump swelling the lower portion of his fly. She wanted to scream, to rip the paper and smash her fists into his naked face. She lay still and tried to erase the violence she felt, to keep it from the precious new being inside her. She let the paper fall to the floor. She raised her head and looked through sparking light to David's face.

"No," her lips said without a sound.

"If you love me and are faithful, you will want to sign it," he began, and as he spoke, the light faded and she closed her eyes.

>>>>>

Olivia pushed herself out of Giershe's dark, safe cavity with very little help from all the assembled experts. One moment it seemed impossible, yet inevitable, like orgasm. She feared she would split into two bloody halves, that nothing could stop this eruption from within. To *give* birth. What nonsense!

"Bear down!" said the blue-eyed doctor. Try to help an avalanche! Try to stop a flood! "Now!" he commanded, and again she tried to make some kind of effort which might be "down," although she was flat on her back with feet in stirrups, and "down" meant nothing. David, in white lab coat and hospital mask, was holding her hand in both of his, letting her dig her fingernails into his palm, soothing, smiling, trying to protect her from pain. He whispered in her ear: "I love you. Try one more time." The white mask tickled. She waited. The splitting began again, and continued. Was she still together, in one piece? David dropped her hand, the doctor got very busy between her legs, and then the furious cry of an infant seemed to suck the air from the room. She tried to sit up; hands pushed her down. David said, "She is perfect! Beautiful!"

The doctor placed Olivia beside her, while nurses cleaned, covered, clucked, smiled. He said, very gently, "Congratulations. You are finally a mother. I'll see you both later on. Rest now," and he squeezed her hand. Giershe was wheeled into the recovery room, and supple, cool hands kneaded her flaccid stomach. She studied Olivia's lips, cheeks, her tiny fingers, and wished she were alone so that she could croon her words:

"*Lovely pink Olivia, you are here now, outside, where there's more room and so much to learn and do. My name is Giershe and your name is Olivia because it's a pretty name. Pretty is not enough. You must fill it with strength so that when someone says, 'Olivia, do this,' you won't have to do it just because they tell you to.*

"*Ah—rosy lips trying to suck. There is no milk yet, but what is there is warm and will taste good. Lots of things will taste good. Try them all. Your hands, long fingers and eensy nails. Will your hands do something useful? Or will they just grow long nails for nail polish and stay smooth to attract? I have important things to show you. There's a place called the ocean where we'll go. The water comes in and then goes out again, in and out, and it makes you feel small and humble, and you want to give thanks for all that bigness and blue, but there's no one to thank. It's just there, like you, like me. There's sand, infinite sand, some wet, some dry, and we'll feel both kinds. We can sing, you and I; we can make up songs to accompany the voice of the ocean. I will carry you with me until you can walk. I will never leave you, not until you want me to. Now, all you have to do is sleep and suck and teach me how to be your mother. I don't know how yet . . . Olivia. . . ."*

Through the flaming days of fall, on into the silent winter, whenever Giershe heard the cry of hunger, she surrendered her body for Olivia's pleasure and nourishment. Her favorite position for nursing was lying on her side beneath a light blanket, with Olivia's curly, red-brown hair tickling her armpit. In deep comfort, she could study her daughter—the inquiring fingers which clutched any flesh she could grab, the sucking mouth, the eyes which had turned sherry brown, the arching, perfectly formed eyebrows, the rounded arm with dimple in the elbow, the sturdy legs with toes flexing—warm, all warm, in dark night with the candle burning, at midday with the phone off the hook, whenever the cry came, the sweetest of alarms.

Sometimes she continued her monologue, or sang the new lullabies she was learning, or she gave herself up to the gentle rise and fall of a distant, rippling orgasm which might accompany Olivia's milking, not urged or looked for, just there, the unexpected linking of the body's pleasures. She remembered all the lying-beside she had done, in so many beds, and all the warring odors rising from bodies which sought to merge—the nicotine, wine, garlic, orange juice, milk, peanut butter, shaving lotion, urine, excrement and sour genital juices, trying to mix and bless like incense at the altar. There was no such conflict with Olivia. Her body gave off the smell of warm milk and baby powder, and when she grew very still, looked puzzled and grunted, Giershe could smell sweet manure laid out on a plot of dark earth beneath the sun.

The more Giershe lay beside her daughter, the harder it was to rise up and go to David, who waited for her in the bedroom, smoking, understanding her new duties but impatient to resume old habits. Each evening, when Olivia had sucked her fill and was deep down in her long night's sleep, Giershe postponed the moment of lifting the baby and placing her in her crib for the night. She made bargains with her guilt. One night she would let herself fall asleep beside Olivia; she knew David would not disturb them, and after waiting for her, would get up, turn off the light in Olivia's room, and return to the bedroom without her. He was too proud to ask her to come to him.

The next night, she would put Olivia in her crib, and go to David. Several hours later, both would get up. Giershe would go downstairs to wash the evening dishes; David would go to his study where he would talk on the phone, smoke, write letters, and brood. He gloomed about her nights away from him, his "enemies" at work, their own past, present and future. She wished she could divide the house into sealed halves with communication by phone on special occasions. She would stuff the cracks with towels so moods couldn't escape.

One day in early spring, Giershe carefully bumped Olivia and the baby carriage down the porch steps. Olivia laughed at each bump. She was sitting up in red knit cap, red sweater, red leggings, and mittens. She kept kicking off her blanket and trying to pull herself erect by hanging onto the side of the carriage. There was a rush of water everywhere, from the ravine at the end of the street, from the dripping trees, the melting gray slush in the streets and front lawn, melting snow gushing off roofs, down the drainpipes, the cold ground sending up wispy vapor as Giershe pulled each boot from sucking water and ice. Olivia squinted into the sunlight, bounced and squealed, enchanted with the puffs coming from her mouth.

Up the middle of the road Giershe slogged, towards Whitfield College, where the hills would still be covered with snow and the cleared paths would make the going easier. Olivia was riding backwards with her red mittens gripping the carriage. She watched her mother's flushed face, the tall telephone poles, the houses, the circling raucous birds, with the solemn intensity she gave to all new sights.

"Olivia! Little Pooch! Let's go see your father. We might as well. We can catch him between classes. He'll throw you up in the air and show you off to everyone!"

They stopped to wait for the light to change to green on the busy street bordering the college. Giershe bent down to tuck in Olivia's blanket. When she raised her head, she saw their blue car, moving fast, heading out of town towards the big city twenty miles away from Centerville. Moving fast, purposefully, with David at the wheel and devoted secretary Angela tucked in beside him, the halo of her fur hat resting on his shoulder, David's arm around her, excited smiles on both their faces. Angela, the clean-copy, fastest typist, the angel who worked nights to keep up with his demand for errorless pages. Angela, everyone's devoted office slave. Angela, who had a husband who was "unreasonably" jealous of the overtime she gave to her job.

"Olivia! Your father's a busy man! Shall I feel jealous? Would he like that? How long has this been going on? Do we care? Answer my questions, silly Little Pooch!"

Olivia went to sleep very late that evening. Querulous, laughing and crying when David had played with her, she raised her head when Giershe tucked the blanket around her, and let out a howl of fury.

"Rage, rage, little daughter. You'll have to work it out for yourself this night. I have other things to attend to."

She heated herself a glass of warm milk. David had not said anything, but she knew he was angry at the rearrangement of furniture. He was upstairs in his study with the door closed, which was the sign. Not that she needed a sign. Even Olivia, especially Olivia, had noticed his rushing through play-time, his tight mouth, and the way he stared at her as though he was not thinking about her at all.

Giershe walked into the study without knocking and sat down in the green chair with her milk mug between her palms. "I saw you today with Angela, on your way out of town."

"Is that why you moved the double bed out of our bedroom into my study? Is that why you hauled a single bed down from the attic and put it into *our* bedroom? Is that why you moved all my clothes into this room? Isn't your reaction a bit excessive in the light of your total lack of information?" He paced, quizzed, glared at her.

"Hard to say why I did it. I've been wanting to for a long time. I want a room of my own, someplace where I can write a bit, play with Olivia with her toys all spread out. But that's not why. I want to sleep alone—and when we want to make love, we'll do it in here, when we both feel like it." Giershe's heart was throbbing with fear. Her hands shook.

"And when might that be?" David snarled. "Once a year? Or perhaps that's too often for your fastidious taste."

"David, be reasonable. Nursing is tiring."

"Am I to believe that if it were not for Olivia's demands, you would arrange your life so that we could be something more than strangers living in a house together? The only time we are with each other is time spent with Olivia. As soon as she goes down for the night, you find hundreds of things that have to be done, millions of ways to avoid me. If I try to hug you, you pull away to mop up the kitchen. If I ask you to a department party, you pretend you'll go and then find an excuse at the last minute. Once, *one time*, this year, you went to a function with me and no sooner did we arrive than you ducked out and left me there. If we have people to dinner, you feed them, excuse yourself to check on Olivia, and forget to come downstairs again. Is this a marriage?"

It was all true. She'd like to tell him he was not as interesting as a song, a poem, the writing of a letter, or best of all, just doing nothing in a rocking chair, moving back and forth, watching a spider climb the wall. He was forever telling her she didn't love him. Was it true? If she truly loved this man, would all moments with him turn sunny? Would she grow like a tomato plant in summer sun, produce ripe sweet fruit for the plucking? Love should be simple, like what she felt for Olivia. His love was not simple, and the more he proclaimed it the less clear it seemed to her, like seeing shattered stained glass at her feet and not knowing what the picture should be. Pretend jealousy. That would please him.

"Where were you going with Angela so snug and tight against you in broad daylight, where anyone could see you, speeding out of town, might I ask?"

"Oh, Angela. I need her to help me get tenure in the department. She's been at Whitfield for many years, she knows all the politics, all the weaknesses of the professors, all the secrets. She knows who is laying whose wife and how much he wants to hide it. She's a big help to me."

"I thought you got tenure by publishing and teaching. I didn't know you had to screw the department secretary." David hated her to use words like "screw" but adored it when "cunt" and "fuck," spoken lasciviously through his teeth like a friendly rapist, made juices flow.

"Angela and I are good friends. We do not 'screw,' as you so indelicately put it. She's much older than I am, you know. We were on our way to a place where we could talk and have lunch. You know I belong to you, body and soul!" David took the mug out of her hand. He sat on the arm of the chair, put one arm around her shoulders, his cigarette dangling from his lips, eyes blinking in smoke, and pushed his free hand inside her jeans. She squirmed away, perched on the other arm of the chair, her feet on the seat.

"What else do you do to get tenure? Tell me more." Ugly, fishwife fury. He politely returned her drink to her.

"I'll ignore your tone. You are very upset this evening, perhaps understandably so. When you are more calm, perhaps we can discuss my future and whether or not it will be your future as well."

Forgetting Olivia in the next room, Giershe hurled milk and mug at David's head and screeched: "I don't give a damn about your future—your precious tenure—our future— I want . . ." But she couldn't think what she wanted. David caught the mug, but not before it had spattered milk on his papers. He turned his back on her, pulled a tissue from his bathrobe pocket, and was meticulously mopping up little spots of moisture when she flung herself at his back. With one hand she dug her nails into his neck. With the other, she reached around him to grab and crumple all the loose papers she could grasp. She swept all the books and papers on one end of his mammoth desk to the floor, stamped on them, kicked the books, and was starting on the bookcase which filled one side of the room to the ceiling when she heard Olivia cry out, a new cry of fear she had never heard before.

The witch left her, dizzy, disgusted. Through tears, she saw the hint of triumph on David's face.

4

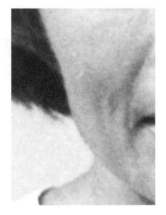

. . . she found herself

falling down

what seemed to be

a very deep well.

I

N THE MONTHS FOLLOWING, Giershe took many hikes with Olivia in the wooded areas north of town. At first, she carried Olivia on her shoulders. Later, in the fall, Olivia was able to climb, run ahead, hide behind trees, collect pinecones and little rocks, worry about bears, wade in streams, and anticipate their return home to David. He would never accompany them, and seemed to feel that their pleasure in the woods was a subtle infidelity.

When the weather turned cold and Giershe realized their outings would have to cease until spring, she began to sink slowly into a climate of doom. There was one tree in front of the house, a maple; it was no different from the other maples, except that it was the first to grow leaves in spring, and it arched over their front porch, giving needed shade in the hot summer months. Olivia could go out on the porch each morning and collect ten red leaves. She put the red leaves in a special box, and when they turned brown, she would crinkle her nose at them and throw them outside on the ground. Soon her leaf box was empty and Giershe felt a weakening of will, an irresistible pull downward towards thoughts of quiet dying.

The afternoon before the first snow fell, she was standing on the front porch, dazed, cold, when a flock of birds heading south flew over the house. The sound of wings beat on her ears. One bird, almost as large as an eagle, swooped down on her shoulders, screaming, tearing at her with spread talons. Giershe fainted. When she opened her eyes Olivia was sitting beside her, peering curiously at her face. One little mittened hand was stroking Giershe's cheeks. They smiled at each other, hugged, and the solid little body snuggled close in her arms. Giershe sobbed happily while playing hide-and-seek with Olivia's brown eyes.

When David came home, the house was dark and he raced upstairs to her bedside. "What is it? What's the matter with you?" he asked anxiously. Again and again she began: "I was out on the porch this afternoon, when . . ." She couldn't continue. The tearing talons, the wings, sorrow. Her body ached, shook with a misery so intimate she couldn't separate it from herself or form approximate words. He held her tightly for a while, then kissed her and told her to get some sleep. He left the door ajar. While Giershe lay quietly in the dark, he read a story to Olivia, gave her a bath, and put her to bed. She listened to the man and the child, to the water running into the tub, to David's questions about bath procedure. She felt a weak urge to get up and reclaim her duties, and a simultaneous counterforce pressing her into the pillows. *If I am weak, I cannot be asked to be strong. If I show joy, that joy is strength, and I shall be asked to divert that strength from my own life, to meet the needs of others, especially David. The wings of madness . . . give flight from work round the clock— cleaning, serving, typing, making love, yielding. Yet I must be careful. Playing slave, I have become slave. Playing mad, might I become Ophelia, floating lifeless down the river? I must be dead to David, alive to Olivia. I wonder what other women feel. Do they love their children more than they care for their husbands? They talk of household, children, sickness, their husbands' careers. They seldom speak of themselves. They don't like me. They ask why my husband lets me go alone to the forest. They turn away from my eyes and voice. They invite me to morning coffee, once, but not again. I wouldn't go again. They are slaves, little mothers emitting hollow mother sounds. I wish I could be one of them, content in discontent, my eyes on a future when house will be bought, the children in college, the rewards of apparent monogamy. What is wrong with me? David says I have no gift for happiness. . . .*

David came into the room. He sat on the side of the bed and stroked her head with hand of lead. She moved towards the wall. "Can you tell me now what happened, what frightened you so much?"

"It was the birds going south. One attacked me. It was huge. I fainted. It's going to snow tomorrow and everything is dying. The leaves are gone. Everything has a purpose out there, and knows its purpose, but I don't know mine."

"There were no big birds going south late this afternoon. I saw a flock of small birds, probably the same flock you saw. Have you been eating or are you still forgetting? You're getting thinner and thinner. I like boyish figures, but there's a limit." His hand moved down to her buttocks. He rubbed rhythmically. She opened her mouth to ask him to stop. The scream rushed past her polite words. Remembering Olivia, she screamed into the pillow, threw up a black liquid and buried her face in it.

She heard David talking on the phone. "Yes. . . . yes. . . . I don't know. . . . She's had a psychotic episode . . . perhaps is suicidal . . . "

She stumbled through the dark room, around the corner into his study. He looked up.

"Hang up that telephone!" she ordered. She couldn't ever remember giving a man an order. It felt strange and good.

"Now Giershe, you're not yourself. . . . I'm—"

"Hang up . . . now! I am not your property! I will tell what I want to tell when I feel ready to. . . . You have no right to . . ."

"I'll call you back," he said into the receiver and placed it in its cradle. She pulled the wire from the wall. She was powered by a new, clean rage. She knew she would suffer for it later which made it all the more enjoyable while it visited her.

"This . . . whatever is happening to me . . . all of it . . . belongs to me.

Mine to tell or not tell. It is as much mine as my skin and eyes. When I want to send out announcements, I'll let you know."

"The college has an outpatient clinic and therapists to help the professors and their families . . ."

She covered her ears with her small fists and returned to her own room. She felt a seeping shame. She had to retrieve her parts and pieces before morning, when Olivia would be needing her again.

>>>——

Olivia's second Christmas was a lighted space in the shadows. The presents, coming to her from grandparents and uncles and aunts, from friends at the college, and from all the members of the Olivia Kinnard Fan Club which David had formed in an excess of pride in his daughter, were a high pile of color and shape around the Christmas tree in the living room.

"Who's the smartest girl in the world?" he asked with arms outstretched. She ran into his arms.

"'Livia!"

"Who's the most beautiful girl in the world?"

Run, hug, and "'tiful." Again and again they played this game. When friends came to call, they first had to proclaim Olivia the smartest and most beautiful before they were allowed to settle into ignoring her. Olivia didn't like to let them withdraw from her. She fussed, brought them spoons and treasures, and tried to climb into their laps. David said "Beautiful girl! Thank you!" each time she pushed a spoon at his chest, until he tired of being interrupted. Then he would suggest that Giershe take Olivia upstairs, or feed her, until the guests left.

"David," she asked bravely one evening after two guests had left, "why don't you just introduce Olivia to the guests and then let her go on playing, and you can have your visit, and I can keep on working in the kitchen, and nothing will be disturbed?"

"Disturbed? What do you mean?"

"I don't think it's good for her to interrupt everything for a sort of false worship of Olivia. People don't feel comfortable and Olivia is learning to expect the world to stop for her. Later on, it won't."

"Don't read your own unhappiness into her life. She will always be adored. She's beautiful."

"David, I *wish* you'd stop saying that! There are many kinds of beauty. You're teaching her to place too much value on how she looks. You can't make a life out of being adored, even supposing it happens."

"You always look for the worm in the apple, don't you? Why shouldn't she be adored?"

She knew they weren't really arguing about Olivia. Giershe hadn't been to visit David since the birds flew south and there was a nasty edge to all their words. She knew she would have to bring her body to him if she wanted to be allowed to follow her own instincts with her daughter. A trade-off, fair as could be expected.

"I want her to grow in her own way, grow strong from inside. She has so much to learn, and being an eternal princess in a world without castles or kings is . . ." She could feel David's scorn scrape sense from her.

"Obviously, you cannot judge what is best for a girl. The Puritan spirit is small and tidy and believes that for every joy there must be pain. I want to free her from that belief. She needn't grow up with that sickness."

"David, haven't you noticed how cranky she gets when your friends pay so much attention to her? And all that stuff about the Olivia Kinnard Fan Club is something you have ridden into the ground. Can't you just allow her to be herself?"

"Is there anything else you'd like to complain about in my dealings with my own daughter?"

"Yes! I want you to stop playing with her that string game with your penis."

"Aha! Now we're getting to what is really bothering you. Schizo mother wants to produce schizo daughter, is that it? Over my dead body will you instill in her your own confused feelings about the penis! It's good for her to see that I *enjoy* my penis and want to include her in my pleasure. I suppose you object to her seeing it at all?" Giershe felt strangely calm. David was very angry. She felt she was leading Olivia up a hill ahead of a tidal wave and nothing she had ever had to do was quite so dangerous. She spoke softly.

"Here is what I would like. Listen carefully. It means much to me. I do not mind your going naked in front of her, but don't want you to sit with her standing at your knee, and pretend that your penis is a marionette on a string to make her laugh. I want you to stop doing that with her. She is a girl baby who will grow to a knowledge of penises in her own time in her own way. Let her do that without your help. I shall not ask you again. I want you to stop that now. You have done it so often that she now wants the game whenever you sit down naked under your bathrobe. Soon she'll be asking other men to play the game. I want you to stop."

Giershe's legs were trembling; all the words were out now, her power shut off. David laughed at her. He could laugh with no mirth, with hatred yelping past his lips.

"You may not order me to do, or not to do, *anything! You* haven't the *right!* I'll do with Olivia what I see fit to do, with or without your knowledge, consent, or approval. Can we consider this conversation at an end?"

Giershe did not answer. Was she exaggerating the danger? How could she know? Was there anyone she could ask without giving private information to the world out there? She knew what would happen if she told Molly, who would tell Harry: Harry would pick up the telephone and tell David, in a transcontinental burn, that David was an insane, ruthless, destructive, egotistical maniac, all things he'd been thinking ever since he first met him. And then David would hang up and do whatever he felt like doing, and Molly and Harry would grieve and never forget or allow her to pretend that her life was quite okay.

Alone in the living room, Giershe stared at the beautiful tree; the lights blurred as tears came. There was one big pink box with silver bows which contained a perfect brown teddy bear. Olivia knew this was her gift from David and Giershe. David kept telling her that all the presents were for her and Olivia smiled happily and leaned on the teddy bear box. Did she not understand, or was she trying to tell them that she cared only for gifts from her parents?

>>>——>——>

One evening in February, David brought home two guests, an orchid for Giershe, a Raggedy Ann doll for Olivia, and presented an aspect of loving father and husband, merriment and goodwill all around. He helped prepare the dinner and gave Giershe time to go upstairs to rest and change her clothes. The dinner was good and wine softened the edge of consciousness. David and the guests helped wash the dishes. Giershe joined the men in the living room, sitting close to David, listening dazedly to academic gossip. Later, she and David stood at the front door, arms around each other, accepted thanks, and said a loving good-bye.

Giershe went to bed and that night the Beast visited her, tears in his eyes. Giershe looked once, blinked, and there stood a prince at her bedside. She held out her arms to him and he lay down beside her. She pulled her nightgown over her head, feeling warm in a bubble of languid desire. He kissed her everywhere, with accompanying slow, fingertip caresses, as though she were a new, unmarked, first woman on earth, and he never before in male form. She writhed and curved towards him, pulling him closer, into her, melting I, she, he.

Olivia found them together in the morning. She bounced onto the bed, pulled the covers back, and squeezed happily between them. She lay there on her back, her wet diaper adding its sour odor to the body smells on either side of her. Giershe climbed over their bodies on her way to the bathroom. She glanced behind her. David had turned away from Olivia and was gazing after her, a yearning in his eyes.

She locked the bathroom door behind her. She turned on the shower water and tried to wash away the queasy feeling in her stomach. She stayed in the shower until the water ran cold. She tried to decide what expression to wear when she unlocked the door. She would be matter-of-fact friendly as though nothing had happened which required differences. She would go downstairs to feed Olivia and would try to avoid David. She would take Olivia for a walk right after breakfast. She would not lose her bed, her right to solitude, her precarious control over her own time and body. If he forced her she would explain, reassert her claim to a self apart from him. She would not tell him just now that she had forgotten the diaphragm.

She covered her clean body with a bathrobe, opened the bathroom door and hesitated briefly before entering her bedroom. Perhaps it *was* a new beginning. Dared she hope for a self *and* love? She stepped forward.

Olivia was standing beside the bed in wet diapers, Bear hanging from one hand, the other hand reaching up to poke a tiny finger through a smoke ring. David was lying naked on his back, pillows under his head, his legs spread out, erect penis pointed towards the ceiling. He was using a plastic doll shoe for an ashtray and ashes had spilled out onto the white sheet. He was aiming smoke rings at his penis. He lovingly gazed at his wife, who stood in the doorway. All of the night's events were mirrored in his proprietary assessment of her rosy cheeks, the long, damp golden-brown hair; he willed her to remember and rejoice in being his mate once more.

She called to Olivia: "Come Olivia, let's go change your diapers and get some breakfast." She turned towards the bureau, her back to David; she grabbed underwear, jeans, turtleneck sweater, and socks, piled the clothes on one arm, bent down for her tennis shoes, and hurried into Olivia's room.

"Get dressed in here, why don't you?" David called. "I like to see you dress yourself. Your body shyness is ridiculous. You look wonderful!"

She didn't answer. She changed Olivia's diapers and dressed her warmly in overalls, T-shirt, knee socks and tennies. She put on her own clothes and with Olivia's hand in hers she was beginning the slow journey down the stairs—step-down-wait, step-down-wait—when David called to her: "Giershe, come here a minute."

"Olivia, you can go down to the kitchen. I'll be down right away." Olivia sat down to begin the faster trip downstairs. They were polished wooden stairs and she loved to slip-bump-slide-push until she got to the bottom, climb up again and repeat. Sometimes she lay on the top stair and slowly pushed a ping-pong ball over the edge. She watched it bounce to the bottom, roll to a corner, and when it was still, chuckled deep in her throat at how funny it was.

Giershe went to the door of her room. "Come here," David coaxed. She remained at the door. She smiled.

"What do you want? Olivia is waiting for me."

David smiled back and flicked an ash in the direction of the doll's shoe. "After you feed her, could you get her to playing in her room, and maybe we could lock the bedroom door?"

"I don't think so. I told Olivia we'd walk to the ravine." She felt a suffocating hatred of him, and wondered for the millionth time where it came from and why it came and went unbidden in spite of her clearest intention to be serene and loving.

"You can take a walk later on. It's important for us to talk about last night."

"I don't feel like talking. I feel like walking and fresh air." She turned from him and ran down the stairs, skipping every other step.

"Then bring me some orange juice and coffee!"

>>>——

On an unseasonably warm November day, David Kinnard III was born. She called him Tony because he looked like a Tony. No, that wasn't the reason. She didn't think fathers should repeat themselves in their sons' names, but she got nowhere arguing this with David. He said he was a junior and of course his son would be number three. She offered many delightful names: Candor Kinnard, Capability Kinnard, or Oliver to match Olivia. No, it had to be David Kinnard III, so she called him Tony as soon as he was placed at her side, and began, in his turn, to suck.

During Tony's pregnancy she had read Professor B.'s book about life and death, and now her pleasure in the infant's sucking instinct was tainted with vague alarm. Whitfield College had published his book and all the professors and their wives were reading it in Laundromats, during office hours, and late at night after the children had fallen asleep. Everyone was proud to be acquainted with such an instantly famous thinker and amazed at his breadth of knowledge, the brilliant sweep of his theories: The child experiences, at the breast, that primal condition, ever after idealized, as Freud says, "in which object-libido and ego-libido cannot be distinguished"; the subject-object dualism does not corrupt the blissful experience of the child at the breast. In the earliest phase, there is no ambivalence in the relation to the object, i.e., the mother's breast. The first stage, the oral stage—the stage in which the child's chief zone of pleasure is the mouth at the mother's breast—is subdivided into a first oral phase distinct from a second phase, the second phase being distinguished by the onset of biting activities, and therefore being called the oral-sadistic phase. The appearance of biting activities marks the first emergence of the ambivalence of love and hate. Man in his unconscious keeps his allegiance to the primal experience of the satisfaction at the mother's breast and seeks to abolish the ambivalence of love and hate.

Again the hands kneaded her belly in the recovery room and the infant sucked the watery liquid. Tony opened and closed his eyes, worked lazily, without urgency, lapsed in his labors and seemed to study her face. The nurse said: "He's a dreamer. You can tell right off. When a boy baby acts like that, he will become a wise man, a poet, or a teller of dreams and legends. God has formed him for His own purposes."

"I don't believe in God. The closest I ever get to belief is when I see outside myself the creature I have carried inside me for nine months. Then, for a few minutes, there seems to be a presence with me. A stop in time. A perfection. I can't explain."

"Everyone believes in God, each person in his own way. Is this your first?"

"It's the third birth. I have a little girl named Olivia at home. The first was a stillbirth."

"I'm sorry"—she leaned over to look into Giershe's face—"but God knows best. He chooses which ones will stay on earth for a while. The others He takes for Himself so they will not suffer."

"I don't believe that. It was a bad arrangement to let the baby grow nine months, let the mother give birth, and then make the mother leave the hospital alone and cry a lot. Big old waste of cells and time and love."

Giershe felt feverish. She stroked Tony's damp black hair, traced his eyebrows, his plump white cheeks. He stopped sucking and seemed to smile. His eyes closed and he gave a deep sigh. She lifted the edge of the blanket to peek at the equipment which had caused David to leave her side during delivery and proclaim, in odd pride, as though he had somehow whittled the organ himself: "It's a boy!"

There it was, the tiny penis with the shriveled sack below. A miniature factory, part of an endless process of being. It seemed so dangerously placed, right out there in front, exposed to weather and injury. Giershe tried to remember whether the penis, little sack with balls, had evolved in man's history, changed in size, or structure, like the hand, brain, skull, and body; but why should it change its shape or working parts when for millions of years its function had remained the same? A sudden awe of Tony took hold of her. She covered him again with the blanket. This was a male child; how could she possibly know what to do with him? She tried to imagine male parts on the front of her and inserting this part of herself into the dangerous, dark, slippery holes of relative strangers. Think of doing all this for the first time in the individual life, with small consolation that it had been done again and again in the life of the species! She ached all over her body, was so sleepy.

"She has a temperature of 103. I don't think the baby is ill, but we'd better put him in the nursery overnight just to be safe," a man's voice said, far, far away. Giershe opened her burning eyes.

"Don't give him a bottle. Promise me. No milk. Wait for mine."

"Don't worry about Tony. We'll take good care of him."

"No! No!" Giershe tried to sit up. They were going to take him away, give him away, to people who had bought him and knew what to do with boys. She struggled and tried to hold Tony, but he was gone even while she reached for him, into the arms of the doctor, to the arms of the nurse, out the door. She tried to throw herself out of the bed. Hands held her shoulders. She couldn't move. Her head was a great ache, and her legs seemed lifeless.

"Giershe, sweet Giershe, it's all right. What they say is true." Where had he come from? Why wasn't he making them keep Tony safe beside her bed? Was he in on the plot?

"David, help me up. We have to get Tony and leave the hospital now, go home to Olivia. You have to help me, please! Where is Olivia?"

"She's home with Rafaela. You remember. She's probably asleep by now. Everything is fine except you're sick and have to get well. Just go to sleep now and in the morning maybe you'll be well enough to see David—Tony."

"Who is Rafaela?"

"Giershe, please, you remember your friend Rafaela, Sidney's wife. She's taking care of Olivia." He put his arms around her and eased her back onto the bed. The nurse and doctor left them together.

"Are you going to stay with me?"

"I'll stay until you're asleep. The doctor doesn't want to give you a sleeping pill, but if you won't sleep, he'll have to." His heavy hand was stroking her forehead, her hair. The weight of it. Her eyes closed. From far away she heard his voice: "She's almost asleep now. I think she'd rather not have a sleeping pill."

"David, I love you. Thank you," she whispered.

>>>>

Centerville, 4.18.61

DEAR MOLLY AND HARRY—

Spring! The maples are green again, early tulips across the street, and we're outside all day long. Nothing gets done, not even beds. But I can't enjoy it to its fullest because I know that we have about three weeks before blistering hot weather and worse, David has agreed to take a year's job at Gorge University starting in July. We'll have to begin packing books right away (he insists on taking all his books—fifty-four cartons the last time we moved) and rent the house here for a year. I have just planted tomato seeds and lettuce and string beans and now the tenants will reap, unless they ignore. We'll be moving to a house with eleven rooms, five bathrooms, three stories, two tenants in the attic. Eight months of winter. I don't want to take time away from the children for all this career management. They will never again be five months and almost three.

Tony is still our lazy laughing bear. He never cries. Olivia spends many hours playing across the street with her friends. I don't think she's pleased with having a baby brother. When she comes inside she fusses and wants to get into my lap. Her vocabulary is deteriorating and her accent, picked up from the street, is full of whiny diphthongs like "lay-up" for "lap" and "wy-a" for "why." She doesn't take a nap and when Tony sleeps I spend time with her guiltily, not quite enjoying it. She suggested today that it might be a good idea to send Tony to you and live in the big house, just the three of us. "Molly and Harry would lie-yuk that, don't you think so, Mommy? We could get him back someday."

Hope the book's coming along and all the plants are in bloom.

love, Giershe

Centerville, 6.1.61

DEAR SISTER—

Don't marry a scholar. I'm so tired I could die. I have all the packing, cooking, housecleaning, care of the children, and still he wants me to type for him if I have a half hour free. He's thesising, talking politics on the phone, or teaching all the time. He spends fifteen minutes a day with the children. I find I don't *ever* want to make love. It just seems like one more duty. It *is* duty. I don't enjoy it at all and he knows it. What's to become of us? Don't tell Molly or Harry.

I came across the following while reading a book on the john the other day (the only place I do any reading):

I met Wilhelm Reich in October 1939 shortly after his arrival in the States. I became his wife, secretary, laboratory assistant, bookkeeper, housekeeper, and general factotum, soon thereafter, the mother of his son in 1944. I had to continue my work, which at that time and place consisted mainly of typing Reich's manuscripts. I also had to take care of the baby. I remember well typing away at a manuscript while pushing the carriage back and forth with one foot to keep the baby quiet because Daddy could not bear to hear him cry. Or Reich, very graciously telling me in the late afternoon to take off for a while and go fishing on the lake while he would look after the baby, then after half an hour, his waving to me frantically because the baby needed to be changed, an ordeal which he could not face.

I wonder if Frau Reich had "orgastic potency" and if she did, did that make her life any happier? How are the men in your life? David drips perspiration over his books and I am swollen and dizzy with humidity. We now have air-conditioning in one room—David's study. Olivia helps me pack. She has packed her own stuff thirty times. She wants to choose what to take and what to store, but she keeps changing her mind, as I do. We're a pair of crazies. She does all this packing running around naked (in the house, of course). She's now very conscious of being covered up properly when outside. State law.

Write soon. I hope you can visit in the fall.

Giershe

Gorgeville, 7.8.61

DEAR MOLLY AND HARRY—

We're here. It took all day to drive a few hundred miles, pulling a trailer filled with indecisions and Western Civilization. The day we arrived—104 degrees, 99 humidity—I felt so ill and goofy. We pulled up to the monster house about four in the afternoon, the whole outgoing family there to greet us. Tony was in my lap, sticky sweat mixed with wet diapers. I put on my company smile. Mrs. Professor took Tony from me, cooing and loving him. Olivia hung behind me, wide-eyed at the house and sloping lawns surrounding their real estate. The professors effusively exchanged handshakes and formal salutations. The air hung on my neck and I couldn't stand upright. I half-crawled, half-staggered towards the porch steps and the next thing I remember I was lying on the grass looking up at the gray sky and voices closing in on me—"doctor . . . carry her . . . weather . . . Mommy, Mommy . . . oxygen . . . what a shame . . . bed . . . tea with whiskey . . . air . . ." I remember wishing I could lift off with Tony on one wing, Olivia on the other, a big mama eagle taking her eaglets to safety out west where the skies are blue and air is of friendly consistency. After I was put to bed in a room upstairs, with whiskey and water, I dozed off and woke to the sound of hammering rain on the roof. The house shook with whacks of thunder. Olivia held a damp, cool washcloth on my forehead and when I smiled at her, she got under the sheet and we listened to the rain together. She said, "I'm not scared!"

The countryside is wild and beautiful, full of dangerous ups and downs, cliffs and gorges, seems like nothing in this town is level. The yard is large, with sandbox and swing. Tony tries to cover more ground and keep up with O. This morning he crawled outside with a small box of Rice Krispies and tried to feed one to a worm. There are two boys living in the attic with their own bathroom. I have to change their linens each week. They bow and flutter when they see David.

I'll write more in a few days when I have more time . . . ha!

love, Giershe

>—>—>

Summer in Gorgeville was much like summer in Centerville. The men drank lots of gin and tonic and seemed to have endless hours to drape themselves over chairs, gossip about where all the other assistant professors were spending their summers, perspire into the upholstery, and leave the care and feeding of children and themselves to the women who were always in the kitchen anyway. No one seemed to be doing any work of the sort which would make it possible to spend next year's summer in a more pleasant environment. It was a time for talking about the sins of others, whether academic or marital, for estimating one's own chance of supplanting another lazy scholar when the book was finally finished or when someone at the top died or retired. Charity towards colleagues was reserved for those who occupied positions by virtue of solid achievement, or those who held places throughout the country that no one could possibly covet.

Here is a partial list of familial disorders which regularly gobbled work time:

1. Illness of wife or children
2. Lack of adequate housing
3. Car breakdown
4. Loss of wife's job
5. Birth of a new baby
6. Visiting grandparents or in-laws
7. Noise of quarreling children
8. Toddler's discovery of file cards
9. Undiagnosed melancholy of wife or husband
10. Husband's infatuation with female, usually wife of another professor
11. Wife's infatuation with professor not her husband

There were never-to-be-forgotten situations when all eleven conditions occurred simultaneously and six to eight months of climbing were lost forever. Giershe tried to be more of a helpmate than a checkmate, but often her best intentions were not enough. It was no one's fault, and everyone felt guilty.

One afternoon, David came home late. He looked shower-scrubbed and fresh. As he bent over to kiss Giershe, she smelled faint jasmine, an elusive scent rising from his moist hair. She hoped that whoever wore jasmine would prove a lasting entertainment for him and would supplant her weary self. How many wives had such hopes for their husbands? Now if they would all understand one another, rise above dog-with-bone sentiments, they could enter a peaceful division of love's labors.

At dinner, David said, while gnawing on a chop bone: "You can move back into our bedroom now that Tony's settled down. I've missed you. You really should take better care of yourself. You look like you've lost ten pounds since we arrived."

"David, I've been meaning to tell you. I think I'll stay across the hall from Tony, make that my bedroom. I can hear him better there. I'm not feeling well. There's a pain."

"Where? Why haven't you told me!" Concerned, solicitous. She had rather hoped he would be angry. Anger would make it easier.

"It isn't much of a pain. Where the uterus is. It hurts to walk, a dull ache all the time. I plan to rest in that room every afternoon. During nap time."

"A good idea. That can be your rest room—ha-ha—and at night you can sleep in our room." He started on his second chop.

"I'm not going to sleep there for a while, not until I feel better."

"You make it sound like climbing Mount Everest simply to sleep with your husband. Do I have leprosy? You turn away from me when I try to kiss you, you move away when I put my hand on you. We can't go on this way, you know that. What are we going to do about it?"

He lighted his after-dinner cigarette, reached for an ashtray, and settled back to discuss. Giershe smelled jasmine on the hand that moved across the table to clasp hers. She willed her hand to stay in his.

"David, I'm too weary to be diplomatic. Your kiss hurts my lips. I don't want to make love and I don't know what's wrong with me. I don't know what we're to do about it. I don't want to think about us, or work on us, or be pressed, or scolded, or— I don't want it this way, it just *is*." She bent over the dinner table and began to sob. David snuffed out his cigarette and put his arms around her.

"Giershe, dear Giershe." He kissed her ear, and blew into it.

"Stop! Leave me alone! It hurts when you touch me!"

She stood up like a jack-in-the-box erupting from closed space, hit his jaw with the top of her head and ran into the living room, bumped the stereo as she rounded the corner into the hallway, fled past his study, past the front door, up to the first stair landing, slid to her knee on the polished floor, up one more flight, three stairs at a time, down the hall to Tony's room, flung herself through the door of the room opposite, and slammed it behind her. She felt pain on her skull, in her groin, in her ear where his lips had touched. Her knee hurt, her throat ached.

She sat down on the narrow cot, almost the only furnishing in the ugly room. Late summer twilight on the faded wallpaper, baby roses amongst pale green vines. Here and there, irregularly shaped patches were torn away, leaving behind a pattern of gray wall and stains of white glue. Her typewriter was sitting on a small table against one wall. The table was wooden, with children's carvings etched on its surface. One leg was missing its last two inches, and Giershe had placed a two-by-four under it, so she could type letters there and hear Tony if he cried. She would try to find a good typing chair somewhere in the basement. She would cover the hanging bulb with a shade—no, she would leave it hanging like that. It was strong light. The curtains were organdy, rather pretty, but could use some Clorox and starch. Maybe there were throw rugs stored somewhere. At least she wouldn't get splinters in her feet, and the children could sit on the floor to play when winter came.

The door had an old-fashioned keyhole. Every interior key would fit it. Did she dare put a padlock with a combination on the closet door? She could lock herself in with the interior house key, a statement that she was wishing to be alone, but when she was not in the room, she needed a way to keep David out of her thoughts. Why was a combination lock on a door more wounding than the words "It hurts when you touch me"? She'd buy the lock tomorrow. She'd memorize the combination. He'd have to hammer it off if he wanted to snoop.

She would give him one more winter. She would care for his children, cook meals, serve guests, be a landlady for two tenants, clean the house, encourage his work, discuss, eat more, take long walks in the falling leaves and early snow, read poetry, be courteous and keep her temper, keep a journal about the children which David could read, another journal about herself which he must not read even if he appeared in the doorway with hatchet in hand. Once in a while, she would climb into his bed, but return to her room after "love."

She turned the key in the door and sat down again on the cot. Pain receded. She was re-seeding her life. She heard the doors to David's study slide open, and a few minutes later, heard them close again. She would not think about his pain. She would go downstairs and do the dishes.

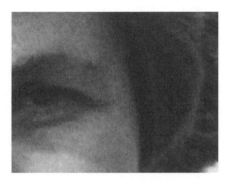

If you drink much

from a bottle marked "poison,"

it is almost

certain to disagree with you

sooner or later.

GIERSHE'S FIRST HOUR in her locked room was on a lovely day in early fall. She forced herself indoors to the typewriter. She made a list:

ALL THE THINGS I DON'T LIKE ABOUT DAVID

1. His ill-formed big nose with blackheads in the nostrils.
2. The smell of his nose when he kisses me.
3. The way he watches to see my reaction when he makes love.
4. His vanity about his smooth, poreless, perfect hands.
5. His heavy step, like Cromwell.
6. His smooth hairless chest.
7. His vanity about his size-32 waist.
8. His skinny arms with girl hairs.
9. His huge, muscular legs with narrow knees.
10. The way he crushes when he hugs (one broken rib).
11. The way he stands with one leg dipping at the knee towards the other knee, like a beauty queen.
12. The smell of his sweat, nicotiny and sour.
13. The smell and taste of his semen.
14. The smell of all of him when he doesn't bathe and has been working, a stench of tobacco, urine, excrement, sperm, my juices, sweat, all going rancid.
15. The way he fawns on ferrets of higher degree.
16. The way he plots vengeance against fancied or real enemies.
17. His perfectionism at his desk: clean copy or do it over, every tiny new thing in a separate folder, no one can touch his typewriter.
18. The way he centers even love letters.
19. The way he folds letters, exactly in three sections, creased with a ruler.
20. His tiny writing, growing tinier each year.
21. His farting in bed, saying "There's more room out there."
22. His ability to make love all night and then sleep till noon.
23. The way he chain-smokes and never gets the ash into the ashtray.
24. The "endless proliferation of parentheses" in his speech.
25. His eternal farewells at the door when we have guests.

26. His telephone gossip—at least twenty times a day.
27. His penis game.
28. His heavy leg flung over my body when he sleeps.
29. The way he flicks an ash into his trouser cuff because he's too lazy to get up and get an ashtray.
30. His total ineptitude about plumbing, car engines, wiring, or anything practical.
31. The way he fixes on one word or phrase and uses it until it pops out of his speech and hits you in the ear.
32. His Olivia Kinnard Fan Club.
33. The way he treats books as though they were made of crystal: "A book that has been written in is a damaged book."
34. His suspicious nature cloaked in friendliness.
35. His refusal to wash dishes, mop the floor, pick up his bath towels, wash a sock or shirt, iron, cook, make a sandwich, clear a table.
36. The way he takes twelve sections of toilet paper, folds them precisely into a square, then wipes his ass, careful not to get anything on his hands, then repeats.
37. The way he insists I have an orgasm and then says, "I guess I know what you need, how to give it to my girl."
38. His calling me "girl."
39. The way he talks about the genius of his mother and father.
40. His saying that Harry's writing is not worth doing because it's shallow, current.
41. His saying "Isn't she beautiful?" when I'm struggling to say something in public.

Feeling guilty, she stopped typing. She wanted to go on to the next list where she would think of all the things she liked about David. She got up to look out the window. There was a woman on the sidewalk below the house. She was holding the hand of a boy about the age of Tony. Two older boys were racing up and down the grass slope, whooping and hollering, hiding in the shrubbery, pretending to shoot each other.

"Jeb and Jason! Get off that property! Now! Stop that!" the woman shouted. They broke off two pieces of hedge and began hitting each other. The older boy butted the younger one in the stomach with his thatched blond head. The woman ignored them and looked up at Giershe. "Hello up there! I think we're neighbors. My name is Leslie Barker. These"—she waved a hand at the screaming boys—"are some of the people who live with me. I think it's safe to come outside."

"Wait. I'll be right down." She put her list on a shelf in the closet, closed the door, and twirled the dial. She opened Tony's door. "Tony-baloney! Let's go see another boy-walker!" He bounced on his mattress and tried to stand on his head. She picked him up and kissed his nose. "Olivia! Let's go meet some neighbors."

"I hope they're not boys!"

Leslie and her littlest boy had moved some distance down the sidewalk when Giershe finally sat down on the grass with Tony. Jeb and Jason stood still with feet planted wide apart, staring at Olivia and Tony. Giershe wanted to call to Leslie but didn't want to display an eagerness the other woman might rebuff. She lay down in the grass and closed her eyes. When she peeked, she could see the woman's long legs in a beige wraparound skirt, her feet in dainty sandals. She paused, bent down to the little boy, two blond heads close together, turned around and began walking slowly towards Giershe. She looked like a blond flamingo—stalky legs, a sleeveless beige top with no bra, long skinny arms. Her face was an inverted triangle on a smooth white column, topped with that shiny haircut where every strand is the same length as its neighbor. She didn't smile or speak as she climbed the slope. She lifted the baby to her hip, hiked up her skirt with her free hand and sat down near Giershe.

"This is Jesse. He's one. The other two are Jason and Jeb, six and nine in that order." She lay down on the grass and closed her eyes. Giershe started laughing. She sat up and tried to control it. "What's so funny?" Leslie asked without opening her eyes.

"I don't know. I'm sorry. I think you are, but it could really be almost any-thing—the day, the hour, the tickly grass, seven tiny people beneath a huge blue sky trading names and ages—anything."

"I don't usually convulse people on first acquaintance and we haven't traded names. Your name is New Female Resident in the House at the Corner of Our Street and your two attachments are Solemn Girl and Roly-poly Brown Boy." Her eyes were still closed.

"Well, I can't introduce myself unless you open your eyes." Leslie sat up. She pulled her skirt up around her hips for greater comfort. Her legs were shaved from just above the knee downwards. The hair on her thighs was dark and grew more dense the higher Giershe looked.

"My name is Giershe Kinnard. This is Olivia, and Brown Boy's name is Tony. He'll be one next month and Olivia was three this summer. David . . ."

". . . is a professor at Gorge U. Otherwise why would we be sitting here on this lawn trading names? Jeb Senior plows the Nineteenth-Century Et Cetera Field in the Literature Department. Let's assume they are both at this moment working in the library."

Leslie's eyes were very blue, set deep and far apart. Her eyebrows and lashes were dark, perhaps emphasized, subtly. Her mouth formed thin double lines below an elegant straight nose. When she spoke, her mouth curved up on one side. In a flat voice, she continued:

"You will have to speak distinctly. I have no hearing in my left ear. All the rest of my parts are in good working condition."

"I like your haircut and the way it shines in the sun. I think I'll cut mine and hope for the same cheerful result."

"The color is Clairol Golden Blonde. Why should you want to cut your hair? Giershes need long hair."

"Giershes get tired of people saying 'Giershes need long hair.' It's time to smash the image." Giershe was feeling alert, happy, and very content with her new acquaintance.

"What else are you smashing this year?"

Giershe hesitated. "I'm going to begin with a haircut—no, I began by claiming one room in that house for my own, with a typewriter and a combination lock on the closet door." Having said it, she wished she could scoop it up and put it back into her mouth.

"The gentleman who lives with you doesn't care for the sound of a typewriter, and is offended by a locked door?"

"I already feel I've betrayed David. I'm going to shut my mouth."

"Betray," Leslie snorted, "what a splendid word! Do you want to go pick apples out in the country on Saturday? We get boxes, a big car, pile in all of our children, drive five miles out, collect all the apples left on the ground (free), settle quarrels with diplomacy and terror, pack them (apples and children) back into the car, drive back home wondering why we ever chose to do such a tiring thing when we could have done something else instead."

"Whew. An invitation like that is a work of art. In one sentence you've given me all the information I need. I don't have to expect to enjoy myself and be disappointed. I could even say in the midst of it, 'Goddamn, this was a terrible idea!' and you wouldn't care. I would come home with some apples, at the very least. The children could all behave like beasts and we would not have to apologize to each other." Giershe looked at Leslie, who was once more lying flat with her eyes closed. "I think I could learn a lot from you. What kind of car do you have?"

"A Bug. I like to confine chaos."

"I'll get the Chevy. And maybe you and your husband can come for a drink or dinner soon."

"Inevitably. And maybe David and Jeb will like each other and we'll serve you dinner and they'll find out who's cleverer, or maybe they'll draw swords while we calm the children or think about how much we're paying the baby-sitter." Leslie laughed, a snort it was, accompanied by a lift of her face on the right side. She sat up and looked around. "Where is everybody?"

"Jeb seems to have gone home. Jason and Olivia are in the house. Olivia seems fascinated. I heard her ask him if he wanted to paint."

"Oh fret, fret. Do you want paint all over your walls and floor?"

"It can't hurt the room. It's already that way. Anyway, I trust Olivia to impose order. She'll tell him the rules as she sees them."

"And he'll break them. How old did you say Tony is?"

"He'll be one next month."

Tony was going down the stairs to the sidewalk, backwards. Jesse was sitting next to Leslie, leaning on her lap, watching Tony from a safe distance.

"Where did you get him? He doesn't resemble you at all."

"I invented him. He's a dream of mine, thoughtful, pleasure-loving, funny, easygoing (until we came here), happy, loving. Excuse me, I have to rescue him from the traffic." Giershe ran to Tony and grabbed him as he was beginning to run wildly down the sidewalk towards Leslie's home. She ran up the grass slope with Tony bouncing up and down on her hip. As soon as she put him down near Jesse, he started crawling towards the steps again. Jesse buried his face in his mother's lap.

"It appears unlikely, but should you occasionally wish to be free of him, I wouldn't mind taking him for a few hours now and then. A reciprocal arrangement between neighbors is sometimes practical. I must go. Tell Jason to come home soon, or sooner if he gets in your way. I shall call you about plans for Saturday."

Leslie stood up, straightened her skirt, picked up Jesse, and walked away from Giershe without looking back. Giershe felt dismissed, rebuffed (for what? loving Tony?), and wondered if Leslie's visit was for the purpose of acquiring an emergency baby-sitter. She shrugged. What did it matter? She wasn't going to let anyone take care of either Olivia or Tony, not while they were awake anyway.

>>>>

The next day, at nap time, Giershe put clean paper into the typewriter and headed it:

SOME OF THE THINGS I LIKE ABOUT DAVID

She sat for a long time, trying to remember. Finally—

1. The back of his neck, smooth and brown.
2. The way he tells jokes, especially shaggy-dog jokes.

After item 2, she sat for five minutes, unable to think of any other single aspect of David she unqualifiedly liked. Hopeless. She ripped that sheet from the typewriter and inserted a new one. She typed:

FRIGIDITY

Frigidity is a word we never use. We have the word in our heads but it is never uttered, at least to each other. If he were to say "frigid" to me, that would mean I am sick and must find help to get well. If I called myself "frigid," that would mean that if I were not sick, I could enjoy making love to him. Frigidity is a state of disease, dis-ease, and disease can be medicated, cured, or perhaps is terminal. Frigid means cold and icy to the touch. I am that, with David. Sometimes I pretend warmth, so we can go on living with one another and raise our children, but then it hurts inside me.

Imagine that David and I are lying beside each other on the big double bed. I am lying there because I feel I ought to be, not because love has led me to him. I lie on my back, stiff, waiting for him to make the first move. I hope he will be quick about it, but know that the colder I am, the longer he will try to thaw me. He strokes my breast. I feel it shrivel, grow smaller and colder, although it is warm in the room. He leans his big face over mine, he puts his lips on my lips. It is like pinpricks and I turn my head away. A sensation of frostbite after walking in a freezing wind. I try to relax. I know that if somehow I can pretend an interest, I will gain time. I turn towards him, and put an arm around him. My arm is cold and has goose bumps. He nestles my head and we lie still for a moment. My legs feel like I've had a spinal. He shifts his weight to his elbow and slowly pushes my head down towards his penis. I close my eyes and think of Tony, Olivia, the sun. It seems impossible. That huge, bulbous column waiting for my mouth. I open my dry mouth and try to take in the tip. His hand presses on the back of my head. I gag. I push up for air. His fingers are in my vagina, in and out, spreading the moisture, clutching the lips, opening them. It hurts. I pull away. He slobbers and sucks the lips, pushes his tongue in and out. I gaze over his head at the moonlight out the window. I know I could feel pleasure if I chose to. Turn a tiny wheel in my brain and I'd be writhing all over the bed, liquid flowing out onto the sheets, arching my back, clutching him, biting, swallowing his saliva.

He is getting me ready for his penis. He hopes that when he begins to piston in and out, in his most expert fashion, I will not be able to stifle the lust he has known from me in the past. He thinks frigidity is involuntary, perhaps physical. He has theories. He puts a pillow beneath my buttocks. My legs are spread wide, they are limp and inert. All of me is inert. He pauses, touches me with his penis, teasing, a perfect technique used millions of times on all the jasmines I don't know about, used on me, warm in my memory. He holds my hips steady, because he knows I won't. He pushes in, watching me. I look into his eyes and think about my bed in the other room. He goes in and out slowly. He watches it go in and out. It hurts. I wince. He pulls out, reaches for a jar of Vaseline, twirls the top with one hand, scoops out a mound of grease and inserts his fingers into the hole. Now he can move faster and faster.

He forgets me. He drips perspiration on my stomach from his chin and chest. He goes on forever while I think of my bed, of sweet funny Tony, of the fever Olivia had when she went to bed, of how many months of snow there will be, of summer in Berkeley, of how to leave him, and when, and how to support two children, of how soon after he comes I can leave the bed and take a shower.

He falls on me, heavy and sweaty, sucks one breast, kneads the other; everything hurts—what he calls my "cunt," the breast he is sucking, the breast he is bruising, his chin in my rib. I will not cry out, not even that sign of life beneath him.

He lies still. I cannot move. I am under a fallen tree. When his breathing is regular, with muted snore, I roll him off and out of me. He puts out an arm to keep me at his side. I duck under his searching limb. My legs, when they reach the floor, won't come together properly. I walk down the long hall like a person who's been on horseback for twelve hours. It is over, for now. He took his pleasure. I did not give it.

Giershe heard Tony talking to himself across the hall. From far away, she felt herself being called back. She had forgotten Tony and Olivia, had lost the sense of their presence in the house, or in her life. She snatched the page from the typewriter, placed it on the shelf, closed the door, twisted the lock. She stood in the hallway, the same hallway she'd walked with aching legs in her fantasy. Not fantasy. Reality lifted onto paper. She felt like a flashlight with new batteries.

>>>>

Winter came early to Gorgeville. It always did, every year. The trees seemed to grow naked overnight. Crickets, bees, birds ceased their warm weather sounds. The wind came up, the rains came down, then sleet, and finally snow on the ground, covering the tree branches where the squirrels used to play. The waterfalls, with their constant rainbow splashes against summer light, froze into sculptures a thousand feet in height. Life moved indoors and stayed there.

They all went to the country to pick apples one nippy October Saturday. Leslie alternately shouted at Jason and Jeb, or coolly removed herself from responsibility for them with philosophical comments about the transitory nature of parenthood. Olivia cried. Tony and Jesse ate apples until they had acute stomach pains. Giershe drove the carload of fretting bodies there and back, and in spite of the cacophony, or perhaps because of it, arrived back home less troubled than when she'd set out.

After the apple trip, Giershe and Leslie began to find free hours for each other after the children had gone to bed—a sign that the passing of mother-time was not their aim. They talked often on the phone—something Giershe had never done before. Once or twice a week, after dinner dishes, Giershe would put on boots, muffler, coat, earmuffs, and mittens, peek into David's study to say she was going to Leslie's, and high-step through snow and ice to the end of the dark street. Her house was the last house before the gorge-out point. Another city might have called it Vista Point, but Gorgeville had an unusual number of students and residents who had jumped into the roaring waters which fell into the precipitous canyon below. City officials, unable to hide nature's grand and stylish invitation to oblivion, had yielded responsibility to the individual. There was a low fence (anyone could climb over it) and a simple sign: DANGER. In winter, when the waters were frozen into icy tails extending several thousand feet to the miniature lake on the valley floor—no one jumped. There was an oppressive silence about the place, as though watery throats were stuffed with white rags to stifle sound. Giershe paused there, in front of the sign, feeling its gentle irony. She could see the little sign atop the world ball, a warning for those who touched down for an earthly existence.

Giershe and Leslie always sat in the warm kitchen while Leslie knit socks and mittens, or absentmindedly made cookies. The boys were upstairs doing homework, or sleeping, or quarreling. Jeb was usually at the library. Leslie's hands were never idle; to the sound of knitting needles going click-click, she questioned Giershe. Giershe tried to answer honestly and keep the tone unemotional. There was a studied lightness about Leslie. She seemed to be saying: "We are all the same in our little lives, are we not?" Giershe didn't feel that way about her life, but found it comforting to try to answer as though she were speaking of a third party, well known to her, but of only casual interest. "You remind me of Madame Dufarge, knitting while bloody heads roll into the street, but your heads get whacked off without blood. Blood would be tasteless."

"Apt. It's *Defarge*. You people from California all like blood," she said, believing each one different enough to merit at least twenty questions. "Let's see, where were we? You've been born, gone to school, child of parents with intellectual pretensions, liberal and pacifist leanings. Second child of three. Moderately unconventional. Your brother? What does he do?"

"He's the black sheep. He's an engineer. He used to lie down on the floor and have tantrums whenever we looked up a word in the dictionary. It took him four years to graduate from a three-year high school, two years in the service to cool off, and four years to get out of a three-year technical school. He's bright, but negative. He's *happily* married."

Leslie uttered her high-pitched snort-laugh and began winding yarn around the back of a chair. They were drinking hot, spiced wine and the fumes were making Giershe dizzy. Leslie's twirling hands moved faster and faster, pulling blue yarn into a ball.

"You graduated from high school, most popular girl in your class?"

"Wrong. I graduated from high school the youngest and most shy and mousy girl in my class. Now this reminds me of the Arbuthnot cliché articles in the *New Yorker*. Aren't you bored?"

"No. In the natural course of events, you enrolled at the university to study what?" Leslie was the only person Giershe knew who could answer a question with a simple "no."

"Unable to think of anything else to do with my life, I wandered onto the campus, took a part-time job to support myself, and took courses in political theory because I fell in love with the professor."

"And he fell in love with you instantly and you contemplated marriage?" Leslie lifted the right side of her face in a mocking smile.

"Wrong again. I was already married." Giershe laughed. Told this way, it seemed quite jolly. Or was it the wine?

"The strands are tangling. You were married *during* your pursuit of political theory?"

"During." She hoped to master the one-word answer.

"This wronged husband was Dino?" Leslie had called David "Dino" since the first day she had met him. She didn't pretend that she couldn't remember his name. She simply said Dino every time she should have said David, to his face, to Giershe, without irony or apology. It was like a buzzing fly to David. He seemed to want to wham it, but was afraid that if he killed it, it would metamorphose into something worse.

"Not David. My first husband."

"So the marriage crashed on the rocks of Infidelity and you left him for Political Theory?" Leslie was watching her now with almost, but not quite, unconcealed interest.

"I just walked away from both of them. The marriage crashed on the rock of not having children. He couldn't, the doctors said."

Leslie was nibbling at the bones of her life, scattered on a desert, bits and pieces drying in the hot sun. Yet talking to her leavened. All the years up to David now seemed to weigh less, as though she'd boxed up all the tears and confusion and left the load on the street for the Salvation Army truck to pick up in the morning. Her cheeks felt feverish from the wine and warmth in the room. She got up from her stool, stretched her arms to the ceiling, and bent down to touch her toes. She began to worry about David all alone in his study, resenting her absence.

"Oh don't go so soon. We're up to Dino, aren't we?"

"Leslie, you are relentless! Have I ever told you that David is very annoyed at being called Dino? His face twitches every time he hears it. Why do you do it? Do you want to make him angry?"

"David is evil strength. Dino is wily, conniving gigolo. He's Dino."

Giershe sat down again. She mutely tested her reflexes. Did she feel like defending David? She knew that Leslie's summation was not just, but Leslie was not concerned with justice. Plot, narrative, character, portraiture, perhaps motivation. Surely habit and behavior. And enclosing all of it, appearance. Satisfied that Giershe wasn't going to cry "Foul!" Leslie continued:

"Enter Dino. Where did you meet?"

"We met in a male house of prostitution where David earned one hundred dollars an hour. There are lots of them in Berkeley, supported by the university, to keep the ladies happy. I went there to get material for a term paper on the psychosocial behavior of undergraduates, but was deflected from my purpose by a wily, conniving gigolo."

Leslie stopped rolling her ball of yarn. "Giershe, if my name for David offends you, I shall stop. In my thoughts of him, it helps me to call him Dino, and keeps him at a safe distance from me. I am not immune to charm, but in this instance I want to be sure I am not charmed. It's my armor. I like handsome devils, but I find him sinister. He frightens me."

"It does not offend me. It compels me to think. I met David in a bookstore where we were temporarily employed at one dollar an hour. He knew everyone, talked brilliantly (or so I thought at the time), made everyone laugh, and stared at me in between, as though he thought me Aphrodite on a windswept hill overlooking the sea."

Leslie's face softened. Giershe sat with her elbows on the kitchen table, chin in her hands, watching her friend count stitches, zip the needles in and out. Both understood that the perilous questioning had run its course for the evening.

"Oh shit! I made a mistake. Did you know that I can hear better in my bad ear when my hands are busy? I always knit at concerts or lectures. And, in reverse, I cease knitting when I don't want to hear the children screaming. My children are very violent, like their father. I am not. Open emotion appalls me. The only violent literary genre I enjoy is the fairy tale."

"When will your book be published? What's it about?"

"In the spring. It's about silly people not too different from you and me and our house residents. Most of the people I write about are silly. Life is very peaceful for me right now. As soon as the book appears in the book-stores, people will read it and think I'm writing about them. Jeb will think I've exposed him to view and will be horrid to me."

"And yet you keep on writing? I've been writing. I have to keep it in a locked closet, and David can't forget or forgive what he imagines is there. There must be a million typewriters clacking away behind locked doors all over America. Drivel, treachery, fantasy, most of it awful. I want to know what all these ladies are *really* thinking, *not* what soap powder they use, *not* how clever their children and husbands are."

Snort-laugh again. "You must never let me be in your house alone. I shall read all your letters, take the door off its hinges and read what's behind the lock, read all of Dino's private stuff (although husbands generally have their locked desk drawer at the office), snoop in your bureau drawers and your medicine cabinet."

Fuzzy with wine, they laughed together, cackling like Halloween witch-es at a children's party. The telephone rang. Giershe rose from her chair, unsteadily, and began putting on the layers of clothing necessary for the trip home.

"Midnight! Dino, how extraordinary! I'm teaching Giershe how to knit and we lost track of time. I'm sure you'll agree that it's a useful art for her to know. . . . Oh . . . a father can comfort a crying little girl, can he not? . . . Oh yes, I agree . . . a mother should certainly be home when her child is crying. Chin up, Dino, she's on her way."

Saying good-bye to Leslie was like her one-syllable answers. All Giershe had to do was walk out the door. No amenities necessary. No arrangements for future evenings, no required thank-yous, no summations. Exit.

6

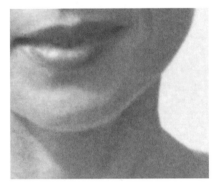

"What a curious plan!"

exclaimed Alice.

$\mathcal{S}$CENE: *Dining room of Kinnard house in Gorgeville. It is late spring, already hot.*
A table is spread with correct hors d'oeuvres, glasses, wine bottles in bowls
of ice; gin, tonic, and ice in a bucket on an antique buffet.

David's colleagues are entering the room, gathering to say good-bye to
the handsome couple. The women are clustered in the adjoining living room,
discussing child care and their husbands' futures. The men stand in groups
of two or three, glasses in hands, looking out the windows onto the grass
which surrounds the house. They talk, laugh, with party manners.

Giershe, her face tense with pain, is wearing a dainty embroidered
Hungarian blouse, with tie-puff sleeves, a long black cotton gathered skirt,
sandals on brown feet. She moves silently among the men, offering sand-
wiches on a tray. She gives each group a wan smile as she offers a day's
labor which will be consumed in an hour. She stops often at the window to
check on the children playing in the grass: four-year-old Aaron (child of
Judson, David's officemate), Olivia, and Tony. Aaron is chasing Olivia.
When he catches her, they roll over and over in the grass. Olivia escapes, is
chased, caught, rolls over, laughs. Tony watches, laughing.

David and Judson stand at the window, glasses to lips, laughing. Both
men are dressed in nylon seersucker suits.

JUDSON: It begins early, doesn't it? The chase-and-catch-me game.

DAVID: I've never seen Olivia behave that way before, except with me,
and I'm not sure I like it. (*Mock severity*)

JUDSON: There's damn little you can do about it. Aaron is irresistible. He's
a four-year-old tidal wave.

DAVID: If he rolls over Olivia, he'll meet a thirty-eight-year-old tidal
wave on the green. He'll have to state his intentions and they'd
better be honorable!

JUDSON: Is that the way you intend to handle Olivia's affairs, in the future?
She may not like that; it's a new generation, not like ours.

DAVID: It better not be like ours! (*Leers and laughter*) I don't intend her
education in these matters to be taken over by some pimple-pus

hot-pants kid on a trial-and-error basis. Do you remember the story about the king and his beautiful daughter . . . (*Volume fades. The two men put their heads together. David gestures with his free hand, Judson watches and listens, then laughs with David, enjoying the story. They look out the window again. Volume up*)

JUDSON: I'm glad I don't have to worry about that just yet. My daughter is only six months old.

DAVID: It's never too early for a daughter to realize that her father is the most fascinating man around! (*Laughter*) Incest is a relative—ha-ha—matter, after all. Liberals like you are afraid to take responsibility for their daughters' educations, and then are dismayed at the mess they make of their lives.

JUDSON: (*Nervously*) I'm not sure I know what you mean.

DAVID: (*Puts an arm around Judson's shoulders*) When the time comes, give me a call and I'll explain it to you. (*They move off together towards the living room*)

           (*Giershe stands with tray in hands, looking after them. People move around her, speak to her, take food from her tray. She does not speak. She is a statue*)

>>>>

SCENE   *Living room. Giershe is lying on the sofa. David is collapsed in an overstuffed chair. Empty glasses, filled ashtrays, crumpled paper napkins, trays with colored toothpicks and crumbs, litter the room. David is perspiring. His tie and jacket are draped over the back of his chair.*

DAVID: Well, I'm glad we made that effort. I think everyone had a good time. Jeb came in for a while. Where was Leslie?

GIERSHE: I'm not sure. I think she and Jeb have been having trouble since the book came out. Jeb didn't stay long.

DAVID: What did she expect after that knife-job, that cheap novel?

GIERSHE: David, I was serving in the dining room. I heard you tell Judson—let me see if I can remember the words—"I don't intend her education in these matters to be taken over by some pimple-pus hot-pants kid on a trial-and-error basis. It's never too early for a daughter to realize that her father is . . ."

DAVID: That's enough. I'm aware of what we said.

GIERSHE: Judson didn't say it. You did. What did you mean?

DAVID: What is this? Room 101?

GIERSHE: (*She sits up. Her face is pale. She presses her hands on her stomach and frowns in pain*) I have to know! What are you planning to do with Olivia?

DAVID: I don't believe you have the right to quiz me about anything I may have said. You are Miss Purity among the savages, aren't you? You really believe that having failed at everything else in life makes you the world expert on human development and child care!

GIERSHE: (*She begins to cry, hands clutching her stomach*) Answer me!

(*David leaves the room. The front door slams. Car engine is heard. Giershe lies down again. She stares at the ceiling*)

—————>>————

During the next week, Giershe packed fifty-four cartons of books to accompany David back to Centerville, cleaned the house, set her departure date, paid the travel agency for a one-way flight to Berkeley (children half-fare), sent her writing in a sealed envelope inside another larger envelope to Molly and Harry with instructions to hold for her arrival, swallowed aspirin every hour, mowed the lawn, was polite and distant with David, stayed out of his way. She felt like a lone miler on an empty track, determined to get to the finish line even though everyone has gone home. Her mind seemed to follow her around the house, detached from her body, like a balloon tied to her wrist. She saw a frazzled lady, pushing a vacuum, with a transparent balloon trailing after her. Inside the balloon were questions:

Am I strong enough to leave David?
Will I have to have an operation?
Will the children be harmed by divorce?

How can I support myself and them?

Have I failed at everything in life?

Do I know how to love?

Do I have enough paper cartons for all the books?

What does David mean when he says those things about Olivia?

She pushed the vacuum cleaner up onto Leslie's feet and thought she'd faint from the shock. "My God! Where did you come from? I didn't hear . . ." she yelled over the noise of the machine. Still dragging herself to the finish line, she made no move to turn it off. Leslie pulled the plug from the wall. "It has a turn-off switch, right here," Giershe said.

"Yes, mine does too. Marvelous!"

Giershe stared at her friend. Leslie's tidy blond thatch was limp, dirty, untidy. No lipstick, red eyes, tearstains on her face. She was wearing a lumpy gray sweatshirt which extended almost to the hem of a skirt which seemed to be fashioned of burlap sacks. She was clutching a soggy mass of Kleenex, dabbing at her eyes and blowing her nose.

"You look ghastly! What *is* the matter?"

"You're a vision yourself. The wracked-with-pain look, very fashionable this season." Leslie threw herself down on the sofa. She sobbed into a pillow and moaned: "Oh—oh—what am I going to do?" Her elegant flamingo stalks were unshaved and Giershe remembered the prostitute in *Threepenny Opera* in Munich whose stubbly armpits had sent a current of shock through an almost paralyzed audience. She thought, "Perhaps I don't know how to love, but I know that I *do* love this creature on my couch." She sat on the floor near the sofa. She wanted to touch Leslie, as she would touch and soothe Olivia, but she was afraid she might deepen the sorrow. She could touch a man, or a child, but how do women touch each other? She sat still, her hands in her lap. She sent hugs and kisses with her eyes. Her fingers itched.

"It's Jeb. He finds me *disgusting*. He won't make love with me. Says I'm an *animal!*" Leslie sat up, hiccuping. "Last night he kicked me out of bed and made me walk around the bedroom on all fours and said he was going to take me from the rear because I was a bitch."

"But why?"

"And then he got on top of me, but couldn't, and so he kicked me and knocked my head against the wall and said I was revolting, and he left and I don't know where he is." She began crying again, blowing her nose, hiccuping. "He hasn't made love to me since the book came out. He says I've made him the laughingstock of the town. He says I didn't make it up and I was writing about affairs I've had with other men. He says . . ."

"Were you?" Giershe asked tenderly.

"Yes. I can't make up anything. I just rearrange and mix it up, but it wasn't in our house, or in our bed, or with his son around like in the book, and it was before Jeb, or mostly, and I *love* Jeb! Oh, what am I going to do?"

"You're going to have some tea with whiskey in it. So am I. Come on out to the kitchen with me." Giershe stood up and put out a hand. Leslie took the tips of her extended fingers, put her feet on the floor and pulled herself up. She trailed behind like a reluctant child. At the kitchen sink, she turned on the water and bathed her face from cupped hands. She dried herself on a filthy dishcloth, then slumped into a blue chair beside the kitchen table.

Giershe turned on the flame under the copper teakettle and sat down opposite Leslie. They had never sat together in Giershe's kitchen and it was as though power had shifted to her, was coming from her own blue mugs, the red tablecloth, the margaritas and marigolds in a blue vase touching Leslie's elbow. "Leslie, you said to me once, 'You get what you want in life, but not your second choice.' I've thought about that so much. Maybe Jeb is your second choice now."

Leslie winced. "As someone said, it's bad manners to remember, and even worse manners to quote a friend to the same friend."

"It was Emerson, or Margaret Fuller. My mind has become a sieve. I remember, it was Emerson. He said—"

"Giershe, we are not at a literary tea! Thank God! Suppose I were to attend one of Jeb's functions looking like this, trailing after him keening 'Oh look what literature has done to our love!' Everyone gawking, tsking. I feel better. Where's the tea and whiskey?" Leslie laughed her high-pitched snort; Giershe giggled. She poured whiskey into the mugs, inserted two Lipton tea bags, and watched the hot water rise to the brim. They sat across from each other, clutching the hot mugs, their noses in fragrant vapor.

"You *also* said, quoting someone, who was quoting someone—"

"Giershe, I'd like my words to lie on a page somewhere, or sit in a friend's mind. I don't like them to come flapping back at me like wet wash in a cold wind."

"Is that metaphor somewhere in your journals? You said, 'We're lucky. Nothing bad can happen to us. It's all material.' This is only true if your first choice is to be a writer."

"I may have said that, but I don't remember saying I believed it. I think I believe it in reverse. Bad things happen to us, and we begin to write them down, almost in vengeance. It becomes a bad habit, and yet necessary, like farting in an aisle in the supermarket where you know you don't need anything, then wheeling away from the odor to an aisle where the air is better."

"Oh! Do you do that too? I love bagels but—"

"Good afternoon, ladies. I hope you realize that the metaphoring mind is a sign of schizophrenia," David said from the doorway, posing. "I just gave Jeb a ride home. Are you two studying to be juiceheads? What's the occasion?"

Leslie stood up. "It's farewell, Dino. I'm going to the Big City for a few days and when I return you will be gone. I hope the years bring you all you deserve." She put out her hand to David. He hesitated, as though considering whether her long fingers had a stinger attached, then smiled, grasped her hand tightly, and walked with her to the front door.

"Good-bye, Giershe," she called over her shoulder. "We'll meet again."

Giershe sat in her chair staring at Leslie's cup. There was a lump in her throat and a buzzing in her ears.

>>>——————

Berkeley, July 2, 1962

DEAR DAVID—

First night here I went to sleep to the sound of drums in the neighborhood and slept fourteen hours. Didn't even wake up when Elizabeth picked up the children for an outing in the park. In the last four years I have slept in bits and pieces.

Dr. G., after examining the doctors' reports you sent him, and my body, sees no reason for an operation, and I have had no pain since the forty-minute stopover in Dallas. He folded the reports carelessly, like yesterday's newspaper.

The plane ride was exhausting. Tony kept squirming off my lap and running through the aisles. People were kind to him. He'd stand in the aisle and study a face. Face would say hello. He'd climb into the lap, examine glasses, look through a purse. Since he was usually wet and/or carrying turds in his diapers, face would grow stern and tell him to go to Mommy. Which he wouldn't do. Olivia couldn't decide whether his behavior was criminal or perhaps she should try the same.

I don't promise to write every day. Muriel's coming over tomorrow with Andrew (I call him Piper because I hear him on the phone piping high and wild). She says Jack is in and out, does and doesn't live there. He's in charge of Piper's education and is very interested in the child. She says he's forcing her to get a teaching credential and she hates it.

The children ask about you and miss you.

love
Giershe

Berkeley, 7.31.62

DEAR LESLIE:

Letters are no substitute for sitting with you in your kitchen. I've tried writing to you many times but each time I sit down and head up the letter I think, "I'm writing to a writer," and then I just stare at the paper. I've written one story—about my stay in London some years ago. It's about friendship and filial duty and music and being, briefly, completely happy in the presence of an intelligent, loving man, without sex or romance as we know it in this here town. In the story, there's a wife on a holiday, with husband waiting for her stateside, wondering what she's up to. And here's the difficulty, aside from the gigantic difficulty of writing anything at all. Whenever I write about the David character, I get scared and cease to be honest because I know he'll read it and I don't want to roil the waters more than they are already. So I keep adding water, as you say, so the mixture won't be so strong, and after the dilution, it's all wrong and I cross out and begin again. But I can't get it right because I can't allow myself to be glad I'm not in His Presence. I bend over backwards to be fair (dishonest) and am left with a character no one could possibly object to, much less want to take a holiday from, permanently.

Writing is such hard work. Doubt of my ability crouches malevolently. I write five pages and can't bear to read them until the next day, at which time I read and am appalled by my lack of skill. Does it get any easier? And yet, writing is like cell development, quite beyond my power to control. When I'm not composing at the typewriter, I'm dialoguing in my head while I clean house or drive the car, and in company, I watch people and rearrange scenes. Sometimes I write the scene in advance of its happening. This morning Muriel Davey was coming over with her three-year-old Andrew and I knew she was going to talk about her decaying marriage to Jack. So I wrote the scene in my head while I was waiting for her, and then when she actually arrived, I dematerialized to the ceiling where I watched the two ladies go through the scene much as I'd written it. When I came down to join the group, I found that everything had already been said, and Muriel was going home. So the part I hadn't written never had a chance to happen.

Oh, by the way, sometimes Jack Davey (old ferret friend who

has left serious ferreting for a less rigorous life at the state college) comes over with Andrew, and when he's here, nothing is replay. I am present. All of me. And we talk about—child development!

Thanks for the invitation to Maine. How about next summer?

love
Giershe

>——>——>

As the summer crested, Giershe noticed in herself unmistakable signs of Romance. She read poetry before she went to sleep. She washed her hair and put on her most becoming clothes whenever Jack Davey might be expected to drop in with Andrew. She sometimes put on and took off multiple combinations of garments in her closet, in rapid succession, when she knew he would arrive within the hour, then pretended not to have heard the doorbell when it rang. She looked at her face in the mirror and wondered what he might see should he stop his pacing and look at her. As the affliction progressed, her former ease with him vanished and she carefully kept ten feet between herself and him at all times when he was in the apartment with her.

He seemed interested only in Andrew; his eyes followed the child and he made no effort at concealing his bondage. While he watched his son, he asked Giershe questions about mothering and education for three-year-olds. She gladly answered, if she could, and tried valiantly to construct into theory her vague instincts about children.

One morning they drove to the park high in the hills. There was an old carousel there, with intricately decorated horses, real stirrups, and poles to hang on to. The music was loud and enclosed in a glass box; they could watch the brass drum go around and the glittering rods fall into place. Jack sat with Andrew on a white charger. Olivia climbed onto a swan, Giershe and Tony rode the pink pony just behind Jack. She kissed the top of Tony's curls. Jack bent down to hear Andrew, then held him close. Olivia turned around to see how everyone was situated. She waved, and as the music began, grew serious, almost frightened, and hugged the swan's neck. The mounts and their riders moved up and down, the music vibrated and surged through their legs, up to stomach, heart, throat, wherever one feels purest joy. They went faster and faster but no one gained ground or moved closer. Jack couldn't stop his smile, Andrew squealed "Faster, faster," Olivia yelled "You stop that, Andrew!" and Giershe shouted into the wind, "I am happy, happy, happy!" "Happy, happy!" Tony echoed.

They rode the carousel three times. When the music stopped, the children chose different animals. Nervous, Olivia climbed the white charger. She seemed to believe that a horse would give her a more lively ride than her gentle swan. Andrew chose a bucking bronco. Tony wandered in and out of tall metal legs. When he stopped to look up at an animal, he would lose his balance and sit down. He paused at the proud ostrich and said, "Up!" Giershe placed him in the seat and he said, "Go way, Mommy!" Jack watched her hesitate. He shook his head. She climbed up behind Tony and thought how pleasant it was to want to obey.

The music began again and slowly gathered sound, movement, up and down, helping them ride their fantasies to a sure completion. She studied Jack. All the adjectives people attached to him swarmed into her mind. Gruff, "black," cold, Machiavellian, lawless, witty, earthy, profane, tender-tough, ruthless, manipulative, self-made, mocking, devious, remote, brave, and Muriel's favorite—"that fuckin' Jack." Yesterday she had said, "That fuckin' Jack, when he *does* sleep with me, he just puts it in, grunts until he comes, then rolls over and snores. He makes love like a longshoreman. He won't stay with me. He has a pad across town where he goes most nights. He entertains all his women there. I'm Andrew's mother and that's the only reason he's ever around. Oh Giershe, what am I going to do?" Her beautiful green eyes brimmed with tears. Giershe handed her a Kleenex and said the first thing that came to her mind:

"Muriel, you wanted a child of his, as a sort of consolation-prize ending to a crummy marriage. That's what you said. Now you have not just 'a child' but a splendid little boy with an adoring father. None of us seems to be able to create the marriage of dreams."

"What do you mean, 'none of us'—is David . . . ?"

"Another time. I have to get the children ready to go to dinner at their grandparents'."

Around and around they went, a third time. Jack stood beside the bucking bronco, his hand tucked firmly into Andrew's waistband. He was short, no more than five foot six, and he didn't seem big enough to have sparked so much fear in those who crossed his path. No one would have called him loving or happy or gentle, yet there he was, shielding his son, smiling helplessly. She had always felt uncomfortable with him, afraid of his mockery. He and Muriel never had a kind word to say about their acquaintances, and Giershe had often wondered what rendering of the Kinnards they served up to mutual friends. With Muriel, he was abrupt and curt, cutting off her chatter by abrasively moving into a new monologue, a different subject, as though not completely aware that she existed. She would have preferred watching Muriel be silly, coquetting, posturing for the men, patting the women. Anything was better than another academic lecture. Jack was boring, like all professors. He would pace back and forth in any room, hearing only his own sounds, infatuated with his theories and their articulation, drowning conversation, until everyone yielded a weak social effort to his strong claim. Except David. David had the energy to shout: "AREN'T YOU FORGETTING THE WHOLE HISTORY OF . . . ?" Muriel and Giershe would go to bed with the sounds of their swords clanging. Giershe always hoped they'd leave the next day.

In each of their visits to the Kinnard household, Jack would wander into the kitchen to pay his respects to the hostess. He would nibble at food on the sink drain board, open the refrigerator, look for cheeses, select a beer, close the door, pace around the room, look out the window, choose something to say to Giershe: "How goes the life of a scholar's wife? You're looking very motherly and pretty in your blouse and peasant skirt. I see you haven't given up the costume of Berkeley. Does my favorite hexa have any words of wisdom for a weary traveler?"

"I wish you wouldn't call me a hexa. Why do you?"

"All of us are fools. You are the only wise one among us."

"That's blather. Hexa doesn't mean 'wise one'—it means that I cast spells and jinxes and if I could I would, but I can't, alas." He was playing with her, and she hoped he'd leave the kitchen soon. She felt tit-witted around him. Jack began opening drawers, looking for a bottle opener. She pointed to the wall above the sink and returned her wet hand to a bowl of lettuce.

"See, sweet Giershe, that's what I mean. You don't prattle. If words are unnecessary, you leave them alone. With that silence wrapped around you, it's no wonder we feel you have powers beyond our ken."

"There's no room in scholarland for my words, and if I were to speak my thoughts, much madness would emerge."

Jack paced the kitchen. "'Much madness is divinest Sense—To a discerning Eye—Much Sense—the starkest Madness—'Tis the Majority—In this, as All, prevail—Assent—and you are sane—'" He paused, looking to her for help.

"'Demur—you're straightway dangerous'!'" she whispered.

"'And handled with a Chain,'" he finished, smirking at her. "Last year, I remembered the time you told me Emily helps you understand. I surely needed more understanding, and I bought a collection of her poetry. She's a fine poet. I wrote you a letter about it, in an airport. Didn't you get it?"

"Yes, I got it. I was touched, but I thought you were copying from the book. I certainly didn't think you'd memorize. I'm sorry I didn't answer your letter, but David . . ."

"Yes, your chain. You are his body slave. How do you stand it? Do you gather rich sustenance by serving his body and soul?"

"Sh-h, he'll hear you. Hush up and let me get dinner ready."

"He's talking. Don't you ever want to break the lock and walk free?"

"Hush! He *will* hear you! Be nice and go back to the other room. Please."

The music had stopped. Tony was wiggling in her grasp, Andrew was shouting "More, Daddy, more, let's go round again!" and Olivia was searching for her next mount. Jack carefully lowered Tony to the ground and then extended his hand to Giershe. He gazed up at her, waiting. His sailor hat sat on frizzy hair backing off a massive forehead. His eyebrows were shaggy tufts shading gray-blue eyes. She wanted to touch his face and trim his eyebrows. The hand waited, delicate with curled hairs. How many things his hands could do! Put radios together, repair cars, install house wiring, button a little boy's pants, fix gas ovens. Could they also make love? Giershe ignored his hand and slid quickly down the opposite side of her horse. He shouted, "Popcorn, anyone?" and instantly they left off their wailing at leaving the carousel and followed him to the popcorn stand. They wandered through a eucalyptus grove, walking slowly, munching popcorn. She wanted to ask him to be alone with her, without the children, just once before she had to leave. But how could she ask him such a thing? They were together in a mutual concern for Olivia, Tony, and Andrew, and Jack gave no sign of further interest. He might laugh at her. She couldn't ask him. He leaned against a tree: "Muriel is fixing dinner tomorrow night in sad celebration of your departure this weekend. She's made me promise to attend, play the host and carve the roast, mix the drinks, all things she can do without me. You'll come? With the children, of course."

"Yes, I'll come. Did you get those books from the university?"

"They're in the car."

"I need support for my own instincts about children, and I'm hoping Montessori will give me some answers."

"What do you plan to do with what you learn? Apply it in the kitchen in between cooking dinner and typing manuscripts? I understand the only training program in Montessori is in your great state of Connecticut. Why don't you enroll?"

"It IS? Oh. Oh." Giershe's heart lurched around inside her. If she could leave David *for* something else, perhaps he would let her ease out without destruction. He wouldn't have to say, "She left me"; he could say, "Giershe is taking the Montessori training for young children." It would be like giving meat to the Dragon and slipping by to Paradise while he ate. Money. She'd have to borrow. Maybe he'd cosign a loan. She could start a school not too far away so the children would be able to see him regularly. They'd have a formal separation eventually, like Jack and Muriel, and a coming together amicably for the sake of their children's care and training. She sat down on a tree stump and hugged her knees. She looked up at Jack, still leaning against a tree. A breeze swirled dry leaves at his feet. Blue tennis shoes, blue cords, blue cotton shirt, hands jingling his car keys, and the face looking down at her, serious now and eyes steady. Always impatient to be moving, get things done, get on with it, decide, plan, formulate, he now seemed content to be the still center of her tempest. They smiled at each other.

"I see you have lots to think about. You'll be up all night reading. Let's get going. Come on, Andrew, it's time to go." He put out his hand to her and this time she grasped it and gave a little squeeze. As Andrew came towards them, he gently pulled away his hand. A three-year-old could talk, could give the history of their afternoon to a mind called Mommy. As could a four-year-old. Even Tony, with his few words, might find a way to report two hands together. She felt soiled, as though the sea gull she'd been watching had dropped a gray blob on her upturned face. She told herself she must be more careful, but careful of what? Of her happiness? Did being happy, however briefly, take something away from David or Muriel?

Jack waited with Andrew in the front seat of his blue '49 Ford while she gathered socks, shoes, Olivia, and a resisting Tony. She climbed into the back seat with Tony on her hip kicking his heels, struggling, working up a tantrum. He threw himself on the floor, which was littered with old newspapers, cigar rings, dirty socks, broken toys, pipe fittings, resistors, and one car battery. While Jack took the curves down the hill with sickening speed, Giershe tried to assemble Tony on her lap. He screamed and hit out at her. Andrew, standing placidly on the front seat, with one arm tightly around his father's neck, put his free hand over his ear, and blinked his big green eyes. Olivia rolled down the window and stuck out her head to "windy" her hair. Tony screamed all the way down the hill. Jack turned around once, looked at him with distaste, and shouted over the noise: "Jesus! What in hell's the matter with him?"

"Popcorn, maybe!" Giershe shouted, apologetically, knowing it wasn't popcorn.

"Tell Olivia to pull her head inside the car!" Jack yelled. Olivia didn't wait to be told. She rolled up the window, stuffed herself into the corner and began to sulk.

⸻ ⟩⟩⟩ ⸻

On the next afternoon, at five o'clock, Giershe and Olivia climbed the stairs of Muriel's second-floor apartment. Tony trailed behind.

"Hurry UP, Tony! We'll be late!" Olivia scolded. She had copied Giershe's frantic indecision about what to wear. She'd tried on all combinations, settling at last on her birthday dress with huge red apples against a white background, and a bonnet to match. She was submerged in the bright print and her little hands kept smoothing down the bouffant skirt as though irritated by its independent life. It was a gift from Angela, who worried that Olivia never "dressed up." Since dressing up seemed to put her in a cross-patch temper, Giershe never suggested it. She recalled the many times the only way Molly and Harry had been able to get their second daughter to accompany them to a fancy restaurant was to agree to her own terms, which were blue jeans and permission to order a tuna sandwich, even if it was not on the menu.

Olivia pressed the doorbell button. Giershe felt faint. She could hear Andrew: "Doorbell! I'll get it! I'll answer it! Let me!" and Muriel's voice: "No, Andrew. I'm giving you five minutes to get dressed! Jack! Put some clothes on this boy!" Muriel opened the door. Andrew was hiding behind her, naked.

"Oh! You are so clean and beautiful and tan! Come in." She smiled at Giershe. She was wearing her Berkeley uniform—faded blue jeans, blue turtleneck, thong sandals, and, for the occasion, a ridiculous white organdy apron with a huge bow tied in back. Earrings of silver, three inches long, dangled to her shoulders; her chestnut hair drooped in soft curls around her face and swirled into a bun in back. She turned from her guests to scold Jack, who was sitting at a table with a tape recorder laid out before him, his hands surrounded by pinch pliers, tape, and plastic parts. "Jack! I told you what time it was. *Please* get Andrew dressed! I need to set the table. Dinner's almost ready."

Olivia stood by Jack's elbow; she picked up a tiny red-and-blue wire. "Good afternoon, Olivia. You're looking very nice. Do you want to learn how to fix a tape recorder?"

"Jack! Get that shit off that table!"

"Olivia, why don't you put all these pieces in this box for me? And if you'll do that, we can set the table for the lady of the house. While you're busy, I'll see if Andrew has put clothes on for company. Giershe! Lovely as always! Berkeley seems to be agreeing with you. Where's Tony? Did he recover from his bout with popcorn?" Jack grasped her arm above the elbow, placed a kiss on her cheek, and without waiting for a reply, went in search of Andrew.

"What can I do to help, Muriel? Something smells good. A roast, new potatoes, tiny peas. They're fresh? And homemade biscuits! You must be celebrating something besides my departure. Have you finished your classes?" Her arm, where Jack had touched, felt hot.

"Finished! My last final was yesterday. The only thing worse than taking education courses is teaching art to high school students. Tomorrow Andrew and I have to drive into that fuckin' hot flat valley to look for an apartment.

Here, put these on the table. And go see what Jack's doing with Andrew, will you? Dinner's just about ready."

Giershe, with Olivia following closely, stepped through Muriel's black-on-white decor to the doorway of an adjoining room (white with one black chest of drawers). The floor was strewn with Andrew's clothes, wires, bulbs, six-volt batteries, flashlight parts, a fish tank with one goldfish. Jack was picking up clothes. Andrew was sitting in the middle of the room in his underpants, wrapping wires around a light bulb.

"Okay, Andrew. Now if you'll just head for the bathroom, I'll wipe the dirt off your face." When Andrew saw Olivia, he dropped the wired bulb and ran past her into the bathroom. He stood in front of the basin hopping up and down, turned the water on full force, stuck in the plug, then pulled it out again. He watched the water go down the drain.

"Dad! Dad! Where does the water go?" Jack stepped past Giershe. Again, he put his hand on her arm without looking at her.

"Leave the water in the basin. We're not playing now, we're getting ready for dinner." There was a hint of controlled exasperation. "The water flows down, out of the drain. Look, see the pipes." He opened the cabinet beneath the basin. Andrew sat on his heels to look. "Notice the pipe has a track in a U-shape, so heavy objects will fall to the bottom and not float out to the sewer." He traced the pipe with his hand. Andrew repeated the motion.

Olivia edged closer to look at the pipes under the basin. Jack smiled up at Giershe. "This is a lot more fun than standing up in front of slack-jawed youth and talking about the gold standard."

In the living room, Tony was piling white pillows in a tower on the black couch, climbing up and letting himself fall over as the tower fell, sometimes to the floor on his head.

Jack fixed three gin and tonics. Giershe took one sip, shivered, and placed her glass on the kitchen counter.

"Ten years in schullardland and still not a drinker! Most of the wives I've known can drink me under the table!"

"And you know what happens under the table." Muriel curled her mouth in a sneer, yet managed to keep her taunt almost light by pretending to be pretending. Jack stared at her. He paced from the kitchen area to the window looking out on the street below. He held his head back as though looking at a distant horizon, one hand tucked into his trouser pocket. His walk had a slight roll to it, like Captain Bligh on deck.

"All righty-o. Let's sit down. Giershe next to Tony. Andrew next to Olivia on that side. Jack, can you bring the meat to the table?" Muriel, falsely gay.

"You should be able to answer this, Giershe," Jack began. "I'm not too surprised that the men stay with the system until they're dead, or have become basket cases—but why do the women put up with it? Are they so wrapped up in the man's fortunes that they . . ."

"JACK! Carve the meat! Maybe the women *like* staying home with their children. It sure beats teaching." The children were staring at one another. Andrew was silent, leaning away from Olivia, with his hand on his father's arm while Jack was trying to carve. Jack accepted the extra weight.

"I think I'll change the subject. Muriel is not ready to count her blessings. Giershe, did you read in Montessori?"

Giershe took a deep breath. "I'm afraid to talk about her. I'm afraid that if I speak, it won't come out right and will vanish. Her wisdom, her clarity, will come out fuzzy from contact with my lazy brain. I wish I'd brought the book with me."

"Good, huh?" Jack asked gently. He passed a plate of food to Muriel.

"I read until about three this morning and I feel wiser and stronger now, so much better able to see what I'm seeing when I look at my children." Giershe cut Tony's meat into small pieces, then got up to cut Olivia's. Andrew was eating his meat with his fingers, his huge eyes on Tony across the table from him. Muriel poured the wine and held her glass high as Jack sat down. Jack raised his glass: "To our children, to Montessori, to us—may we all get off our asses this coming year and contribute our talents to the community!"

"Fuck the community!" said Muriel, daintily sipping her wine, with little finger arched. She looked from Jack to Giershe and back to Jack; she took another sip from her glass, set it on the table, and began to eat, somehow mocking theory with her robust appetite.

"Last night—don't laugh—I wanted to become a Montessori teacher so badly that I understood what 'to be called' might mean. I . . ." Giershe couldn't continue. She didn't trust them. They would laugh at her as soon as she left. She turned to Tony, mussed his hair, and lifted his glass of milk to his lips. He pushed her wrist down until the glass sat again on the table. Using both hands, he tipped the milk into his mouth, gulping until it was gone.

Jack decided to rescue her. "I don't have intellectual love affairs anymore. But perhaps, for you, this love is necessary to carry you through to action." Did Jack talk in bed with a woman? Did he make love with his mouth pouring words over a quivering body?

After dinner, Giershe wanted to leave, Muriel wanted her to stay and talk, and Jack wanted to continue fixing his tape recorder. The children were happy enough stumbling over junk in Andrew's room. Olivia was ordering Tony not to touch Andrew's light bulbs, and Tony was having fun stepping on objects and trying to keep his balance. Muriel excused herself to go to the bathroom.

"Come on, kids. Time to go home. It's eight o'clock."

"Well, Giershe, it's been interesting. I hope you're prepared for what awaits you when David hears of your response to Madame Montessori. You'll keep me informed?" His hand on her upper arm again. Her legs trembled.

"Jack . . ." She let herself lean against his shoulder, "Would you come to say good-bye to me tomorrow night, about nine?"

He stared at her, into her. He removed his hand. "Of course," he said.

Muriel returned. "Oh Giershe, I wish you wouldn't go! Jack could stay with the kids and we could take a walk or go to a show. Are you ever coming back to Berkeley? Who's going to listen to me when you're gone? Not Jack, for sure." She hugged Giershe, pretending to shed tears, and caressed her head.

"Muriel, leave her alone. You're always pawing people," Jack muttered.

>>>>>>

The day after Muriel's dinner party, the world of people and objects fought Giershe. Her hair was washed twice but refused to shine. She burned the pancakes and boiled the maple syrup. The percolator broke when she took it from the burner and set it on the cold tile counter. Coffee spilled to the floor and onto her bare feet, just missing Tony, who was building a railroad track across the kitchen floor. The orange juice sat in her stomach. Molly called three times and was worried about her. She said Giershe seemed nervous, and shouldn't she return to David immediately so that the "family can be together for a while before winter"? Harry called to ask if she'd remembered to change the oil in his car and did she want him to help her pack? Elizabeth wanted to come to dinner and couldn't understand why Giershe was sounding so distant. She reminded her that some time should be spent with her family, didn't she think? No, she didn't think, couldn't, wouldn't. Olivia tried to pack and things wouldn't fit; Tony touched something of hers and she cried.

"I wish you'd help me today by being happy, Olivia."

"I *can't* get happy, *because* I'm so *un*happy," her daughter wailed.

"What would make you happy?"

"I think I might get happy if we went to the park." Olivia was not a devious person, this four-year-old. She always told the exact truth and although she enjoyed fairy tales, she wanted her mother to label them "pretend" and sometimes asked in the middle of the night if the "realio, trulio dragon" was real or pretend. She was missing her father. Giershe didn't have to guess this. Olivia told her several times a day: "Mommy, I miss Father. I want to go home. We have to go home and take care of Father." Giershe would try to explain that the hot weather had made her sick and that Father had to work hard to keep his job. But Olivia knew, beneath words, that her mother was trying to decide not to go home.

When Tony heard the word "park" he went to the front door to wait. He was naked, except for the peanut butter on his face. So they went again to the merry-go-round and it was pleasant not worrying about doing or saying something which the children might tell David. They ate peanut-butter sandwiches and tangerines beneath the eucalyptus trees and Olivia collected all the pods she could stuff into a brown bag "to make my room smell nice at home." Giershe lay on her back in the hard-packed dirt, and the drifting clouds gave her the illusion of movement. Tony sat beside her with his elbow in her stomach. He kissed her cheek and pinched her nose until she made the gasping noise which was the whole joke. He laughed and kissed her on the mouth and bit her lip. Olivia sat down beside them. "Mommy, when we go back to Centerville, will Father be there?"

"Yes."

"And then we'll all be together and live happily ever after?"

"I don't know. Father and I fight a lot and we can't seem to stop."

"Mommy, a long time ago, did you live by yourself without Tony and Olivia?"

"Yes."

"Without Father?"

"Yes."

"Then you said, 'I want Tony and Olivia and so I must find Father,' yes?"

"No"—Giershe tried to sound convincing—"I said, 'I want to find Father.' "

"Oh—*then* you found Father and *then* you said, 'Now we must get Olivia and Tony,' and *then* we came!" She lay down on her back to look at the sky. Giershe sat up and hugged them both. The three of them together, how peaceful they were when they paused and took the time, when they escaped ceilings, schedules, relatives and friends. "The sun is saying it's about four o'clock. We have to leave. Tony, hand me your socks and I'll put them on."

"*I* do!" Tony said, and struggled to stuff his brown foot into a sock.

"Oh boy, he thinks he knows how to do everything!" Olivia whispered.

><><><

Giershe sat quietly in the dark. Somewhere in the neighborhood drums were beating bum-bum-bum-te-bum, without pause or alteration. A fire siren climbed up to join the beat, then faded out in the distance. Tony slept so peacefully, Olivia with her mouth open. Adenoids? Tonsils? She closed the bedroom door behind her. The apartment was small but had three levels: liv-

ing room and kitchen, up four stairs to the bathroom and the children's bedroom, down four stairs from the living room to a second bedroom—a convert-
ed garage with closets and carpet. The floor of the upstairs bedroom was the
ceiling of the garage bedroom, and in the morning Giershe would hear Tony
shake his crib to make it roll around the room. Olivia would say crossly, "Be
quiet, Tony, you'll wake Mommy. I want to slee-e-e-p!" Silence. Then a crash as
Tony threw himself over the bars of the crib to the floor. "Tonee-e-e!" Silence.
Tony's footsteps running across the floor, pause to open the door, down the
stairs, around the corner, pause, jiggle the doorknob, peek in, five more steps
to Mommy's bed. She would keep her eyes closed, pretending sleep. Wet-dia-
per smell. Sweet baby breath on her cheek as he inspected her. Then two tiny
fingers would try to lift her eyelid, pulling gently on her eyelash. She would
wait while he tugged. Suddenly she would come to life with a fierce growl.
Tony would squeal and climb onto the bed, jump up and down, then tuck himself under the covers beside her. She would go back to sleep and he would lie
still, watching the morning light, the breeze lifting the curtains on the open
window. Every morning of the summer.

Giershe heard a car door bang. Jack so soon? She hurried downstairs,
down four steps to her bedroom and over to the window. Her stomach was
throwing darts again. A black man visiting the girl next door. Door opened. A
flash of white teeth in the moonlight. He went inside. Door closed. Drums.
She threw off her bathrobe, put on white panties, white bra against brown skin,
black velvet pants, emerald green sleeveless blouse, sandals. She rushed to the
bathroom to stare at her face. "What the hell are you doing?" she quizzed her
reflection. "You! A mother! At your age! Oh God, dark circles, crazy eyes, skinny neck." Getting the tremblies with Jack. Jack, the opportunist. Will he come
say good-bye to Giershe? Of course, why not? The lonely, unhappy wife on
vacation. All over town they waited for car doors to bang, the children asleep,
the moon high in the sky. A transcontinental game of forbidden bodies. No,
she would listen to Jack talk, she would thank him for the good days of summer. She would not—then why the sexy pants and why did she feel that the
deed was already done and she was looking back on it, remembering?

Lipstick, Yardley lavender toilet water, pearl earrings. Crazy nervous.
Down to the living room. Turn on a light. Too bright. Turn it off. Turn on the
pole lamp with its lamps reflecting light off the ceiling. Where should she sit?
In the big easy chair, curled up like a little girl with legs tucked in tight? Buried
feeling, trapped. She sat on the couch, legs outstretched, one brown arm dangling down languorously, pillows piled at her back, her other arm resting on a
stray pillow. Cross the legs. Kick off her sandals. She had a giggling fit. Oh,
men and women were too, too funny.

She moved to the kitchen, an environment where she felt at home. She put beer in the refrigerator and filled the teakettle. The percolator was broken but there was a fancy electric percolator in the closet. She got it out and was staring at it, trying to discover its secrets, when there was a knock at the door. She leaned against the counter, her knees wobbling. "Whatever comes, let it be light and sweet," a small prayer spoken to moon and crickets. She opened the door.

"Good evening, Giershe." Jack glanced briefly at her and moved into the living room. "Christ, what a night! Moon, drums. Do you have a beer for a weary traveler? Muriel couldn't face house-hunting unless I went down with her. She stayed down there with Andrew and I think she'll find something tomorrow. Fuckin' freeway. Kids asleep?" He followed Giershe into the kitchen. She stood beside the counter, unable to remember why they were in the kitchen. He looked at her, judging what he saw. "You must have had a good day! Very lovely, fresh and cool. Have any cheese? No dinner. I just had time to shower. Just crackers, maybe some coffee later. Oh goddamn, it's good to be here. You have a precious gift of making peaceful any kind of hole. How do you do it? Eh? If you could tell others how, the world would be a happier place."

Giershe prepared a plate of cheese, crackers, pumpernickel bread. Jack nibbled and paced the kitchen. "I'll start some coffee if you'll tell me how to work the landlord's percolator. I broke mine this morning. That's how peaceful I am. You prefer to see façades."

"Façades, that's all I ask. Who wants to look into dark interiors? They're all alike. Dank, messy, poisonous. There you go, just put the coffee into this part and punch the button. It works by itself and we can retire to the living room where I want to hear what else you've discovered in Montessori."

"I didn't read today. Everyone was fretting so we spent the whole day in the park. I feel all smoothed out." Giershe draped herself on the couch. Jack walked back and forth, his eyes fixed on whatever wall moved towards him. "Do you feel like talking? I'd like to know how you made up your mind to leave prestigious university-hopping and settle on the second-rate, as they say." Get him talking. Like a windup toy. When he runs down, start him again. That's what women do. It's a support system which professors' wives develop to an art. If they listen, sometimes they learn a thing or two.

"Talk, I can always talk," Jack began wearily. "After the last big-time stint, I refused to be a schullard any longer. It took me ten years to pull myself free, and I haven't recovered from the damage. Whatever creativity I had before grad school was destroyed and I am still incapable of independent thought or action. But there's one thing I'll tell you. The stuffiness of academic society I'll no longer tolerate. I don't like professors, their wives, their children, their casseroles. They spend all their money on microfilm and books and eat stuff that rots their guts, if they have any left to rot. Professors are impecunious, ungenerous, and Pecksniffish."

"And always use predicate adjectives in groups of three."

"Do we? Do they? Did I?" Jack halted his journey across the room.

"It's a minor speech defect I noticed one day. I haven't been able to stop noticing. Sometimes I just count three and forget to listen."

"*What* three did I use?"

"Um—Pecksniffish, impecunious, ungenerous."

"Christ! Some of the damage I'm not even aware of!"

Giershe turned herself around on the couch so she could watch Jack pace from the front door to the kitchen. It was going to be a long evening. He hadn't even looked at her yet, unless you counted his brief interest in threes, and his kitchen survey. "Why did you go to all that trouble if it was so distasteful?"

"I was a poor boy from Missouri. All I had was brains. I went to graduate school because the professor said that was what you did if you had brains. It wasn't whether or not, but which one? Is the beer in the refrigerator? Don't get up, you look lovely sitting there. I'm talking too much. Do you want to go out somewhere? Oh, I forgot the bairn asleep upstairs."

"What do you think of your present colleagues?" If she asked questions all night long, would he answer in complete sentences until dawn? Would the children pull away from sleep, warm and damp, open their bedroom door, sit together on the top stair, their tousled heads turning to the right, then left, trying to follow his words and feet?

"At State College one doesn't have to be a dismal *careerist!*"

"What's a careerist? Is David?"

"Quintessentially!" Jack snarled. "There is no indignity he will not suffer, no ass he would not kiss, no boring labor he would not undertake if it would advance his career." Then, more kindly, as he saw Giershe shrink back into the pillows, "You know that! You have suffered it for years, not always quietly. It has driven you—sometimes—almost insane." Jack stopped talking and Giershe knew she didn't want to wind him up again. He was standing at the front door. He might open it and walk out. She stood up, hesitant.

"Jack, it's getting late."

"Yes, and we both must get some sleep before our labors begin again."

Three feet between them, but she couldn't walk that far. Dizzying fear. Of what? He stepped forward. They pressed together like folded hands. Shorter than David, fitting face to face, body on body. Gentle fingers caressing her head.

"Sleep? Together, do you mean?" She tried to recall if this was what she intended.

"Yes, of course together. We made a contract. Last night. Don't you remember?"

"But do you promise—not to betray? Not to tell?"

"Silly Giershe. I promise. You do me honor, kind lady." They smiled and hugged and swayed and couldn't seem to pull apart. He whispered in her ear. "I'll turn off the lights. You go get in bed."

>>>——>

At 5:30 a.m. Jack left Giershe's rumpled bed. She raised herself up to peek through the window after he had closed the bedroom-garage door. She watched him climb over the fence, saw him wave one hand at her face in the window, turn away, sprint down the sidewalk. She couldn't see his car. Had he parked it away from the front of the apartment to hide his presence? How deeply secretive he was! How much she knew of him, and how little. She slept, hugging the sheets and pillow which smelled of his warm body. No remorse, no sadness. No bite of guilt or sorrow.

Later, when Tony stood beside the bed, she said: "Oh, Tony-baloney! I'm a happy mommy and ferocious. Look out! I shall eat you!" Tony's wet diapers were clinging to his knees. He lay down and kicked until he was free of them. He staggered back and forth on the bed, his little penis bobbing up and down. She stared at him. Was there any way to teach a male to make love like Jack? No one ever talked about it. No man she had known, no book she had read, told of learning an art so intricate that to speak truly of its mysteries would paralyze the initiate at the start. Most boys learned early to pursue and take what they could get from swift encounters. If one pursues, the other must flee and be caught, yield, and taste sadness. Wait for her, Tony. Wait until it's a necessity as natural as peeing when you need to, or sleeping when you're weary. And practice while you wait! Stroke cats, dogs, rabbits, birds fallen from a nest, horses, the petals of flowers, hot sand, water in the bath, tree trunks, leaves, piano keys, the paper you write on and the penis you aim at a toilet bowl. Practice!

"Want a helicopter ride, Tony?" She lay down on her back in the middle of the bed, her knees together and pulled up almost to her chin. She lifted Tony high and placed his stomach on the soles of her feet. She wiggled her toes. He giggled. She held his hands tightly and slowly straightened her legs until he was riding her feet, high in the air. He stretched his legs behind him, arched his back, and became the big machine. He sputtered bubbles from his mouth for exhaust and tried to dip and turn his naked craft. "Look out, you're going to CRASH!" She let him fall down to safe sheets and blankets.

"Me too, Mommy! It's my turn now!" Olivia cried. She stood at the door, rubbing sleep from her eyes. Giershe gave Olivia a turn, then Tony again, then Olivia, then Tony, until sun filled the room.

"Okay. Stop now. I'm tired." They lay quietly together on their backs, watching sun patterns on the ceiling.

"It smells *funny* in here." Olivia wrinkled her nose.

"Funny? I think it smells like sweat and skin and sun and hair and Tony's diapers. Is that a funny all-mixed-up smell?

"Yes! And it smells like walls and curtains and sheets and windows . . ." Olivia listed everything she could see. Tony lay still and pulled on his little knob.

>>—>——>——

Eleven days of postponing air flights, eleven nights with Jack. Eleven days of insufficient explanation to Elizabeth, Molly, and Harry. Eleven days of lies to David. Eleven nights when tongues traded biographies, when they had the time. Eleven days of dazed wonder at the body's regenerative powers. One night of fear and tears. She would return to Centerville. She would take the Montessori training if they would accept her. They would be mature. They would postpone. They would write every day. They would not forget. They would meet again and unite in a new radical marriage without clutch or bad temper. Surely discarded mates would be reasonable. The children would adjust. David and Muriel would be glad to start new lives. In the meantime, she would prepare herself for a career with young children and he would write his book on social theory. Chin up, be brave, be strong. "Be a dreadnought!" he said. On the twelfth day, Elizabeth took Giershe, Tony, and Olivia to the airport.

7

"I don't know,"

Alice said doubtfully.

"I don't want to be

anybody's prisoner

I want to be a Queen!"

DEAR JACK:

Confusion! We've had night after dismal night of confession and semiconfession and where are we? He's confessed all sorts of females I knew, or assumed, were something more than coffee dates, but I feel nothing more than a faintly derisive tolerance for the foibles of men-children. He claims he loved me throughout and still does. I deny you, perhaps because I'm reluctant to disturb, at this exhausted moment, his pride. And don't wish to share you. I don't understand where we are, who we are, or how any of us got from there to here. Your letters are wonderful! The P.O. box works well. If you don't hear from me, don't worry. I no longer have a room of my own.

your
Giershe

Centerville
8.30.62

DEAREST JACK—

Last night he came to me with urgent love, and because I was roused from dreams, I moved through the farce without once taking my mind from you, and even while engaged, composed this letter to you. In the morning I was assaulted by loving looks and adoring eyes. I fled to the kitchen where I dispensed malignancies of sound all around and claimed a headache I didn't have. Strange that we discussed so calmly the next summer, or a distant future meeting, but forgot to take up the question of this week, and the next.

love
Giershe

Centerville
8.31.62

DEAREST JACK—

David guessed. He said: "I suppose it was at your invitation
and was brief, clean, impersonal." I've denied you many times. I
don't smile. Sometimes now, as I walk the streets of Centerville, I
am without warning visited by you. I feel you and am faint. I had
thought I might not answer your letters or keep them, but I read
them again and again, and preserve them like nuts against winter.
I answer whenever I can be alone for long enough. My first letter
to you was composed in a parked car, in fetid humidity, with
cross children eager to be off. It was the first time I'd been away
from David in five days.

I'm so tired of being the cause for another's pain. My job now
is to put myself loosely apart from him, find a way to earn a good
living and keep the children within easy reach of both parents.
What heaven it would be to live with someone one wants in
every way to please!

It's underwater weather and I'm back on Diuril, the balance of
which is never sure. Only last week I was well, happy, and you-
and-I was all that was important. Now we've lost our hyphens
and are in a mess. What intellectual tomfoolery it is to expect the
pen to continue what was wrought by all the swift senses. Are
you frightened of the downslope of our twelve-day love? It's all a
piece with leaves falling, birds departing, all the eastern events
which tear me each year. It's a child's reluctance to awaken the
day after Christmas.

Sorry this letter is so jittery. It has been written in at least
eight pieces of time, place, health, and mood.

Always love
Giershe

Berkeley
August 30.62

DEAREST GIERSHE—

I have never been a lover of the telephone but now I want to call you a dozen times a day. Your voice is perfect reflection of your mind and spirit. It is complex in tone and has dozens of subtly shaded nuances. It hovers and expresses in sound those things that are beyond mere words.

My darling, don't despair. David will return to sanity. He will stop trying to hold you when he sees that you only want yourself. He will see, unless he is mad, that we all belong to ourselves.

No one in his right mind wishes not to love the mother or father of his children. I have spent hour after futile hour wanting desperately to love Muriel simply because it was the most sensible thing to do. It was no use.

Each night at this time I imagine how delicious it would be to come to your bed, wrap you around me, and fall into a perfect sleep.

Jack

Centerville
September 3.62

DEAR JACK—

I'm sitting on someone's grave, headstone as backrest. This is not metaphor. I ran from house with pen, paper, and envelope, leaving behind a furious David and two small children. The sun is shining gently on me, and I can see Connecticut's tame landscape from high atop a lovely Indian graveyard where I have come, winter, spring, and all seasons since I've been here—to reclaim myself. It is very quiet here and after the angry shouts and brutal words, this absence of sound is itself a balm.

I found out today that the Montessori training is school from September through June, an hour away by highway, and costs $1,000. There is a guarantee of a job with one of their schools in California and a permanent career in a booming cult. Both children could attend same school. Today, while I was trying to find out by phone whether a fellowship was possible, David told me I'm a mess, a tramp, a failure at living and loving, I shall destroy the children, am death-centered, there's no joy in me,

Olivia will crack up if I leave, I'm frigid, and I've never been able to love anyone. I feel like a building tagged for demolition. Last night we were quite serene, and he accused me of feeling fine. I told him I was trying to keep calm, sort the necessary possessions, and not act hastily. He approved, yesterday.

How shall I ever recover from hurting David?

love
Giershe

San Jose
Sept. 9.62

DEAREST GIERSHE—

This is the last love letter I will write to you for the month of noninvolvement with me that you asked for today. I will resume them sooner if you request me to do so. Today I finally received some of what you've been absorbing for two weeks. First, there was a long conversation with you, and then tonight a much longer one with Muriel. I was a big winner today. At one p.m. you asked me to get out of your life, to go love someone else, anyone else, and at one a.m. Muriel asked me to get out of her life and go love you, or someone else, anyone else was also fine with her. Tomorrow Andrew will probably hand me my shaving kit and sleeping bag and I can wrap up the bloody lot of it. I suppose I can now move into my utopian community as the sole tenant.

I'm not interested in another nuclear marriage. If I must die before the grave, I prefer to die alone. You spoke once of a radical marriage or union. Such things are not constructed in moments of passion. Such a union is built to preserve life and passion in a world which has conspired to eliminate them and to form mankind into a seething mass of hatred. To build radically in this world requires care and negotiation. It must be based, of course, on a contract, but not contracted between those who are not equal. If I said to you now, "Fly to my arms," and you did, you would be standing here defenseless, and would have little choice but to take love as I administered it. Why trade a known for an unknown misery?

You also said today that I should never have allowed you to leave California. My darling, you can't come here until you leave Centerville. I'm not a home-destroyer. I didn't kill your love for

David, and I didn't take your body away from him. Love had died in you and your body was a useless thing. I allowed love to be reborn and gave you back your body. What you now choose to do with this soul and body that's once more yours is entirely up to you. You may give them to David or to me, but you might also choose another or even decide to keep them for yourself!

What a dull love letter this has turned into. Thank God I've said everything serious I think needs to be said for the next ten years. It sure as hell has drained all passion from me.

Goodnight
Jack

Centerville
September 10.62

DEAR JACK—

All of your letters are in David's possession, including several I've not even seen. Centerville's postmaster gave them to him upon request. And when I realized he had the written notice of your love for me, all will flowed out of me. All I could do was *beg* him to return the letters. Scenes, wreckage. Two telephones (one of them red) pulled from the wall (to keep me from calling you), wires torn from the engine of the auto (to keep me from escaping), light fixture in kitchen dangling from its gut, one broken newel post, and a crying Giershe. Disgusting. I know he will use the letters to attempt to claim Olivia and Tony.

Today was the day I was going to Greenwich with Olivia, but David said he wouldn't take care of the children or borrow money for Montessori unless I *promised* a future. I can't move my will. I must write letters and request sums. I must pack. I must cuddle my babies, but I'm so cold and there's no mail. I feel I don't exist. I'm afraid of this man I've loved, in my way, for so long a time. My only sense of movement in all the silence is that the U.S. Gov't will take my words to you. You will groan, wish you had steered another course, then you'll try to help. And if you were with me, we would laugh and love and you'd begin to retreat, knowing your limits, and mine.

love
Giershe

Centerville
September 11.62

DEAREST JACK—

Yesterday about three, Natalie (she's perhaps a friend, an English professor here) came over to talk to me. We laughed and tried to be jolly. Then David returned looking very pleased with himself. He announced that he'd just spent an hour with a psychiatrist and had arranged for a Dr. Gerz to come to the house to see *me* in the evening. I wanted none of it but Natalie whispered to me that it would be "master diplomacy" for me to agree. I called Dr. Gerz to cancel the appointment. "I'll be honest with you," he said. "Do you know that your husband thinks it might be necessary to commit you?" I handed the phone to David and walked calmly (heart crashing) out the back door, threw myself into the car, raced over to Natalie's house where I locked myself in, then talked with her, phoned you, and finally went home about 10:30. David called once and demanded that I return to feed the children. Natalie told him for Christ's sake to open the refrigerator and feed them himself. I noticed I was barefoot.

Natalie told me it is indeed the law in this state that a husband, with signature of a psychiatrist, may commit a wife for thirty days' observation in the state insane asylum. I could have turned to ghee on her living room floor, but I didn't. Throughout I felt deep fear and solid purpose. I slept well, and David for once didn't poke at me.

This morning Olivia and I chattered the seventy miles to Greenwich. Don't want housekeeping again, in California. Don't want marriage—yet—or perhaps ever. Do want Montessori. You. A parting from David. David burned your letters this morning on the back porch with Tony saying "Hot! Hot!" Some of the evidence against me has been destroyed.

I love you and thank you for being . . . Jack.

Giershe

San Jose
Sept. 13.62

DEAREST GIERSHE—

Until now, I have said nothing unfriendly about David, but when a person calls in the authorities which are provided by a corrupt society, to fight against one whom he professes to love, he has gone too far. He's a cad. I hope to Christ that his actions have at last led you to realize that you are in a fight *for your freedom and your children*. Stop worrying about David and exert your will to live. You are also fighting to preserve the good that is in David.

In the past few days, there has been time to think about just how I feel towards you, and no matter how I look at you, the answer is always that I love you. I have felt this incessant pull towards only four women in my life. That averages out to about one for every ten years, so it's likely to be some time before another such makes herself known to me.

love,
Jack

Greenwich
September 24.62

DEAR JACK—

Cruel red sumac along the highway—a beautiful day! This life has begun. Olivia bid me good-bye with smiles and kisses. She said "I didn't realize today was the day you start school." This Tuesday, Wednesday, and Thursday I'll be at the Y. You've no idea how this pleases me. Home on Friday. Friday, Saturday, and Sunday I'll be in Centerville. Monday I take up residence in what appears to be an old ladies' home. No typing after 10 p.m. Share bathroom, room of my own. Train noises and fire sirens. The room is amazingly ugly. Ten dollars a week. They hug and pat me. I must look frightened.

love you,
Giershe

YWCA, Greenwich

DEAREST—

First evening away from Olivia and Tony, the day an ooze of pain. Free at twelve noon, I walked down Greenwich Avenue, so rich, perfumy, prosperous, settled, policemen everywhere giving personal directions to station-wagon occupants in tweeds and cashmere. Guilt tracked me, a little for David (vanishing), swamps of it for Olivia. I am hurting her, and though I feel it's for the best, I have doubts. I walked to the P.O. to see if by some miracle you could be knowing what hell it is. I find this sentence—"I do not like to speak of it, but I know you'll be bitterly lonely during . . ." How did you learn to love this way if you've had as little practice as you claim?

love
Giershe

Greenwich
October 11, 1962

DEAR JACK—

Since Olivia and Tony joined me, living in households with others has not worked out. The kids were too active, and no one was able to say grace at table. Olivia said, "We've got to stop moving. Winter is coming." Therefore, we've moved to a cheapo apartment and we pay by the month. Unfurnished, with our mattresses on the floor, a few card-tables, and various borrowed pots and pans. It's heaven to be alone and devise our own rules.

Two weeks in a Montessori school and I don't recognize Olivia. Tonight she bustled with "purposeful activity." She set the table, took a bath by herself, put away her clothes, played blocks and built a Renaissance palace, put away the blocks, tried to read a book, printed a letter to Father, and did some watercolors. All Montessori and without prompting from me. Tony followed her lead. Oh, thank you!

Giershe

San Jose
Oct. 12.62

DEAREST—

Now that I love you, I'm not suddenly going to use you as an emotional crutch. If you withdraw, I'll suffer, but I'll never again live without love. If I don't love you, I'll love another. If not another, then many, an idea, a creed. The world is too various for anyone to live a desiccated life. Xmas can take care of itself. It always has. I will not mention it further.

Jack

Greenwich
October 21, 1962

DEAREST—

It was hard to type "dearest"—you are a man, are you not? The telephone company installed a phone but only with a $25 deposit and the bills sent to David. I tried to get a bank loan but couldn't because I exist only through David's person. David says he's figured out that if he sends me $100 per month he'll only have $118 a month to live on, after rent, etc. So now he says he's going to send $75 a month. I told him I was *determined* to get through this year and come out at the end SELF-SUPPORTING if I had to entertain in the evenings to do it. He said, unkindly, that I was too old.

He had an offer. If I would try to reconsider his "reappearance" in my life, he would eliminate all redheads and would get a bank loan for as much as I needed. What I must do for this money is cut off all communication with you at once. I told him no, sweetly, and said that when I began to receive a salary, I would be glad to help him out of what he calls "grave debt." All unhooked by this offer, he renewed his own. By this time, the kitchen was spread evenly with peanut butter, milk, Wheaties, cheese, watercolor, the gas man had arrived, and I had a headache. Suddenly, I told him that if it was to be $75, he could keep it but without the children on weekends.

So, no more weekends for work, and no $75. Oh woe! I feel much better, and have probably given you my headache.

Giershe

San Jose
Oct. 23.62
CUBAN CRISIS

MY DEAR GIERSHE—

It is morning and we are still alive. I wanted to call you after cretin Kennedy's speech, but I was first too stunned, then too depressed. I think there'll be time for you to receive this, and my message is brief. I love you and am grateful to the providence, divine or malignant, which made this love possible. In the eerie nuclear silences, I want you to know that I think of you countless times each day. My fear is deep. I would riot in the streets but one man cannot make a riot. Everyone moves in his accustomed rounds, but now everyone is frightened. Even the jingoes are quiet. Never before did I understand historical descriptions of a society which has lost its compelling ethos and whose members turned to personal values and the subjective life. Now only the people one loves seem important. You are very important. If I feel up to it tonight, I will phone. I do wish to say good-bye—shit!

love
Jack

Greenwich
October 30.62

DEAR JACK—

I've been talking to the women around here. It's amazing how many thought they had cancer last year when they had a regular life with husband and family. This year, no cancer, no husband, disrupted family. One woman, whose husband is a lawyer who forbade her to take the training, has received no funds from him since her arrival in September. She baby-sits and types for cash. When she told him she would go to Greenwich with or without his permission, he locked her out of the house and stood guard on the front porch with shotgun pointed at her car. She told her two children to "hit the floor" and drove away.

Montessori: "The three-year-old still carries within him a heavy burden of chaos."

I'm still working on Xmas. My first preference is a spot where we can provide ourselves with every possibility of driving each other crazy, all irritants not of our own devising removed from

the experiment. I can't discuss it with David—I fear his retaliation. We must be grubs producing a winged thing.

loving you,
Giershe

Greenwich
November 9.62

DEAR JACK—

Tony has a raging fever and Olivia has croup without fever.
Tony lies uncomplaining and quiet, on his back, cheeks bright
pink, eyes the same, and my heart goes thump every time I look
at him. Why must they have pain? As Faulkner says, in a different
sense, "Children hurt."

can't write
Giershe

Greenwich
November 13.62

DEAREST JACK—

Am scared of Xmas meeting. We two would be on trial with
everyone saying "Well, you've caused so much trouble, you'd
better enjoy yourselves!" I have work to do.

The nicest thing that's happened to me lately is that after
sweating out a reply from Leslie to my announcement that I no
longer live in Centerville came a letter scolding me for going
Catholic Montessori, and telling me that whatever profession I
took up was lucky to have me. On the same day the postman
brought from Gorgeville a huge poster—white with enormous
black letters:

SEE, THE WHOLE LAND
IS BEFORE YOU!
GO WHEREVER YOU
THINK IT GOOD
AND RIGHT TO GO
Jeremiah 40:4

Love me, Jack, I say, when I should say, "I love Jack."

Giershe

P.S. I am *so* happy these days! Found this in Wm. James: Nothing is easier than to familiarize one's self with the mammalian brain. Get a sheep's head, a small saw, chisel, scalpel and forceps (All three can best be had from a surgical instrument maker), and unravel its parts either by aid of a human dissecting book, such as Holden's *Manual of Anatomy* . . .

There was a *Super*-ferret!

San Jose
November 25.62

DEAREST GIERSHE—

Physical work with machines and tools makes three-year-old boys happy all day long. I spent the day getting my old '49er ready for the winter. The local garageman quoted a price of $60. I did it myself and saved $47. In addition to the savings, Andrew had about $53 worth of fun so I put it down as a $100 day. He smiled his puckish smile and said: "We're winners, Daddy."

This morning we lay in bed together and made up a dozen versions of his favorite song: "'Twas once in the crosswalk I used to trip gaily, Once with the light I used to walk free, First to the drugstore, then to the café . . . Got struck by a car, and I'm dying today. . . ." Muriel returned full of guilt at having enjoyed a weekend with some guy. She annoyed me enough to begin a quarrel. How could this match have produced a child I love?

Jack

Greenwich
November 26.62

DEAR ONE—

Sick all weekend. In Centerville, I did nothing but sleep and throw up for two days and David considers this a good sign. He launched a campaign for us to chalk up some good hours between now and Xmas so I'll not see you and will save Marriage, Children, Honor, Morality, Love, etc. He wants me to return "home" each weekend and he'll hire Nonny and turn over his office, stripped for my "work." He wants to Start Over. David's Large Nouns have the most depressing effect on me.

While wandering through the Centerville house, I wondered what Lawrence said about sensuality. So I went downstairs to find your gift copy of his *Selected Poems*. I pulled it from the shelf and opened to the front, expecting to see your teasing inscription: "All my love, Jack." There instead, in tiny careful handwriting, were these words: "For Giershe, with all my love, David." I looked again. No page was torn out.

love,
Giershe

San Jose
Nov. 29.62

DEAR—

I'm still laboring away on Christ and the fall of Rome. Imagine a small group of barely literate farmers and craftsmen gulling half the world for two thousand years. They commit larceny upon the Jews, deck out the message in the more obvious frills of Greek philosophy, invent a monotheistic trinity that absorbs Magna Mater, Attis, Mythra, Isis and Osiris (the greatest shell game of all) and then find saintly jobs in the Lord's workshop for every local deity. My own task is to convey to my students my own sense of wonder at this miracle without alienating them by any seeming irreligion. I think they might even become better Christians if they could see the cleverness of the whole operation. In a contest between Caesar and Christ, who in his right mind would have bet on Christ?

I now lie awake almost every night with a throbbing erection, and wish you in my arms. I love you, Giershe.

Jack

CHAPTER SEVEN

Greenwich
Dec. 6.62

DEAR ONE—

    I am not confident this time before Time begins in another way. Will he like what he sees? Will I? Is it too late? Can I be me?

Giershe

San Jose
December 9.62

DEAR LOVE—

    Not all the yellow foolscap in the world can prepare one to meet the reality which steps from or greets a plane. Nothing can be done about it. We shall meet in a great hollow cavern with our heels echoing in the morning silence—we can play Last Year at Marienbad.

I await you . . .
Jack

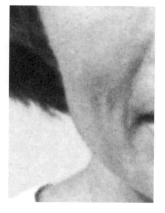

"And when I found

the door was locked,

I pulled and pushed

and kicked and knocked."

A
S A LITIGANT, I should dread a lawsuit beyond almost anything else short of sickness and death.

—*Justice Learned Hand*

"The doorbell. Answer it, Giershe. No, wait. I'll answer."

Giershe watched Jack's back at the front door. A tall man in a yellow slicker handed him an envelope. Jack signed, closed the door, glanced briefly, too casually, and handed it to her. "A special delivery for me? But no one knows I'm here except David. What is it? The children—they're sick?"

"Giershe, slow down. Look, while you're reading your mail, I'll fix more coffee. Christ! It's freezing in our idyllic mountain retreat! How does Fred keep his balls from dropping off into his lap? Do you suppose it's raining all over the valley? Let's get out of here and find a cozy café." Pacing, not looking at her.

She stared at the envelope in her hands. Her stiff, blue fingers stuck out half an inch beyond the scratchy wool of Jack's warmest turtleneck sweater. Her vision blurred. Yes, it was her name, Giershe Kinnard, and in the corner, embossed and wiggling, Superior Court, County of Middlesex, State of Connecticut. Her fingers twitched as she tried to force them under the flap. Jack placed his hands on her arms and sat her down gently on a chair. He pulled the envelope from her fingers and swiftly tore off one end. He pulled out a white sheet of paper, read it silently and handed it to her. "The fuckin' bastard! Read it, Giershe. Don't panic. It's just a formality."

SUPERIOR COURT, MIDDLESEX COUNTY

December 14, 1962

DAVID KINNARD v. GIERSHE KINNARD

NOTICE TO GIERSHE KINNARD

It appearing from the application of the plaintiff in the above entitled action, returnable to the Superior Court for Middlesex County on the first Tuesday of January, 1963, that the Plaintiff is claiming a divorce and custody of two minor children, and that the Defendant is . . .

"Jack! Who's the defendant? Me? Who's the plaintiff? Tell me!"

"Have you finished reading it?"

"No . . ." Giershe was holding the paper with both hands, staring stupidly; the sentences merged, separated.

> . . . or shortly will be residing in California, and that notice of the institution of this action most likely to come to her attention is that hereinafter ordered . . .

> Dated at Centerville,
> state of Connecticut,
> this 14th day of December, 1962

Bernard Carlson

> Bernard Carlson
> Clerk of the Superior Court
> Middlesex County

"Jack, the dates, December fourteenth. I was still there. He knew he was going to do this. He knew it all the time we argued about Christmas plans. He knew it when we agreed that he would have Tony and Olivia on Christmas Eve and I would arrive Christmas Day. What day is it? Does this mean . . . Is he asking for . . . *custody?* Jack!"

"No. Yes. No. Now just hang on. Now you need to be calm. You need, *they* need you whole, rational, thinking. I'll make you a hot milk with whiskey. Now just sit there and pull yourself together. What he's doing is what you should have done last September. He's beginning a divorce action, and he's chosen a devilish time to do it. Just like him. Bastard! Okay. You're returning to Centerville on the twenty-fifth, which is a holiday, but the next day of business you have to find yourself a lawyer and contest. You have to do exactly what that lawyer tells you to do."

Jack busied himself with a pan of milk. Giershe stood up, her knees shaking. She held onto the oak table. Sausage and egg were bubbling up inside her. She stumbled across the living room to the bathroom. Throwing up was something she knew how to do, and she did it expertly, not a drop anywhere, her whole breakfast deposited neatly in the toilet bowl. She pushed down the flush-knob and watched yellow and brown clumps swirl out of sight. She stood up, shaking and shivering, cold inside her where the night's warmth had been. She washed her face with warm water and with fastidious concern for Jack, brushed her teeth. She went into the bedroom and climbed under the covers with all her clothes on. She lay there listening to the rain beat down on the roof.

Jack padded into the bedroom, his feet in his host's fur-lined slippers, in each hand a steaming cup of hot milk. He kicked a chair to the side of the bed, set one cup on the chair and held the other over her chest. "Now, sit up and drink. Feel better? If I had such an instant reaction to trouble, I'd be imperially slim forever. Drink!"

She drank. He drank. They smiled at each other. Hansel and Gretel in the woods.

"In an hour or so, I'll call my lawyer to find out what your next move should be. In the meantime, would you like to call Centerville to remind Olivia and Tony you'll be with them on Christmas Day? *After* you finish that whiskey. Then we'll dress up and go to the city."

"Jack, I don't feel like . . ."

"And I don't feel like sitting around in this rain forest glooming just because David doesn't want us to enjoy the Christmas season. We've got to keep moving. Come along, drink up. You can't let David wrap his sickness around you. Please." He held her cold fingers in his hands and searched her eyes for help. *He's thinking of Muriel and Andrew. He's afraid. I must not collapse. I have to help us both.* Giershe pulled herself upright in bed, kissed his nose, twitched a smile across her face, and said:

"Right. Where's the telephone?"

Jack lifted himself wearily from the sagging bed. He pulled a black phone from beneath a pile of pillows in the corner of the room and placed it in front of Giershe's buried feet. He left the room, closing the door behind him. She picked up the receiver. It was black ice. She tried three times to dial. Each time her finger fell off midway through the sequence. The fourth time, she completed eleven digits without mishap, and waited while blizzard noises, bleeps, faint voices vied for control. Five rings. She grew dizzy.

"Hello?" David's voice, faint, crackling on the line.

"Hello, David. May I speak to Olivia?" She waited. "David?"

"Yes, I hear you."

"May. I. Speak. To. Olivia?"

"The children are not here."

"Not there? Where are they?"

"I don't believe that need concern you. They're not here."

"Where can I reach them? I'd like to tell Olivia that I'll be there, as planned, on Christmas Day."

"The children are not here. You will never see the children again."

"DAVID!" she screamed. "Where are they? I have a right to talk with them! David! What have you done with them? Where are they?"

"Giershe, there's no need to break my eardrum. Olivia and Tony are well. They're being cared for elsewhere."

"WHAT? David, I got your communication from Superior Court. You are a total RAT! What do you mean I'll never see the children again? What is the matter with you? I'll be there Christmas Day and I expect them to be there. I *promised* them I'd spend Christmas with them! *You* promised!"

She knew he had hung up. She kept on talking to operator voices. She dialed again. She let it ring and ring and ring.

>>>>>

Five days later, in Centerville, alone in a silent house, Giershe couldn't remember how she had traveled from the state of California to the state of Connecticut. She remembered Jack's wordless farewell at an airport terminal, and she was aware that she'd left not on Christmas Day as she had promised, but one day later. All planes had been grounded because of high winds, rain, sleet, and zero visibility. Terminals and telephones were her route. Sitting on her baggage, dialing David's number, waiting, no answer, hang up. Two minutes later, dial again, wait, hang up. A stranger had taken her from the train station ten miles outside Centerville to David's door—a nice lady who talked about her grandchildren and looked worriedly at the wraith on the seat beside her. She remembered sitting on the porch in the snow waiting for the college's representative to bring her a key. Sorry she'd lost her key and too bad he had to be inconvenienced. No, just let her in, she'd be all right as soon as she got warm. Thank you. No, no need to call anyone else, she was *all right!*

It was cold inside the house and evident that no one had been there for several days. There was no Christmas tree, no wrappings in wastebaskets, no food in the refrigerator. The beds were neatly made, and the children's little suitcases were not in their room. Their winter clothes were not in the closet. Giershe turned on the heat and stood over the floor furnace in her coat, burning the soles of her snow boots. Ten feet away from her was the red telephone and lying beside it was their address book, filled, she knew, with the names, addresses, and phone numbers of everyone they knew in this city, this state, other states, this country, other countries, everyone who had the pleasure of their friendship, now, ten years ago, and even a few hopefuls seeking future friendships. Without bothering to remove her coat and earmuffs, she began to dial.

First, she called all the people they knew in Centerville. No, they didn't know where David was. Yes, he planned to be in Chicago at the end of the month for a conference. No, they hadn't seen the children. They were sorry they couldn't help. Next, she called people she didn't know, but David had mentioned. She called the president of Whitfield College. He was out of town. She called the provost. He listened to her story and promised to make a few calls and get back to her. David was really very thoughtless, wasn't he? He was sorry for her pain.

She widened the search. It wasn't her telephone; the bill would be sent to David. She called all the people who might know something. They didn't. She called everyone on the East Coast who might like to hear such a story. Let's not have any privacy any longer. Everyone was glad to hear from her, and no one knew anything. They complained that David had been most unresponsive for several months, even secretive, and they told her not to worry, everything would be all right soon, they knew, didn't she know? She would write as soon as she returned to Greenwich, wouldn't she? Sid Freeman in Washington, D.C., gave her the name of an "honest shyster" in Centerville, and Rafaela Freeman offered to come stay with her for a few days if Giershe would promise she wouldn't have to see David. Maybe she'd like to see her in Greenwich? No, Giershe assured her, she felt like she had leprosy and she particularly didn't want to see anyone she *liked*, for the time being. She might infect.

There were no more names in the little book and it was getting late. Giershe looked up Carl Adams in the telephone book. In the Attorney section of the yellow pages, she found "Adams and Anderson, Dissolution—Family Law—Domestic Relations, Wills and Probate, Tax, Personal Injury." She dialed his number and gave her name to the secretary.

"And what is the nature of business?"

"I beg your pardon?"

"Why do you want to see Mr. Adams?"

"Oh—my husband has disappeared with the children. I want . . ."

"That's terrible! How long have they been gone?"

Giershe had been dry-eyed for several days, but as soon as the voice erupted in sympathy, her throat clogged and she couldn't speak.

"Why don't you be here at our offices at nine o'clock in the morning. That way you'll be sure to catch Mr. Adams before he goes to court. Don't worry, Mr. Adams is a very good lawyer."

The receiver now weighed twenty-five pounds. She let it rest. She locked the front door, turned on the porch light, picked up her suitcase, and climbed the stairs to the children's room. The sun was setting across Olivia's bed. She lay down for a minute and slept without dreams until dawn.

>———>———>

On the morning of her first visit to a lawyer, Giershe dressed carefully. She wanted to look neat, calm, motherly. Her wits were returning to her, and she knew she would have to win his approval if she wanted him to fight for her. She was going to have to walk to town and that meant wool socks, snow boots, earmuffs, and heavy mittens, but beneath winter's ugly necessities, she wore a soft, pleated gray skirt and a black cashmere sweater. Pearls at her neck, pearl earrings. The chaste look. Olivia's red wool scarf around her neck, for courage, and in the pocket of her coat, one of Tony's stray socks, pale blue.

The weather was mild—sun, ice melting on the streets, drifts of fog spliced with warm, moist air. As she walked she tried to remember if ever in her life she had talked with a lawyer. No. Of all the interesting people who visited Harry, she couldn't recall one lawyer. He believed that lawyers, like policemen, bankers, and military men, were by nature unclean. 201 North Main Street. She pushed open the entrance door and climbed the marble stairs. The building was old and its hardwood floors echoed footsteps, the taps of heels hurrying to places behind the gray opaque glass windows in doors which opened onto the long hall.

She turned the knob, pushed open the door, and moved forward. A secretary sat at her desk by the open door. She placed a cup of coffee to the right of her typewriter. She looked up and smiled. "Are you Mrs. Kinnard?"

"Yes."

"Let me take your coat—it's warm in here. May I get you a cup of coffee? Mr. Adams will see you in a few minutes." The sympathetic voice. (*Please let me not cry.*) She handed her coat to the outstretched hand, removed her earmuffs, and sat down in a chair near the door. The telephone buzzed.

"You may go in now, right through that door."

"Good morning, Mrs. Kinnard. Please sit down." He was tall and looked like a Texas senator. Wavy white hair, glasses, and the complexion of the hard drinker, red veins on plump jowls. Not quite as old as Harry. He puffed on a pipe, trying to make it stay lighted. One match. Two. Puff-puff. She waited. "Yes, Mr. Freeman recommended me? He's a fine fellow. We've worked together a bit on Democratic politics. He called me last night at home, left a message with Mrs. Adams, something about your husband being a professor at Whitfield, a difficulty over two small children. And a notice you received in California from your husband's lawyers. Did you bring it with you?" She pulled the envelope from her purse and handed it to him. He glanced at it, relit his pipe, puffed. "Mrs. Kinnard, may I ask you, have you sought help from any other attorney in this matter?"

"No, I thought I'd give him time to get used to the idea that I was going to go to school and would not be returning to him."

"That was your first mistake, but I don't want you to think I'm criticizing you. He's made the first move and that makes it more difficult for me. We have a lot of work to do to catch up with his action. While we're waiting for a report from the courthouse, please fill me in on the events which have led up to this—abduction—removal of the children. Answer my questions carefully and as honestly as you can. How long have you been married?"

He was kind. A gentleman. And Giershe pulled answers from deep inside her memory. She gave bare facts, he took notes; back and forth they plowed, digging up events, births, travels, infidelities, the bedrock of her married life. Twelve years in thirty minutes. The secretary entered, smiled at Giershe, and placed a folder on Mr. Adams' desk. He glanced, read, marked, and handed Giershe one of the sheets of paper. "This will be waiting for you when you return to Greenwich. They've been busy."

TO THE SHERIFFS OF THE COUNTIES OF MIDDLESEX AND FAIRWEATHER, OR THEIR DEPUTIES

GREETINGS:

By AUTHORITY OF THE STATE OF CONNECTICUT, you are hereby commanded to summon GIERSHE KINNARD, of the town of Greenwich, in the County of Fairweather, to appear before the SUPERIOR COURT to be held at Centerville, in and for the County of Middlesex, on the first Tuesday of January 1963, then and there to answer unto DAVID KINNARD, of said town of Centerville and State of Connecticut, in a civil action wherein the plaintiff complains:

FIRST COUNT:

1. On divers days between August 10, 1953, and the date of this writ, defendant has been guilty of intolerable cruelty to plaintiff.

SECOND COUNT:

1. The plaintiff is the father of two minor children, issue of such marriage, David Kinnard III (Tony) and Olivia Kinnard.
2. Said minor children have been in the custody and control of defendant during most of her separation from the plaintiff.
3. The defendant was and is an unfit person to have the custody and control of said two minor children, and the circumstances surrounding their life with the defendant were and are not conducive to their best welfare.

WHEREFORE, the plaintiff claims:
1. a divorce
2. custody of said two children, both pendente lite and permanent.

Hereof fail not but of this writ, with your doing thereon, due service and return make according to law.

Dated at Centerville, Connecticut, this 14th day of December, 1962

Joel Smith

Commissioner of the SUPERIOR COURT

Giershe's hands trembled. She locked them together in her lap. The white sheet of paper slid to the floor. She leaned over and felt a cloud drift into her brain, blocking her light, throwing her off balance. Mr. Adams' feet were suddenly next to her snow boots, and she felt his hand on her shoulder. "Mrs. Kinnard, don't be frightened of legal documents. Do you feel better? Here, drink my coffee. I haven't touched it." She took a deep, gasping breath, reached for the coffee he was holding beneath her nose, and drank with hiccupy gulps. Mr. Adams resumed his seat, put his elbows on his desk, and began again to coax his pipe.

"If you retain me, I'll represent you in court on the first Tuesday in January. In the meantime, I'd like you to return to Greenwich as soon as possible, and wait for the children there. There's no way to force your husband to return the children until a court orders him to do so. He's employed by Whitfield and won't needlessly damage his career. You'll just have to be patient. I want you to do nothing, preferably not even talk with him. Keep yourself busy while you wait. You must write down everything about your marriage which might be of use to me in court. Do you understand?"

"Yes. Is that all? Does he have custody now?"

"It's a no-man's-land. He has *possession* of them, but until a court renders an opinion, neither of you has custody. You might think of people who would be willing to appear in court with you to vouch for your character—people who have seen you with the children."

"Yes, I'll do that. Good-bye, Mr. Adams." He bent to shake her hand, and as he reached past her to open the door, she thought she smelled whiskey.

>>>>>

San Jose
12.28.62

PRECIOUS GIERSHE—

I want to tell you not to worry. When one deals with the marginally sane, one has to treat them as strange and stop worrying about how sane they used to be. David is acting out some boyhood petulance, and when it's all over, he'll have a monstrous hangover. You, my love, must use your time well— Montessori exercises and the methodical chronicling of every enormity you can dredge from your memory. If you like (make carbons) you can send them to me as letters filled with interesting anecdotes. I'll want to talk with you the night before the court appearance, and again when it's all over. Be a good actress and abstract yourself from the emotional crap that surrounds these legal charades. Cry when you should and be confused when you should, but keep that old brain going every second you're in that courtroom.

Remember, Jack loves you, thinks you're sane, clearheaded, and of sound moral character. Your only relapse from these qualities has been to listen to the shit David puts out. Build a countersuit so appalling that David's lawyer will refuse to go to court.

Damn, I miss you most of every day—alone in the house, in the car, in bed—no loving voice, face, or body to comfort and delight me. If nothing else, if I were there, I could hold your coat when you went in to fight.

love
Jack

Greenwich
Dec. 31.62

DEAREST—

Do you know the song? "Why did you leave your house and land? Why did you leave your babies? Why did you leave your own wedded lord? To go with the Black Jack Davey." It's time for a thank-you. Night's here, it's 10 degrees and falling, with a hurricane wind, and when I realize that my babies are not tucked safely in their beds in the next room, but are wandering around in my imagination—it's time to pace the floor, repair their clothes, write Jack. Our week together seems the only right week in a lifetime. Your tact and love gave our foolish tryst an eighteenth-century elegance. All the dear props of those days with you, most of them attached to your person. Your hands. I could watch you forever at work on a car, a toilet, opening a bottle, cleaning a windshield, turning the pages of a book. The smell from hands that work. David has beautiful Michelangelo hands, smooth as satin. He will not get them dirty or touch excrement, grease, dirt, or dust. If he has to change a diaper or a tire, he asks afterwards for hand lotion. You prowl with a cat's grace. Sometimes I glimpse the youth behind the man's face and am delighted, but no Alcibiades face could be loved as much as Jack's.

Giershe

Centerville
Jan. 3.63

DEAR JACK—

I'm existing between appointments. From two to six, Olivia and Tony at David's house; six to six-thirty, dinner with the O'Dwyers down the street; seven p.m., pick up Leslie at train station; nine p.m., Leslie and Adams conference; ten a.m., Natalie, Leslie, and I go to court.

David, that wounded beast. His face is an ugly hate mask. Yet I also hate. Need I tell you of the many half-truths and lies which are forced on me and I must juggle in court tomorrow? Instinct leads me, tells me when to lie, when to tell the truth. I turn around each day and look back to September, surprised at the tactical accuracy. I'm becoming a foul crook.

love
Giershe

San Jose
Jan. 2.63

DEAR ONE—

Bite on your knuckles when you feel like crying off cue, don't give an inch, offer no quarter until you get those children. Then get out of that town and stay out. I shan't tell you of my difficulty in getting past the thirteenth anniversary date. It's looks of love that undo me. Why in God's name would anyone whom I have treated as I have Muriel love me in a romantic fashion? I could understand a grudging admiration based on emotional exhaustion, but to have sweet soft feelings can only mean that she has experienced none of the pain I imagined we had *shared*. There is indeed a philosophical problem of whether or not there are other minds.

My love is with you,
Jack

Greenwich
Jan. 4.63

DEAR JACK—

Court Day: Leslie, Natalie, and I drive to the courthouse. On the way downtown, they talk about David as though I'm not there. Leslie says: "I don't like people to touch parts of me that I reserve for my friends." Leslie asks Adams for a "program." Adams advises us to be solemn when in court. Adultery! It's everywhere, ripe boils on married bodies. Everyone I know (except Leslie's Jeb) has experienced it.

David comes in with his young lawyer and refuses my smile. He is grim. During an intermission (a recess), Leslie talks with him. Leslie: "Dino, I had no idea you were being so naughty in Gorgeville! Shame on you!" David: "My body has needs and Giershe doesn't like sex."

Just before we begin our hearing, the judge has a short discussion with the lawyers and threatens to throw the whole mess to the Family Relations Department, then bangs the gavel for lunch. Adams cuts through people who want to see him and takes his ladies to lunch at a fancy restaurant. Leslie eats heartily and confesses to him that she's written a novel on adultery but assures him he doesn't know any of the characters. Adams looks steadily at me and says: "There is nothing to worry about." My life is in this man's hands and he's on his third highball. I eat nothing.

We return to court. The lawyers leave the room with the judge, called "going into chambers." They bring back a proposal: custody to me, *pendente lite*, weekends with David. I cry. David turns pleasant for his audience, says: "Would you like to take the children this weekend to make up in part for what you have unfortunately suffered during the last ten days?" "Yes," I say.

Have you ever been in court? Lawyers *cringe* before the judge and he likes it. Looming bench, black robe, the intricacies of procedure. No citizen can be safe or assert confidently that the system works. The Grand Guignol knows he can do anything! I am so weary, too weary to be happy with my prizes.

love
Giershe

Greenwich
Jan. 5.63

DEAREST JACK—

All of Whitfield College has now heard that I am frigid, that David has "physical needs" and therefore took his body elsewhere, that I "threatened to kill the children and went upstairs with a butcher knife," that "she always has gone into a tailspin when she has stopped nursing," that "there is no joy in her and she has an overdeveloped death instinct." Mr. Adams said this morning that I must remember during the interview with the psychiatrist that I am being examined for the court, not to forget it for a minute. The appointment is for Friday in New Haven.

love
Giershe

Greenwich
Jan. 6.63

DEAR—

The day before Court Day I had my first visit with the children, accompanied by Natalie (the witnessing adult requested by Adams). Olivia ran whooping into my arms. Tony wouldn't come near me. After David left, Olivia climbed into my lap and began cataloguing my face. She traced my mouth and cheeks. She said: "I'm going to pretend to get off your lap and you must say, 'No, I won't let you go!' and put your arms around me and don't let me go." Tony circled closer. Olivia finally left my lap and began showing me her Christmas presents. Tony climbed into my lap and snuggled down. I fed and bathed them. The wind began to blow. Tony, the fearless one, the child who walks into dark closets and closes the door, became almost hysterical and kept saying "It's dark outside." He buried his face in Olivia's lap. I couldn't get him to sit up. He kept saying "Wind . . ."

After dinner Don O'Dwyer and I went to the station to collect Leslie. There she was in a slinky brown otter coat, long skinny legs, the same blond thatch, distorted face, all-seeing eyes, the hands forever at their knitting. Later, with Adams, she got so worked up over the Gorgeville year her fingers went faster and faster and she spluttered.

Tonight Tony has the croup. He weeps for Father. I've been with them now long enough to begin scolding, but when I do, Olivia cries and Tony screams, "Don't spank me, Mommy—don't, don't!" You must never let anything like this happen to Andrew. I write this in hope of teaching those who are contemplating similar destructions.

Your
Giershe

Greenwich
January 11.63

DEAR—

Tony is well again and most affectionate. I asked Olivia where he's been getting all the words which spill out of him. "From me," she said. "I give him lots of words every day. Yesterday I gave him 'sheriff' but he didn't know what to do with it, so I took it back."

Psychiatrist hour went very well. One hour we talked and did not mention adultery—David's, mine, or his. In conclusion, he wished me success in my career and urged me out to California. He said the knife story has several versions. First, I supposedly threatened both children with a butcher knife (we don't own such); second, I supposedly singled out Tony and threatened to go after him with a hammer (we do have a hammer). David has been going to a female psychiatrist every week since September.

Should I mention? Yes, I shall. I have wanted the child of every man I have loved. Let's see, that's one, two, three, and Jack makes four. Be warned. Don't come near me if you aren't prepared. I won't ask permission or lie. My objection to Enovid is that it prevents conception!

love,
Giershe

Santa Cruz
January 14.63

DEAREST LOVE—

It is another place and mood in which I write. Freedom from the hang-up is already beginning to tingle my member. Tonight, for the first time in weeks, I sat down and wrote easily on the book.

If you're going to have a child from my loins whenever you feel like it, as of now it behooves me to plan for the petty financial troubles which might ensue. I think your biological hots for me is quite the most flattering expression of love you could show me. I am hereby warned. But remember, I never take precautions, ask questions, or worry about consequences. It is entirely up to you. Oh, I love you so much!

Jack

Santa Cruz
1.25.63

DEAREST—

You asked if I ever feel jealousy. Yes, occasionally. The more I love a person, the less I feel it. Complete love is complete generosity. The assumption must be that each person knows what gives him or her happiness and the other person should be pleased if his or her love is happy. One way to analyze the problem of past marriages is to use a standard economics approach. Analyze it from both micro and macro theory. Your discussions tend to be all micro theory. In micro theory you examine any system by seeing how much each part relates to all the other parts. Presumably, one knows how a successful system operates, so you examine the particular marriage, which has failed, and try to find the malfunctioning part. If you're successful, and one always is, because there's always a painful malfunction, then you say, "Ah, if this had been different, then it would not have failed. Maybe I should go back and try again."

If, however, you use macro analysis, the whole problem looks quite different. In macro analysis, one doesn't ask what are the internal conditions of a successfully functioning system. One simply asks: 1) What is the system supposed to produce? and 2) What is its record of production? In your marriage, you could say it was supposed to produce a) healthy, happy children, b) a bearable level of pain, and c) a minimum of happiness. What is the annual record of production? Not good. Why? When output is unsatisfactory one measures supply conditions. A successful marriage requires W units of good humor, X units of willingness to live and let live, Y units of ability to give, and Z units of adequate and assured income. Can this system ever have adequate aggregate-supply conditions? No. You could tinker with it till doomsday and it would never yield satisfactory output.

Is this a love letter?

Jack

Greenwich
Jan. 27.63

DEAR ONE—

Work, work this weekend. My ass is forever aching. Last evening, between telephone calls, Olivia and I followed Tony around and cleaned up his rebellions. He flooded the bathroom with potties of bathwater. While we mopped that, he took a black crayon and wrote on the kitchen walls. While we erased that with soap and water, he sprinkled a path of Ajax from room to room. Finally, when he was discovered peeing on Olivia's precious Bear, I spanked him. He raged. Olivia said she wished she didn't have a brother. I said: "I'm tired of him too. Let's throw him out the window. He'll break into millions of pieces like Humpty Dumpty. We'll try and try to put him together again." Olivia, eyes big: "But we won't be able to put him together again. (Long silence.) Let's throw him out the window tomorrow, not today." Yet when I go in to check his progress in the bathtub, he says: "Glad to see you, Mommy!"

your Giershe

Santa Cruz
Feb. 11.63

HI LOVE!

Andrew has been asking me about sex and reproduction lately and I've been filling him in as the need arises. At breakfast he asked where the seed I used to make a baby was lodged. The testicles. How does it get out of the testicles? Through the penis. Show me. Later. Why not right now? I'm fixing breakfast. Where does it go when it comes out of the penis? Into a female. Mother? Yes. He also asked me what his erections were for. For fertilizing a female. Mother? No. I told him he had to grow first. How big do I have to get? Not very much bigger. I trust Andrew's sense of discretion. I've convinced him he'll get hurt by other people if he doesn't watch what he says. If I could see him emerge unmarred by guilt, I would feel a great sense of triumph.

I understand your wish to smash David's face, but your wish to understand him seems less rational. Objectify him, and guard against responding to any of his symbol words. Be flat with him.

A month ago I took Andrew to an old graveyard and spent an hour reading tombstones to him. He was not overly interested. Yesterday he was nattering to himself about something: "Oh, I'm telling the story of Mr. Bompkins who was born in 1894 and got killed in the war but he had a little boy before he died so it's all right." You and Andrew, you never, never bore me.

Jack

Greenwich
Feb. 20.63

DEAR ONE:

I spent most of the day in the library. "What is all this juice and all this joy? / A strain of the earth's sweet being in the beginning / in Eden garden. —Have, get, before it cloy, / Before it cloud, Christ, lord, and sour with sinning." That old monk Hopkins.

I suffer from a loss of feminine work. I like keeping a man happy, in spite of my bad record. Even living with David there was much which gave me pleasure. Keep the environment clean around him, serve meals, bother about his health, tell him to wear warmer garments out-of-doors, scold him for not remembering his dentist appointment, etc.—any male would do. I need a certain amount of this kind of work to keep me juicy.

Olivia and I have a truce. We've agreed that she's old enough not to test my love by wailing and paling for hours. When she feels like that, I'm to hug her and she'll go to her room for a while (Tony was imitating). I've agreed not to get cross but to love her even while she's departed. Today was our first day; all went well.

The crocus in front of the library is just about to—dare I hope? Soon, my love.

Giershe

Berkeley
February 23.63

DEAREST—

The sap is rising—dammit. I asked Elizabeth whether she thought you could make the transition from a semirecluse to a woman who could care for a family, do a first-rate professional job, and cope with the public. She answered that she hadn't the slightest doubt you could do it brilliantly. She also told me that some Berkeley ladies placed an ad in the paper announcing the formation of a Montessori study group. You must get control of that little operation as quickly as possible. If you are doubting, remember the workbooks are growing, the children are still mostly sane, David has not won yet, and "the hounds of spring are on winter's traces."

love
Jack

Greenwich
March 5.63

DEAREST MATE—

The ring! It is light and I cannot feel its weight on me. Precious gift! The pigeons are mating on the roof next door in slush. I know why pigeons are so healthy. Food, bird love, family, exercise. The sun is shining, steam rising. I want your baby. Some might say this is immaturity, but I think of myself as a breeder and you have fine genes, the only similarity to David that occurs to me. Why is this very rational urge not valued in our society?

Tony knows the words "story" and "knife" and uses them, but he has a new construction. "Give me a sharp," he says, and "Tell me a once-upon-a-time." Olivia calls him "bad boy" when he transgresses and now when I do something he doesn't like, he calls me "bad-boy Mommy." He likes to open an overnight case which contains a mirror. He peeks in and says: "Hello, bad boy," then "Bye-bye, bad boy!" and bangs the case closed.

Your
Giershe

9

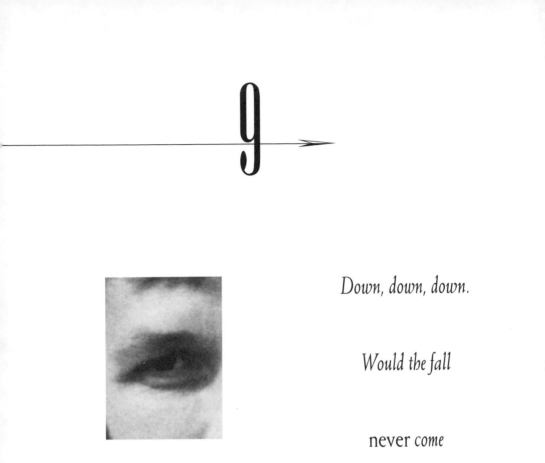

Down, down, down.

Would the fall

never come

to an end?

Greenwich
March 13.63

H ELP! Where are you?

David, in my memory, has spent whole days playing with his penis and talking down his enemies. Olivia has become a kisser, charming and pathetic. She tells me, "Mommy, I love you more than you love me. Millions and trillions more," and kisses me to prove it. This evening she asked to kiss my secret parts. "Where did you learn that?" I asked.

> Olivia: Father does it.
> Me: Father does what? Kisses your secret parts?
> Olivia: No— (giggle) I kiss his penis!
> Me: When do you kiss his penis?
> Olivia: Oh, we kiss it and play with it all the time. Tony and I take turns. But last night I got up in the *middle* of the night and went in to Father's bed and climbed under the covers and kissed his penis!
> Me: What did Father do?
> Olivia: Oh, he giggled. He liked it.

Oh my love, what am I to do? What *should* I do? When Olivia was about a year old, David began tickling her in her secret parts. She wouldn't let anyone wash her, and on the rare occasions when he bathed her, he made a game of it and tickled her unmercifully. This continued until now the response is so conditioned that when she has an infection there (and how, I now wonder, did that happen?), she can't bear to have me put Desitin on, so ticklish is she. With David, when he fondles it all day, his toy poking out of his bathrobe, there is no sun or earth or sky, just cigarettes, coffee, and talk, talk, admire it, rub it, flop it up and down. I have wanted to shout, "GODDAMMIT! WILL you put that thing away, OUT OF SIGHT, and play with something else for a change?!" and then have spent the rest of the day asking myself what's wrong with *me*. I've told you Olivia's a truth-teller. She said the washing machine in Centerville leaked so much that water rose and went upstairs, into the bedrooms, the bathroom, up over the side of the bathtub and down the drain. I showed proper horror. Then she said: "It *really* only leaked a little bit around itself."

I'm weeping without tears.

love
Giershe

San Jose
3.17.63

DEAREST—

Your letter on Olivia just arrived and I hate David as never before. I can't bear to think of him. I've had an intimate relationship with two women whose fathers introduced them to sex, and both were flipped. I'm not saying that a father-daughter love couldn't be successful, but how in this world? David is a fool, malignant and strange, and the danger to Olivia is enormous. If it continues, it will not stop at kissing, and will progress to a heterosexual union with her. At any time, an innocent remark by Olivia could lead to acute embarrassment for her and for David, scandal, even a jail sentence. I don't know how you can handle it. Can you afford to leave the children with him at all? Should you tell his psychiatrist? Your lawyer? I am *certain* you should not doubt your own instincts. NOTHING IS WRONG WITH YOU! If David wants to sit holding his penis for the next twenty years, that's his business, but the children have a *right* to their own sexuality and, in this society, I can't think of an easier way to rob them of it. You may be driven to the conclusion that David is twisted in such a way that complete separation is the only solution.

Oh yes! David's a most sensitive type, just the tutor Olivia needs. He's applied his theories of sex and love to you for many years and you ended frigid and loathing him. (Well, Trilby, if he's made you a novelist, it may have been worth the thirteen years.)

love,
Jack

Greenwich
March 21.63

DEAREST—

I may write the psychiatrist, may tell Adams. My first act was to call David. I made something of a joke about it to deflect his anger. I took a Paul Goodman tack, said our society wants blood and this sort of revelation makes them wild. He confirmed the story and laughed about it. He disclaimed provocative behavior, but he has set up a sexual flow from Olivia since her infancy. He's done this from an ideological standpoint which I think stops short of the act, but how can I be sure? He has stressed the physical union of father and daughter and the mystical connection between father and son. When I've objected to his tickling her, his answer has always been the same: "Just because *you* don't like it!" He was good-humored and agreed that she must be protected from society and made to realize that these things are private. (That's supposed to comfort me?) He told me a sequel. One evening a student (male) was with David and the children. Olivia said to David: "I'm going to kiss your penis." David laughed. Olivia went to the student and said the same. "I have a book near my bedside which speaks of the phenomenon but doesn't tell you what to do about it," David says he said. The student laughed and replied, "I have a book near my bedside which speaks of the phenomenon but the solution isn't applicable to four-year-olds." Worms. What haunts me is that I know David feels that the more sexual play between himself and Olivia, the better for both of them.

love,
Giershe

Greenwich
March 30, '62

DEAR JACK:

Last night a nightmare. I went to California, where I fell into the Slough of Despond. Sent a telegram to Molly. MRS MOLLY GAVIN STOP AM WITH JACK STOP MY TWO SELVES WERE TOO MUCH FOR ME STOP RETURN ON FIFTEENTH STOP. You waited patiently for me while I pulled myself from muck. You had a beard, sad eyes, a beige jacket, a green skirt, very long bobby socks, and tennis shoes. You slithered from place to place and projected yourself through objects.

I spent several hours today at the DIVORCE shelf of our ivy-covered public library. Did you know that children don't belong to parents? They belong to the State.

"Why don't you *ever* extend a hand to help?" is what you asked me on the phone. I once told Leslie that I was going to be the first case on record of someone driven insane by *adverbs*. The only word I hear is *ever*. Habitual. You're telling me I'm negative, mean, bitchy, and horrid. David says: "You've *never* loved me. You *always* think of yourself, *never* of me."

Giershe

$\Longrightarrow$

"Good morning, Giershe—Mrs. Kinnard—I received your letter. I'm sorry I didn't return your call. I've been ill and had nothing to report. I thought I'd wait until I had something definite to tell you. Can you talk now? Are you alone?"

"Yes, Mr. Adams—Carl—I hope you're feeling better now. I'm alone; the children are at a friend's house."

"First, I want you to tell me the 'explosive material' you refer to in your letter. Can you do that?" He sounded very tired.

Giershe's arm began twitching. She switched the phone to her right hand but wasn't sure she was speaking into the correct disc. She returned the receiver to her left hand and steadied her elbow on the kitchen table. "It's hard to begin. A month ago— I keep a diary of the children's sayings. Perhaps I could read my entry? No. Olivia returned from Centerville with stories of kissing David's penis, of a game they play, she and Tony, and she said she gets down under the covers at night and kisses it and that . . ." She pressed her elbow into the table until it numbed. Her shoulders were shaking and there a sharp pain where spine joined neck.

"Mrs. Kinnard, I am a lawyer. I hear much that is unpleasant. Don't worry that my aged ears will burn with embarrassment."

"I asked him. He laughed and confirmed it. He said he discussed it with a student. Olivia asked the student if he'd like her to do it to him, and they agreed they didn't know how to respond to her overtures. And Tony, she said that she and Tony take turns and that 'Father likes it.'" She waited. For the opinion of the world.

"Mrs. Kinnard, you say the children are at a friend's house?"

"Yes."

"And they're to go to Centerville this afternoon?"

"Yes, the usual arrangement."

"Could you invent something to prevent their going this weekend? An illness, or a Montessori gathering, something plausible?"

"It's most difficult to lie to David."

"Here's what I have in mind." Mr. Adams' voice was stronger now. "I want a day or so to think and make some calls. I want to try to get hold of Dr. Bennett, who probably hasn't responded to your letter because he's not your doctor and is in fact a branch of the court. I know that within the week the court will move to make it official that you're not to leave Connecticut. That restriction was inadvertently omitted from the court order about custody pending litigation."

"But Mr. Adams, I cannot stay here, I won't allow—" Giershe's voice was tight and shrill.

"Listen carefully. I can't advise you to disobey a court order. I can't tell you what course of action to follow to protect your daughter. I can say, privately, that if Olivia were *my* daughter, I would not allow her to see her father again until I had assurances that the behavior you describe, and Olivia reports, is either a child's fiction, or, if not that, has ceased."

"Olivia wouldn't invent it. I know enough about David to know that."

"Please listen. I want you to prepare a letter for the judge. Tell him just what you've told me. Be specific. Quote from your diary. *Do not* mention that I've advised you to write the letter. Don't say anything at all about me. Make a copy of your letter to Dr. Bennett. Put both letters in a sealed envelope and hold them until I tell you what to do with them. Can you do that?"

"Yes. Thank you, Mr. Adams—Carl."

"Good-bye, Mrs. Kinnard."

>>>——

Giershe sent Olivia and Tony to Centerville that last weekend. She had warned David; surely he would behave. She wrote a careful letter to the judge. She didn't mention her plan to flee to California. On Saturday and Sunday, she packed their few belongings and arranged rail-freight pickup for Wednesday. She found Mrs. Rambusch working in her office and received permission, "under the circumstances," to postpone her exams and practice teaching, until they could be arranged in California. TWA was pleased to reserve seats for her for Thursday morning. Could she be at the ticket counter one half hour before departure time?

On Monday morning, the mailbox was stuffed with legal motions.

Adams had been busy, and although her legal position was not clear, Giershe felt relieved to know that she was not the only person in doubt. In any case, she was leaving and they could argue in her absence. She couldn't believe it was not her natural right to remove the children from an unsafe environment, especially since there was still no written restriction upon her leaving. Legal machinery was far too slow to respond to the swift changes in the lives of human beings. She told herself that when the judge received her letter, he would understand. Perhaps he had children of his own and would be able to imagine her state of mind. And wasn't he a friend of Mr. Adams? There was nothing to worry about. As soon as she arrived in California, she would explain everything to another lawyer and crawl in under her home state's protecting wing.

>———>———>

Tony: (*As plane circles the airport*) Mommy! I could skate on those tiny cars, couldn't I? Mommy, those are *not* ladybugs!

>———>———>

MOLLY GAVIN'S DIARY:
APRIL 25, 1963

> The girls and I to a Montessori meeting in the evening. Giershe spoke to the group. She looked beautiful and answered all questions fully and with lovely poise. They are eager to get a school started here and want Giershe to teach. Harry told Tony not to carry peanuts around or he'd spill them. Tony said: "It's all right, Harry, I already did."

APRIL 28, 1963

> Giershe down to the lawyer this morning. Two years before she can get a divorce. Tony threw a footstool at Olivia. Harry difficult.

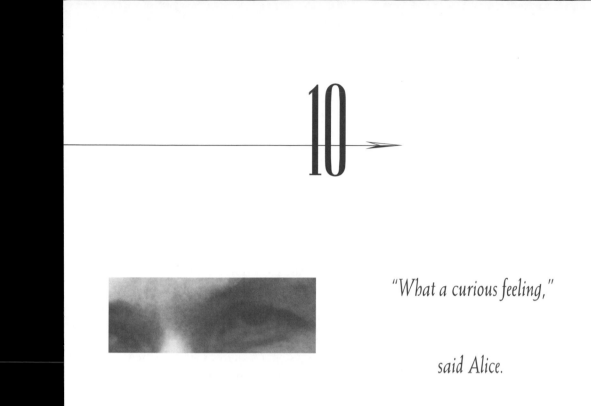

10

"What a curious feeling,"

said Alice.

"I must be shutting up

like a telescope."

G IERSHE KNEW she wasn't feeling safer in the house by the sea. She told herself that her sense of foreboding was a natural consequence of having escaped from danger. She was three thousand miles away from David, and yet she felt she might meet him on the sand dunes, or at the local post office, or find him sitting on the front porch when she returned from a walk among the pines and redwoods.

Certainly the house was not at fault. If she pushed hard against just the right surface, it might topple in on itself, but this did not bother her. Squirrels, mice, bats, and stray cats peaceably shared quarters with her little family. There were many rooms, each less finished the more stairs one climbed. They collected firewood for the huge fireplace, and each night they camped in front of its warmth and roasted hot dogs on willow sticks gathered from the tree which drooped over the porch. During the day, the children played happily in the high grass surrounding the house, and while she worked on one of her five thick Montessori albums, she could hear Olivia shouting to Tony: "No, Tony, you're supposed to be hunting for *me!* I already found you. Now do it the right way. Now it's my turn."

Jack visited on weekends, or whenever he could get free of his writing, and while it was not ideal to have to wait until nine o'clock to be alone, they were happy enough, in the beginning, to be allowed to sit together in the sunshine and stare at each other. The children didn't like to share her with Jack and were cranky when he was there.

There were five unfinished bedrooms upstairs, each with its bed. On the nights when Jack was visiting, they scrupulously separated before dawn so that . . . They didn't discuss why they erected a façade for Tony and Olivia. Was it consideration for David the Father, or was it fear of the Court? Courtesy to the children? Whatever the reason, Giershe kept an alarm clock beneath her pillow, set to ring at 5:30 a.m. Buzz-z-z-z and she would kiss Jack one more time, pull her naked body from his warmth, slip on her flannel nightgown, and tiptoe into the adjoining room. Tony always found her there in the morning.

One night, after a long walk together in the May moonlight, Giershe forgot to wind the alarm clock. Bright sunlight! Covers tugged from her body, Tony, quite naked, standing at the bedside shrieking "Mommy! Where's your nightie? Put your nightie *on!* My Mommee-e-e!" Jack clutched the covers. Giershe grabbed her nightgown, which Tony tried to yank from her fingers, and with sleepy dignity, she covered her nakedness. She picked up the kicking, screaming child and took him to her second bed. He lay quietly, his long lashes dripping tears onto his fat cheeks.

"Tony, I love Jack. I want to sleep with him when he's here. That's what people do when they love each other."

"I don't want Jack to visit. I want Father to visit."

"Father's not going to visit. We don't like each other. Father likes you and Olivia, and when the court gets it all settled you'll visit him."

"Now, can we go now?"

"Not now. Maybe not for quite a while. I have to finish my work, and Father has to teach, and the court has to decide. You'll have to wait. It's a beautiful day! Want some pancakes?" Bribery. In two weeks by the sea, Tony had fainted twice, once in a supermarket and once on the porch beneath the weeping willow branches. She lay now beside him, his curls twining around her fingers. She wiped his tears with the sheet and tapped lightly on his cheeks. Anything, Tony, anything, but faint no more, my lovely boy.

"I get to flip them! Jack like pancakes? Jack! Jack! Pancakes for breakfast! Livia, get up! Pancakes!" He was out of the bed at a run. Giershe dropped her face into the pillow. Jack fled after pancakes and said they were burning a hole in his stomach.

Giershe had a new lawyer, Mr. Arthur Baker. She had no money to pay him (he was a Gavin family acquaintance) and took up as little of his time as possible. He spoke crisply and asked her a minimum of questions. She gave a short, flat speech setting forth her reasons for leaving Connecticut. He asked for a copy of her diary.

"Is that necessary? Isn't it possible for me to receive protection here without that?"

"California has various reciprocal arrangements with Connecticut. The judges honor these ties with a sister state. We cooperate if we can. It's possible that if Connecticut finds you in contempt of a court order, California may be asked to return the children to the court of original jurisdiction. We have to assert unusual circumstances. I believe your diary supports these unusual circumstances. It's up to you. You may do what you wish." He folded his hands, swung around in his desk chair, and gazed out the window. Would he be more interested if she had paid him? Jack, Elizabeth, Molly, and Harry were all contributing to her support until she could finish her training and take a job. She was in debt to everyone she knew and the chains of gratitude were rubbing her sore.

"Mr. Baker, I'm grateful to you for taking my case. I know you have a busy schedule and are making a place for me out of regard for my parents. I want you to know I shall pay your fee when I get a Montessori job, and until then, I'll do whatever you ask. I'll send you a copy of the diary on Monday."

"Thank you, Mrs. Kinnard." He extended his hand to her, and before she left the room, he was again staring out the window.

>>>>>>

GIERSHE'S DIARY:
MAY 1, 1963

Tony fainted. Olivia stopped up. She said: "I should breathe through my nose, not my mouth. If I use my nose for what my mouth is supposed to do and my mouth for what my nose is supposed to do, everything is going to be all mixed up."

MAY 2, 1963

Olivia calls hands that have been in water a long time "shrinkled hands." Tony works with play-dough. He pounds it and rolls it. "This is my bosoms," he says. He pretends he has a book in his lap. He tells the Jack and Jill story. He interrupts himself to say "Turn the page!" and pretends to flip a page. He says: "I'm going to get a job and make some money for Mommy."

>>>>>>

IN THE SUPERIOR COURT OF THE STATE OF CALIFORNIA
IN AND FOR THE COUNTY OF ALAMEDA

GIERSHE KINNARD   v.   DAVID KINNARD
PLAINTIFF   DEFENDANT

COMPLAINT FOR
SEPARATE MAINTENANCE

The Plaintiff complains of the defendant David Kinnard

I
That plaintiff is a fit and proper person to have the sole custody, care and control of the minor children of the parties.

II

That the defendant is an able-bodied man, gainfully employed, and is capable of contributing a reasonable amount per month to plaintiff for her support and maintenance, and further, of contributing a reasonable amount per month to plaintiff for the support and maintenance of the minor children of the parties.

III

That plaintiff has always been a good, true and faithful wife to the defendant, but that the defendant, unmindful of the solemnity of his marital vows, duties and obligations, against the wish and will of the plaintiff and without her consent, and without any just cause or provocation on the part of the plaintiff, has been guilty of extreme cruelty toward plaintiff, and has thereby wrongfully inflicted upon plaintiff a course of grievous mental and physical suffering.

IV

That plaintiff has employed counsel to prosecute this action and has incurred reasonable attorney's fees and costs incident hereto.

WHEREFOR, plaintiff prays judgment of the Court as follows:

1. That plaintiff may live separate and apart from the defendant.
2. That plaintiff be awarded the sole care, custody and control of the minor children of the parties.
3. That defendant pay to plaintiff a reasonable sum per month for the support and maintenance of plaintiff.
4. That defendant pay to plaintiff a reasonable sum per month for the support and maintenance of the minor children of the parties.
5. That defendant pay to plaintiff reasonable attorney's fees and costs incident hereto.
6. For such other and further relief as to the Court may seem just and proper.

_____

Arthur Baker, Attorney for Plaintiff

>———>——>

"But Mr. Baker . . . paragraph three is not true. Could you omit it?"

"Mrs. Kinnard, paragraph three is part of the Complaint for Separate Maintenance in California. Its inclusion is proper."

>———>——>

SUPERIOR COURT, MIDDLESEX COUNTY
MAY 15, 1963

DAVID KINNARD   v.   GIERSHE KINNARD

MOTION TO MODIFY TEMPORARY CUSTODY ORDER
AND CONTEMPT

That the plaintiff respectfully represents:

1. That the defendant was granted temporary custody of the two minor children by order of the Court dated January 4, 1963, with reasonable rights of visitation in the Plaintiff.
2. That the Plaintiff has filed a motion in this Court dated April 19, 1963, praying that the Court modify the temporary custody order of January 4, 1963, to conform with the agreement of counsel for the parties to this action with respect to custody of the two minor children, which motion has not yet been heard by this Court.
3. That since the date of said motion of April 19, 1963, and *contrary* to the *intended* order of the Court restricting removal of said children, the Defendant has fled the jurisdiction of this Court with said minor children.
4. That the Defendant has deprived the Plaintiff of his rights of visitation by removal of said children contrary to the *intended* order of the Court.
5. That the Defendant by her actions since the date of January 4, 1963, has become an unfit person to have custody of said children.

WHEREFORE, Plaintiff respectfully moves that:

1. The temporary custody order of January 4, 1963, be modified to grant custody of said minor children to the Plaintiff and

that the Defendant be found in CONTEMPT by the order of the Court of January 4, 1963.

PLAINTIFF

By _____

His Attorneys RONALD RATCH

"Jack, how can I be found in contempt of an order of the Court of January 4 which did not exist when I left and still does not exist? Can they just insert stuff into court documents like that, ex post facto?"

"My love, we shall see . . ."

"Jack, they like words in triplicate or duplicate as much as David does. Does that mean—"

"Sh-h-h."

>>>———<

IN THE SUPERIOR COURT OF THE STATE OF CALIFORNIA
IN AND FOR THE COUNTY OF ALAMEDA

GIERSHE KINNARD   v.   DAVID KINNARD
PLAINTIFF   DEFENDANT

ORDER RE CUSTODY OF
CHILDREN PENDENTE LITE

IT IS HEREBY ORDERED, ADJUDGED AND DECREED that pending further order herein, it appearing that the best interests of the two minor children will best be subserved thereby, the custody of the minor children of plaintiff and defendant, to wit: Olivia Kinnard and David Kinnard III (Tony) is awarded to plaintiff.

Dated: July 1, 1963

_____
R. BOSTICH
Judge of the Superior Court

>>>>>

SUPERIOR COURT
MIDDLESEX COUNTY

JULY 18, 1963

DAVID KINNARD   v.   GIERSHE KINNARD
PLAINTIFF   DEFENDANT

ORDER

It appearing that the Plaintiff's Motion to Modify Temporary
Custody Order and Award of Counsel Fees, dated April 19, 1963,
should be granted, in order to express the full agreement of
counsel at the time of *prior* orders of this Court, it is ORDERED
that the Court's Order of January 4, 1963, be and hereby is
modified to state as follows:

Temporary custody of the two minor children named in the
writ is granted to the defendant subject to reasonable rights of
visitation in the plaintiff; *the minor children shall not be removed
from this State pending the final determination of the matter;*

and further that modifications of the aforementioned orders are
to be effective *retroactively* to the original dates of such orders.

JOHN LEGALITY
Judge of the Superior Court

SUPERIOR COURT, MIDDLESEX COUNTY
JULY 18, 1963

DAVID KINNARD   v.   GIERSHE KINNARD

ORDER

It appearing that part of Plaintiff's Motion to Modify Temporary
Custody Order and Contempt, dated May 15, 1963, should be
granted inasmuch as Defendant has *violated* the Court's Order of
January 4, 1963, and denied the Plaintiff's rights of reasonable
visitation, by removing the two minor children from this State to
the State of California, it is ordered and adjudged that the
Defendant, Giershe Kinnard, is found in CONTEMPT of this
Court and this Court's order of January 4, 1963.

John Legality
JOHN LEGALITY
Judge of the Superior Court

Why, in yonder village (the village is named Morality) there
dwells a gentleman whose name is Legality, a very judicious man,
and a man of very good name, that has skill to help men off with
their burdens as thine are from their shoulders; yea, yea, to my
knowledge he hath done a great deal of good this way; ay, and
besides, he hath skill to cure those that are somewhat crazed in
their wits with their burdens.
To go back is nothing but death; to go forward is fear of death,
and life everlasting beyond it: I will yet go forward.
— *J. Bunyan,*
Pilgrim's Progress

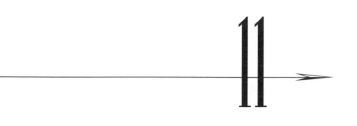

11

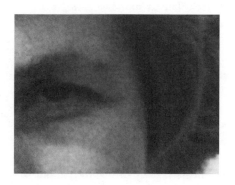

"I'll be judge, I'll be jury,"

said cunning old Fury.

"I'll try the whole cause,

and condemn you to death."

G IERSHE SUSPECTED that her Berkeley summer apartment was being watched. A beige Ford was often parked across the street, a young man slouched behind the wheel, one knee up, resting on the dashboard, tweed cap pulled down over his face. He never seemed to be awake, or looking her way, but he was there when she turned off the lights at night, and sometimes early in the morning. Professor F. was in town. He came to call, bringing with him an urgent despair. When she took walks with Jack, late at night, she was sure she saw the professor ahead of them, walking fast, turning a corner like the White Rabbit.

Jack and Giershe were night friends. He avoided the children and left Giershe's bed just before dawn. They amused each other by writing an essay on "What America Means to Me" and sending it to a *Reader's Digest* contest. They researched a teasing half-serious article on "The Female Orgasm: Vaginal, Clitoral, or Mythical?" But the article (which didn't get written) was merely a diversion to take their minds off conflicting ORDERS from the Superior Court judges of two cooperating states. Giershe had offers for the fall from the southern, the middle, and the northern parts of California, but there was no money for July and August. She begged (and miserably accepted) $50, $100, another $100, then $40, from Molly and Harry, Elizabeth, Jack, and even Professor F. She took an afternoon job at the university, and placed the children with a baby-sitter, with instructions *never* to let them out of sight.

Awake, she expected David to descend like a human helicopter, with two claws like those candy machines they used to have on ferryboats, scoop up the children, and roar off into the summer fog. Asleep, she began to have a dream she would have many times. She was walking barefoot—stumbling, weeping, through bombed buildings, pulling at a smoking rafter, turning over cracked pavement, listening for the sound of two kittens. The wind whipped black rags around her body; snow crusted on her shoulders and formed icicles of her tears. She would clutch the sheets and sit up in bed. Jack would murmur, "Same dream?" Listen, listen to the silence in the apartment and hear a child turning over, a sigh, a cough, the mockingbird beginning its night recital. Slide down into warmth again. This night would pass without event. Awake or asleep, there was a burning in her stomach and throat. Her food did not digest. A great State was protecting her, and her body knew it was just so much puff against the force of a David Kinnard.

MOLLY GAVIN'S DIARY:
JULY 31, 1963

We are exhausted but plug along. I'm very tired of *Little Black Sambo*. Harry very difficult. Tony said to me in the dining room: "Harry is mad at you. Don't go out there!"

GIERSHE'S DIARY:
JULY 15, 1963

Tony asked me to lie beside him before he slept. He checked to see that I was not too close to the edge. He said: "I won't let you fall off, Mommy." He kissed me, on the lips, as he always does. He caressed my hair, gently, with his brown hand and said: "Such pretty hair! Don't say bye-bye, Mommy, say night-night."

JULY 17, 1963

I was angry with Jack on the telephone. Olivia said: "Why don't you like Jack? You've *got* to like Jack! *I* like him. You've got to love *someone* so I can have a father!"

AUGUST 5, 1963

Olivia: "Why doesn't Jack live with his wife?" Me: "They don't live together." Olivia: "Why can't we go back to Centerville and live apart from Father, but close enough so I can ride my tricycle to his house when I want to?"

AUGUST 10, 1963

We went to the doctor to see what's wrong with me. Tony: "Is he going to give me a shot?" I said, "No Tony—you're all right." Tony: "Then who's wrong?"

AUGUST 17, 1963

Olivia: "Tony, you can't have babies because babies come out of your secret parts, not out of your belly button. My secret parts have a crack in them. Want to see? See? Your penis doesn't have any crack in it." She's been drawing earthquakes.

"FATHER"
Olivia, Oct. 1963

MORNING OF AUGUST 12, 1963

"Hello, Giershe? Is that you? The line's crackling. It's Dianne. I'm calling from Eugene, Oregon. What are your plans for the fall?"

"Dianne! What are you doing there? I thought you were in the East. Are you coming to Berkeley?"

"Not right away. I want to leave, but I'm stuck up here getting a school started. Is there any chance you could come relieve me? They need a teacher until their fancy Irish teacher arrives in January, and I've convinced them you're the best of the crop."

"But I've signed a contract with the south. I don't want to go down there. I want to stay here. There's a school opening here in January. Do you suppose I could get out of my contract?"

"Just do it. But you have to be here by August twentieth so I can spend a week getting you started. Olivia and Tony attend free. Well?"

"I don't know. That's about fifty miles from David's hometown. His goofy sister. His mother. Yes! I'll do it! Tell them yes. Wait, I just thought of something. I'm not supposed to leave California. Maybe the court would give me permission to leave. It's just temporary and I *have* to begin earning some money. I'll find out and let you know. Whoopee! Sweet nourishment to see you again! I think of you so often—ol' Computer-Brain."

>>>——————

Berkeley
August 27, '63

DEAREST GIERSHE

I was terribly disappointed at missing your call. Elizabeth said you found a lovely apartment and that will certainly make Eugene easier to take. I went over to your apartment to get your things, thinking I might sleep in your pajamas for a couple of nights, but all I found was a pair of slippers and a shower cap. Your absence will soon generate an epistolary urge in me, and, fed by longing, it should produce acceptable letters soon.

I had hoped we could integrate the children more closely, but it hasn't worked out that way. Mostly, it's been my own incapacity to adjust to your domestic establishment. Olivia and Tony do upset me. You have exposed me as more of an authoritarian than I could possibly have imagined. I'm educating Andrew for the role of social critic. I want him disciplined, taught to deal easily with society so that he can step outside of it. I want him tough, with a *cast-iron ego*. Such plans are not your mode, and there's no reason why they should be, but neither is there any reason why yours should be mine. We both have hostages to fortune, and we owe our first loyalty to them. What we have left, we can give to each other.

Muriel wants a divorce, and full custody. I'm not willing to play that game. Whatever happens, I'm going to keep my hands on and control over Andrew. The pattern might take some time to work out. I can offer you a great deal of love, affection, aid, and comfort, if you don't demand that it come in just the form you want it. I miss you, sweetheart. I'll do everything I can to make the time pass swiftly for you. Please let me love you.

Jack

GIERSHE'S DIARY:
AUGUST 30, 1963

Tony stood on his chair and pulled his pants down during Grace this evening with board chairman's family. He pointed his penis at the bowed heads and said: "I'm gonna pee on you!" Some of the children giggled. I shushed him and adjusted his pants.

AUGUST 31, 1963

Tony's first day in school with Dianne. The children have been taught to kill spiders and bugs. Tony was solemnly watching a bug when Demeter stepped on it. Tony socked him and screamed: "You! Don't dead the bug! I'll dead you!" His rage spent, he cried quietly by himself and murmured: "He shouldn't dead the bug."

SEPTEMBER 1, 1963

Had to leave Tony at school with Dianne while I went to a board meeting. He was furious and closed the door after me. He tried to lock it and told Dianne: "We won't let her in when she comes back."

SEPTEMBER 2, 1963

River picnic with summer group. Tony spent time by himself. He watched the river and ate alone, indifferent to the other children. He sang: "I am the sun, Olivia is the moon. You are the sky, and Father is a tree." He paused. "Is Father the tree or is Jack? Mommy, we have to go get Jack." He calls oars "rowers," propellers "twisters," and skates "rollshoes."

Olivia is with Molly and Harry in the mountains. I miss her so.

SEPTEMBER 4, 1963

Board chairman (a doctor) arranged an overnight stay for Tony in hospital to determine cause of his fainting. He was curiously brave. He asked for a kiss and then went off with the nurses without tears. He submitted to electrodes and blood extraction with a great deal of interest.

SEPTEMBER 5, 1963

Tests yielded no information. All is normal. Tony greeted me this morning: "Mommy! I didn't cry at all! I'm so happy. Are you happy, Mommy? I'm glad you came back. Are you glad?"

>>>>>>

Eugene
September 10, 1963

DEAR JACK—

I'm working so hard, in so many different directions, it's impossible to write a coherent letter. Taking up the reins of a horse I've never ridden is perfect exercise for my weak character. I'm at it sixteen hours a day. The school is open from nine to twelve this summer with about twelve kids, more arriving each day, but the environment still must be painted, the playground covered with something to soak up the mud. The equipment hasn't arrived from Holland, an aide must be hired, parents interviewed, and study groups formed. I'm in charge of all of the above. Nuns pop in to chat and spread their glad tidings. My mother-in-law has been phoning daily to beg me to bring the children to see her. Helen Kinnard is not a person I like to think about, but she *is* the children's grandmother, is an invalid, and is only fifty miles north of here. I plan to go see her on Saturday morning, pay my respects (I have none), and cut out of there before any part of her total disease infects me. I'm usually a philo-Semite, but five minutes with her and every anti-Semitic stereotype hisses at me. She adores money, professional status, social rank, and power. She's devious, two-faced, malevolent and ugly. A flat face with bulbous nose and weasel eyes, perched atop a ruined body confined to a wheelchair. She had a stroke fifteen years ago, and everyone in the family resurrects her prestroke personality as a defense against the witch she is today.

Before, she was beautiful (never!), talented, loving, kind, a gourmet cook, a loyal and faithful wife, a philanthropist, witty, charming, and friend alike to low and high. Now, she has a plotting mind. Her right arm is paralyzed; she lights cigarettes with her left hand, holds the cigarette between the first two fingers while her thumb goes round in a circle. She watches her thumb. I watch her thumb. I've tried to attach meaning to the action. The best I've come up with is that once she had a loom and was a weaver. Try to visualize a weaver at her loom. The thumb makes an arc as the hand pulls skeins up, over, through. Her thumb remembers, protests impotence.

She's in a fancy Catholic nursing home, courted by nuns and priests who hope she'll convert before she dies. Her children gather at her bedside and say things like: "Oh, Granny, shut up!" or "Boy, do you stink today!" or "Hurry up and say it, Granny. We can't wait forever for you to oink a thought." She giggles. It's the family style, but sometimes I see tears in her eyes. I should feel sorry for her, but I remember that she didn't speak to me until Olivia was born. Wrong. She talked to me during the first pregnancy. I became a person when I carried her blood in me. That's where I'll be on Saturday, should you call.

love
Giershe

>>>—

LAW OFFICES
Arthur Baker
Berkeley, California

October 13, 1963

Dear Mrs. Kinnard:

As you must have anticipated, your husband's attorney is moving to vacate the California proceedings on the grounds that you've violated terms of the Order and have removed the children from the jurisdiction of the California courts. There would be one way to stop this move to vacate, namely, if there were some assurance you were returning to California with the children within a reasonable period of time. Please advise me immediately.

Sincerely,
Arthur Baker

San Jose
October 14

DEAREST—

You must try to live somewhere on the safe side of hysteria. Your crazy talk of giving up Olivia and Tony. It is impossible for me to imagine you apart from them. I suppose you must share them with him and I pray he'll not be a monster. Cannot love and compassion win even that adamantine pride? Sweetheart, please don't harm yourself. Stay whole, and return to health.

love
Jack

Eugene
October 21

DEAREST JACK—

November rushes towards us. A weekend with you! David says he's visiting his mother and sister on November 1. He wants me to spend the weekend there. I've told him that's not possible. He pleads and *promises* to behave. He wants so much to see the children and they're begging me to allow it. I feel as though it's not happening in my life, but in a story. The only precaution I've taken is a postcard to lawyer in Berkeley. I'd rather not talk about it. We live lives based on selected fictions. "Each psyche is really an anthill of opposing predispositions. Personality, as something with fixed attributes, is an illusion—but a necessary illusion if *we are to love*. In the end, everything will be found to be true, of everybody; Saint and Villain are co-sharers" (Pursewarden).

It is, has been, and will be raining. But in the distance is almost a Flemish landscape with changing colors and Jack is coming soon.

your
Giershe

GIERSHE'S DIARY:

SEPTEMBER 27, 1963

> Olivia came to me while the schoolchildren were resting. I was singing to them. Olivia: (*whispering*) "I'm thinking of you last year, Mommy. Typing, typing, working so hard. You did it for this, didn't you?"

OCTOBER 5, 1963

> Tony asks again and again: "When is Father coming?" He asks male strangers two questions: 1. Do you know my father, where is he, when is he coming? and 2. Why do people have mothers?

OCTOBER 30, 1963

> Olivia can't decide which of two outfits to wear for the visit with David: "Oh, I have two minds."

>>>>>———

Salem, Oregon, sixty miles north of Eugene, was David's hometown. In November 1963, there were thirteen Kinnards listed in the telephone directory, but only one—Helen—was a relative. David had two sisters: Betsy Kinnard Swan, eight years older than her brother, had lived in Salem all of her life; Anne Kinnard Levine, two years Betsy's senior, had escaped to the southland after her marriage.

Hotel Kinnard (no relation) was the largest hotel in town and in 1950, Giershe had spent two migrainy days in room 142 while David tried to convince his parents that she did not have horns. While David held audience with his father, Dr. Kinnard, or quarreled with his invalid mother, Giershe vomited all of the family into the toilet. After each skirmish, David phoned to report progress. His sister Betsy called to apologize and proclaim that "David should have been castrated at birth—the misery he's caused women all of his life." Betsy's estranged husband urged Giershe to shake herself loose from all the Kinnards and flee before it was too late. At eleven p.m. Helen Kinnard rang the room to bid David good night.

Giershe let Harry's old green Chevy poke along in the slow lane of traffic. Olivia and Tony sat beside her in the front seat. They were solemn and well behaved, unusually subdued. She tried to remember whether she had ever actually met Dr. Kinnard, or whether she could see his face so clearly because she had sat in the Kinnard living room with only his portrait for company. David had driven her on that Sunday afternoon to the elegant house on the hill. Exotic plants flanked the circular driveway. Betsy had opened the door, playfully poked David in the ribs, and had placed Giershe on a couch opposite the portrait. David went upstairs to see his father; Betsy left the room. She sat with her future father-in-law staring down at her, his eyes following her movements, like those life-size Miss Sailor chocolate ads they used to place on the sidewalk in front of drugstores. She was alone with him a very long time. His face was long, austere, controlled. The eyes burned above a lengthy thin nose. He was dressed in a brown business suit; one hand lay in his lap. The manicured, sculptured fingers held a slim ivory cigarette holder. Smoke curled upward, shadowing his brown tweed vest.

Dr. Kinnard, why don't you want to see me?

My dear Miss Gavin, you are not important to me. My son's moral life is all that concerns me. He knows the Path he must choose, and I have faith that he'll find his Way again.

When you say Path and Way I suppose you mean the Church?

David knows whereof I speak. I need not explain it to you.

Of course you needn't. I understand, but David and I love each other and want to marry.

Miss Gavin! I don't want to hear about it! David has a wife and a daughter. My little granddaughter. They pray for his return. They are my solace in this time of trouble.

Dr. Kinnard—I've known David almost a year now, and I know other people who've known him for four years, and they tell me that in all that time, they've never seen any evidence of belief in—

My son was raised in the Church and he tells me he is guided yet by its Truths. This morning he bowed his head in prayer and confessed his sins.

And early this afternoon, he climbed into b— Dr. Kinnard, your son loves you and wants you to be happy. Has David told you that we're leaving in two weeks, that we shall marry as soon as we can, and that we're here in hopes that you'll give us your blessing?

David will send for his wife and child as soon as he gets settled. When he does that, he'll receive my blessing and the blessings of his Lord.

Amazing. Two fathers, both pigheaded. My mother and I tried to keep it a secret from Harry that David was raised a Catholic, and your women keep it a secret from you that your children long ago left the Church. Oh, Harry is my father.

Miss Gavin! Your family is of no interest to me! My heart! It hurts me now . . . There is medicine in the kitchen. . . . Please cease your chatter and bring it to me. . . . Hurry . . . That's a sweet lady . . . pretty lady.

>>>>

"Mommy, did Father have a father?" Tony was looking out the car window.

"Of course he had a father, dumb Tony. He's dead, isn't he, Mommy?"

"Yes, dead. He was an old man and he died before either of you was born. I was just thinking about him and couldn't remember if I ever met him. He was a doctor. He was Big Boss of the family while he lived, and maybe that's why I can't remember. He frightened me."

"Don't be afraid of Father. I won't let him hurt you." Tony climbed over Olivia and put his head in Giershe's lap.

"Oh Tony, I'm not afraid Father will hurt me. I'm afraid he'll *steal* you. He *promises* he won't, but I worry all the same."

Giershe parked the old Chevy just behind Betsy's lavender Cadillac convertible. Whatever Betsy wanted, she talked herself into getting. She needed a car to take her mother places, one that was dependable and would give her mother fresh air. She had to have new furniture, for her boys, so they wouldn't be ashamed to bring kids home. She had thirty-seven pairs of shoes because her feet hurt, and although Giershe had never seen her in anything but a muu-muu or a bathrobe, her closets were filled with expensive garments she was planning to wear when she lost a "little weight."

Betsy was fat, short, and looked like an Indian squaw, with her brown face, high cheekbones, bare feet, stubby fingers, and straight brown hair, which she often wore in a braid down her back. Her tongue was tart, witty, vulgar, and constant; she had an opinion on all family matters and was interested in little else. She grumbled about having to take care of her mother but subsisted entirely on Helen's capital (rapidly dwindling). She didn't work, and although her sister and brother often devised perfect "schemes" to set her up in a business which would sustain her when the money ran out, Betsy was agile in avoiding the first step into independence. She didn't have time, she had to be on call in case Helen needed her, she wasn't feeling too well this month, perhaps next month. She didn't want to bring up latchkey children. Two boys. Really good kids, and proof that youth could survive any sort of mothering. There was nothing about Betsy that Giershe completely approved of, but she had to admit that somehow the whole mess functioned in a way that she envied. Betsy was trivial and would surely come to a bad end, but meanwhile, the food got to table, the boys were cared for, money floated in for all necessities and more than a few luxuries, and Betsy herself was a fleshy monument to the victory of short-term folly over long-term planning.

The sun was setting. It had been cloudy with intermittent rain, and as usual in this alien land, sunshine, misty showers, clouds, and rainbows mixed to conclude the day. Giershe sat behind the wheel. One of Betsy's boys was studying meteorology and had set up his equipment in the backyard. A wooden tower he had built could be seen through the side gate. He liked to sleep in his tower, ever hopeful the sun would rise and submit to observation.

"Mom," Olivia asked tenderly, "do you have a headache?" Her mittened hand touched Giershe's cheek.

"Yes. Let's go in." Betsy came down the front steps. Her purple-and-black muumuu was cut low over bulging bosom. Behind her, standing in the doorway, posing, not smiling, was David in a brown bathrobe she hadn't seen before. This family, they seemed to prefer bathrobes for all occasions. Betsy even went to the market in hers, if that's what she happened to be wearing when she came to the end of a carton of cigarettes. They weren't wash-and-wear robes. They were wool challis, cashmere, satin, or silk, and they were worn at night after sweating all day, or for two days on a weekend spent at home. The pockets carried used toothpicks, shredded Kleenex, broken cigarettes and even ashes, gathered from moments when it was too much trouble to find an ashtray. The fronts were stained with soup and soft-boiled egg, jism, and red wine. The rears were shiny.

Giershe followed Betsy up the front steps. She glanced at David as she brushed past him, but he was crouched to receive the children, arms stretched out in front of him. They crowded into his arms, both of them talking at once, Olivia shoving Tony out of the way, saying "Shut, up Tony! I was here first!" Betsy led Giershe into a bedroom. "This is the boys' room where you'll sleep. Donny's on a Boy Scout trip and Bobby's sleeping in his tower tonight. Two twin beds, one for the children, one for you—or however you want it. Really, Giershe, cheer up! My brother has promised to behave himself and I think he knows it'll hit the fan if he doesn't. You look very tired. Been sick? Or just working too hard?"

"I didn't sleep last night, and I've been working very hard. Maybe I'll perk up after a sherry. Let me wash my face and then I'll be out. Why is David's stuff in here?"

"Christshit! I don't know, I told him to put it in my room. He can either sleep on the couch in the living room or in the extra bed in the back room. I figure that's his business. I've got a casserole in the oven. Come out when you've washed up."

Giershe stood in the middle of the room. Choo-choo-train wallpaper, toys everywhere she looked, models, stuffed animals, airplanes hanging from the ceiling, Boy Scout awards, science kits, sneakers, a dirty Little League uniform lying in one corner, two twin beds with identical baby-blue quilted satin comforters, neatly made up, purple satin pillows with crimson fringe.

She tied her car keys to her belt and turned on the hot water.

"Olivia—it's my turn— I WANT TO TELL FATHER."

"Tony, I'm going to smash you! Now let me sit in his lap . . ."

"Now, now, we have lots of time and I can hear everything. There, we can all fit in this chair. M-m-m, you look good enough to eat. I think I'll take a bite."

Hot water steamed the bathroom mirror. She pressed a hot washcloth into aching eyes and bent her head over the steam rising from the basin.

Why hadn't she realized she would need all of her strength? She could have taken a sleeping pill last night. She'd never be able to sleep in this house, not with David in the next room. Who was the queen who awaited execution, night after night? Had she slept while they decided the day and the hour?

David was singing a song about a cowboy. Betsy called everyone to dinner. Giershe sat across from David and felt she was no one and nowhere. David talked of ferreting troubles. Betsy talked of her new beau who was really quite all right, good to the children, but had two problems—alcohol and impotence. Giershe's head weighed two thousand pounds—the children's voices, rising now in volume, shrieking, cutting the air like squealing pigs when the garbage is thrown out. She stood up and began to clear the table. "I think it's time we went to bed. I'm not feeling well and they obviously are ready for sleep."

"I'll put them to bed. You lie down on the couch for a while. And Betsy, you just leave the dishes. I'll do them later." David, tender, smiley, in command. He pulled an afghan over Giershe and told the children to kiss her good night. They asked where she would be sleeping. She told them she would sleep with them. They wanted to know where David would sleep and there was no answer. She lay on the couch, her eyes closed, listening to every sound in the bedroom. She pressed one side of her head into the pillow and rubbed her temple. David's heavy step in the kitchen. Low angry voices. ". . . what about what she did to me! A lie-detector test, an investigation!"

"I'm sure you're capable of it, and she's sure. What was she to do? I'm your sister and I . . ."

"She's a killer. She'll wreck their lives!" Laughter. A dish breaking.

"Now see what you've done. Look out for your feet!"

Giershe murmured good night to Betsy and David and went into the bedroom. She closed the door behind her. No lock. She placed a chair in front of the door, removed her jeans and climbed into Olivia's bed. Olivia stirred, and snuggled close to Giershe's back.

>>>—————

"Giershe? Are you awake?" David whispered.

"Yes. What are you doing in here?"

"Do you want some hot milk and whiskey to help you sleep?" He sat down on the edge of the bed. She turned over on her back. She could see his face in the streetlight shining through the window. His bathrobe was open in front.

"No. I feel better. What's the plan for tomorrow? I have to leave by noon. I have lots of work to do before Monday's class."

"I'm going to put Olivia in Tony's bed so we won't disturb her."

"David, we're okay. Just leave." He picked up Olivia and placed her beside Tony. He lay down next to Giershe on top of the covers. "David, I don't want you to sleep in here. I need to sleep and I can't if you're in here. Why don't you go to bed?"

He lay on his side, his head propped up with one hand, his other hand massaging her head. He felt her face, her neck, pushed sheets and blankets down over her T-shirt, fingers into her panties. "So beautiful! So lovely! Oh . . . oh . . . I've missed you." The huge hand covered her mound, one rude finger going in and out; he was on top of her, the covers separating them. His weight was squashing her.

"Get off of me!"

"Oh Giershe, let me show you what you mean to me!" His face was against hers, his tongue in her mouth, his chest mashing her breasts, his penis ramming the bed covers. One of her arms was pinned to her side. With her free hand she grabbed his hair and pulled. He jerked his head back.

"I shall scream, David. I will!"

"You won't. No, no, Giershe." He lifted himself from her in order to pull back the sheets and blanket, and in that instant she pulled up her knees and rolled out of bed. She scrambled to the door and stood with her hand on the knob, shivering and hiccuping. He stared at her. "Oh, what the hell. Come back to bed. I won't bother you." He pulled the covers over himself and turned his back. She ran to the children's bed, squeezed down between their warm bodies, one arm around each, and for the remainder of the night, she watched the willow tree branches cast shadows on the airplane hanging from the ceiling.

>>>>

In the morning, while Tony and Olivia slept and David snored, Giershe took the fastest shower of her life. She put on a fresh white turtleneck, black tights and skirt (for visiting the nursing home), and went into the kitchen to make coffee. Betsy was already up, hair a mess, sitting at the kitchen table with a coffee cup and a cigarette.

"God, Giershe! You look like a cadaver dressed for a ride to the cemetery. I suppose my brother misbehaved last night?"

"Best not talk about it. I can't remember what it's like to sleep. What are morning visiting hours?"

"Ten to twelve but we can go anytime. Or you can go. I see Helen quite enough. She just wants to see her precious son and the children anyway. She can yell at me any old time. Would the kids like pancakes?"

"Would they! Show me where the stuff is and I'll help."

"Why don't you go get them dressed? Preparing food is just about the only thing I like to do by myself, that and taking a shit."

They all ate breakfast together in the dining room. Olivia ate six pancakes; Tony ate ten. They chased David around the house and vice versa.

"We'd better get ready to visit Helen. It's ten-thirty," Giershe said.

"I have two grandmothers and one grandfather," Tony announced. "I have one mother and two fathers."

"Tony, shut up! You have only one father. Jack is just a friend," Olivia said.

"Which car are we taking?" David asked.

"My Cadillac needs gas. You'd better take Giershe's car." Giershe was standing near the front door. The room tipped and grew fuzzy. She sat down on the floor with her hand over her mouth.

"Giershe, you're not well. Do you think you could trust me to take the children to see Helen? I've promised Betsy and you. You *know* that to steal them would be an insanity." David crouched in front of her.

"No, David. No. I can't. I don't want to see Helen, but I just can't let you."

"You should help us begin to trust each other again by letting me take them. We'll be back by noon—no later—and you can keep a check on us by calling the nursing home. You can't drive back without some rest. I know you didn't sleep last night, and I understand why and I'm sorry. Can you trust? Try." He looked into her eyes.

Giershe handed him the car keys. They said good-bye and closed the door. She stood at the window and watched then drive away. They were laughing, Tony in his black knit cap next to the window, Olivia in a blue coat with a big collar, sitting beside David. She lay down on the couch and closed her eyes. Betsy washed dishes. She opened her eyes. The cuckoo clock on the wall said "Cuckoo" eleven times. Betsy sat down in a rocking chair and began to knit. Eleven-fifteen.

"Betsy, I shouldn't have done that, should I?"

"Done what? Oh, let David take them. I don't know."

"How long does it take to get to the nursing home?"

"Fifteen minutes."

"Does David know the way?"

"Oh yeah. His father was there for a while."

Giershe stood up. "What's the phone number?" Betsy dialed the number and handed the phone to Giershe. "Hello? This is Giershe Kinnard. Has Mr. Kinnard visited his mother yet this morning? He has. Already? He's left? Where was he going? Were the children with him? Never mind!" She banged down the receiver. "Betsy! Where are the car keys? We have to go find them! Oh GOD DAMN DAMN DAMN!"

"Giershe, you're jumping to conclusions. You haven't given him a chance. Now calm down . . ."

"SHUT UP! If you won't give me the car keys, I'll call a taxi!"

"All right! Let's go."

Betsy drove so fast through the streets of Salem that most of the refuse on the floor of the car whirled out into the air. Giershe rocked in her seat, hugging her knees, and once almost went through the windshield when Betsy unaccountably decided to stop for a red light. They screeched to a stop in front of the nursing home. The car door stuck and Giershe climbed over it and landed on the sidewalk running. She pushed through the glass door, past the receptionist, down the hallway to Helen's room. Nuns in black frocks flapped behind her, their hands outstretched to hold her back. The door was open. Helen looked up at her—stupid, vacant.

"Where are they? Where did they go?"

"They visited. They left. They said they had to go."

Giershe grabbed Helen's shoulder and shook it. Two nuns pulled her back. She wrenched around, jabbing her elbow into a white-framed face. "GET YOUR ROTTEN HANDS OFF OF ME! CREEPS! VULTURES! Where are my CHILDREN?"

"Mrs. Kinnard! You must calm down. The children were here with Mr. Kinnard. They are all right. They're with their father. They left."

"Yes, they've left . . . and I hope they've escaped. They belong with their father." Helen was smiling and the thumb was going around and around. The nuns were holding Giershe's arms. She lunged at Helen.

"You GHASTLY OLD UGLY WITCH! I HOPE YOU DIE, DIE! Today, this minute! You are evil, EVIL, HELEN KINNARD! YOU AND YOUR SON!"

"Mrs. Kinnard, you cannot do this in a nursing home. People are very sick here . . ."

"SHUT UP, IDIOT PENGUINS! How can you care for a woman who would plot to take away a mother's children?"

"He is their father, this is their grandmother."

"Yes, the father who has his daughter kiss his penis! WONDERFUL father." They began to pat and soothe her. They folded her into their black gowns, and for a moment Giershe let herself rest against their strong bodies, let their cool hands brush the hair from her eyes. She sobbed into their pleats, breathing in the soapy fresh smell, then suddenly pulled from them and ran down the hallway, out the doors to Betsy, who was sitting calmly behind the wheel.

"Betsy, they've gone. Your mother helped them and is glad. Betsy, did you know? Did you?"

"Believe me, I didn't. I'll never forgive him for this. Let's go home."

"We have to call the police. Hurry, hurry!"

12

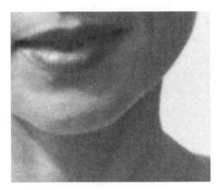

"And things are

worse than ever . . .

for I never was

so small as this before."

Eugene, Nov. 18.63

D EAR NATALIE—

I'm learning about Courts and find that I'm not as strong as I'd hoped to be. I feel myself a pariah, cut off from decent society, everyone's bad news. In case you haven't learned from someone by now, we ran up against an insane judge whose name I refuse to remember. He has turned over all documents to Camelia FAHEY, Domestic Relations Officer, Family Relations Division, for a complete report, and has postponed a hearing until after December 10. Until then, the children reside in David's house, with a court-appointed person living there round the clock. He also stipulated that I couldn't see the children. Leslie Barker traveled a thousand miles to witness but was not called. Nor was I.

The day after the court nonhearing I went to New Haven to see Camelia Fahey. She took my life history and asked me, with all the "casual relations" and the marriage overlap, if it didn't look pretty awful? She believes that this particular judge, who banned Henry Miller in Connecticut, is capable of putting the children in a foster home.

I'm now back in Eugene where I'm experiencing what Montessori says is the reward the directress receives from her children when she's been very disciplined with them and has given them tools for constructing themselves—love, eagerly expressed in hugs and work. I am needed here and can do nothing in Centerville. Jack says: "Don't be a loser—stop sniveling and fight," or "Dammit, I wish you'd get off the hook—compassion interferes with love." He makes me laugh. I dare not touch their toys.

love to you
Giershe

Gorgeville, Nov. 20.63

DEAR GIERSHE—

Are you all right? Do you want me to come to Centerville again? I am still shocked by the stupid behavior of that judge and the mean, selfish behavior of Mr. Kinnard. Too bad about Mr. Adams. Wrapping oneself around a tree at two in the morning is pretty much what one might have expected from his lifestyle. I wouldn't have said so before, but he was not the greatest lawyer that ever lived. The next one will be better. As for the Family Disservice officers, my advice is, don't tell them anything unless you know Dino already has. And don't feel guilty about their references to "casual affairs." Most people I know, and I, are still ahead of you; also most Family Relations folk. Jeb isn't home, so I can't ask him to help steal O. and T. Can I help?

love,
Leslie

><<<<

In Montessori's teaching, there is a period of the day which she calls *"il gran lavore"* time. The child has come to school after a night's sleep and an adequate breakfast. His body and mind are ready for maximum effort during the morning hours of nine to eleven. He will want to work or play vigorously until he feels hunger or fatigue.

Il gran lavore time was Giershe's busiest part of the day. As soon as each child had hung up his coat on his hook, he was expected to choose work, to take it from the shelf to his table or the floor, and to concentrate on the task until he lost interest. The "work" is usually what is placed on the shelf. It isn't "work" to imagine you're a flamingo and try to stand motionless in the middle of the room on one leg, or to pretend you're a snake and move across the floor on your stomach without using your hands and legs. "Work" is cleaning up your mess after polishing your shoes. It's cutting and scraping carrots for lunch, pouring milk, and setting the lunch table. It is not going outside to climb the one tree in the yard, but it might be sweeping the path to the school door after the wind has blown leaves and redwood bark all over, and it might be washing the windows after a storm has left muddy stains.

Giershe suggested work and introduced new equipment. And usually, around ten o'clock, she liked to sit quietly in a corner of the big room to watch or make notes. Each day that she observed the big-work period, she felt herself in the presence of an energy so compelling that it was like sitting inside a huge kaleidoscope, herself part of the multicolored pattern which could shift and take new form in the next minute but always re-formed itself into pleasing, harmonious beauty. Eighteen tiny children, all of them quietly busy!

On the morning of November 22, at ten minutes after ten, she sat in a little chair with her clipboard on a low, pink Formica table. Suddenly she heard noises outside the schoolroom. A shriek, high and wild, like a sea gull above a cresting wave, and then a falling wail, another shriek, and mingled voices—"Oh Mother of God— Oh—oh dear Lord!" As Giershe stood up,

Sister Monica and Sister Ursula flapped down the corridor towards the door to the schoolroom, their black frocks billowing behind them. They bumped into each other as they hurled themselves through the door. Their faces, usually serene, pale, clay-colored, were red and blue, cracked, fragmented pieces held together by stiff white frames. Sister Monica's white hands fluttered in front of her, and in the instant before she wrapped herself around Giershe, her face gleamed wet.

"The children— Olivia— Tony— What?" Giershe struggled to free herself.

"The president—our beloved president—he has been shot . . . in Dallas . . . Oh Mother of God . . . Our president!"

Giershe struggled. All around her the children were staring. A hand on a pink cube. Gi-Gi dripping water from a sponge. Frederika crying. Kirby flat on the floor with his arms covering his head.

Is it so monstrous that a President be shot? There was no flicker of kindness in your faces when I told you the father had stolen Olivia and Tony. You didn't inquire if there was pain or even say, "God's will be done." A shot in Dallas and you crumple beneath the weight of one death.

She smiled at Ursula and Monica, merely women wrapped in costume, hiding from the world their breasts, white shoulders, moist places. They could cry, shudder, cling, doubt the support beneath their hidden feet. She kissed their wet cheeks and turned away. "Children, put away what you're doing. Come to me at the story place, quickly. Gi-Gi, get a mop. Benny, can you get all the color tablets back into their box? Frederika, help Benny if he'll let you."

Peter Henley stood in the middle of the room. "I want my mommy!" he cried, and couldn't seem to move backward or forward. He dropped his puzzle. His brother John put an arm around him and with his free hand put the puzzle together. The children put away their work sloppily and hurried to the back of the room where each day they rested after lunch. Giershe sat on the floor and asked the children to form a circle. Peter was still crying and wanted to sit in her lap. Frederika was hanging from her shoulder and tried to push Peter to the floor.

"Take a friend's hand. Make the connection. Good. Kirby, take Benny's hand and sit down please."

"Who got shot? Bang-bang!"

"What's a President? Is he dead?"

"I want my mommy!"

"I'm hungry!"

"I want to pee."

"I can walk home by myself! All by myself!"

"Did God get shot?"

Giershe hung the Silence sign over the back of a chair. She waited. Would they be able to control themselves? Every day, once a day, the silence game was played. She placed the sign with its wooden lettering in a different place each day, and waited for a child to notice. The first child who saw the lettering whispered (never shouted) "Silence" to one child, that child whispered to another, and as the children heard the news, they left what they were doing and gathered at the story place, silently. Today, it was difficult for Giershe to wait for the hush and peace which was the reward of the game. She closed her mouth and pointed to the sign. Peter tried to swallow his sobs. She rubbed his shoulders and closed her eyes. She waited . . . and waited . . . almost . . . a sob . . . a whisper . . . (Who shot? . . . Sh-h-h) . . . silence.

"Oh, that's nice. I feel much better. Thank you, children. Okay. Sister Monica and Sister Ursula came into the room. You saw them. What did you see?"

"I saw them crying," Frederika said.

"Yes, they were crying. They were very sad because they heard on the radio that President Kennedy has been shot in Texas. A president is the leader of the United States and he was visiting Texas. Someone shot him. Is there anyone who knows where Texas is on the U.S. puzzle map?"

"I know. I'll go get it." John Henley left the circle and walked to the big frame which held the geographic puzzles.

"Bring the whole United States, John. Good. Now which one is Texas?" John handed her the large pink wooden piece. She balanced the puzzle in her lap so that all the children could see where Texas fit. "Over here is where President Kennedy lives with his wife and two children, in a place called the White House. He went in an airplane to visit in Texas, and while he was visiting, someone shot him."

"Is he dead?" George asked.

"I don't know. We hope not. He's in a hospital and all the doctors are trying to make him well again."

"My father could go to Texas and make him well," John said.

"Let me hold Texas," George begged. He pointed the panhandle at Kirby. "Bang-bang! You're dead, Kirby."

"George, let me put Texas away and we'll talk a bit more. Thank you. We're going to stay in school for a while, but Sister Ursula will ask Dr. Henley to call your parents to come and get you as soon as they can. We'll fix our lunch, just like always, and when your mother comes, you can go home. Now *maybe* your mother will be crying when she picks you up. She might be very sad about President Kennedy getting shot and she's going to feel better if you're with her to make her feel better. Tonight you'll be watching TV and you might even see your father cry."

"I saw my father cry one time. He broke his leg," Liam said.

"My father never cries and I don't cry even when I'm hurt!" said George.

"*If* your parents cry today, can you comfort them?"

"I can hug her if she cries."

"I got a cough drop I can give my father."

"I'll go to bed and not fuss."

"I have all the money in my piggy bank. *That* will make my father feel good. If I give it to him."

"Ah kiss Mommy," Kirby said, shining with his plan.

"I don't cry. Not today."

"I can help Mommy set the table. I can scrape the carrots."

"I'll put my toys away."

"When's Mommy coming? I want to go home!"

"Bravo! That's good comforting. You do know how. Now, Frederika, Gi-Gi, Kirby, and Liam are going to help me fix the lunch and set the tables. All the rest of you, what are you going to do? George?"

"Wash tables."

"And you, Jackie?"

"Wait for Mommy at the door."

"And you, Bobby?"

"Read a book. Is the president in heaven?"

"And you, Andy?"

"Polish my shoes."

>>>——>

Eugene
December 5.63

DEAR MR. ANDERSON:

I was saddened by Carl's death. I'd grown fond of him. I hope you're willing to stand in for him, since you were his law partner and perhaps know something about the case. David told me *he* had devised thirty-four questions on the basis of my allegation to the judge and had been given a private polygraph test which he passed. Surely this is not the customary way of taking a lie-detector test? I'm willing to withdraw my charges if that would pacify the judge, but I have to remember that David's own statements about me are not gentle and place my reputation in a sensitive profession in jeopardy.

Yours sincerely,
Giershe Kinnard

MOLLY GAVIN'S DIARY:
DECEMBER 20, 1963

Called Miss Fahey and learned *we* are to be given custody! She was very friendly and says twenty-four-hour housekeeper is costing David a fortune. We are scared. What is happening to our lives? Giershe, so stubborn and lawless!

DECEMBER 21, 1963

Giershe arrived looking tired and thin. When we told her of the talk with Miss Fahey she pounded the table and said she *would* have the children! Harry excited, eating and drinking too much.

>>>>——>>——

Jack and Giershe's time together in December and January took on an unvarying pattern. Giershe arrived at his apartment in San Jose, distraught and trying to smile. Jack greeted her with courtly courtesy and a glass of sherry. They drank their sherry and she told him of her new Montessori colleagues, the talks she had given to parents, and the work she was doing to prepare for the school's opening in late January or early February. Jack talked of college politics, of his book chapters, and occasionally, deftly, of Andrew. Giershe paced and listened, glad to be hearing his voice, and to smell the stale odor of his workplace. Talk would continue until Jack said "Let's go to bed." She always waited for him to say it, and he always delayed until sherry had blurred her hectic contact with the world. She took off the clothes she chose so carefully for her visits with him, and lay down on the cool sheets which were never quite clean. As she closed her eyes and waited for him, the dark room would revolve and suck her deep into its space, adrift from memory. He was always warm-skinned, and she was ice beside him until he wrapped himself around her. They seldom spoke to each other in bed. They returned to the first room where they had "met" and allowed their bodies to bridge distance.

Sometimes they put on their clothes at midnight and walked wet streets or wandered into a Chinese restaurant and slurped wonton soup, hungrily, then walked back to the apartment and clung together until dawn. They usually ate breakfast together in silence, at a restaurant with orange-and-mocha decor, while Jack read the morning newspaper. Giershe stared at her grapefruit or Jack's hands. They would speak calmly of their next planned meeting and Giershe would drive back to Berkeley, never sure whether she felt better or worse.

New York
January 14.64

GENTLY, JACK JINGALO!

I'm here, frozen but happy. I just called Miss Fahey and Sam Anderson. Both were friendly and informative. She said the transfer of children to Molly and Harry was a transfer to me. "The report will favor you and your parents." The judge is furious at David because he told Miss Fahey, apparently without apology, that he's the father of the baby of a friend of ours. Who? Mr. Anderson promises more scandal when I see him, which should be Saturday. I have the feeling, not pleasant, that David tells these things because he plans on a conversion to middle-class sainthood. Haven't slept for twenty-four hours. Feel fine.

bye my dearest
Giershe

Centerville
January 17.64

DEAR—

I've been here three hours and already my tooth aches. I feel farther away from Tony and Olivia than ever before. I spent an hour with Sam Anderson this evening and found him fluent, witty. Snow is everywhere. I'm in a house in the woods. It's a big house with a small couple—newlyweds. David just phoned and promptly I'm loco. He says: "The court has given permission for you to see the children from one to three-thirty today. I cannot have my life upset by your visitations. How long are you going to be here?"

"Until the hearing."

"Oh, that will be many weeks."

love you
Giershe

Centerville
January 19.64

DEAR JACK—

I've sent for Harry because I can't balance. What Anderson tells me, whatever he says, only makes me nervous. Likewise Miss Fahey. Somehow they're not straight. Today I saw the children and though they are splendid, even this weakens me. Olivia now has a missal, Tony a "church" jacket. I loathe David. Olivia understands this and makes allowances for it. We discussed a possible journey and she said: "But Father won't be able to see us. How will we get all our toys there?" Tony wanted to go right away, but he thinks any arrangement that includes either of us is fine. My children—can I take credit for the sparkle in their eyes and their upright manner? I'm eating myself. I remember that I have loved you and know I'll love you again.

Giershe

13

"Tut, tut, child,"

said the Duchess,

"Everything's

got a moral,

if you can only find it."

HARRY WAS PACING the depot waiting room when Sam and Giershe arrived. He was wearing a brown tweed overcoat, a soft gray hat punched down at its center, black rubbers, a brown suit and thick black gloves (where had he found warm gloves?). On a bench nearby was a battered yellow suitcase with straps. He looked smaller than she remembered him. His face was red with the cold, and as he circled his suitcase, he looked anxiously over the heads of travelers. A cigarette drooped from a corner of his mouth.

"Harry! Over here! Harry!" He located her face, raised a hand in greeting, flipped his cigarette into a spittoon, picked up his suitcase, and walked towards her. He didn't look tired, just nervous, a condition which afflicted him all his waking hours. Giershe felt relief at seeing him so perky, and as he hugged her and shook hands with Sam, a pride in him filled her, almost like love. The men chattered together on the drive to Centerville, Harry asking reporterish questions about Sam's background and his memories of the South, Sam answering with an almost poetic surge of nostalgia for the landscape of his childhood. Then politics. What did Sam think of Johnson? Would he vote for him? Harry had a way of offering his own opinion without condemning another's, but when Sam asked: "And you, sir, would you vote for Johnson?" Harry snapped: "Don't call me 'sir.' I hate it. If you call me 'sir' I'll call you 'Mac.' I'm not sure I'd ever vote for a Southerner. I don't believe they can represent the country at large."

Giershe stared out the window from the backseat and listened to them arguing amicably. As they neared Centerville, Sam asked: "Mr. Gavin, would you and Giershe join me for lunch tomorrow? We have a bit of talking to do before the hearing."

"Of course. Has the date been set?"

"No, but it won't be long now. Miss Fahey is holding us up. She's a tricky lady, and I have to be careful how I press her. She knows she has the power right now, and isn't rushing around to make things easier for others."

"I would like to talk with her. Could I see her tomorrow?"

"I'll try to make an appointment for you for after lunch. That way we can be sure we agree on what to say to her."

"I don't believe a rehearsal is necessary. I can speak plainly and truthfully of myself, Mrs. Gavin, and Giershe. I'm only curious about what should be said of my son-in-law, a man I do not respect or like."

"That's what we'll discuss at lunch. She leans sometimes one way, sometimes the other, and I've a feeling she is sensitive about criticism of Mr.

Kinnard. He's quite a ladies' man, isn't he?"

"That's his reputation. Women often respond to his attention and flattery. To me, he seems unclean and has the nature of a gigolo. Not an attractive person at all." Harry sank into his seat, tired of talk. He gazed out the window. Sam parked in front of the house and lunged from the driver's seat to remove Harry's suitcase from the trunk. He led the way up the snow-covered path to the front door.

"Watch your feet. It's slippery," Sam said.

"I'm *quite* all right. I've been in snow before."

While Giershe unlocked the door, Sam shook hands with Harry. "Thank you, sir—Mr. Gavin, for a most enjoyable talk! I wish you lived in town. It's hard to find someone of your interests and knowledge in Centerville."

"Well, Mac, I'm glad you enjoyed yourself, but I'm very happy with my permanent residence."

Old Harry. Not exactly rude, but not gracious either. Again she felt something like affection for him. Sam bounded down the walk, not watching his feet, and drove away. Giershe let Harry into the large, high-ceilinged hallway, and closed the door behind him. She felt an uncertain gaiety, a leavening and lightening of inert surroundings, a playfulness at being hostess to her father in this immense lonely house. She led him up the stairs to a bedroom much like his in Berkeley, with a bathroom next door which he would share with his daughter. His bed was ready for him, with clean white sheets and a thick red-and-white comforter folded back on itself. She had felt odd pleasure in preparing a bed for her father. Such a simple act, and in thirty-nine years she'd never made up a bed for Molly or Harry! Millions of times they'd done up her bed (usually before she had a chance to help) and had said to her, "Giershe, your bed is ready. Don't be too late going to sleep." Molly never said "Here are your sheets," even when she was tired, ill, or cross.

"This is an interesting house. I wonder how old it is." Harry was opening doors, closing them again, looking at the ceiling and inspecting the window frames.

"It's old. Everything in this town is old, even the young people. Everyone is hunched over with history and no one looks at the lovely river except the blacks who are confined to shacks down there. They fish in the river even in winter."

"When did you start calling them 'blacks'? Can you see the river from here?"

"That's what Don O'Dwyer calls them, and since he's from the South and takes leave of the college to register them to vote down there, I figure he ought to know what they want to be called. The river—you can see it from anyplace in town—and on the far bank, the state insane asylum. See, there it is—all gray and white, like a bunker. There are a few professors there and some professors' wives. Are you tired? Hungry? I bought groceries for dinner. We don't have to go out."

"I'm not tired. You sound like your mother. Oh, I have to call her after six. She'll be worrying whether I survived the trip. This is very hard on her, on all of us of course, but especially your mother. She's not well and I'm afraid she's failing in health. Maybe I'll lie down for a while and read." He smiled at Giershe and tried to look cheerful. She stared at his red ears, the blue congested veins on his nose, his drooping eyelids, the beautiful white hair, still abundant and wavy, and she knew he didn't want to be with her and missed Molly and was wondering why he had left her alone to go to a daughter whose affection for him was sporadic and lukewarm.

"Harry, thank you for coming here to be with me. I don't feel very brave. There's something about Centerville and David that strips me of backbone, like a fish on a platter."

"Insist on metaphors like that and you'll be eaten. Call me at six. And I'm glad I came." He lay down on his bed, groaned, and closed his eyes. He raised his arthritic right hand, and after removing his glasses, rubbed his eyelids with his left hand. Giershe took his glasses from his fingers and set them on the bedside stand. She closed the door halfway and turned on the hall light. He would sleep for a while, and later he would say he had not slept. She would lie down on her bed and think of Olivia and Tony as darkness came, or of Jack, and she would not sleep and later she would tell him she'd had a fine nap. Their conspiracy to encourage each other had begun.

Harry and Giershe sat across from each other at the kitchen table. They had prepared scrambled eggs and a green salad for supper, had washed the dishes, and Giershe was beginning to wonder how to close the day. At home, Harry was never idle, was always busy with household chores, or writing, or reading, or standing out on the sidewalk talking to neighbors. He slept no more than six hours a night. What could he do in Centerville? There were no neighbors. She wasn't sure he'd enjoy making repairs on a house not his own, although just in case he asked, she'd been making a list of windows that didn't work, doors that wouldn't close, molding ripped away, one window pane missing in the storm door, light fixtures which popped when you put a plug into the wall socket, the dripping faucet in the master bathroom, the sliding glass door which was stuck.

"Harry, do you remember the last time we stayed in a house alone together?"

"Yes, I do. I was thinking about that on the airplane. It was in the mountains and you were eight years old. I remember we had a damn good time."

"Right! Let's see, that was thirty-one years ago." They stared at each other. Harry pushed his chair away from the table, filled the kettle, and lit the gas burner. "Thirty-one years—where has it all gone? No, cancel the question. Do you remember what we talked about under the stars up in the mountains?"

"Of course I remember. Constellations and Mooney-Billings. I fancied you were interested in the history of the labor movement. At that age, you never tired of hearing the story, and I remember I told you a great deal about corrupt connections between the police and the legal system, but I never thought I'd be spending my mature years confronting the legal apparatus in a Catholic state."

"Oh Harry, this is not a Catholic state."

"Isn't it? You might be able to insert a razor blade in the space between Church and State in Connecticut, but I doubt it."

"Come on. The judge is not Catholic. Sam isn't. I suppose Miss Fahey is, and so is her organization, but that's no reason to jump to conclusions."

"Perhaps not, but in this state you still, in 1964, can't buy contraceptive devices unless you have one kidney or mongolism in the family. I know a few things about this state and you should do your homework."

"That sort of homework is depressing. I don't want to talk about it. Do you ever wonder why we stopped talking?"

Harry slumped into his chair. His face was very red, his nose a maze of swollen veins, and his gloom-lines cut an inch into his jowls.

"Stopped talking? I wasn't aware that we stopped talking. Is this how you view the thirty years? Millions of words have passed between us in those years, some of them angry, but most merely informative and— Christ! What are you talking about?" Anger, then a swift smile, a hand across the table, a pat of Giershe's hand. Remember the woman is upset, and no wonder. Keep the peace.

"Oh, I don't know what I meant. I think we're tired. Let's go to bed. Tomorrow, if we're stalled for things to do, there are jobs around the house I'd like us to attempt."

"What jobs? Where?"

"Not now. Bed now." They climbed the stairs to the bedroom together, and after Giershe had washed her face and teeth, she met Harry in the hall. He had removed his teeth and it was not Harry who kissed her cheek. There was an old skull topped with white living hairs, watery, yellow-gray eyes, lips so collapsed they couldn't meet her face for a kiss—a grotesque grin, a mumble, "G'ni . . . Gisha." She stared, touched her lips with her fingertips, and watched him shuffle into his bedroom and close the door.

MOLLY GAVIN'S DIARY:
JANUARY 28, 1964

Harry phoned to say that the report from Fahey was twenty-one pages long and advised neither parent having the children nor us either, because we are close to Giershe. Giershe in a frenzy. Hearing postponed a week and Rafaela Freeman is going to Centerville to testify to something she saw while she was caring for Olivia. Stirred myself to go out and lift the fragrant rhododendron and put it in a large pot. I should get out somewhere, but where?

>>>===

Between January 19 and February 12 (court hearing), Giershe and Harry did the following:

1. Giershe wrote twenty-four letters to Jack and talked with him fifteen times.
2. Harry wrote twenty-two letters to Molly and talked with her thirteen times.
3. They ate twenty dinners together, fifteen of which they prepared themselves in peace.
4. They ate dinner once at the O'Dwyers', three times at a Greek restaurant where Harry liked to talk with the owner.
5. Giershe went to a black dentist six times. He sang the talking-dentist blues while he worked: "That ol' court—it gonna, it gonna postpone yo' case . . ." Bill sent to David Kinnard.
6. Harry fixed all the defects Giershe listed, and went on to insulate the attic, repair both toilets and one shower fixture, and set up a bird-feeding station on the front porch.
7. Giershe repaired the drapes, polished the woodwork and the wooden floors, cleaned the black off all the pots and pans, and washed all the dishes in the cupboards.
8. Giershe visited the Freemans in New York and prepared with Rafaela her testimony for the judge. Could anything so shadowy be true? Rafaela was angry with Giershe's doubt. "I believe it! Why shouldn't the judge? It's as true as any of the other testimony in this stinking mess. I'll enjoy myself in court. Don't pull me into your Protestant pit!"
9. Giershe spent one afternoon with Tony and Olivia at Sam Anderson's house. Tony circled Sam and called him "Rat fink!"

10. Giershe walked a mile to David's house in early evening six times, trying to catch glimpses of the children in the lighted window. She failed six times. Harry frantic at her absence.

11. Giershe called Miss Fahey six times.

12. Harry called Miss Fahey five times.

13. Giershe talked with Sam Anderson twenty-one times and had lunch with him four times.

14. Harry talked with Sam Anderson seventeen times and had lunch with him three times.

15. Both called the courthouse too many times to count.

16. Giershe spent many hours trying to learn to play the xylophone, an instrument which it seemed to her lacked soul.

17. Giershe visited five elementary schools.

18. Giershe cried at least once a day, and sometimes all day on Sundays.

19. Harry cried once after seeing Olivia and Tony and David. He didn't sob and carry on like Giershe; tears dripped down his freezing face as they walked up the street in the snow. (It might have been the cold wind in his eyes, but Giershe didn't think so.)

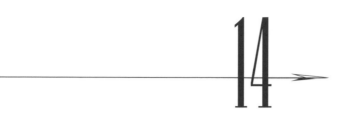

14

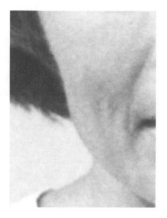

But it was of no use—

the Anglo-Saxon attitudes

only got more extraordinary

every moment, while the

great eyes rolled wildly

from side to side.

AT NINE-THIRTY IN THE MORNING, with snow lightly falling on the twenty-eight steps in front of Centerville's courthouse, Giershe pulled her arm from Harry's gloved hand. "You go on in, Harry. I'll just stay out here a minute. I want to think." But she didn't want to think. She felt light-headed, without substance or presence, as though she had only to rise on tiptoe, look to the horizon, and push off to join gray clouds. She was wearing Millie O'Dwyer's fur coat, and when she looked down at her arms, she could see the brown fur spotting with white flakes. Something was supposed to happen today. There was some reason why she was standing in the gentle snowfall. She pushed her mittened hands into the coat's pockets and pinched the skin on her hips as hard as she could through layers of woolen clothing. Nothing. No pain, no feeling at all. *I'm asleep or dead. I'm dreaming. How can I wake up? All of it, it has gone on so long. Dreams cover years and seem to last forever, but are only an instant.* She tilted back her head and closed her eyes. *I could go to them now. No one will be there. I could hold them in my arms and tell them stories. They don't need me here.*

"Well, if you're not going to go inside, neither am I. I am *weak* with fear! I've studied theater and was *never* afraid on the stage and this morning my hands are trembling. See, look at them." Rafaela held out two hands in front of her. Giershe stared at the hands. She lifted her own. Four mittened hands twitching in the air. Rafaela's red hair was blowing across her freckled face. "Jesus Christ, Giershe! Only for you. No, only because that bastard seems so powerful and all this Fahey crap. God, I don't know why I'm here, but I'm here. And we should go inside. Where's Mr. Anderson? Inside? Sid's staying at the O'Dwyers'. He doesn't trust himself. Come on, I'm freezing!" She linked her arm through Giershe's and pulled her up the stairs.

>>>>

CHARACTERS

Judge:	JOHN LEGALITY
Plaintiff:	DAVID KINNARD
Counsel:	RONALD RATCH
Witness:	PROFESSOR RALPH GROPER, Chairman, Department of Humanities, Whitfield College
Defendant:	GIERSHE KINNARD
Counsel:	SAM ANDERSON
Witness:	RAFAELA FREEMAN, Housewife and Mother

SCENE: *Centerville Courthouse, Centerville, Connecticut.*

The courtroom fills slowly, Giershe's group on the right-hand side, David Kinnard and Ralph Groper, with counsel, on the left. Stray people wander in from the foyer and take seats here and there. They are perhaps waiting for their own hearings, or are there for the entertainment. Bailiffs and police officers walk back and forth, trading papers, giving whispered orders.

The Judge enters from the front and all stand up. The Judge sits down. The audience sits down. Judge John Legality is of medium height, sober face but not stern. Perfectly regular features, blue-green eyes, tufty eyebrows, glasses. He is forty, and has been a judge for seven years. His pose is calm, almost serene; his hands rest on the table in front of him, thumbs and fingertips together. His gaze is distant. When irritated, he leans forward with a pencil in his hand, which he points at the offender. The lawyers are respectful of his power, in his presence and out of it. They cannot peg him as this, or as that. A man known to be unpredictable in his reactions but fair in his decisions.

JUDGE: You may proceed, gentlemen. I don't know who is the plaintiff and who is the defendant.

RATCH: I represent the plaintiff, Mr. Kinnard, Your Honor.

JUDGE: Then the defendant will proceed.

(Giershe, led by Sam Anderson, walks to the front of the room, climbs up the stairs to the chair beside the Judge's platform, and takes the oath)

JUDGE: What is your name?

GIERSHE: Giershe Kinnard.

JUDGE: Where do you live, Mrs. Kinnard?

GIERSHE: In Berkeley, California.

SAM: Mrs. Kinnard, you are not now living with your husband?

GIERSHE: No.

SAM: Would you mind telling us when you were separated?

(The chair beneath Giershe is brown leather which squeaks when she shifts position; it sucks on her gray wool pleats. When she places her right arm on the puffed surface of the chair's arm, her shoulder hikes up to her ear. She doesn't like chairs, preferring the floor with big cushions or lying on her stomach on a hard bed, a book open beneath her nose. Her anklebones are pressed tightly together above the black pumps buried demurely in the thick carpet. She wants to wind or cross her legs, stop the shivering in her thighs, look calmly at Sam's face which no longer looks familiar. She moves her hands to her knees and presses down with the palms, careful to leave her fingers loose, unclutched. She can feel their tremor transmit from wool to nylon to bone. She must not shift again. She has to answer the question)

GIERSHE: I left in September 1962.

(Questions are answered. Ronald Ratch and the Judge search the report for Olivia's words, told to Giershe, told to Miss Fahey, told to a secretary, typed, Xeroxed, now being read to the Judge, who reads the passage for the stenotypist, so that all these words can crawl into something called "the record." Giershe would like to help them, like a secretary or a wife, point out to them that they could lift the report, all twenty-one pages of it, and place it in the stenotypist's lap, with instructions that she include it in her transcript. She wonders what would happen if she were to snatch the report from Ratch's hands and run down the aisle with pages flapping, out the door, down the steps, to her favorite graveyard where she could sit in a snowbank and read, for the first time, Little Bitch Fahey's words, the cold, black, bleak, frozen history. Would the bailiff shoot her? Would Judge Legality scream, "Stop her! She has the unbiased report!")

SAM: Now, Mrs. Kinnard, could you be a little more specific about the games that you mentioned?

GIERSHE: Well, Mr. Kinnard had a game which he used to play with his penis when he would come down in the morning at breakfast time. He would pretend that it was attached to an imaginary string, and he would pull this string up and down like this—and the penis would move in correspondence with the movement of the string, and Olivia thought this was great fun.

(Giershe sees that her hand, pale from a month of winter, looks too delicate when she makes the motion and she wishes she had a penis so the audience might have the whole performance. In the silence which follows her words,

her eyes brush the faces, speeding from Rafaela to David. He sprawls in his seat, his crimson tie parted like his legs, his brown eyes waiting, aware that his composure is a weapon which has never failed to scatter her wits. In the second she meets his gaze, she wonders if Judge Legality believes her and is sure he doesn't. She can report a beating, or infidelity, but imaginative breakfast games are ranked with wartime propaganda stories—too self-serving to be considered in history books. Is it then all over? Is a football game stopped in the third quarter because the score is fifty-seven to six?)

SAM: Now, Mrs. Kinnard, may I ask what you did after Olivia reported what you say she reported, which is in the report from the Family Relations Department?

GIERSHE: I told Mr. Adams, who was my lawyer at that time.

SAM: As a result of your conversation with Mr. Adams, did you do anything further?

GIERSHE: Mr. Adams listened to the account. He then advised me—

JUDGE: No, what did you do?

SAM: What did you do?

GIERSHE: What did I do? I told him about it, and he told me to write down— I can't say he told me?

SAM: No. Just say what you *did* as a result.

GIERSHE: I wrote it, in chronological form. Olivia's testimony, my reaction to it, plus the things I've done to prevent its recurrence. And, as I say, he gave me—

SAM: What did you do?

GIERSHE: I left Connecticut as a result of that conference.

RATCH: Your Honor, may I have just a moment?

JUDGE: Certainly. (*Counsel and Judge whisper*) No, I don't see *any* reason for a *closed* hearing. I have never ordered one yet!

SAM: Mrs. Kinnard, the question of your stability has been raised in the report, and I'd like you to tell the Court whether at any time, to any person, under any circumstances, either in excitement or deliberately, you have made threats of any kind against your children.

GIERSHE: Never have I threatened Olivia or Tony! I can't imagine that. Never, NEVER! I haven't the heart even to spank Olivia when she seems to need it.

SAM: That's all, Mrs. Kinnard.

GIERSHE: May I go now?

RATCH: I have a few questions. Mrs. Kinnard, if you were granted custody of these children by the Court, what visitation would you suggest that Mr. Kinnard have?

GIERSHE: May I tell you something my little girl said?

RATCH: No. I wish you would answer my question.

JUDGE: I will hear what your little girl said.

GIERSHE: She said she realizes we can't get along, but she would like to be within tricycle-riding distance of her father, and for me, that's the ideal situation. I would like their father to be in their lives to the same degree as their mother.

JUDGE: But Mr. Kinnard is rooted here. I assume he has tenure.

GIERSHE: But as recently as last November, he was negotiating with the University of Oregon—

JUDGE: We must deal realistically with the situation which exists and that is that he is in Centerville and you're in California, and although it would be lovely if Olivia could be within tricycle-riding distance of her father or mother, it is not realistic. Even if Mr. Kinnard were at the University of Oregon, from where you are in California to where he might be in Oregon is several hundred rough-biking miles.

RATCH: Your Honor, I'd like to get to the major attack—as far as I know, the *only* attack on Mr. Kinnard—the alleged charge which is the basis for the claimed unfitness on his part.

JUDGE: The whole thing is terrible! According to *normal* morals it is very terrible. When you get into terrible, it doesn't make too much difference what the degrees are. Terrible is terrible. In the usual case, I have found that the report is a better indication of what the facts in a case are than the testimony of the parties, for the simple reason that the parties are emotionally charged up. But the investigator hasn't supplied us with a solution, only a recommendation. So, the whole matter is open.

RATCH: Mrs. Kinnard, I believe you stated that you felt you were under no prohibition to leave Connecticut in April 1962?

GIERSHE: My feeling at that time was that it was not in a document, a court order.

RATCH: The documents speak otherwise, but I want to go on, Your Honor. Mrs. Kinnard, you took the children to California, and is it not correct that there you procured a court order that neither party should remove the children from the state?

GIERSHE: Yes.

RATCH: You then *did* remove the children from the state of California, did you not?

GIERSHE: I consulted—

RATCH: I want a yes or no answer!

GIERSHE: Yes.

RATCH: And you didn't go to the court for permission? Answer yes or no.

GIERSHE: It can't be answered yes or no.

RATCH: You procured a court order, and without having it revoked, you left for Oregon. What did you do when you got to Oregon?

GIERSHE: I set up a school. I had to earn a living. It was understood by California that I would return within a few months.

RATCH: Mrs. Kinnard, do you remember writing Mr. Kinnard that his litigation was in vain, the children would *vanish* if he got a court decree in his favor? Is that your handwriting?

GIERSHE: There is nothing in this about their vanishing.

JUDGE: He asked if you wrote the letter.

GIERSHE: Yes, I WROTE THE LETTER!

JUDGE: Exhibit F. Letter dated October 16, 1963.

RATCH: Tell me, Mrs. Kinnard, do you go to church with the children?

GIERSHE: No.

RATCH: Do you recall the last time you yourself were in church?

GIERSHE: I used to belong to the Presbyterian church in Berkeley when I was in high school.

RATCH: And since that time have you attended church?

GIERSHE: No.

RATCH: Do you believe in God?

GIERSHE: Yes, I do.

RATCH: You then believe in the court oath you have taken?

GIERSHE: Yes.

RATCH: Have you given the children any religious instruction?

GIERSHE: I regard all of my treatment of Olivia, from the time she was born, and Tony, from the time he was born, as open-ended education which can bring God to them if and when the time is right.

RATCH: Have you told them Bible stories?

GIERSHE: I've told them Bible stories as seemed appropriate.

RATCH: After you separated from Mr. Kinnard in 1962, you went first to Greenwich. Where did you live?

GIERSHE: With a family.

RATCH: How long were you there?

GIERSHE: Two weeks.

RATCH: Then where did you go?

GIERSHE: I moved to an apartment.

RATCH: When you got to California, where did you stay?

GIERSHE: After a few nights with my parents, I found an inexpensive home on the coast where the children could run free and I could finish my work. I stayed there two months.

RATCH: Then where did you go?

GIERSHE: I moved to Berkeley

RATCH. How long were you in Berkeley?

GIERSHE: I was there two months, but—

RATCH: Then you left for Oregon, is that correct?

GIERSHE: Yes.

RATCH: I have no further questions, Your Honor.

SAM: Nothing further, Your Honor.

JUDGE: You may step down. Court recess. Until one P.M.

Rafaela was the first to reach Giershe as the witness and her counsel walked down the center aisle. "You did great! You looked lovely and were so calm. You were terrific!" She took Giershe's cold hand, pressed it tightly, but veiled her excitement in gentle whispers.

"I'm proud of you," Harry said.

"Sh-h, we mustn't talk here," Sam warned. "I need some coffee. May I bring some for you, Giershe?" She nodded and stared out over the mahogany seats. She could see David and Ronald Ratch, David's arm around his counsel, heads together, both men smiling.

"I'm here if you need me. Sorry I was late," Millie O'Dwyer said. She kissed Giershe's cheek.

"Why in HELL didn't Sam stop that questioning on religion?" Harry's voice was too loud. "I'm going to go talk with him." Harry jingled the house keys and loosened his tie.

"Sam is not fighting. His mind is not on it. He's weak," Giershe murmured.

"Sam knows this community. It's better to say nothing. He's doing all right. How awful it is, how can David let it go on?" Millie fretted.

At 1:05 on the schoolroom clock behind the witness chair, everyone again takes a seat in the his-and-her arrangement of the morning and Giershe notices that the scattered public is missing. It is lonely and ominous without them, as though a flock of friendly beach birds has suddenly departed in advance of hurricane winds. She wonders if David has objected, and feels his power riding the back of her neck. She sinks down into the soft leather chair. Rafaela takes Giershe's hand into her lap. "Christ! I hope I'm first so I can enjoy the rest of the show!"

"*The judge wants Giershe on the stand again, or maybe Ratch does. While we were at recess, they—*" Sam bends towards Mr. Gavin.

"No! No, not again. I cannot, Sam, no!" Giershe plucks at his sleeve.

BANG! BANG! "*THE COURT IS IN SESSION! PLEASE TAKE YOUR SEATS!*"

Again the long walk, the climbing up, the turning around, sitting, arranging limbs and face, swallowing air.

JUDGE: Mrs. Kinnard, I have excluded the public because we're approaching a subject which concerns your sexual activities in the recent past, and I didn't want to embarrass you in the presence of other people in the courtroom.

GIERSHE: Sure.

JUDGE: You can start by telling us whether you have any present relationships which involve physical relations of one kind or another with other men?

GIERSHE: Yes. With Mr. Davey.

JUDGE: Can you tell me a little bit about this relationship? Please speak up.

GIERSHE: I love him very much. It has lasted a long time.

JUDGE: And he is the gentleman who is getting a divorce? Is it your intention to get married?

GIERSHE: It is.

JUDGE: You have sexual relations with him periodically?

GIERSHE: Whenever it can be arranged out of the presence of the children.

JUDGE: Where does it take place?

GIERSHE: The children haven't been with me now for three months. When they were with me, Mr. Davey used to come to see us with his little boy in the daytime, and then a couple of times a week, he would return around midnight and leave before dawn.

JUDGE: I assume that if the children were placed in your custody, that this relationship and this same course of conduct would probably continue?

GIERSHE: We've been very careful from the beginning.

JUDGE: I don't want to probe into you about it, but is there anything more you can add?

GIERSHE: I don't want to replace their father. They love him very much.

JUDGE: You think you have kept that father image alive?

GIERSHE: I have.

JUDGE: What about your neighbors and people in the locality? What about their reaction to a man coming to your house at midnight and leaving before dawn? You know how they are.

GIERSHE: There were no neighbors.

JUDGE: The report mentions a Professor F. Has he come back into your life? In a physical way?

GIERSHE: No.

JUDGE: There's been no relationship?

GIERSHE: No!

JUDGE: There was formerly?

GIERSHE: I've said so. To Miss Fahey.

JUDGE: Would you consider it dangerous that the children become aware of your physical relationship with a man you are not married to?

GIERSHE: Eventually, when we marry, it will be apparent.

JUDGE: But that will be different because it will be acknowledged before the world. Then they will sense that this is a *normal* relationship. But at this time, might they not sense that society doesn't approve of this kind of relationship?

GIERSHE: I don't know but I don't think so. We don't live together.

JUDGE: Mr. Rath, you may, if you wish, question Mrs. Kinnard along this line.

RATCH: It is Ratch, Your Honor. Do your parents know of this relationship with Mr. Davey?

GIERSHE: Yes.

RATCH: How soon after the beginning did your parents know?

GIERSHE: I didn't send out announcements.

RATCH: Do they have any objections?

GIERSHE: Mr. Ratch, I am not sixteen.

RATCH: Did your parents know the full extent of your relationship or did they know only of your friendship?

GIERSHE: They now know the full extent.

RATCH: Have any of your intimacies with Mr. Davey occurred in their house?

GIERSHE: NO!

RATCH: Wasn't one of the attractions of Mr. Davey that he relieved you from the pressures of marriage?

GIERSHE: I don't know what you're talking about. Nothing could relieve me of the pressures of marriage!

RATCH: Is one of your reasons for taking up with Mr. Davey the fact that he wasn't married to you?

GIERSHE: I didn't "take up" with him, I fell in love. You are getting psychological.

RATCH: Answer the question.

JUDGE: She has given you her reason. She fell in love with him. Do you mean is this something in the nature of an escape?

RATCH: That's it.

GIERSHE: It wasn't much of an escape to love someone for two weeks and then return to Centerville to try to work it out with Mr. Kinnard, to move to Greenwich, to take an intensive year of study without Mr. Davey. Is that a relief?

RATCH: Mrs. Kinnard, just prior to leaving for California, at Christmastime, in 1962, you called Mr. Davey on the phone?

GIERSHE: I was in constant touch with Mr. Davey. Don't pull out my telephone bills because—

RATCH: They're right here.

GIERSHE: Of course they are!

RATCH: Now wasn't your plan really, Mrs. Kinnard, to get a job with the Montessori people in California?

GIERSHE: My plan was to go there and look around. I had to find a job where I could spend summers in good health.

RATCH: Tell me, Mrs. Kinnard, did Mr. Kinnard know of the loan from Professor F.?

GIERSHE: Knew that I'd asked for it. Didn't know I'd received it.

RATCH: Did he approve?

GIERSHE: Need he have approved? I asked him to cosign a loan at the bank. He refused. He read the letter I sent. He was neutral. It's difficult for women to borrow.

RATCH: No further questions.

JUDGE: Mr. Anderson, anything you want to add?

SAM: No, Your Honor.

JUDGE: I think we should adjourn for lunch and return at two-twelve. One of the witnesses is going to testify to something of a scandalous nature?

SAM: Yes.

JUDGE: Then I'll tell the bailiff to continue to exclude the public.

Lunch in a sparkling tearoom, with bar attached. Harry and Sam ordered highballs for each other and wine for Giershe and Rafaela. Giershe felt scoured of thought and said nothing. The men wanted to talk; like dogs after a bath, they shook themselves, sprinkling words around the table.

"Sam, have you ever had a case of this kind before?" Harry asked, with a hint of derision.

"No one has *ever* had a case like this! The judge is a puzzle—can't figure out why he's taking such a hard-nosed attitude towards behavior which is relatively commonplace. But to answer your question, I've stuck pretty close to tax cases. Carl handled all the domestic stuff."

"When will I be called before His Majesty?" Rafaela sipped her wine and stared across the table at Giershe.

"You're on right after lunch. I think we have to go ahead with it, but the judge is clearly unhappy about all the unsavory testimony."

"What the hell is Groper going to testify about?" Harry asked.

"He's an asshole! David's been toadying up to him ever since he came to Whitfield. He's dull and stupid and has left off being a Jew—hopes to garner salvation from High Church Episcopalian." Rafaela wrapped her long, freckled fingers around her glass. "He's the only ally David has on the faculty, and wouldn't you know it would be the chairman of the department!"

"Ronald Ratch looks just like David," Giershe said softly.

"Oh, I don't—" Harry began, then closed his mouth. They stared at her. She gazed back at them. Her composure hung about her like a new garment, filmy, soft, a chrysalis which wrapped her in precarious detachment, hanging from a thread of will.

"Yeah, I see what you mean," Rafaela said. "They're both skunks. Will Ratch be questioning me?"

"Yes, in cross-examination. I'll go first with you and then he'll take over. Just answer slowly and honestly. Don't let him rattle you. Mrs. Kinnard—Giershe—you'd better finish your soup. We have to be getting back."

Giershe stood up first. Her soup was high in its cup. She had eaten the soda crackers and had drunk one gulp of wine. She felt cold and when Harry put the fur coat around her shoulders, she stumbled forward beneath its weight. Rafaela put her arm around the fur and held her tightly. They marched together through the door, giggling a bit as they tried to match their footsteps.

The wine has lengthened my limbs, softened my skin, subdued the lights. Harry's nose looks rosy, no longer raw and skeletal. He wants the judge to call him, more to show what an important citizen he is than to speak Justice, or denounce his son-in-law, or beg the court to bring life once more to his dear daughter, which I am not, or have arrived so recently, he tends to forget.

>>>>

RAFAELA: I was to take care of Olivia while Giershe was in the hospital with her new baby. Mrs. Kinnard felt it would be easier for Olivia to have someone she knew. She knew me fairly well, since I dropped by the house a lot. So, I heard some laughing and talking from upstairs. I started to walk up the stairs. As I got near the top, looking over to the left, I could see right into Mr. Kinnard's bedroom. He was lying on the bed, had a smile on his face, and as I went a little further up the stairs, I could see that he had an erection, and Olivia was lying on the bed near his hip, and that was all I saw. I continued up the stairs—

JUDGE: Wait a minute!

RATCH: I missed some of that, too.

JUDGE: I guess we all did. He was lying on the bed with an erection and Olivia was lying on the bed near—

RAFAELA: If I said *lying*, I didn't mean that. *She* was sitting.

JUDGE: Sitting on the bed near his hip?

RAFAELA: Yes. I continued up the stairs and went into Olivia's room, which was straight ahead. I sort of picked up a few toys and said, "Hey, is anyone home?" I made my presence known.

SAM: For how long did you observe Mr. Kinnard and his daughter in the position you just described?

RAFAELA: Maybe five seconds. Time enough to go up two or three steps.

JUDGE: You continued to walk without stopping?

RAFAELA: I did not stop.

SAM: Then what happened?

RAFAELA: David said, "We're in here," and I went in. He was sitting on the bed with his back to me, and I said, "Have you had some coffee?"

JUDGE: What was he wearing?

RAFAELA: A bathrobe.

SAM: Did you mention what you had observed to Mr. Kinnard?

RAFAELA: I certainly did not!

SAM: Did you mention it to anyone else?

RAFAELA: I told my husband when I went home.

SAM: I have nothing else.

RATCH: Mrs. Freeman, when you witnessed this alleged incident, I believe your testimony was that you did not mention this to Mr. Kinnard at the time.

RAFAELA: I believe I just said so.

RATCH: And you haven't mentioned it to him since. Is that correct?

RAFAELA: Correct.

RATCH: Isn't this sort of a serious thing, that should have been brought to his attention immediately?

RAFAELA: I didn't feel it was my place—

JUDGE: I agree with the witness. I don't think it was up to her. I think it was very embarrassing for her, something she wishes she hadn't seen.

RATCH: Did you make any effort to bring it to the attention of the authorities?

RAFAELA: I did not.

JUDGE: What difference does it make? The only thing we're interested in is whether it happened or didn't happen. That, I will be the judge of. It would be absurd to bring it to the attention of the authorities, because they would have laughed at her and said, "What do you want us to do?"

RATCH: How old was Olivia at this time?

RAFAELA: I think she was two and a half.

RATCH: Mrs. Freeman, you took an oath here to tell the truth. Are you an atheist or not?

RAFAELA: I am an atheist.

RATCH: But you took an oath, based on your belief in God.

RAFAELA: I don't believe in God, but I do believe in truth and justice, Mr. Ratch, and the oath has a great deal of meaning for me.

RATCH: The next time you're asked to take an oath, indicate, if you're in court, you would rather take an affirmation. That would be technically correct in your case.

RAFAELA: I'd be glad to take the affirmation now, if that would help.

JUDGE: It is kind of an unusual situation. On the other hand—stand up, please. Do you solemnly affirm that the evidence that you are about to give and that you have given concerning the case now in question is the truth, the whole truth, and nothing but the truth?

RAFAELA: I do.

RATCH: No further questions.

JUDGE: Witness dismissed. Mr. Ratch, your witness Mr. Groper? There's probably more of a scandalous nature coming from him, is there?

RATCH: I don't believe so, Your Honor.

>>>>>>

"Fuckers! Only for you, Giershe—no, not even for you, ever again."
"Sh-h—forever in your debt. Eyes front."

>>>>>>

Professor Ralph Groper, a short man, almost a dwarf, walks towards the witness chair. His head is large, bald with wispy tufts around his neck and ears. He is wearing glasses without rims which distort small, pale blue eyes. His thick, loose lips ooze saliva from the corners. He wipes his mouth with a white handkerchief as he seats himself. His dark gray flannel suit has three buttons and a narrow collar. The vest bunches over a protruding stomach. His white French cuffs stick out an inch below his suit sleeves. His feet are tiny in shining black elevator shoes. He crosses his legs, and immediately decides not to. He settles on an upright, stiff posture, leaning slightly forward, his hands in his lap. The hands are startlingly white, as white as his handkerchief. His posture makes his head appear to be enormous, his body too small to support it. There is an uncertainty about him, as though the scene recalls an earlier time when his performance fell short of perfection. His speech, when it comes, is without regional accent—slow, hesitant, convoluted, with fretful backups and ponderous marches forward, stiff-tongued.

RATCH: What is your position, Mr. Groper?

GROPER: I am Professor of Humanities at Whitfield College. I have administrative duties which, in the normal course of events, I take a turn at, such as the Chairmanship of the Department of Humanities and the Cochairmanship, as it is now called, of the College of Humanistic Studies.

(*On Giershe's left, Harry says: "What a jackass!" On Giershe's right, Rafaela says: "Smelly little fart!"*)

RATCH: At the time of Mr. Kinnard's assumption of tenure, did you or the tenure committee make an investigation of his background, his extramarital episodes?

GROPER: Before we recommended tenure for him, this was brought up and, of course, discussed at some length, by several of the senior members with Mr. Kinnard.

JUDGE: What did he say?

GROPER: He did not deny that such events had occurred, and we then went on to discuss his *meanings*. And the view of the meanings I had, and others with me, was that these represented not a professed or ideological kind of occupation, something he gloried in, but rather, something he was ashamed of and was in conflict with his basic outlook on life.

JUDGE: Explain, briefly, what he meant when he said these things.

GROPER: Affairs with other women.

JUDGE: How many?

GROPER: I didn't presume to ask that question!

JUDGE: I have the impression that one of the purposes of your testimony is to lead the court to believe this man has been thoroughly investigated by Whitfield. I realize your investigation would cover more fields than his extracurricular activities, but I assumed, in view of the fact that you knew about it, you might investigate that too, but apparently you haven't.

GROPER: We investigated only those things he agreed to. Certain acts of marital infidelity.

JUDGE: With how many women and over what period of time?

GROPER: Your Honor, that degree of detail would have been beyond my business to ask.

JUDGE: Professor Groper, the report says this: "The plaintiff has consistently violated accepted social mores. He has had a long series of admitted illicit associations continuing into the present." Does this have any influence on your judgment of him?

GROPER: Your Honor, I am unaware of any illicit association now being practiced. The main point was, from my highly puritanical outlook, any deviation from the marital relation is repugnant. How many is not the point. It was something he was unhappy about.

JUDGE: They go back to the time he was at the University of California and have continued consistently to the present.

GROPER: Your Honor, I would be most inclined, sir, to discount consider-
           ation of the University of California days, because, at that time,
           in that part of the country, and certainly right after the war, there
           was a deteriorating of morals, according to my standards, and I
           would guess he was a *victim* of that.

JUDGE: You think that the morals of this country sort of went to pot after
           the war?

GROPER: There was a great amount of it, sir!

JUDGE: That explains this?

GROPER: No generalization can explain a particular case. I did not ques-
           tion him on this wild behavior—

JUDGE: The behavior has gone on *at all times*, up until his separation from
           Mrs. Kinnard.

GROPER: I have found that at no time did any of Mr. Kinnard's personal
           affairs affect his performance as a teacher. We had to satisfy our-
           selves that this man was not a *moral reprobate.*

JUDGE: Aren't there people of normal habits and morals who would look
           at this and say, *"He is a moral reprobate"*?

GROPER: If he himself condoned it and gloried in it—yes. I think it is a
           question of guilt and redemption, Your Honor.

JUDGE: Is that *all* it is? This man was very close to a moral reprobate for
           many years and you now feel he no longer condones it and has
           been redeemed?

GROPER: Let me put it in very concrete language. I think that here is a man
           who was in conflict in his actions, with his basic religious com-
           mitment and his basic outlook, and he was torn inside. I think
           these actions came out of his own personal unhappiness—

JUDGE: Couldn't this apply to Mrs. Kinnard as well?

GROPER: I can't speak to Mrs. Kinnard's motivations, Your Honor.

JUDGE: How can you speak to his?

GROPER: I have talked with him at great length. *I am used to passing judgment!*

JUDGE: This man was looking for tenure. He wasn't going to run himself down.

GROPER: The one thing I look for is consistency.

JUDGE: When did he start to get consistent?

GROPER: Ever since I've known him, he has been consistent as a person, a colleague, as a teacher in the classroom. Had he been a person of gross personal immorality, I would have fired him!

JUDGE: How far does it have to go before you achieve a sense of it?

GROPER: There have been people at Whitfield who have held to a position that was grossly immoral by *doctrine.* Their number has diminished.

JUDGE: In other words, the only time you're excluded from Whitfield is if you're grossly immoral by doctrine. That disqualifies you. Highly immoral acts over a long period of time do not!

GROPER: Not necessarily. Not in this case.

JUDGE: Sorry to interrupt, but I'm trying to do the job I have to do.

RATCH: Your Honor, I think the conclusion in the report is somewhat different from the details, but be that as it may.

JUDGE: Mr. Ratch, I'm not going to argue with you. We have here *rampant immorality*—according to the contemporary mores of our society. I can't see that he's any worse than she, or vice versa. And when this man attempts to give me the impression he has passed Whitfield standards, I want to know what Whitfield standards are!

RATCH: I've no further questions. Do you, Sam?

SAM: No.

JUDGE: Witness dismissed. Mr. Ratch! This case is taking too long. You have one more witness?

RATCH: Yes, Your Honor, the plaintiff.

JUDGE: This is the last! I don't want to see Mr. Gavin. I know what he would say. I have letters on his virtues. Sam, do you have any more witnesses?

SAM: No, Your Honor.

>———>———>

"He sure made a fool out of Groper, didn't he? He's on our side," Harry whispered as he pulled from his pocket a dingy gray handkerchief. He blew his nose loudly and Giershe felt a sticky moisture settle on her cheek. Rafaela watched Giershe, then leaned her head onto her shoulder. "I'm cheered. The judge doesn't seem to like any of those bums. I don't understand why David confessed to all that junk. Makes me nervous—but you feel better, don't you, honey?" Giershe swallowed and tried to speak. She closed her eyes and felt her hand wrapped in cool fingers.

"All of my life is in reverse. Today is not different."

"Oh Giershe—"

"Sh-h," Sam said.

>———>———>

David Kinnard strides vigorously up the center aisle. He offers his hand to Judge Legality.

The Judge looks startled, but accepts, and smiles vaguely. David sits down, pulling up his trousers at the knee, carefully, before sitting. The Judge settles back in his chair and stares at the back wall. Mr. Kinnard is dressed in a brown gabardine suit, white shirt, gold cuff links on French cuffs. A Countess Mara tie with a paisley pattern in brilliant crimson and Persian blue is held in place by a gold tie clasp. His hair is wet-combed, abundant, curly black with silver side-strands. He leans back in the leather chair, his legs spread languidly, one arm resting on the chair arm, one hand in his lap near his fly. His shoes are brown with a high polish. Black, silky socks. He nods in Ratch's direction, but Ratch does not respond.

JUDGE: Mr. Kinnard, according to the report, you had a sexual relationship in the spring of 1963?

DAVID: That's right.

JUDGE: With whom and over what period of time did you know her?

DAVID: Her name was Janet Cavo, and I have known her from roughly
          the spring of 1960, down to the present, although there have not
          always been relations of the same kind, and I have not always,
          during that period, been seeing her.

JUDGE: Over what period was there a relationship involving sexual
          intercourse?

DAVID: During the period from say, March—that's rough but close—I
          don't want to be held to it—within a month—of 1960, until
          May—June of 1963.

JUDGE: Was there an explanation for it—some rift with your wife?

DAVID: The *specific* background is, very simply, that my wife was very
          seldom willing to sleep with me at all, and took considerable dis-
          tress in it when she did.

JUDGE: Considerable what?

DAVID: Distress. This is not absolutely all the time, but most of the time,
          and it was a rare event, even at best.

JUDGE: She suffered physical pain during—

DAVID: Psychiatric and emotional pain, I would say.

JUDGE: It was not physical? Or is this your interpretation?

DAVID: No, she would have admitted that, although she really thought
          there seemed to be a physical complication during the last six
          months of our *active* married life.

JUDGE: When did this *psychic* and emotional pain—

DAVID: It started very early and increased, with occasional periods of
          warmth.

JUDGE: Was it present during your premarital relationship?

DAVID: The signs of it were already there.

JUDGE: Is Janet Cavo married or single?

DAVID: Single.

JUDGE: The report says she followed you to Gorgeville.

DAVID: Yes, for a time.

JUDGE: Do you have some emotional attachment to this Janet Cavo?

DAVID: I am very fond of her and regard her as a good friend. I have no commitment to marry her or intention to marry her.

JUDGE: A good friend. But with the sexual relationship there is emotional attachment?

DAVID: Yes, I am not an animal.

JUDGE: This seems to have been a troublesome relationship. It had a hard time making up its mind. Off again, on again. Your wife has been very honest with us and I expect you to be equally honest. I think you will be. Unfortunately, sex is involved in this case to a very large extent and unpleasant though the job may be, I have to find out all I can about its possible effect on the whole situation. What about subsequent to the spring of 1963—with Janet Cavo? The report does not say.

DAVID: We broke absolutely. We resumed on a basis which was more compatible with the position I was in, and which was that I would see her from time to time, and for the most part I have seen her with other people around, as a friend.

JUDGE: Do you have any attachments that don't involve sex, at the present time, with a girl? Or girls?

DAVID: I have many women friends.

JUDGE: You mean you date?

DAVID: No, I do not date.

JUDGE: What are the manifestations of their friendship? You say you have many women friends, and you say you don't date. To me there is an inconsistency. Perhaps you can explain?

DAVID: If a movie or a concert is a date, there's that. That's all.

JUDGE: Is there any possibility, assuming this Court grants you a divorce, that this thing with Miss Cavo might mature into something more than mere friendship?

DAVID: Let me try to explain. I have a *very complicated* feeling on this, although I think I can express it in two or three seconds. I feel very chary, being a two-time loser, of swiftly making a decision of this importance again. I think I must be out from under the pressure of all the misery and entanglement.

JUDGE: To make a decision.

DAVID: In order to make a *valid* decision. I would not foreclose Miss Cavo, but I have no commitment, and I have, out of sheer *honesty*, made a statement roughly like I am making now some time ago to her, in which I said anyone in my position cannot predict how he will feel and must be careful not to repeat.

JUDGE: What do you think was wrong, went bad, with your marriage to Mrs. Kinnard?

DAVID: I think we are two very different people. I would sum it up very simply—

JUDGE: My impression is that neither of you are what they call promiscuous people. There is an emotional attachment involved, apparently, in whatever relationships you have had. There hasn't been anything smacking of casual infidelity on either side.

DAVID: Well—I have a few times— There have been fleeting incidents— which there is no point in concealing. Why did the marriage go bad? It is a very difficult question, and I certainly would not swiftly pass the buck to Mrs. Kinnard. I thought the marriage still redeemable in the fall of 1962, though I thought it was going to take really an *heroic* effort on both our parts, and I tried to talk her into that heroic effort.

JUDGE: What brought about your initial separation?

DAVID: Two things. First was her departure for California in early July of 1962. I was very strongly opposed to that. She returned in late August, and the second thing was that she had acquired, over the summer, an attachment to another man which seemed, at least for that period, to be decisive and overriding as a commitment.

JUDGE: This is Jack Davey?

DAVID: Yes, Jack Davey. I was in *great* distress over this, but I did believe if we could both make an heroic effort, something could be done, and it would be *worth* it, in terms of the way we once felt about each other, and also in terms of the children, who basically need two parents.

JUDGE: Very true.

RATCH: What happened then, if I may interrupt?

DAVID: Two things. I was unsuccessful in talking her into an attempt and this corresponded to the strengthening, rather than weakening, of the attachment to Jack Davey. That was one. The other was a decision, becoming clear, to remove herself and the children to California. At that point I decided I was in grave danger of losing not only my marriage, which I realized I had lost, but my two children as well.

JUDGE: I thank you for your candor, Mr. Kinnard. The record may show it is no longer necessary for Mr. Kinnard to retain the services of a court-appointed full-time housekeeper.

DAVID: May I make one more statement?

JUDGE: Certainly. Anything you wish.

DAVID: I think it is desirable to marry again, and doubly so if I get the children, because I think the children should grow up in an atmosphere of two people who love each other. I think it's a good dream to have before them, all the time, an open and easy warmth between a man and woman, as something they grow up with, looking towards, as their own hope. Another thing, I think the sex relations of parents is none of the children's business, and I try to keep it that way.

JUDGE: I should think you would. Is there anything more, gentlemen?

SAM: Do I understand, Your Honor, that *this is it*? We are not expecting Mr. Kinnard to come back tomorrow?

JUDGE: No.

SAM: Then I have a few questions. Mr. Kinnard, do you expect to pursue your studies in Europe?

DAVID: That would depend very strongly on the determination of the Court and what restrictions the Court would put upon my movements. If I were given the children and left free to go to Europe, I would take a flat there and would provide the children with schooling—a school run by English nuns—and would have a woman in to take care of them.

JUDGE: How long would you be in Europe?

DAVID: Nine or ten months.

SAM: You intend to go, is that right?

DAVID: Let me say what I put first! Olivia and Tony!

JUDGE: I believe Mr. Kinnard would ask the court's permission, and in view of the fact he has tenure here, I think it is *very* unlikely he would flee the jurisdiction of the court on a permanent basis.

SAM: That's not the point at all! The point is visitation!

JUDGE: Mr. Anderson, are you arguing with me?

SAM: I beg pardon, Your Honor. Mr. Kinnard, do you have any honest concern for the safety of your children in the event they are given to your wife?

DAVID: May I answer yes *and* no?

SAM: You will anyway.

DAVID: It will take two or three minutes. Normally, in her usual state, twenty-three hours and fifty-three minutes out of even bad days I have really no concern at all. She loves them and would do a great deal for them. The reason I do have concern is that I did hear a *screaming*, out-of-control scene at midnight one night by a woman with a hammer in her hand, and I'll never forget that scene! And I have seen her—

GIERSHE: DAVID KINNARD! YOU ARE A DISGUSTING LIAR!

SAM: Mrs. Kinnard—SIT DOWN!

GIERSHE: I SHALL NOT SIT DOWN! WHO MADE UP THESE DUMB RULES? HE IS LYING. HE *WANTS* ME TO SHOUT IN COURT! HE—

DAVID: . . . seen her out of control as recently as . . .

JUDGE: What was that?

DAVID: . . . two weeks ago. She smashed in the front window in my house.

GIERSHE: LIAR! I DID NOT, DID NOT, DID NOT! And what am I to do without them—when you're in Europe?

RATCH: This is in the report, Your Honor.

GIERSHE: AND WHERE IS MISS FAHEY? WHY CAN'T *I* READ THE REPORT?

SAM: Your honor— Mrs. Kinnard—sit DOWN!

(Giershe rocks in her seat. Rafaela's arms surround her. Red hair falls over Giershe's hunched back)

DAVID: . . . completely out of control! She may not realize it herself. Not normally, no. In crisis, yes, and I can't tell what is going to provoke a crisis. I know *I* provoke crisis, but I know Jack Davey, and know perfectly well *he* is going to provoke many! Life provokes crises. People have to be able to maintain control through crisis. So, yes and no. At any moment, when she gets upset, I would be worried. My son has been talking about the window broken when she slammed the door for three weeks, it distressed him so.

JUDGE: Witness dismissed.

(*Judge Legality reaches across the table to shake David Kinnard's hand*)

>>—>——

At 6:00 p.m., Giershe's little band of supporters dispersed. Rafaela hugged Giershe and climbed into the car with Sid. She leaned back in the seat and closed her eyes. Sid patted her hand. Sam excused himself, saying he had several hours of work at the office before he could go home. Millie and Don gave Harry and Giershe a ride to their borrowed house. Millie held Giershe's hand and didn't ask questions. Harry slumped in the back seat, too weary even to grumble.

"Thank you, Millie and Don. We'll call you when the judge's report comes. Or rather—Harry will call. I'm returning to Berkeley tomorrow if I can get a reservation. I *must* get back to open my little school on Monday."

"Giershe! What the hell . . . ?"

"Hush, Harry. I'll clear it with Miss Fahey before I go, but I'm sure she'll agree. Any more postponements of that school's opening and I'm out of a job. I have to do something healthy and courageous!"

"What am I supposed to do? Sit around and read *Tom Jones* to catch up with you?" He blew his nose noisily.

"I think she's right, Mr. Gavin. If you're staying to take the children when— You're very welcome to stay with us. We'd enjoy your company." Don stood beside the car and shook Harry's hand. Harry was too tired to argue. He stumbled up the path and stood mutely at Giershe's side as she unlocked the door. Giershe turned to wave good-bye. The O'Dwyers waved back and waited until Harry and Giershe had gone inside.

>>—>——

SUPERIOR COURT, MIDDLESEX COUNTY
FEBRUARY 26, 1964
DAVID KINNARD v. GIERSHE KINNARD
MEMORANDUM ON MOTION TO MODIFY
TEMPORARY CUSTODY ORDER

. . . It is the first and natural inclination of the Court to consider an award of custody to the defendant mother. "That, under normal circumstances, the interests of a young child, particularly a little girl, will be best served by growing up in the care of her mother does not admit of question." *Claffey v. Claffey*, supra, 110.

. . . However, after sustained and thorough consideration of the whole situation and all the facts, in respect to many of which the less said the better, the Court cannot persuade itself that the best interests of these children will be protected and served by placing them in the care of the defendant mother, as much as she loves them and as well-meaning as she may be. Under the circumstances which now exist, the Court is of the fixed opinion that it would be imprudent to do so, despite the Court's sympathy with, and understanding of, a mother's overwhelming desire to have her own children. The plain and simple fact is that the defendant mother's *present situation does not lend itself to the kind of a life which society and this Court, in GOOD CONSCIENCE, can approve.*

. . . The Court is fully aware that Mr. Kinnard has made a number of mistakes, perhaps too many. Nevertheless, without question he is completely devoted to the children and he is well qualified to exercise a superior judgment in regard to their education. The present situation of the children is excellent and ought to be continued indefinitely. The Court is satisfied that the plaintiff's sense of responsibility to his children and the society in which he and they must live is such that he will strive successfully to conform with the normal requirements of that society insofar as they relate to the manner in which he personally and these children should carry on their lives and to the moral standards with which compliance is expected.

While the Court is satisfied, and therefore finds, that the plaintiff is *not* guilty of the specific charges made against him in respect to Olivia, his conduct with the children hereafter must be above any possible suspicion on the part of any reasonable person.

. . . It is further ordered that the defendant shall have the right to reasonable visitation to and with said children, provided the same shall be within the *view* of the plaintiff or some other person designated by him, in order to prevent the defendant from removing the children from this state without the prior written approval of this Court.

It is further ordered that the award of custody to the plaintiff hereby made shall be subject to the supervision of the Centerville *Diocesan Bureau of Social Service.*

The above Order is a *temporary* one, as the Court cannot do otherwise at this stage of the proceedings. A change of circumstances may be the basis for a modification of the Order. At all times the best interests of these children, their welfare and happiness, are the primary and paramount considerations of the Court.

John Legality
_____
JOHN LEGALITY
Judge of the Superior Court

>>>

I took the Law to be a person of malignant temper from whose cruel bondage, and from whose intolerable tyranny and unfairness, some excellent person was crying out to be delivered. I wished to hit Law with my fist, for being so mean and unreasonable.

—*Edmund Gosse,* Father and Son

15

"Why, there's hardly

enough of me left

to make one

respectable person!"

GIERSHE ALLOWED ONLY two people—Molly and Jack—to glimpse her grief, and there was no one she knew whose despair resembled her own. She felt herself to be uniquely marked, stigmatized by a society she'd never troubled herself to understand. She wished she had a distinctive costume she could wear daily, perhaps with a Croix de Guerre pattern of white crosses against a blood-red background, with a black hood and a long dirty skirt trailing in the dust, to set her apart from more ordinary folk. The identifying garment should be designed by her judges, and she should be required to wear it, like the Jews forced to wear yellow stars, or lambs at Easter time in Athens who bleated through the streets with red crosses on their heads to mark their journey towards death.

Each morning, Monday through Friday, as she dressed for school, she redesigned the costume she wished she could wear. With her hair bouncing-clean and shiny, she carefully selected her prettiest garments and renewed her smile for the children, their parents, the school board, and the garrulous kvetching ladies of the host synagogue where the school was housed.

Each morning she left society's pariah sitting behind the wheel of the same old green Chevy and walked beneath olive trees, through the huge doors with the brass Tree of Life, down the hallway, turned the key in the school's blue door, and stepped into the tranquil, brightly colored environment she had designed—and which teams of fathers and mothers working nights and weekends had meticulously provided, while she had shlumped through the webbed deceit of Connecticut.

She went each day among young bodies, earnest young mothers, bright, beautiful teaching materials from Holland, twenty-five new little tables with colored Formica tops, a live plant on each, soft little mouths with white teeth and smiles and "Good morning, Giershe Kinnard" twenty-five times in greeting; she entered looking her prettiest and smelling like soap and lavender, caught in a recurring tableau of deeply comforting order.

And each morning, Mary Finley brought her son to school. She was the prime mover of the school, the wife of the chairman of the board, mother of six children. She would stand at the door and look into Giershe's eyes. Mary's eyes were deep blue and her voice was quietly melodious. Giershe would smile at her and shake the child's hand and Mary would ask if Giershe was all right. Giershe would tell her that John had worked with decimals the day before and seemed to like math, and Mary would say good-bye to John and leave, after peeking to see if he went first to the math cabinet.

Twenty times a day, in silent demonstration, Giershe passed on the secrets of the work materials. Each exercise began with her own gathering of herself in readiness. Sometimes she invited a few children to watch. More often, she simply took from the shelf a pair of leather shoes and a tray of shoe-polishing equipment. She sat on the floor with the equipment in front of her. She looked at the polish, the shoes, the wipe cloth, and waited. Two, three, four children left their work and sat down near her. They chattered and asked questions:

"Giershe Kinnard, what you doing?"

"I want to do the shoe polish! Let *me!*"

"Do we get to do it?"

"My shoes are tennies. Do I get to?"

"Wait for Giershe. Don't touch! Be quiet!"

She did not answer. She was very quiet. The children grew silent. Four children waiting. It was a little like putting on *Hamlet* without selling any tickets—no curtain, a shifting stage, and the audience free to come and go when the show ceased to interest. The art of silent demonstration was a skill she had learned in her training and each time she performed the ritual, she was flooded with a peace she felt in no other part of her life.

Top off the round Kiwi container. Put lid underneath. Square cloth inserted into polish. Look at cloth. Smell it. Left hand in one shoe. Rub polish on toe end of shoe. Put cloth on top of Kiwi can. Look at toe of shoe. Blow on it. Wait. Blow again. Wait. Wait until it grows dull. Look at tray. Find clean polishing cloth. Rub toe of shoe until it shines. Put polishing cloth back on tray. Take left hand out of shoe. Put more polish on cloth resting on top of Kiwi container. Put hand in shoe. Polish side of shoe. Et cetera. Return shoes to shelf. Move on to another demonstration in a different part of the room.

> I tie my Hat – I crease my Shawl –
> Life's little duties do – precisely –
>
> . . . .
>
> And yet – Existence – some way back –
> Stopped – struck – my ticking – through–
> We cannot put Ourself away –
>
> . . . .
>
> Therefore – we do life's labor –
> Though life's Reward – be done –
>
> . . . .
>
> With scrupulous exactness –
> To hold our Senses – on –
>
> —*E. Dickinson*

Jack and Giershe continued to meet. Elizabeth and Molly knew when Giershe was with Jack, but Harry was told that of course she was obeying the judge's implied wishes. He licked the wounds of Centerville, helped Giershe with her school environment, and left the room if she grew melancholy in his presence.

When she drove to the valley, she went north on the freeway until she came to a freeway cloverleaf jammed with weary motorists. She edged into a line of exiting cars, looking into the rearview mirror to check the car behind her, drove in and out of gas stations, and doubled back onto the freeway going south to San Jose. She always parked her car several blocks from Jack's apartment and walked in the darkness, first away from, then towards, the two rooms where Jack waited.

The little alarm on Jack's wristwatch would buzz them awake in two hours. She never saw him set it, and knowing him to be a man of plans, she assumed he had their pleasure scheduled before her arrival. Buzz-z-z-z-z. "Shut that thing off. Let's sleep. I'm tired, Jack."

"Time to get to work. If you think *I* want to get out of this bed, you're crazy. Come along, I have some stuff to show you."

"No, I'm too tired. I need to sleep. See, I'm going back to sleep. I don't want to work, it's no use."

"Oh, right! That suits me! We'll just let the Law and Judges and the Church and foul Husbands cut you up and throw you to the hounds. It's not *my* life. If you want to sit in a corner and snivel, don't do it here. I don't want to hear it." Jack glanced at her sleepy face, her brown hand clutching the sheet, then turned and walked away from her into the bathroom. She listened to the pee-sound, the toilet flushing, the splash of water, the shluff-shluff of footsteps to the refrigerator, opening, closing, the clink of glass on the drain board. It was unthinkable to lie abed while he wandered around the apartment. She followed his route to the bathroom, panties, stockings, skirt, and blouse draped over an arm growing chill in the breeze from the bedroom window. She washed her face and combed her hair, staring at her eyes in the mirror. She saw the fear and wondered again how Mary Finley could leave her son with her. There were two decorative etched lines down the mirror which gave to her reflection the caged look of a prisoner on death row. She felt she knew why such prisoners wanted death more than they wanted loved ones to seek reprieve.

Giershe walked into the lighted living room where Jack was busy pulling papers from his briefcase. "Here—read this first. To your friend Sid. He can use his ACLU connections." He handed Giershe a letter written in pencil on the familiar legal-size yellow paper. He had never learned to type.

DEAR SID:

Legality's decision was worse than an outrage, it was stupid. I
have worked long enough in civil liberties to believe that it is
indefensible. If we work implacably enough, I am convinced it
will be thrown out. I am even enough of an idealist to think that
if we succeed, it might help reform what is obviously an
antiquated set of legal procedures. Furthermore, it might smoke
the fuckin' Catholics out of the Family Relations Division and, to
one who loathes the Church, this is perhaps the best thing about
it. Please do not believe that I am one who loves Mankind but
not my fellowman, i.e., Giershe Kinnard. I wish to see this
injustice repaired and her children returned to her, but I fight
better when I can unite principle with interest.

I'll shortly be sending you copies of two communications.
One is to Judge Legality, the other to the Connecticut branch of
the American Civil Liberties Union. In the first, I beard Legality
in his own den, politely, but make no bones about his stupidity. I
see no harm in this. We can't reverse this thing by being nice.
Any man who would write such an opinion is not likely to be
amenable to any arguments we present. I hope only to raise
doubts.

The letter to the ACLU is a narrative of the case which
presents the civil rights aspects. In all of this, I make the
assumption that Giershe's "reform" is not going to change
matters. We must:

1. Force them to reopen the case so we can prove David had
   an illegal sexual relationship with Olivia. If necessary we
   can take the evidence to the D.A.
2. Get David fired from Whitfield, quietly if possible, pub-
   licly if necessary.
3. Blast the case out of the court-imposed secrecy into the
   public domain.
4. Force the court into proving the validity of Miss Fahey's
   report. If the court has to prove the "facts" which it says
   Fahey "established" are indeed facts, I don't think the court
   will have a chance.

We should also have some idea of how we shall proceed if we
want to go to the press, radio, and TV—who has contacts, can
the report be read by the press, which news media hate
Whitfield, who are Legality's political enemies, who hates the
Catholics. We need a smart, aggressive, civil-rights-minded

lawyer who isn't afraid of being held in contempt of court. No lawyer who takes on this thing is going to get anything but personal remorse or satisfaction from it. He must have an emotional or ideological commitment.

Sincerely,
Jack

Jack paced the floor while she read. When she finished, she held the yellow papers in her lap. "Well? May I send it?"

"Yes, you may send it. I feel better now and thank you again. How do you find time for this?"

"I don't waste time looking back. I keep moving. When my enemies get to where I was yesterday, I'm already six miles ahead churning up the dust. The stuff we did last week—I've pulled it together and it's got to be typed. You brought your typewriter?"

"In the car."

"Okay, tomorrow I have meetings all day, but while I'm gone, you can type it, with about six copies, and then—there's a little restaurant south of here where no one goes and we'll drink wine and— What's the matter?"

"I'm interrupting your plans for the next twenty-four hours to say I love you."

"The best way to show me is to keep a smile on your face and continue to work your magic with the Montessori folk. I like to back winners, and it's all conceptual. You have to think it, walk it, sleep it, and keep moving. Are you ready to go over the chronology with me? No, let's do the thing for Legality first. Sid might need it. Here's the first page. Make corrections on fact or opinion, and while you're doing that, I'll get us some milk and whiskey. Goddamn, I wish we could sleep. My bones ache. Christ, I hope we have some milk."

Giershe propped a pillow against the wall and sat down. She let Jack's "we" cover and include her while he was far away in the kitchen, and when he returned and handed her a blue-and-white cup of hot milk, he bent over and licked her face, just once. She read the careful, detailed presentation of fact and opinion. She read until she was dizzy.

"Are you finished?"

"No, but Jack, there's not a humble word so far. You're supposed to humble yourself before the Law. And I'm not sure it's exactly true."

"TRUE! If there's a line of study which I'd recommend to you, it's epistemology. Exact truth, as you call it, has brought you where you are today."

"I keep wanting to laugh as I read. It's the nineteenth-century language sitting astride a twentieth-century runaway horse. I try to imagine what Legality will make of it."

"Read on; perhaps you'll change your mind."

> . . . no sooner did Mr. Kinnard hear of Mrs. Kinnard's plans for taking the Montessori training than he rejected them. She turned to me for moral support and I willingly responded. Very quickly Mr. Kinnard discovered my affair with Mrs. Kinnard and expressed moral outrage. I found this so completely hypocritical that I wrote him off as a cad and every action he has taken since has only confirmed me in this opinion . . .

"Jack, really—CAD?"

"It's a fine concept and I didn't think 'prick' would sit too well with the judge."

> Miss Fahey has characterized the Gavin family as unstable, while nothing is said of the Kinnards. This is ludicrous. Except for the Gavins' association with David Kinnard, the family has been unmarked by any scandal. By contrast with the stability and decent conduct of the Gavins, the Kinnard family history is etched by scandal and public display of the seamier side of the human heart. David's father was for years a morphine addict. In 1951, while under the influence of this drug, he administered a lethal dose of medication to a girl patient. His partner locked the door against him and he was never again allowed to practice. He died still an addict.
>
> The failure of Miss Fahey, and the court, to put Mr Kinnard's cynical use of his Catholic faith into proper perspective is a disgrace. Doubtless, as a pious Catholic, Miss Fahey is much impressed by Mr. Kinnard's miraculous regeneration and his return to the faith of his father. However, when seen in the light of the fact that during thirteen years of marriage to Giershe Kinnard he never entered a church for religious purposes, her credulity is astounding. The use to which he put his Catholicism in his scheme to take his *first* daughter away from her mother— by papal annulment—is the capstone to this.
>
> By confessing to some fifty affairs—Mr. Anderson's count— Mr. Kinnard established such a dazzling image of healthy heterosexual virility that any untoward behavior with his daughter was held unthinkable. It was a perfect smoke screen and it worked so

well that even you, Judge Legality, gave him forgiveness for his venial sins. I quote: "The court is fully aware that Mr. Kinnard has made a number of mistakes, perhaps too many. Nevertheless, without question he is completely devoted to the children." You've been Tartuffed by a consummate liar. Read Molière's classic on hypocrisy.

I now consider my moral responsibility in this matter has been discharged and I need not take further part in this case, unless you request me to do so.

Giershe gathered the yellow papers and carefully placed them on the carpet beside her. She lay down, her face in a pillow, and tried to see Tony and Olivia behind closed eyes. Olivia had been fading of late, and she saw only her sturdy legs in white knee socks and Mary Janes. She could see Tony walking away from her, with the little hitch to his walk, as though he had to pull up his pants every other step. Jack stretched himself out beside her, groaning elaborately at each level of descent. His groans always made her laugh and she opened her eyes to watch his mock pain. "I wish Olivia were here right now. She would say, 'Don't worry, Mommy, it's only a story!' Do we *have* to work anymore tonight? Is there any way we could disinfect the room?"

"Right now we're going to open all the windows, take a walk around the block, and then fall into bed. Christ, it's three a.m. I'll go out first. You follow in a few minutes. Oh, my bones!"

>>>>

In the months that passed like snails, Jack and Giershe prepared for June, the month of earliest possible renewed combat in Connecticut, and the date beyond which Giershe could not dream. Harry, Molly, and Elizabeth maintained what Giershe called a "suicide watch" over their balancing relative. They tried to know where she was at all hours when she was not teaching school, and Giershe, aware of their concerns but resenting their fears, learned to check in with them in order to avoid a late-night telephone call. She did not feel steady, optimistic, healthy, or whole, but she was quite certain that to die or not to die was her own business, and of small importance.

Weekends, unless Jack was in them, tipped her over into blind grief. Everyone always vanished into families and left her sitting out on a dangerous perimeter of memory. She called the children in Connecticut, but they too were in a family, or had to go to church, to somewhere for dinner, with someone else to a park. Even Jack sometimes had to be with Andrew.

In April 1964, chronologies, depositions, affidavits, letters, and phone calls from San Jose, California, to New Jersey, to Florida, to Connecticut, produced a candidate, Mr. Lewis Cohen, to replace the reluctant Sam Anderson, as counsel for the defendant.

CHURCH AND LAW STRS.
New Haven, Conn.

April 11, 1964

My dear Dr. Davey:

Please accept my gratuitous advice to you *not* to forward to Judge Legality the original of your proposed letter and memorandum on this case. It is my considered judgment that both the letter and the memo would hurt rather than help Mrs. Kinnard's cause now and in the future. After I study this situation carefully, I'll consider how to produce for the record the information which you've offered in this inappropriate form. Please don't be offended by my suggestion, but your approach is *academic* and therefore not practical. I plan to handle this as a *legal* problem. Mrs. Kinnard must also approach this case as a legal problem. Staging a sit-down in Centerville will *not* produce the results which Mrs. Kinnard wishes. My objective will be to obtain for Mrs. Kinnard her objective of custody, without any more complications than now exist. It's going to be very difficult to rectify the situation, but I've never been one to duck a difficult matter. Trust me.

Sincerely,
Lewis Cohen

16

"Well, in our country,"

said Alice,

"you'd generally get to

somewhere else—if you

ran very fast

for a long time

as we've been doing."

DON'T SAY IT, WRITE IT!

To: Mrs. G. Kinnard
From: Lewis Cohen, Church & Law Strs., New Haven, Conn.
June 5, 1964

Message:

THIS IS THE BEGINNING! WE ARE ASSIGNED FOR THE
NEXT FRIDAY, JUNE 12, 1964!
     I would like Dr. Finley or his wife Mary to come voluntarily
to testify about your character, integrity, ability, and your
reputation in the school and in the community where you now
live. We are now on the way, we are on the offensive. I want your
complete backing.

Sincerely,
Lewis Cohen

MOLLY GAVIN'S DIARY:
JUNE 10, 1964

     Giershe left for Connecticut today. Mary Finley went with
her—what a person! Her husband and parents at the airport.
Lovely people. I hated to see both these superior people take
their chances in the air.

JUNE 12, 1964

     Waited and waited for a call from Giershe which didn't come
until quite late. NOTHING had happened. Nothing. At five-ten
Judge Mezzadeo said he was tired and court was over for the day
and for the summer! Nothing possible until September. Incredible! She seems low and Cohen is crushed, says Giershe has been
"hacked by the New England viewpoint."

GIERSHE'S DIARY:
JUNE 14, 1964

     Olivia looked years older. She came directly to me and

hugged. Tony stood off, smirking and chattering. We went to the backyard to the swing set and laughed merrily. Olivia kept demanding attention, Tony impish. We looked at stamps and I told him the names on them: Andrew Jackson, Abraham Lincoln, George Washington. He gave back: Andrew Jacks, George Lincoln, George Jackson. O. and T. brought blankets from the house and we lay on the grass. Tony was positive the blanket should be placed just so. Olivia drew pictures for me and I knew she'd done nothing for months, school her excuse. Tony came running out of the house: "Mommy! Father says I can go to California with you!"

JUNE 17, 1964

David three feet from me at all times. When we were outside he sat on the back stoop and stared. His car is placed in the driveway, ready for chase. I asked Olivia for a sandwich: "I can't remember how to make sandwiches, Mommy. I never do it anymore." Tony set me up outside with a footstool for a table and two little chairs. He stayed very close to me. Kept asking me when I would return. Tomorrow, I said. Olivia and her friends came outside to play games. I had planned various activities but they played so well together, it was enchanting just to watch. I can't take Olivia from her friends, because I can't take her away. I haven't been alone with her for eight months. David said: "I do not intend to go to Rome unless the children go with me. My plans are very flexible."

JUNE 18, 1964

Arrived at four. Came a little blue VW Bug. Ted Painter and Freddy Heywood tumbled out. We hugged and danced around in the grass. So good to see them and together still! I asked about Lenny Kampfer but they weren't sure where he was. We skirted all talk of present trouble and remembered the good days in Germany when the three of us shocked Kultur Vultures with our laughter at concerts and exhibits.

Children arrived at five-thirty. I pulled sleepy Tony from the car and he snuggled. Olivia smiled wanly. She used to smile radiantly. Now it is a careful act. The kitten and turtle I had brought perked her up. Olivia asked: "Mommy, where was I when I was inside you?" I placed my hand over the spot and it grew warm with memory.

"Stomach?"

"Womb."

"And where did I come out?" Last January she asked me: "How did I get out?" and I answered: "By pushing hard." This time, before I thought of an answer, she ran off. Am I the only one she asks? At this rate, she'll have the whole picture by 1985.

JUNE 19, 1964

Tony sat in my lap out on the grass for about two hours. He took my compact and powdered his cheeks, nose, chin, eyelids, lashes and knees. Then all the children (friends) did same. David seemed quite upset by the kitten. He's lucky I didn't give them a horse or an elephant. Olivia asked about my school, Molly, Harry, and California. She asked to go with me. "Girls should be with girls," she said. Tony began to get cross as it approached five. He went to the kitchen and hit David, who said, "Don't hit Father, sweet boy." Just before I drove off, Olivia whispered in my ear: "Good-bye, Mommy, I love you. I'll tell you a secret, you're a pretty mommy!" Then she solemnly waved good-bye.

>>>>

YWCA, June 20.64
New Haven, C.

DEAR JACK—

Cohen has forced a hearing set for week of July sixth. Mary Finley coming again. (They insist.) YWCA is the craziest place. I can't think why they went to all the trouble of setting up all over the U.S. A place of locks. Every room has a lock and in each room is a closet with a lock. You're to put all your stuff in the closet and then lock the door to your room whenever you go out. The first thing you hear upon awakening is the sound of metal keys in locks, echoing down the halls. Each female unlocks herself to get out of her room to go to the bathroom, and locks the door behind her. Five minutes later she returns, unlocks, locks, etc. As long as I can keep my mind on the metals, the turning, the key, I'm all right. But the mind slips easily into symbolism and then I miss you *so* much.

love
Giershe

In late afternoon of a visitation day, Giershe returned to her room at the Y just as the daily rain, which was supposed to clear the air, burst from black clouds. There were sixteen stairs up to the second floor. Her thin white skirt, damp and smelling of healthy mildew, was streaked with car stains and clung to her body. There was a film of moisture on her skin and as she sat on the stairs, halfway up, her heart seemed to be trying to leap from her chest. If she collapsed in the YWCA, would that look like psychic instability? She had to keep going, every day, like a soldier slogging through to front-line combat. She was dizzy and confused. She tried to remember the number of her room. Every afternoon she forgot it, and forgot also to look at her key where the number was plainly etched. It was as dark as winter in the hallway, and she couldn't see the number on the key. She held the hot metal in the palm of her hand and wondered how many females had used it, had climbed these stairs, had rushed to answer the phone at the end of the hall, had crossed their thresholds and wept, had cursed the weeds growing in cracks in the concrete wall outside the window. Why had they lived alone, and did anyone visit?

Lightning flashed across the key—224—she climbed six more stairs and stood in front of 224, inserted the key, pushed open the door, and waited a moment before entering. Let all those women leave, if they would. She closed the door behind her and put the chain-lock in place. She took off her damp clothes and lay down on the bed. She tried to separate her limbs from torso. The chenille itched. *Living in this room is for something, has to be, flagellation of spirit and pride, it's good for me.* She tried to sleep, but the lightning lifted her eyelids, demanding sight for its show. She decided to take a cold shower in the moldy communal room in the basement, get dressed, take a walk in the rain, and eat her usual at the restaurant around the corner.

After a cold shower, she felt much better. She walked quickly through the ground-floor lobby, past the front desk, looking at no one; she had tried friendly smiles and received stares from the listless attendant. Giershe had observed that there was a camaraderie among the hired help which vanished when she appeared as though they knew she was marked and troubled, and like dogs who take no interest in wounded birds on the shore, they sniffed and turned away from her.

She walked to the corner and crossed the street. The rain was gentle and mixed with orange light. Children were playing in the puddles of muddy water at curbside. Mothers and fathers scolded and urged them on towards the city park where each night during the summer they could stroll, eat hot dogs, perhaps listen to a band concert. Halfway down the block was Travatoli's Bar and Grill, where she ate every night; she could sit by herself in a booth, write in her journal, order what they called a salad, and stay as long as she liked, drinking iced coffee with rich cream. Every evening the same people were there—two elderly married couples, five lone burned-out men in soggy suits drinking beer at the counter, one old woman dressed in black who talked to herself of disasters in the daily world and admonished herself to be careful because the world was "getting worse and worse ev'y day"—and Giershe. The noisy air conditioner (which brought the temperature down to eighty-five degrees) sent greasy breezes down the aisle. It struggled to function, sometimes wheezing and clanking ominously, but never gave up.

Giershe liked returning each night to this unvarying scene of stagnant comfort. She required only that her table be wiped clean before she placed her journal on its surface; she reached behind the cash register for a damp towel and wiped crumbs and beer puddles from the tabletop, then returned the towel to its hook and sat down. The proprietor had stopped asking her what she wanted to order. He brought the "salad" when he chanced to notice she was in her booth, and as the old man placed it in front of her, he nodded his head in greeting, then waddled down the aisle to his place behind the cash register. Iced coffee near her right hand, salad pushed to the center of the table, Giershe began to write: "June 20, 1964: Arrived at three, as planned."

She chewed on the pen and looked at the brown wooden seat across from her, the names etched—"Manuel loves Maria." It was so hot, but she must write it all down, to keep it, these words. *Man standing in the aisle. Just standing there. Don't look up, he might think*— Voice, low and soft: "Giershelein?" She turned her head and stared up at him. Gentle brown eyes, blue shirt, wet and rumpled. Dead white skin, moist black hair receding from smooth forehead.

"Lenny? Lenny? How . . . ? Am I having a dream?"

"Giershelein. Freddy Heywood called me in Boston and told me. I tried to call you. I left a message at the Y. Didn't they tell you?"

"LENNY!" She tried to slip across the plastic seat which clung to her skirt. He put out a hand to help her. She stood before him in the aisle. His arms went around her, hugging her closely. He was sticky with sweat. He rumpled her hair and swayed back and forth on his sandals. She tried to drown in his comfort, shutting out sound and memory. The air conditioner wheezed. A voice—"worse and . . . worse." She remembered where she was. She pulled away from him and laughed.

"Lenny! Sit down. In my parlor. Sit and have some iced coffee. The help will serve you whatever you wish. Cold beer? Lenny, how could you be here? I thought you were in Germany. No, I knew you'd returned, but I thought you were studying in New York. No, no, I don't remember. Much has happened since I last—"

"Giershe, hush up. Yes, I'll sit down and yes, I'd like a cold beer, any kind. Where do I get it?"

"They'll bring it. They heard you. Everyone heard you and saw us. It's all right. But what are you doing *here*? I don't mean in this town, I mean *here*, in my parlor?"

"I asked at the Y and they told me you ate here every night. Very helpful old lady."

"What? How did they know I eat here every night? Oh my God! It's unbelievable. I've never said so, to them or to anyone. Why should I?"

"Relax. Take it from a seasoned, happily *former* spook for the U.S. government, that everyone always knows everything that is none of their business. Especially what's none of their business. Giershe, Freddy said you didn't look well, and you don't. You're probably not taking care of yourself, and he said you might even like a helping hand from a friend and admirer."

"Admirer? Of me?"

"Yes—well—Ted, Freddy, and I remember when your cheeks were plump and rosy in Germany, your hair long and glossy, and you didn't mind walking two miles in the snow to attend a Nolde showing and laugh at the note takers. Now we're all note takers, and I've been sent on a mission to restore that picture. You really do look half-alive. It's a difficult assignment, but they trust me to carry it out, with skill and delicacy. We shall begin with a walk in the plaza park, preferably with Sousa thumping at us."

"Lenny, if I'd been asked to choose, of all the people I've known in all the world, or could invent, you'd be the person I would most want to have around. Now. But I can't let you. I'm not that person anymore. I have to do this alone. I want to protect good people from David and me. There's no need."

"There's every need. Have you finished that . . . what is it? . . . salad? Come along. Let's walk. Walking always helps, even in this heat. That's what you used to say. After we've walked, I'm going to feed you. Carbohydrates and milk shakes. Come—get up!" He took her sticky hand and pulled. Giershe laughed. Lenny paid the check and pushed her through the door and across the street to the path bordering the bandstand. "Better. A laughing wraith. How do you expect to win in court if you look so—tarnished? Judges like to punish the punished. Don't you know that?"

"You sound like Jack."

"Jack?"

"He's the other man."

"I hope he's worth it. But if you were one to weigh worth, you wouldn't have married David Kinnard. I never could figure why . . ."

"Hush. Let's just walk and look at all the families. They make me feel so ghostly, as though I've returned to Earth for a night to see what combinations Earthlings arrange for themselves. Have you married or brought children to birth in the six, seven years since I last saw you?"

"It's not that long. I saw the two of you in Gorgeville, remember?"

"Oh yes, a terrible evening, with David trying to make you look foolish because you were a friend of mine. Answer the question."

"What question? Oh, no, I haven't birthed or married. I've scarcely even had time to fall in love. I'm teaching in Boston this summer and I work on my dissertation. In the fall I'll have my first real professional job at a girls' college in New York. *If* I've finished the dissertation. I'll be here in town every week-end, on mission to restore Giershe, and to work in the library."

"I don't believe you have any work to do in this library. I think you're just being noble. I'm remembering your nature. You just can't help it. You adhere to victims like a snail to glass. Oh, disgusting image." She linked her arm to Lenny's and let him lead her, let herself pretend to depend. Their arms stuck together.

"Lady, part of my work here this summer, or as long as you're in need of me, will be to make you realize that you're a very nice person. I was going slowly crazy in Germany, working with fascists all day, and utterly alone at night. You and Freddy, and Ted, you included me in your happy times, let me tag along with you to operas and shows, on walks. Do you remember how you used to celebrate the coming of spring? Little things, like carrying dachshund puppies in bicycle baskets through the park for no good reason, or reciting poetry out loud to the first crocuses. You were so American and pagan, harmlessly goofy at a time when goofiness was scarce." Lenny talked fast, rushing through his words, licking his lips to wet them.

"We were all pretending. Freddy was trying to decide that he was not a novelist, the first to write honestly of homosexual love. Ted was ready to return to grad school. I was telling myself I was frivolous and selfish and must show David I loved exclusively and forever. We were all hysterical puritans scattering our frantic energy onto a sullen, conquered landscape."

"I know that, and knew it then. The point is: a)—"

"Oh no, already you're sounding professorial. Why do all the best people I know turn into ferrets?"

". . . a) blah blah, b) blah blah, and finally, c) blah blah. When do you have to check in?"

"Midnight, of course. Where are you staying?"

"It works out very well. A former student of mine works here during the week and visits a girl in Boston on weekends, and I sleep in his room while he's gone. What's your visitation schedule?"

"*My* schedule is to make an appearance every day. *Their* schedule is to complain and bitch and throw Catholic Charities at me."

"Catholic? Oh yes, Freddy told me. I'll walk you back to the Y. You're looking too thoughtful. Tomorrow we'll have breakfast. Eggs Benedict and

Viennese coffee with whipped cream. Tomorrow afternoon, I want to drive you out of here to look at the ocean."

"Wait! I don't know that we should."

"No one will see us. You have to get yourself out of this town regularly, and I know a lovely place on the sea where we can have dinner. We can even stay there if you like. Separate rooms."

"What are you going to use for money?"

"I have a grant for the summer and it has a liberal living allowance which I don't have to use for lodging."

Giershe removed her arm from Lenny's. She walked ahead of him gulping tears. "Giershe!" Lenny walked fast to stay at her side, his big feet flapping on the damp sidewalk. He touched her elbow. She pulled away. "Giershe, stop! You can cry all you want or throw yourself on the ground, or laugh, be irresponsibly gay! I don't care what you do, but let me help. We have to talk about how I can help. I have some ideas of my own, and I want your permission to meet your lawyer. Say yes, lean on me, don't be such a bloody Protestant! Let me hear it. Yes? Yes?"

"Lenny, if I lean, I give away my strength, I divide it, and when I need it, it's not there."

"Rot! Say yes, or I'll storm the Y, or report you to the authorities for something kind you've said or done. Yes?"

Giershe laughed. He looked so desperate, sweat dripping from his chin, his pants rumpled and soggy, his white face mirroring the moonlight. They stood together in front of the YWCA. She extended her right hand to him for a formal good-bye. "Yes, on one condition. That you will run away without looking back if it gets to be too much for you. Do you agree?"

Lenny shook her hand. "Thank you. I shall not run away. This is my Summer Impossible Task on the road to Glory. Thank you. I'll meet you in front of Travatoli's Bar and Grill at nine-thirty. I'll be disguised as a frog."

>>>———

GIERSHE'S DIARY:
JUNE 21, 1964

> Arrived at three. Olivia and Lisa playing in sprinkler. Tony came out of the house with a pink rosary in a box. We all tried it on and I asked: "What do you do with it?"
>
> "You count it."
>
> "One, two, three."
>
> "NO! Not like that!" he protested.

"You pray with it," Olivia whispered. "First you pray on one bead, and then you move to the next and make another prayer." She turned to Lisa. "Are you Catholic?"

"No," Lisa said sadly.

"What's this?" I asked, fingering a broken crucifix attached to the rosary.

"It's the Lord," Tony said.

"Where is the Lord?" I asked solemnly. He pointed his finger up to the sky and he grinned. "Where?" I searched the sky.

"He's invisible," Olivia said.

"Then how do you know he's there?"

"Because they tell me that at church and in school."

"What about Jesus? Who was he?"

"He was a man who had no friends because he thought he was so great, and they got tired of hearing about it and killed him on the cross," Lisa said.

"Jesus was God," said Olivia, her catechism fixed. Tony was trying to get the rosary back into the little box.

"Jesus has to go in *first*, and then all the beads plunk down on top of him," he explained.

I went to the O'Dwyers'. Half an hour later, up the sidewalk came Olivia and Tony, giggling. "We fooled you, Mommy," Tony said. "Now you can steal us, Mommy," Olivia whispered in my ear. I laughed and told her to run along home.

>>>——

NEW YORK TIMES
JUNE 22, 1964
3 IN RIGHTS DRIVE REPORTED MISSING
Mississippi Campaign Heads Fear Foul Play—
Inquiry by FBI Is Ordered
Philadelphia, Miss.—Three workers in a day-old civil rights campaign in Mississippi were reported missing today after their release from jail here last night. Leaders of the drive said they feared that the three men—two whites, both from New York, and one Negro—have met with foul play.

GIERSHE'S DIARY:
JUNE 24, 1964

Arrived on a regular visitation day. They were not at home. Went to the market. Not there. Walked to the college to see if they were there. Phoned David at 5:30. "No, you can't see the children. No visitation until Saturday. Diocesan Bureau says so."

"How come it's Diocesan Bureau and not the Protestant Family Service?"

"Millie O'Dwyer is one of the trustees of Family Service and I don't trust her."

I hung up and walked down the street to the house. Tony and Olivia came out and we sat on the steps. We planted their houseplants outdoors and I read to them, bid them good-bye, and climbed into the car. Wouldn't start—shorted out from sweating. Two men from across the street tinkered with it for an hour. I was faint from hunger—*everyone* had eaten except me. The children offered me dinner but David vetoed it. Didato's couldn't tow until morning so how was one weary pilgrim going to return to New Haven? I trudged off down the street, got as far as the O'Dwyers', who were not at home, and along came a man from across the street. "I would be pleased to take you to the bus depot, young lady. My wife and I, we got *manners*, which I guess they don't need at Whitfield." I thanked him, and tried to sit on his seat, in my sweaty clothes, like a mannered person.

NEW YORK TIMES
JUNE 24, 1964

FBI AUGMENTS MISSISSIPPI FORCE
Kennedy Tells NAACP That He Cannot Order Any Federal Action

NEW YORK TIMES
JUNE 27, 1964

MISSISSIPPI DRAGS RIVER FOR RIGHTS AIDES
Rise in Tension Feared

Centerville
June 27.64
waiting for car

DEAREST:

I'm obscurely and constantly depressed over the rights workers—depressed because they're missing and because I wasn't concerned over the others who have disappeared. Millie O'Dwyer says that the next war—civil, that is—will be a government slaughter regardless of our laws to safeguard states' rights people. That household is in its usual civil rights furor, and while Don was in the South, Millie got anonymous threatening nigger-lover phone calls from Centerville's citizens.

Oh, please let them be ALIVE!

Giershe

GIERSHE'S DIARY:
JULY 1 AND 2, 1964

Too sick to go to Centerville.

JULY 3, 1964

Arrived at four. Olivia and Tony bounced off the porch. Tony snuggled, looked at me, kissed. I laughed at him and said: "Tony, you're a snuggler." He spread his hands, palms upward, and hunched his shoulders:

"That's just the way I am. I can't help it. You like snugglers?"

"Oh yes! I like them very much!" He settled himself in my lap.

"Little Tony," I said. "Little Mommy," he said. I laughed. He sat up straight: "Don't *laugh* when I say 'Little Mommy.' Now, we'll do it again." Later, he fussed and put pebbles into a cup and threw them at me. "I want you to go away and not come back until you can come and take me away with you!" he yelled.

New Haven, July 6.64
at work, my boss not here

DEAR LEMUEL Q. PITKIN—

I talked with you last night and today three letters! We're very busy preparing for the hearing. Had a talk with Cohen this morning. He'd been over to the courthouse to take notes from the Family Relations report and was in a rage. (They'll not let him have a copy.) He was compiling stuff for Dr. Milton Penn, who has agreed to testify for me. He'd broken his Xerox machine stuffing Camelia Fahey into it, and was cursing. He read me passages from it. "Mrs. Kinnard has no moral sense whatsoever," and "Mrs. Kinnard is unstable, confused, and totally lacking in a moral sense," and "Her visits to the children (January) were infrequent and very upsetting to the children."

"Bitch! Conspiracy!" he shouted, and ordered around his "fine staff." He looked very foolish.

I love you and ache for you. Tonight Mary Finley comes in around nine, perhaps with baby Sam in her arms, then we talk with Cohen, then sleep. Tomorrow, it's Cohen's day.

wait for me,
Giershe

Berkeley
July 7.64

DEAREST GIERSHE—

I tried to call you last night and again this morning. I wondered what bed you'd spent the night in, but thought, She isn't sleeping with anyone the last few nights before the hearing unless she's daft! At nine A.M. I was awakened by Mr. Luigi Cohenovitz asking me for another affidavit. He told me you had gone to Centerville and that lovable David had tried to get you arrested for trespassing. He was delighted and thought it a fine thing to have come on the eve of the hearing. He thinks he'll get the kids for you on Tuesday but that you'll probably have to stay in Connecticut with them for the rest of the summer. Why don't you just get a rifle and shoot David? With Cohen's consent, of course.

love you
Jack

YWCA
July 8.64

JACK HONEY—

As you know by now, Judge Doyle refused to hear any witnesses (including Mary Finley and Dr. Penn), and only the visiting rights were changed. I've been called rotten, a whore, a woman without moral substance, so many times in Connecticut that I do believe a change of scene is indicated. Could you give the Chronology to Bill Peaceman and ask him:

1. If I can get the children to California, will California protect them long enough to go to court there?
2. If Lenny takes them to California and *if* he doesn't cross the Connecticut state line with them, will he be safe from kidnapping charges?

I told Cohen I was going to ask you to ask Peaceman and he said: "But he's the lawyer of your *paramour!*" I feel myself slipping into a world without moral brakes—except that I'll do no harm to people without ample warning, like Hitler, and shall not take lives.

Your Giershe

YWCA, July 9.64

DEAREST—

It has been pouring rain since yesterday afternoon. I'm so nervous. One moment I feel I'll settle down and get some work done, next moment I plot escape, then follows a dramatization of California's returning the kids to Connecticut, then I resign myself for the long wait until we can be heard in Connecticut, then I remember my job will disappear. I remind myself that custody of the children is all-important for me *and* for my job, and then I hear the judge calling me rotten, and I plot escape again. The accomplice seems not to care whether or not he's charged with kidnapping, but I care. I suppose the best way to avoid this is for me to go with the escape car, rather than meeting it out of state. I'm so confused! Oh, to be tangled up with you!

Your Giershe

GIERSHE'S DIARY:
JULY 11, 1964

A young man guarding. We took a lovely walk marred only by his distant presence. We picked gazanias and Lisa caught a butterfly. Bath time. We were very sticky and sweaty so I ran a bubble bath. I climbed in and quickly washed off, then called the kids. They got in and I got out. They watched me dry off and put on my clothes. They said they liked to have me give them baths. Olivia: "I'm going to have hair on my secret parts when I'm twelve." Me: "How do you know that?" Olivia: "There's a girl at camp who's twelve and she has hair." I read them a story. There was a mountain of dirty dishes. I left them. I offered dinner to the young man but he declined. I told Tony the story of Floppy Ears the Elephant who left the zoo and came to Centerville looking for a friend and found two at this very house. He would stand next to the house and Olivia and Tony could climb out the upstairs window onto his back.

>>>>>>

YWCA, July 11.64

DEAREST—

Cuckoo with nerves. On Saturday, July 18, we'll try it. Tomorrow will be spent casing the joint. Then we'll do our best next week. We won't try if there's no chance of success, but plan to be prepared up to the very minute. We'll head for the nearest airport out of state. If Peaceman says I have no chance in California, then of course I won't proceed. Chance, chance. Shakes. I'm going to bed

love,
Giershe

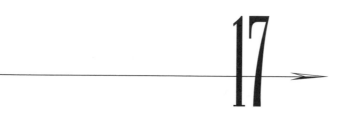

17

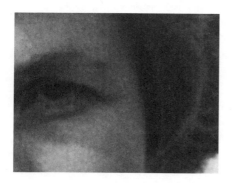

. . . but Alice had got so much

into the way of expecting

nothing but out-of-the-way

things to happen that it seemed

quite dull and stupid for life to

go on in the common way.

G IERSHE? COHEN on the line."

"Yes, what's the matter? It's midnight!"

"Damn right it is! I've been trying to reach you for five hours! We have to be in court tomorrow morning with that bastard Schizzinoso. The judge has a letter from Poltroono and Family Relations with charges from David that you did something squirrelly in the bath with the children. I know you didn't."

"WHAT ARE YOU TALKING ABOUT?"

"Now calm down. All I know is that I got a call *ordering* me to show at nine A.M. for a special appearance in front of that madman. You have to be there too. Now if you didn't do anything, you have nothing— Whatinhell *did* you do anyway?"

"Mr. Cohen, the kids and I were hot and sticky and we took a bath. First me, then the kids. What did Poltroono say?"

"I don't know. The letter is with the judge. All I know is that we'll have to have breakfast and you're going to tell me everything you did and they did. You'd better write it down."

"I've already written it down. And don't take that tone with me. I'm not a criminal. What is the charge?"

"Perversion. I'll see you tomorrow morning at eight in front of my office."

"WAIT! *What* perversion? WHAT PERVERSION!"

"I told you I don't know! Good-bye. Get some sleep, you'll need it."

>>>>

SCENE: Superior Court, Middlesex County, New Haven, Connecticut. July 17, 1964.

The Honorable SAL SCHIZZINOSO, Judge, sits in robes. His eyes are hidden in rolls of fat which extend up over a bald head. Glasses down near the tip of his nose. When he talks, his jowls flop up and down.

JAMES POLTROONO, Family Relations Director, sits in the last seat of front row. He wears thick-lensed, horn-rimmed glasses, and stares down at four stacks of white papers at his feet.

GIERSHE KINNARD, in white peasant blouse and black skirt, sits in seat on aisle; LEWIS COHEN, Attorney, sits next to her. She stares up at the Judge, as though trying to memorize a UFO sighting.

SCHIZZINOSO: This morning I have received a letter from the Diocesan Bureau in which certain facts concerning the conduct of the defendant have been called to my attention. In the light of these statements, I hereby modify visitation privileges of the defendant: *Visitation privileges are suspended until further order of the Court.*

GIERSHE: NO! NO! NO! (*She stands in the aisle below the Judge's bench*)

COHEN: Be quiet, Mrs. Kinnard!

SCHIZZINOSO: What was that?

COHEN: Nothing, Your Honor.

SCHIZZINOSO: I now direct the Family Relations officer to investigate the matter and make a report. I will *retain* jurisdiction of this case for the purpose of acting upon the results of the investigation.

COHEN: Your Honor, if there have been facts or accusations made, I would certainly feel that they should be made part of the record, and I would like to know myself, so I can advise my client what her rights are, what she should do, and what is proper in the premises.

SCHIZZINOSO: Well, among the information in this letter is a statement to this effect: "We have now known from reports of the children and also statements from very close friends of the Kinnards that some of Mrs. Kinnard's activities while visiting with the children are very peculiar and should not be allowed to continue." A recent visit, on July eleventh, the younger child (a boy) casually mentioned to the father—and his statement was confirmed by the older girl—that the mother bathed the children by having herself and the two children take baths at one time! From some of the statements made by the son, Tony, the mother conducted herself in a very improper manner and certainly was trying to carry on acts of PERVERSION with these children. That is part of the record. I WANT THE MATTER INVESTIGATED!

COHEN: So do I, Your Honor, very fully. Your Honor, I realize that Mrs. Kinnard is at a great disadvantage in this matter. In fact, she's being penalized because she did take the children. Your Honor, I have great respect for the Court, and I have a duty to my client, and I wish to state to Your Honor that there is almost open warfare in this matter.

SCHIZZINOSO: I'm here concerned with the welfare of these children and not with the desire or wishes or welfare of the plaintiff or the defendant. I have concluded that the matter should be investigated, and pending that investigation, visitation privileges are *suspended.*

COHEN: Yes, Your Honor. I would ask Your Honor if you would consider this. May I request, Your Honor, that as part of the investigation some form of play therapy under qualified child-psychiatric guidance be employed? There is a technique, which I'm sure Your Honor is aware of, called play therapy. There might be two or three people involved in this who actually can determine the veracity of the children. I know that children are sometimes misquoted.

SCHIZZINOSO: That is the purpose of the investigation, and I'm sure the Family Relations officer will arrive at the proof. I have a statement here by a responsible agency!

COHEN: I realize that, Your Honor.

SCHIZZINOSO: AND I WANT AN INVESTIGATION!

COHEN: I welcome it, Your Honor.

GIERSHE: Your Honor, may I say something?

SCHIZZINOSO: Do you wish to represent yourself, or do you want to be represented by counsel, Mrs. Kinnard?

GIERSHE: I *am* represented by counsel, but I want to say something. I want a Catholic Charities person to be with me on visitations—

COHEN: Just a minute! Mrs. Kinnard, please be seated.

GIERSHE: . . . whenever I see the children.

SCHIZZINOSO: She wants to consult with you. I suggest you do that.

COHEN: Before I do that, Your Honor, may I inquire as to whether it would be possible for a representative of the Charities to be present at visitation *while* this investigation is going on?

SCHIZZINOSO: NO! I am suspending visitation privileges until the investigation is completed. I already did that.

GIERSHE: But I haven't seen them since November, really, almost nine months . . . except for—

COHEN: I'll discuss this with Mrs. Kinnard. Excuse me. (*Whispering*) Giershe, you have got to shut up! You're not to say a word! Do you understand? (*Giershe's hands are locked together in her lap. The knuckles gleam white. Cohen pushes his clipboard against her shoulder. He dips his head. His hair is awash in bubbles of perspiration. "But it's all so cockeyed. You and the Judge, you're crazy, both of you"*) Mrs. Kinnard— She points out, of course, she came at great expense, and she has a typing job which just barely pays her living expenses here, and I wonder if we might have some idea, Your Honor, as to how long this investigation and this suspension would take.

SCHIZZINOSO: I can't tell you. They'll get at it as is convenient.

COHEN: Yes, Your Honor. Incidentally, Mrs. Kinnard advises me that she categorically denies this charge.

SCHIZZINOSO: I WANT FURTHER INVESTIGATION ON IT!

COHEN: Yes, Your Honor. There is another element, Your Honor, which I wish they would investigate. I understand there is some charge that she has attempted to interfere with the children's religious beliefs, the Catholic belief.

SCHIZZINOSO: There is something in the letter. I think from what I've seen of the family life of this case it would seem to me that *some religious training* would be of great help to these children. But we're not concerned with that. We're more concerned with the more *serious* aspect.

COHEN: Mrs. Kinnard says she has encouraged the children to follow
           their religion.

SCHIZZINOSO: Dismissed.

>>>>>

Mr. Lewis Cohen, Counselor at Law, took Giershe's elbow in his tight
fingers and led, pushed her down the courthouse steps, walked fast to the
corner, and across the street to his black Cadillac, which was parked in a no-
parking zone. He opened the door, roughly released his hold, waited impa-
tiently for her to pull in her limbs, slammed the door, and ripped the ticket
from his windshield and sailed it into the street.

He threw himself behind the wheel and roared up the engine like a
teenager on cruise night. He narrowly missed the parcel post truck in the
right-hand lane of traffic, and, gripping the wheel with his whole body, did
fifty in a fifteen-mile-an-hour zone, spinning around corners and throwing
Giershe from side to side like a bag of laundry. Once out of town, he drove
ninety miles an hour until he found a fancy bar open at eleven in the morning. He braked his big toy at the bar's door. The engine died and Cohen
hugged the wheel tightly, his face turned towards Giershe, the sad brown
eyes blank and misty.

"Feel bad?" Giershe asked kindly, although she felt something more like
pity.

"Come on! Let's go get refreshed!"

Giershe followed him through the front door into a large dark room
with windows looking onto an inner garden of groping ferns sprinkled eter-
nally with water from a Cupid fountain. Water spurted from granite mouths
and penises; a stone maiden with mouth open was having a drink beneath the
legs of the center angel.

"Hello, Mary. This is Mrs. Kinnard. I want six scotches in a line, right
here in front of me, and I want them as fast as you can bring them."

The waitress placed her hand on his neck. "It's only eleven o' clock. Had
a bad day already?"

"The worst! Schizzinoso. Giershe, what do you want? The same?"

"You can line up mine too. But I'll have a Shirley Temple and an iced coffee with gobs of cream."

Cohen stared at her. "Don't you *ever* drink?"

"Yes, sometimes. With friends. I don't mean you are not one. I just don't
feel like drinking. I have to get through the day."

"Exactly."

"Lewis—it's hard to use your first name, you're so fierce. Lewis, do you enjoy your profession?"

"Goddammit! Of course I enjoy it! I *love* being made a fool of and toadying before ignorant asses and getting chopped up like a piece of meat! I can scarcely wait to rise in the morning and keep my appointments with beasts in black robes."

"Do you know anything about Darrow?"

"Christ, Giershe, you're such a fool! This is 1964, not 1905. I live in a snarled web of favors and loyalties which I have to think about. I can't just go into court and give speeches. I'd spend the rest of my life in jail for contempt of court."

"But the things you say in court don't even make sense in *your* terms. What was that stuff about play therapy? The children were not misquoted. Why did you imply that they might have been? And why don't you guys ever express outrage? Don't you feel it?"

"I thought I brought up some good points."

"Whatever made you say I had said that I've always encouraged them to follow their religion? I *never* said that. The reverse. I think I said I don't knock it. I fear future perjury because of your misrepresenting me for reasons of your own."

"Would you care to represent yourself?"

"Come now, it's long past that, and you know it. There's nothing much you can do for me except tidy up. You won't lift your eyes to a higher justice. You won't allow yourself to cut through the snarls. You want to play by the rules. I'm not accusing, I guess I'm just sorry. I don't like to see a delightful man crushed by a cranky old ass."

Cohen was starting on his third drink. "Giershe, it's going to take time. It's a very crazy case, the strangest I've ever had. There's something about you and your effect on judges that I don't understand. I'm trying my best and it isn't working. You must be patient. I can't believe that this can go on much longer." He was pleading with Giershe for time, and she knew she wasn't going to give it. She had seen him cringe, had heard him say "Your Honor" to a fathead, again and again. If he was Connecticut's bravest and finest—

"Giershe, you must not do anything rash. YOU MUST NOT!"

"I don't think you can advise me on rash acts. I'm trying to get advice from California, and when I do, I'll let you know what I'm planning. There's no need to talk with you about any of it. You're too much a part of Connecticut's strange ways."

"You're very composed. You must be onto some different track. I can see it, in the way you talk to me. Last week I was your white hope. Today, you're treating me as though I have six thumbs and am feebleminded. But I'm telling you that I'm not going to give up and I'm going to continue to fight this thing and get results."

Giershe said nothing. She felt, as she had felt so many times in the past, that the requirements for full manhood, laid on by society, were impossible to fulfill. Achieve, perform, know, be kind, be tough, be tender, don't cry, win every hour of the day, provide for your family, tip the waitress, open doors, screw, compete, stay young and vigorous, make money, set an example, repair the screen door, fix the faucet. She felt sorry he hadn't won his latest contest. He needed to win, perhaps as much as she did.

>>>>>

DON'T SAY IT, WRITE IT!

From: Mr. Lewis Cohen   July 24, '64
To: Mrs. Giershe Kinnard, YWCA, New Haven

ENCLOSED PLEASE FIND TRANSCRIPT OF SCHIZZI-
NOSO APPEARANCE. SAVE IT FOR THE BOOK WE SHALL
WRITE WHEN THIS IS OVER.

>>>>>

YWCA, July 28.64

DEAREST—

The radio still bleats that the boys are not found, and morbid-ly I dream of their bodies in the mud, gouged, beaten, shot, and their parents waiting for—for what? Waiting, because human beings are capable of believing in reversal, which they call Miracle.

I play a game. I lie on my bed in the YWCA. I move up and out. Soon I am on the roof, looking around me at New Haven and all its beauty and decay. Then I move on up until I can see Centerville to the west and the house where abide my Olivia and Tony. I climb until I'm in a nonplace which allows me to exist as a dot in human time and space. I now see the world as sphere. There is no New Haven, no Centerville, or Berkeley, only me, and far away, the gray-green ball. And while I'm a-settin' up there, I notice that romantic agony does not exist. All male part-ners coalesce into a decorative blob of matter, not an essential part of the picture. You are exchangeable and expendable. If not you, then someone else. You are not prime, but *I* am, because I am the viewer. After me, who else? Olivia and Tony. In their lives, David and I are replaceable. But they are not, in *my* life. I gave them birth and they come from me. I can't let them go any more than I can let go of my left hand, or my eyes. It has to do with time, my time on earth. What must I do with this time? Care for them, and do whatever work only I can do, whatever that be. Then I dive back to my cot in the YWCA, and I remember that you've expressed this to me, guardedly, for you knew I would think you were spitting on the romantic vision of our love. You feel the same regard for Andrew. It is blood, a thing of genes. He is your charge and friend as long as you both live. The women may come and go in greater or less pleasure. They are not finally important. I love you, dearest Jack.

When Cohen calls today, I'll tell him my new plan. Flowing black cape, shapeless black garment, black shoes and stockings, black head covering. Steps of New Haven courthouse, a sorrowing C-shape, woman in mourning there from sunup to sundown, weeping for her children. The Press. I've become something more than an anarchist. Gangster. A gangster can't love, be fair, or of use to you. Gangsters just hate.

Your Giershe

MOLLY GAVIN'S DIARY.
JULY 29, 1964
CABIN

Harry down the lake early to send telegram to Giershe saying we will send the bond money so that G. can see children without guards. Colder, some wind. While I was resting in our cozy bedroom, my dear Harry came and surprised me—surprised us both!

NEW YORK TIMES
AUGUST 4, 1964
FBI FINDS 3 BODIES BELIEVED TO BE RIGHTS WORKERS;
GRAVES AT A DAM

>>>>

YWCA, Aug. 5.64

DEAREST JACK—

Be patient with me. I still talk about Olivia and Tony with anyone who will listen. I feel I'm recalling two dead children. All the dear things I find to say about them are at least a year away in time.

Cohen just called. Schizzinoso is back from vacation! He meets tomorrow with Poltroono at nine. We have a hearing scheduled for Friday. We're moving again. Love you.

Giershe

>>>>

NEW YORK TIMES
AUGUST 5, 1964
FAMILIES OF RIGHTS WORKERS VOICE GRIEF AND HOPE

18

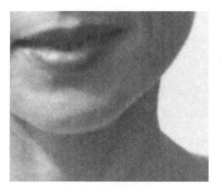

"It's too late to correct it,"

said the Red Queen.

"When you've once

said a thing, that fixes it,

and you must take

the consequences."

O N FRIDAY EVENING, Giershe and Lenny Kampfer ate dinner together at Napoli Cafe, ten miles north of New Haven. They were careful to choose a different place each time they met, and if Giershe forgot to be cautious, Lenny always reminded her of the rules which must be followed. "Your car is out in front. You were supposed to park two miles south of here, and wait for me to pick you up."

"Oh Lenny, I'm sorry. I'm fuzzy today. I promise to remember next time." She smiled at him. He looked so disappointed in her.

"It's okay this time. *I* parked some distance away and walked. So, what happened at the hearing?"

"Seems I'm not guilty of perversion but now there's divided visitation. The Solomon decision. They are clever, imaginative even. I see only one child each visit. And Cohen was idiotic in front of Schizzinoso. They repeated and repeated themselves, and they don't make much sense. I can attend Olivia's party for one hour, and I think I trapped myself in perjury. I'm not sure."

"How did you do that?"

"I said one thing last February, and another thing to Poltroono in court today. About whether or not I go to church."

Lenny studied the menu. He always chose what she would eat, trying to fatten her, convinced that food would restore the "fresh beauty" he remembered from Germany. He liked good food, and nothing could prevent his enjoyment of thick steaks, green salad, Prinzregenten tortes, and ice cream. "I'm going to order two veal plates and I want you to try to eat. If possible, it's a good idea to avoid perjury, but it doesn't matter. Don't worry about it. You can lie, but don't lie so that on internal evidence you can be trapped. Anything you say about religion is probably going to be a lie, and I think Cohen should protect you from all such questions. Why is he getting paid? Did Ratch bring up religion?"

"Cohen led me into it. He . . ."

"Never mind, I can see that you're very tired. So, you're going to see Olivia tomorrow? Is there any way I could meet her? Perhaps not meet her, that would be too dangerous. But observe her. When we snatch them, I don't want her to be frightened, and if she's at least seen me, in a friendly setting, she would be less alarmed."

"I thought I'd take her to the Morgan Museum tomorrow to see the dinosaurs. You could be there, make a kindly comment to the darling little girl, without introduction. And pretend not to know me. Would that work?"

"Good idea. Then tomorrow night, we should case the area around the house. I bought walkie-talkies. We'll try to determine the broadcast distance they're capable of. They might be put to use."

"You're a goof! I'd mess it up somehow. I like it though, like a Marx Brothers movie. Oh Lenny, I'm very lucky to . . ." Giershe's eyes filled. Lenny placed his hand tenderly on hers.

"Listen, I checked on a pleasant place to stay, just a few miles from here. Tonight. You don't want to spend the night before Olivia's party at the Y, do you?"

She pulled her hand from his and let it sit in her lap. "Yes, I do. I want to wash my hair, press something fresh and pretty, wrap a few presents, and write her all my feelings about her. I want to be at the Y, above suspicion."

The waitress brought their dinners and Lenny carefully unfolded the red cloth napkin and placed it in his lap. Giershe stared at her food, wondering if she was going to throw up. Lenny always ate too fast, shoveling the food into his mouth, watching the plate as he took a bite, thinking about the next bite. She stared out the window. The veal smelled dead. The rice with brown gravy looked like brains lying in mud.

"Sh'good, very good. Try it, just a few bites." He wiped his chin, but missed a patch of grease on his left cheek. She gazed at the shiny spot. His skin was so white, and black hairs curled at his throat. They looked like daddy longlegs crawling out of his shirt. She was dizzy. The fumes, the noise of chattering eaters.

"I talked with Sid and Rafaela this week. They want to come down next weekend to help us plan. I told them I'd discuss it with you and you would call them. Next week is full moon, and we'll be able to see clearly what spots can be obscured from the house. The following week, with less moon, will probably be the best time to go for broke. Giershe, tomorrow night, after we try the walkie-talkies, I hope you'll be willing to go with me out of the city, for a rest. You looked so much better after Cape Cod."

"Lenny, you cannot take care of me."

"I can try, can't I? We walked on the beach, we laughed and lay in the sun, and you did me the great honor of letting me make love to you. In the morning you were calm and rested."

"In the morning I hated myself *and* you! I growled over breakfast and poked nasty fun at all the other bodies stoking themselves with dripping, revolting pancakes and slimy butter. I didn't *let* you make love to me, as you put it. I wanted to, the night before, and in the morning all feeling for you was gone, temporarily, *even* friendship. Is that what you want again? Lenny, try to *see* me. I'm a miserable woman, almost insane, hanging on. You're seeing a laughing woman beside the Isar. This zhlub you see at this table gets through each day by will, not grace."

Hurt in his eyes. Brown, brown eyes. "I can take you out of the city, and not make love to you. It would be good for you."

"Oh fine. I lie in one bed and you in another. We pay for two beds. I lie awake feeling bad because you're feeling bad. Marvelous!"

"I'll snore for you. Then you'll know I'm not lying there hungering for you."

Suddenly it all seemed comical and they clasped hands over the cold plates and rocked back and forth. People stared and that made them laugh more and more.

"Wipe your face! Disgusting grease all over it!"

Lenny whipped the red napkin out of his lap. A corner trailed in the gravy. He wiped his face like Putzi Hanfstaengl, bloated Nazi aesthete, then pretended to dip manicured fingers in an imaginary finger bowl.

"Oh lawsy! Now you have gravy all over your face. Go take a bath in the rest room."

"That bad?" He dipped the napkin in ice water and rubbed his face again. They sat silent, staring at each other.

"Giershe! I'VE GOT IT!"

"Got what?"

He was emptying his pockets, searching for dimes and nickels, which he put carefully on the table. "Ratch! His first name? Ronald? I'm almost sure. Lives in Hartford. I've been trying to remember for weeks. I'm almost sure. The bastard!"

"*What* do you remember?"

"I'm almost sure he's the bastard in Germany who testified against me for calling U.S. agents fascists and nearly got me court-martialed! There couldn't be two of them. I'm going to call him."

"You're not!"

"Oh, don't worry. No connections made. I just want to make sure. Come on, there's a phone in the lobby. Never mind the check. We'll come back for dessert. Ice cream."

Giershe scurried after Lenny, who was lunging towards the lobby, his big feet leading, his hands still searching his pockets for change. He flipped through the Hartford telephone book, found a number and dialed, listened, put money in the little hole and waited. He smiled at Giershe.

"Hello? Yes? Hello—does a Ronald Ratch live there? Yes, I'll wait."

"He's married, I think."

"Yes, is this Ronald Ratch? . . . Well, well, this is Lenny Kampfer. . . . Yes, the same—from Germany days . . . . Yes, I ran into Harold the other day and he told me he thought you were getting rich in practice in Hartford. I thought I'd call and say hello. . . . Yeah. I'm calling from Boston. . . . I'm getting my degree and teaching— What? . . . Well sure, are you ever up this way? . . . No, once in a while I'm in New Haven, but not often. . . . No, I've not seen Roy, but I heard he'd dropped out, into the Village. . . . How's the law? Pretty lucrative? . . . Yes, well, it takes time. . . . Sure, I'd be glad to. I'm in the book. Just call me and we'll have dinner. . . . No, no I scraped by that one. They knew they didn't have anything on me. . . . Oh you did, did you? I've got better things to do than get shot in the South. . . . Well, nice talking with you and I'm glad you're doing so well. Clients pay on time? . . . No, I wouldn't think a domestic case would bring much money, but interesting, eh? . . . Yes, I shall. Good-bye." Lenny banged down the receiver.

"The same?"

"The same. We slept in the same quarters for three lousy years. He's lucky he came out in one piece. An informer, a fink, a prig, a Catholic inquisitor. Sometimes it seems like there are only about twenty-five people in the whole world, and I keep running into them over and over. Do you ever get that feeling?"

>>>>>

GIERSHE'S DIARY:
AUGUST 10, 1964
OLIVIA'S PARTY

We went to Morgan Museum. It was heaven to have her by my side. So beautiful, so grown-up, so friendly I gave her pearls, a little knife for Tony, a brass candlestick. She read her letters from Elizabeth, Molly, and Harry. We chattered. We went to the top floor of the museum and a very nice man, with brown eyes, sad and serious, asked her if she was enjoying herself. She said: "Yes, I'm with my mommy." He smiled at her and looked up at the huge Tyrannosaurus rex.

She strutted down the street and showed me how you walk when you're going downhill. She pushed out her stomach. We ran and had fun. We rode back to Centerville for her party and she said, "We'll get to the party in time, I promise you!"

Back home, Olivia was gravely excited, Tony somewhat feverish. We went to their bedroom and I collapsed on the bed. I listened as Olivia gave a lesson to Tony on saying "remember" and not "berember." He said he had a headache but kept on with the lesson. Docile. She's a fine teacher. We went downstairs. Olivia was dressed all in white and she asked that I stay close by. I discovered Ralph Groper and was furious. I asked him to go into the kitchen. It was rude, yes, yes. In the kitchen David said that all the claims against me had been substantiated in court. Groper spoke of his "conscience."

>>———>>———

YWCA, Aug. 11.64

DEAR JACK—

A long time ago, when Olivia was suffering from having a younger brother, you told me you thought Andrew should be allowed to grow up without interference from a sibling. Now, perhaps, it may only be possible to take Olivia and leave Tony behind. She takes care of him. She keeps his head on. At day camp, she collects and distributes his lunch, sees that he gets dressed and ready to leave and that all of his belongings are in her satchel. She propels him to the bus. He's the most helpless almost-four I've yet to see. He's dominated at school and at home, however gently. He drifts as others pull him. Peaceman feels I'd be in a better position with both children and Lenny says that some time after August 12 he will absolutely snatch two children. The thing is beyond figuring.

love
Giershe

Berkeley
August 17.64

DEAREST GIERSHE—

I spoke with Molly and she said she is heartily in favor of your current plans. She's now more radical than you. Only one exciting moment since last writing. Andrew was playing with Alan while he was shaving. Alan is six foot six so Andrew can walk through his legs. During one of these transits, he bit down on the head of his penis. Alan screamed, fell to the floor, sobbed out: "Andrew! You rat fink!" Andrew rushed down the hall white as a sheet and jumped into my lap, Alan crawling after him. I prevented mayhem, calmed them both, and prevailed upon Alan to see the macabre humor of it. Finally, when he was able to ask Andrew why he did it, Andrew said: "It's just my nature."

Kisses,
Jack

YWCA, Aug. 18.64

DEAREST—

I don't like this game Lenny and I are playing. Lenny shows no sign of hurry or nerves. The night in the graveyard when the police spotted us with our space-phones, we both ran, but he ran calmly and I ran like Dillinger, expecting to be shot in the back.

I'm so vexed with having someone love me. Truly, being loved is unbearable and the one who loves is in a moronic state. I hiss at Lenny and he usually rebounds by going into some kind of training for the Event. Looks like Saturday is going to be the big day. I am determined to take Olivia on that day—but shall try to get the whole booty. We are ready—the Freemans, the two of us, space-phones. Could you do this? I'm too nervous to write more.

love
Giershe

>>>——>

GIERSHE'S DIARY.
AUGUST 19, 1964
SOLOMON VISITATION DAY

I took Tony to the lake nearby for the full time. He was ever so precise about spreading the towel on the sand, keeping neat, taking sand out of his shoes. He said, with his little hand outstretched in gesture: "The trouble with Santa Claus is that he *only* knows about toys. He doesn't know anything about *people.*" Once he said: "I promise you!" "What are promises?" "What you said *before.*" He pooped on the beach and asked: "Mommy, why don't girls poop?"

"They do. Don't you know any who do?"

"Olivia is the only girl I know who poops. I don't think other girls do." It grew cold. We sat in the car and I gave him another installment of Floppy Ears. Lousy visitation conditions. There's no place to go to get away from going someplace.

>———>———>———

YWCA
August 20.64

DEAREST—

Tension near madness. I'm not sure I can do it. Both children were with me today. A mysterious change. The housekeeper didn't follow us when we took a walk. This suggests there's a detective watching me.

Last night with manic Cohen. He shouted at me and I threatened to walk out. He apologized and we settled down to reset the patterns. He told me Judge Doyle has been doing some thinking about the sex aspects of this case, and more or less believes the charges against David. He's talking of a FOSTER HOME. I've *got* to act on Saturday. Cohen says wait a while, but I think not. Can't.

Can you pray?
Giershe

Berkeley, Aug. 16.64

DEAREST!

I know you are ready. Good luck. Don't panic. Be a winner!

I LOVE YOU
Jack

>———>———>———

MAY 15, 1979

"Hello? Lenny? I need your help. I've been writing and writing for months with no trouble at all, and I'm at the heist. I *cannot* remember what happened."

"I don't understand. Of course you remember. We picked up the kids from the backyard, drove to Boston—"

"No, I don't mean that. Of course I remember that. But it's like sitting in a room with a lot of money after planning to rob a bank. Here's all this money spilling out of boxes and there's a memory of a plan, but blank where action should be. I know you were driving the car, and that you picked up Olivia, but was Rafaela there? I have a faint recall, but nothing definite. Something about Crestline Motel and the night before."

"The night before the heist we checked into—you and Rafaela checked into—the Crestline Motel. I slept in my car. Rafaela and I worried about you all the next day because you were in a trance, like a sleepwalker. But that didn't matter. We rented a car, a gray Valiant."

"I think I remember that car. Did we use my name, my real name?"

"Yes, I believe so. Does it matter?"

"I want to remember. We must have used my name for the car and the motel, to protect you and Rafaela."

"Right. We parked your Chrysler on a road heading out of Centerville in a direction we did not plan to take after the heist, and left it there. Rafaela, I think she spent the day with Sid at Whitfield. I'm not too sure. You and I went to see Cohen."

"We did?"

"You must remember that! He stopped all incoming calls, locked his office door, and the two of you sat staring at each other for about fifteen minutes. He pulled his chair up to yours and held your hand. Every time you or I started to say something, he said 'Sh-h,' so you just sat. For a talky fellow, that day he had damn little to say. I wandered around the office getting nervous. I guess I thought we might get arrested for *thinking*."

"It's coming back to me, that part of it, anyway. I stood up and put out my hand to say good-bye and that crazy mensch hugged me and the tears came down his cheeks."

"Right. And then you started to cry, and I thought *I* would cry, and I headed for the door and he broke from you and shook my hand. I don't remember that anyone said anything except 'Good-bye.' He knew you were taking all the risks he'd been too chicken to take. I don't know, who knows what he was thinking?"

"He was probably crying in relief at getting rid of me."

"More like he was crying for the death of his soul. And I know he was genuinely fond of you. He told me so enough times. But he just couldn't seem to do anything but shuffle papers around and yell at secretaries. So, are you beginning to remember now?"

"Wait, don't go away. How did we all get together again?"

"We knew the kids would return from camp about four o'clock, that it would be hot in the house, and they'd probably be out in the yard soon after they returned. When we reconnected with Rafaela, she told us David wasn't at Whitfield and that she'd driven around the block and his car wasn't parked in the driveway or in front of the house."

"Where did we all meet?"

"We kept the Crestline Motel room."

"We did? Did we think we might have to stay another night? It must have been *expensive*."

"You really don't remember, do you? It was a dump. You ladies had the best room in the joint for three dollars a night, and I think you were their only customers."

"Then what? This is the part that's a total blank."

"You and I, in the rented car, parked near the grocery store in the rear. We could see—"

"We could see down that path around the side. We could just barely see the swing set at the rear of David's backyard."

"Not *we*. I sat in the driver's seat with my spook hat on, and took an alligator nap, one eye open. You were lying on the floor in the backseat, under a blanket. Out in the air it was about ninety-five degrees and I was afraid you'd pass out. The plan was for Rafaela to watch from a block or so away and drive to us if she saw David's car, and for me to signal to you when I saw two children out in the yard. We hoped both would be there, but I think we had agreed to wait only a few minutes if just one appeared—no—"

"I'm not sure on that either. I know we had decided that if they appeared, I would pick up Tony and you would lead Olivia by the hand."

"You got it. That's just what we did. My car was parked ten miles out on the road we'd chosen. We cut on out of town, I switched hats and put on my blue sailing cap. Rafaela met us at the car, my car."

"It's coming back. I think I can write it now. I'm going to have to reconstruct it from your memory, and Rafaela's, but I think I can do that. Lenny, thank you. When will you get out my way?"

"Not this summer, maybe next. Call me if you have other questions. I'm not likely to forget my finest hour. Afterwards, I was sorely tempted to give up scholarship and hire out as a child snatcher at ten thousand dollars per job. Pay in advance."

>>>>

MAY 16, 1979

"Hello? Rafaela? This is Giershe! Yes, yes, the same!"

"Giershe! I can't believe it. How many years?"

"Oh, countless. I'm calling long distance from California."

"Are you all right?"

"Perfect. Everyone is just fine. Right now I'm writing a book about all that mess and I've reached the part about the removal of the kids from Centerville and I'm trying to remember *exactly* what happened. My memory doesn't cooperate and I'm hoping you can help. I talked with Lenny yesterday but I still have some questions."

"A book! Wonderful! Is it truth or fiction?"

"It's not *Rashomon*. It's my point of view, for the most part, but the part you played is hard to remember. Do you have the time right now?"

"Shit yes. Oh, I've missed you! Let's see, that summer we were in Provincetown. I know I drove to Centerville twice, alone, while Sid or someone took care of the kid. I can remember the long drive very well. One of those times I met you and Lenny. I don't remember where we met, but I got there late at night and we signed into a motel."

"Two times? I certainly put you to a lot of trouble."

"Yes, you did. But we were passionate to help bring forth justice from its hiding place. We would have helped even if you hadn't asked. As a matter of fact, I don't think you did. In the motel, on that first visit, you and I had a room and Lenny had a room."

"He says he slept in his car."

"Maybe he did. The three of us talked about the plan and then Lenny left. You and I got ready for bed. Then you said you would go talk with Lenny for a while. I can remember lying on my bed and thinking to myself that you and Lenny were lovers and asking myself what I thought about that."

"We weren't, at that point."

"Then the next day, you and Lenny drove together and I followed you. At some point, he pulled over, and I did the same. You got out, and you were laughing and breathless, like a TV ad, and you asked if I was listening to the Brandenburg Concerto on the radio. You said you were and it was great! Then you went back to your car."

"Yes! I remember that. Then what happened?"

"I know it was a beautiful day and I thought to myself: 'This is crazy! Here I am following these two nuts to help steal kids, and we are zipping along and Giershe wants to know what I've got on the radio.' Then I remember sitting for a long time in my car on a side street in Centerville, and it was *very* depressing. The time inched along. It was lonely. Finally you came and said that the kids had not come out of their house. So I drove all the way back to Provincetown swearing I wouldn't do it again."

"Oh, poor Rafaela! And you say you came a second time?"

"Yes, and once again I waited on a side street. I had a hat so people wouldn't recognize me. You and Lenny had a rented car and I was to be ready to drive you to another car, or something. Seemed like there were three or four cars. But you didn't use me at all, really. I remember thinking, 'I've been here twice. It has happened without me, even though I'm here.' Have I helped any?"

"Yes, this minute and back then so long ago. As soon as I hang up, I'm going to write you a long letter bringing you up to date. Are you still with Sid?"

"Oh yes. Neither of us knows quite why. Habit, I guess. The kids are fine. Something else occurs to me. You had a talent for attracting defenders. You were blond, good-looking, tall, thin, idealistic, and a bit kooky. Probably if you'd been short and fat your knights and courtiers would have been fewer. Anyhow, your need for help was real. So was the kids'. And your quality as a person made it easier to lend support. Shit, I hope you tell it straight. Quite a story. Did I tell you I'm getting my Ph.D.? I'm good at research, that's why. You'll write us soon? I'll be waiting."

"Bye. Give my love to Sid. Damn the distance!"

＞＞＞＞

"Giershe—" Lenny's voice was low and calm.

"Yes?"

"It's six-thirty. Are they still likely to come out? We've been here an hour. The grocery has closed. Might they go out in front, rather than in the back-yard?"

"No. They're not allowed out front." Giershe came up for air, blinking in the light.

"Down! I can see— It looks like Tony. He's got a Popsicle or something and he's dawdling on the grass. Here comes Olivia. She's going to the swing! Giershe, steady now. I'm going to count slowly to five. When I say 'five,' you get out first, and *walk* to the backyard. I'll be right behind you. Remember, I take Olivia. You pick up Tony. One . . . two . . . three—wait! Housekeeper at the back door. She's gone. Begin again. One . . . two . . . three . . . four . . . five!"

Giershe's heart beat on her chest. Her sandals tangled in the blanket. She opened the car door and stepped out onto the hot asphalt barefoot, per-spiration dripping from her hair into her eyes and mouth, salty sour taste. She walked down the path to one side of the grocery, a route she had taken a thousand times before. She was on fire with fear, her tongue swollen and dry. She felt Lenny behind her.

"I'm here . . . steady . . ." His voice was now urgent. She squeezed through the hole in the fence.

"Tony." She bent over him, hesitated.

"Mommy!" He smiled and turned towards the house. She scooped him up into her arms and walked him to the fence.

"Go through. Fast! Go! I'm right behind you."

He scuttled through. Again she picked up the solid brown flesh and ran with her bundle to the Valiant, Olivia and Lenny on her heels. She held the door open for them.

"In! Under the blanket. I'm coming too!" She tumbled in after them, their bodies all mixed up together. "Down, sweeties! Down! Stay with me *under* the blanket!"

"We going to California?"

"Quiet, Tony! Be quiet. Mommy said get your head down."

"But we going to California? Who's that man? Where we going, Mommy?"

The car was moving, slowly, and when it began to pick up speed, Giershe put her arms around the children. They huddled close to her, both of them smiling.

"Calling, calling, front to backseat, front to backseat? Are you there?" Lenny spoke over an imaginary space-phone. Tony tried to stand up to see the man with the voice.

"Tony, get down. Listen, I'll answer. Calling, calling, back to front seat, back to front seat. We're here. Tony, Olivia, Giershe."

"I want to see that man. Are we in an airplane?"

"You'll see him later. I'll tell you when you can look. He's a friend, and he's helping me take you to California. I can't tell you his name. He doesn't have a name. Let's just call him 'Front Seat.'"

Olivia let out her wonderful giggle.

"Mommy, you're all wet. Sticky wet. It's *hot* under this blanket!"

"Don't complain, Tony. *I've* been under this blanket for an *hour*, waiting for you to come out of the house. What took you so long?"

"But Mommy," Olivia pleaded, "we didn't *know* you were waiting."

"*I* knew she was waiting. She told me but I forgot to berember."

"Tony, you're a liar. She didn't tell you anything!"

"Calling, calling, front to backseat, front to backseat. Get ready to change profile. Pulling alongside change vehicle."

"Okay, kids. The car is going to stop. We're going to get out and get into another car. You must get into the backseat and get down flat again. I'll be there too. We have to stay down until it gets dark. Ready? Let's go!"

Giershe led the children from under the blanket and held the door for them while they flattened themselves onto the worn floor of Lenny's clunker. Lenny started the engine and turned on the radio for news. Bach! *Erfreue dich, mein Herz, denn itzoweicht der Schmerz . . .* She breathed the air and lingered outside a moment, looking across fields of tobacco plants. Beneath the shade of a tree, Rafaela sat in her car. She waved a hand from the window. Giershe looked at Lenny. He nodded. She ran to Rafaela. "Rafaela! Bach is on the radio. Turn it on! Thank you—thank you." They awkwardly hugged through the driver's window. She ran back to Lenny's car and climbed in. He swung the car around and stopped near Rafaela.

"Could you call the car-rental place and tell them where they can find their car?"

"Okay. Aren't we fantastic? *Arrivederci!*" Red hair falling over one eye, she waved and drove off towards Centerville.

Lenny drove steadily, by back roads, until they crossed the border into Massachusetts. It was almost dark and they stopped to buy milk shakes and hamburgers. They spread napkins and ate in the car, the children bouncing up and down on the backseat. They listened for news broadcasts, expecting to hear that two children had been stolen from a backyard in Connecticut, but the news was of auto accidents, the heat, Johnson's quarrels with Congress. The children called Lenny "Front Seat" and laughed at its silly sound, until it no longer seemed strange.

Lenny's old car carried them swiftly to his garden apartment near Harvard. Honeysuckle, ferns, moist rich smells. Wearily, they stood in the middle of his room. He opened the windows and closed the curtains. "The children can sleep in my bed." Tony and Olivia looked around the room, their heads wobbling. Giershe took off their clothes for them, and realized they had no clean clothes to put on in the morning. It didn't matter.

"Will you stay in this room with us, Mommy?" Olivia asked.

"Yes. Go to sleep." Giershe looked at Lenny.

"Giershe, it's all right. We've done our job. You don't have to think of things to say to me. I'm going to have a drink and then take a walk. I'll sleep in the car." His face was haggard, his sad eyes drooping, the white skin in the soft light gleamed with sweat.

"Lenny—I—" How could words tell him? She wanted to flutter her wings over the children and close her eyes.

"Never mind, I know. Go to sleep."

He went into the bathroom and came out with his bathrobe for her to put on. She lay down beside Olivia and Tony, one arm flung over their bodies, and slept.

19 →

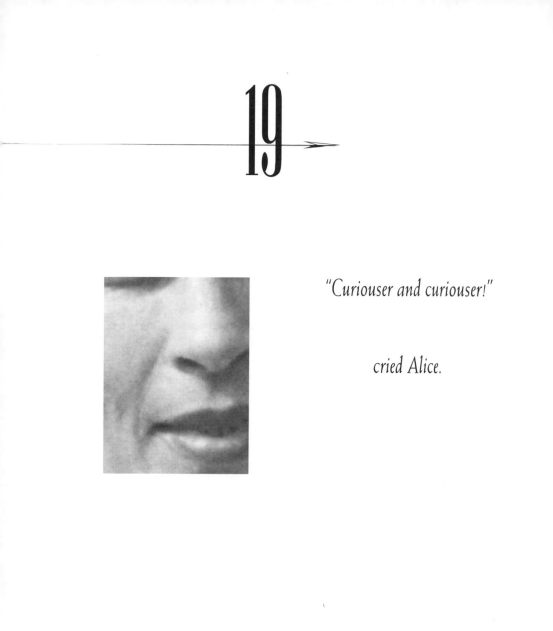

"*Curiouser and curiouser!*"

cried Alice.

N THE MONTH OF SEPTEMBER, Giershe did her best to assume an aspect of normal, busy schedule. She opened a second class at the temple, talked with parents and school board, led study groups, gave speeches. She enrolled Olivia in a public school near the Gavins' new home. Harry drove her to school each morning and was there at the close of school each day to escort her home. He didn't like this responsibility and grumbled at having to spend his retirement years in child care. Molly scolded him each time he complained. Tony went to school with Giershe and did his best to reverse the curriculum. Again and again she heard his voice, high and insistent: "She is *not* Giershe Kinnard! She's my Mommy! Her name is Mommy!"

At two o'clock each day, Giershe would lock the school's doors, drive to the Gavins' to pick up Olivia, then drive to her "secure" house. But it wasn't secure. There was no safety possible as long as David was living his life on earth somewhere. There was a churning ball of undigested food in her stomach which sent hot gas into her mouth. If the children were outside in the lovely backyard, she could not stay inside. She piled up her work and carted it outside. If the telephone rang, she let it ring. If the doorbell rang, her heart jumped in her chest and she found a place in the kitchen where she could view the visitor without being seen. Tony and Olivia knew they were being guarded, wherever they were, awake or asleep, and seemed to be quite used to it and take it for granted.

At night, after the children were in bed, Giershe closed all the curtains, locked the doors, and tried to settle her stomach with long hot baths, warm milk, and Ovaltine. She played a game of extracting each thought in her head and discarding it until her mind was empty. She tried to fill up again with tranquil images—sunlight on mountain streams, baby cheeks, sandpipers ducking under the surf, blue violets in a clay pot. When all the cars were tucked into garages and house lights turned off throughout the neighborhood, she could begin to expect a tap at the kitchen door. One last look at the children, a kiss on Tony's fat cheek, pull up Olivia's cover but do not touch her lest she awaken, close their door softly, walk through a dark kitchen, turn the key, open the door for Jack, the night-stealth on him, his cap pulled down above a grinning face. Two big steps into darkness, press his cold face to hers, feel his hands walking down her back, over her bottom, inside her bathrobe, cold hands on feverish flesh, smile foolishly, hug and hug. Talk, light a candle, heat warm milk and whiskey, set the alarm for 4:30 A.M., go to bed. Get up, walk around the house or the backyard, pace the kitchen, laugh at their predicament—or rant (quietly)—stalk the impossible future, peek at sleeping hostages, wonder at their love's endurance, mix their juices and not wash off the conspiring scents. And when the buzzer went off under their pillow, their warm fingers would tangle together on the knob, and Jack would groan (quietly) and rise up in the darkness, reach for socks, sink down again next to Giershe, kiss her warm breasts, lick her face, pull the covers over her body. In four minutes, he would be gone. Giershe listened, each night, but never heard a footstep or a car engine. She would move over to the warm place he left behind and sleep until Tony climbed onto the bed at six each morning, chattering his dreams at her, bouncing up and down on her stomach.

At six-thirty, the rush began. Urge the children into their clothes. Make breakfast and nag until both children had consumed enough milk and cereal to satisfy Giershe's estimate of minimum early-morning nutrition. Scoop up school items, run to the car, deposit Olivia at her grandparents', drive on to school with a protesting Tony, set up daily environment for her class, pacify Tony while she tried to clear her mind for the influx of students at eight-thirty.

She was aware that her work with her students was not going well. Each day she began anew in the hope that past excellence would carry her forward into the future. The environment was beautiful, the children eager to begin, the parents unaware of inadequacy in her performance. Mary Finley was the only observer who knew that the directress was scattering her talents like a hungry dog who at sight of a biscuit tries all the tricks he knows without pausing to hear a command. She couldn't concentrate and the faces of the children blurred. She rushed through a demonstration, talked when she might have said nothing, and scurried to another child without looking back. She gave commands rather than setting an example of behavior a child could imitate.

Gentle Mary Finley, dressed always in fresh cotton frocks of pastel hue, asked Giershe: "How do you feel it's going? Are you satisfied?" (Answer the question yes or no. If yes, you're lying; if no, you're a failure.) Giershe couldn't make excuses to herself or to Mary. She would not ask for time. To draw on accumulated credit was possible, but Giershe felt she had emptied the account.

After the children had gone home, Mary continued: "Giershe, we need your help. The first class is not going well. The teacher just doesn't have your touch. She's let the room get messy, the children aren't working, the parents are complaining and asking that you put it in order again. The temple people say the children are running wild and the teacher doesn't call them back. We need you as Head Teacher, as well as teacher of this class, and I don't know whether or not you can take on that responsibility." Mary's station wagon was filled with children, and Giershe knew she couldn't delay its departure more than a few minutes. It was tempting to stall. She gazed at Mary's troubled face, the intelligent eyes, and wondered at her aura of dignified competence without imprint of past error. She leaned down to pick a blade of grass. Her hands trembled as she brought it to her mouth. She touched it with her tongue and let it drop to the ground.

"Mary, I can't pretend with you. I've lost *my* touch. I can't bring the other class back into order, nor can I do what I should be doing with my own class. My advice to you, and the school board, is to hope that I can bring my own class up to standard, but not to depend on its happening, and to begin a search immediately for a teacher to replace one or both of us, and perhaps reduce the school again to one classroom."

"I don't believe that you cannot—"

"You *must* believe it. While I'm waiting for the other shoe to drop in Connecticut, and guarding the children, I'm tit-witted. What do you suppose that means? Tit-witted?"

Mary giggled. "I'm sure I don't know. Better ask your father. He always knows things like that." She put her arm around Giershe while they walked together to the car. Giershe felt the tears starting in her throat and heard Tony calling "Mommy!" She turned away from Mary, waved a hand in her direction, and ran back to the grass to pick up Tony.

>———>———>

MOLLY GAVIN'S DIARY:
SEPTEMBER 24, 1964

   Very proud of Harry. He went to Olivia's school at two, and went in for Olivia. She came out and headed towards him. Suddenly there was David, who picked her up and started off fast in the opposite direction. Harry grabbed his shoulder, struck his arm, and he dropped Olivia. She was quiet but cried some over her modeling-clay animals being broken. She wouldn't tell Tony what had happened. We wonder if we should take the children off somewhere. But I am tired!

>———>———>

CHURCH AND LAW STRS.
New Haven, Conn.

Sept. 23, 1964

Dear Mr. Peaceman:
Remember that Mrs. K. cannot come into Connecticut while a warrant is out for her *arrest.* Judge Lodge noted the fact that the

warrant had been issued for violation of *Section 53-26* of the Conn. General Statute. The statute has been construed in *Kuzner v. Police Dept. of City of NY* and refers to "either parent who *decoys* or *forcibly* takes . . ." (It hasn't been used since 1890.) There has to be a lack of consent of parent, and *decoy* or *force*. I would guess that neither such element existed here.

> *Most sincerely,*
> *Lewis Cohen*

Giershe had an arrangement with Elizabeth which provided food for everyone and extra cash for Giershe. Elizabeth paid ten dollars a week, and arrived every night at the house to eat dinner with her niece, nephew, and sister. There was really no "extra cash." Giershe had long since discovered that she must pay rent and utilities when due, take anything offered by parents and friends that one could safely eat, and if there was anything left in the checking account, pay whichever lawyer yelled the loudest, *if* he was working closest to the heart of her case. But Giershe liked cooking a meal for another adult and sitting down like a family, with candles on the table, at six P.M. Tony and Olivia helped prepare the food and set the table. They awaited Elizabeth's arrival each evening, climbed into her lap, fought for her attention, and vied with each other to see who could tell her the most interesting detail of the day. The contract of money for timed services enabled the sisters to avoid the unpleasant investigation of mood. Elizabeth liked to eat, often and in ample quantity; it was a pleasure to cook for her.

On the evening of September 25, Giershe prepared spaghetti and meatballs, which she hated. Her family ate heartily, with seconds, while she pushed the red worms around on her plate. Tony and Olivia helped clear away the plates and they all sat down again at the table to eat slices of watermelon with vanilla ice cream. Tony said: "This is my *most* favorite dinner!" and Olivia said: "It can't be your most favorite. Favorite means *most* already." Elizabeth laughed and hugged Olivia. Giershe sipped her coffee and watched the candles burning low. They had closed the curtains in the dining room as they did every evening. They told each other they did this so that they could light candles, but each knew they feared being observed from the street.

"Come along, kids, time for your bath. Elizabeth has an engagement and if you want her to say good night to you, you'd better hurry it up." Giershe turned on the lights and was blowing out the candles when the doorbell rang. Tony ran to the front door. Elizabeth spoke sharply: "Tony! NO! Don't open the door!" Olivia grabbed hold of Giershe's jeans, her head against a rigid thigh. Elizabeth turned on the porch light and looked out through a crack between window frame and curtain.

"Two cops and David," she said calmly. Her face was white, a mask of paste, etched with lipstick. "We have to open the door. Tony and Olivia, please go to the bedroom. Go, Tony, go with Olivia." She pushed at their stiff backs. Olivia began to cry, shoving Tony in front of her towards the back of the house. Giershe stared at Elizabeth. Her legs were numb. The door opened.

"Yes?" Elizabeth said, imperiously.

"Are you Giershe Kinnard?"

"No. That's my sister. What do you want?"

"I have a warrant for the arrest of Giershe Kinnard on a Connecticut statute."

"Ridiculous!"

"Ma'am, the warrant is right here. You may show it to your sister." Elizabeth took the paper in her hand, left the door ajar, walked to Giershe, and handed her the document.

"Mr. Kinnard must leave. He must! The children are frightened. He has no right to be here!" Elizabeth rushed her words. The second officer, at least seven feet tall, bent beneath the light.

"Ma'am, he's going to wait out in the police car. We have two officers and two cars. There's no need for you or your sister to see him until we get to the station."

"Station? Why are we going to the station? Why is *he* going? What will happen to the children?"

"Ma'am, do you think your sister could read that warrant now?"

"Warrant? Oh." Giershe tried to read. The words danced and fuzzed, the paragraphs fused, slithered together. "ARREST! What for? For taking my children from a terrible man? For taking care of them and protecting them?"

"Ma'am—"

"What is to happen to the children when I'm arrested? Are they going to be taken away by a father who would do *anything* to destroy me? Why do you allow this to happen? What kind of a man are you? You, in your spiffy uniform, hauling off women and children."

"MA'AM!"

"Just be quiet. No one asked you to talk. What you're supposed to do is act big and tough and dumb. How *can* you let yourself do this?"

"Oh God! Everyone hates cops. Everyone! Why didn't I become a fireman? I try to do my duty, obey my orders, and everyone screams at me. Ma'am—"

The second officer interrupted. "Jake, let me handle this. You take it so personally. Can't you see it's a real messed-up situation? Naturally she feels bad. She's probably never been arrested. And she wants to keep her children. Mrs. Kinnard—"

"DON'T CALL ME MRS. KINNARD!"

"I have to ask you to get some things together for the children, and accompany us to the police station. That's what we have to do. We'll wait on the front porch."

Giershe remembered little of the journey downtown to Berkeley's police department. She climbed into the backseat of a black-and-white car. Elizabeth had Tony in her lap; Olivia sobbed and clung to Giershe. Mr. Seven Foot said something into his mike and they drove through familiar streets. At the station, the children were received by a huge matron in khaki uniform who took the struggling, wailing Olivia in her arms. Tony grabbed Olivia's foot and followed behind, sober, brave. David was there. He started towards the children but was intercepted by an officer. He sat down in a chair against the wall.

Giershe listened to the cries and closed her eyes. Elizabeth held her tightly. "Yes, officer, can you wait a minute? My sister is— JUST WAIT!" Giershe's stomach cramped and she thought she was going to vomit. The cries echoing down the hallway, growing fainter. Elizabeth asked courteously: "Where are they taking the children?"

"To the facility."

"What facility?"

"They'll spend the night in the county juvenile facility. They will be well cared for. There are other children there and a good staff, trained for these emergencies."

"But can't we say good-bye to them? We'd like to tell them it's temporary. It's indecent just to cart them off like that! Where is this facility?"

"About ten miles away, out in the country."

"TEN MILES! In the middle of the night?" Elizabeth's control was departing. Giershe opened her eyes. The lights were blinding. There seemed to be officers everywhere, and she was standing in front of a high counter. They were waiting for her to do or say something. She blinked at the uniform behind the counter.

"Your right hand, please, Mrs. Kinnard."

"My right hand?"

"Give him your right hand, sweetie." Elizabeth lifted Giershe's hand to the counter. A big paw took her fingers in a strong grasp and pressed them firmly onto a pad of black ink. She stared at her inked fingers. The paw pressed each finger onto a white paper, then reached for her left hand. While he worked with her left hand, someone said:

"After she's booked, she can go into the other room and make any calls she wants. A lawyer, family. You'd better go with her. She seems kind of out of it." Mr. Seven Foot, helpful, but still guarding them.

"Harry always said, 'Don't let anyone fingerprint you unless you have no choice.' I must remember to tell him I had no choice." Giershe's voice was remote, speaking far away inside her head.

><><><

GIERSHE'S DIARY:
SEPTEMBER 26, 1964

Visited Snidely Cottage, a no-exit place. Visitors and residents under guard at all times. The children were brought to me in the entrance lobby by a huge matron in a white uniform. Olivia ran to my side and clung to me. Tony stood next to the matron and seemed not to recognize me. He stared and I said: "Hello, Tony." He didn't answer, just stood there. Suddenly he ran at me, struggled onto my lap and raked my face with his fingernails. I tried to hug him. He made a fist and beat my chest. The matron moved in and picked him up as though he were a struggling frog.

"Leave him alone!" I shouted at her. "Get away from us!"

"Little boy! I can't let you visit your mother if you're going to treat her like that!" Tony beat on her massive starched chest. She turned away with him to take him from the room.

"Stop!" I yelled. "Mind your own business! If he wants to attack me for what has happened to him, let him. Let him go!"

She turned around with Tony slipping to the floor. He ran to me and we sat down on the bench. He climbed again into my lap, his tiny arms wrapping me tightly, his head pressed against my breasts. I stroked his curly head, kissed his cheek. The matron stood in the doorway, on guard, waiting. The children seemed to know without asking that I had no answers for them. We sat without speaking for the duration of our time. We hugged and kissed and dared a few smiles. When the matron said the time was up, Olivia asked when I would return. I told her I would come again as soon as they would let me. She began crying again and shrieked as the matron picked her up. "NO! NO! I want to go with Mommy! MY MOMMY!" Tony took the matron's hand and walked at her side out of the room with no backward look.

><><><

MOLLY GAVIN'S DIARY:
SEPTEMBER 28, 1964

Harry and Giershe found a criminal lawyer named Schonfeld. Giershe says he's evil, but he's supposed to be splendid. His fee:

$3,000, just to keep her out of jail, or try to, and prevent extradition. In afternoon, down to Snidely Cottage in Schonfeld's black Cadillac. David there, with his lawyers. Long wait. Mr. Peaceman was there—such a tidy, human, nice man. He lacks one arm. Learned that the parents can't see the children because they get upset. Don't know what the judge will decide, but he's our own Kamilian.

SEPTEMBER 29, 1964

Giershe must appear each day before the judge, in criminal court. She seems drugged. Judge Kamilian said he would consider only the welfare of the children and couldn't go against the Connecticut decisions, nor take them from David unless it could be shown he was not a proper parent *after* the last Connecticut decision in August. But the lawyers do not despair. There's a warrant out for arrest of David for nonpayment of $14,000 in support payments in his first marriage. He has disappeared.

SEPTEMBER 30, 1964

Juvenile court at eleven. Kamilian said he had changed his mind and would open the case and admit testimony. Hours of waiting outside. Giershe was questioned endlessly, called an adulteress by David's lawyer, a Mr. Hardy. Did not leave the courthouse until seven.

>>>>>

Early in October 1964, Giershe turned forty. The month was sunny and beautiful, as she had remembered it to be in Berkeley. Every weekday at ten a.m., throughout October and on into November, she had to appear in her own body at the Hall of Justice to assure the judge she was still in earnest desire to remain outside in the sunshine, "on her own recognizance" as they termed it, "O.R." for short.

It was not practical to be in criminal court and continue teaching a class in the morning hours, and on October 2 she packed up her teaching materials at the temple and turned over the key to the new Dutch teacher (pretty, calm, competent, unmarried). It was also not legal, by the laws of the State of California, to teach school while charged with a felony.

Documents multiplied. Giershe listened as carefully as possible to the explanations offered in support of what they called "pleadings" or "writs" or "briefs" or "amendments" but was often surprised at how little effect each pile of paper was expected to produce. There were six lawyers producing documents: two for David in California, one for David in Connecticut, one for Giershe in Connecticut, and two in California. If each lawyer produced a modest eight pages a day, times six, add to that three Xerox copies for everyone, the grand total per day might be close to two hundred. She tried to understand what the lawyers turned out, but her intelligence seemed to be diminishing in direct proportion to the growth of documents. She could never remember who was the plaintiff and who the defendant. Sometimes she was one, sometimes the other, and it didn't seem to matter from which state the document originated, a clue which she had used in the beginning but had had to abandon.

One afternoon in early October, Giershe and Bill Peaceman ran through the corridors of the Hall of Justice as the clocks ticked towards five P.M., searching for *one* judge who would sign a writ of habeas corpus. Bill had patiently explained to her why they were doing this, and she knew he wasn't a man to kick up dust merely in order to earn his fee. She panted down the halls after him and tried to remember her college course in jurisprudence. She had written in a blue examination booklet, "The ancient writ of habeas corpus is one of the glories of Anglo-American jurisprudence." To "have the body"—but whose body, and who wants it, and where was it? Was it hers, or the bodies of the children? And why was David's lawyer trying to get a writ of habeas corpus on behalf of *his* client?

On the day of their frantic search for a judge, the halls were filled with armed peace officers who were on extra duty to quell student uprisings in Berkeley, and Giershe noted as she passed them in the halls that they seemed pleased with the prospect of an extra evening of pay. They jollied each other and stood in small groups making jokes about how many "kids we can haul in tonight."

At three minutes to five, Bill found a judge who would sign his writ. He was pleased. Bill was calm even when running down hallways past armed cops; he never raised his voice, or lowered his head before a judge. He didn't extend false hope. He was a legal technician, without vanity, and Giershe trusted him as she had trusted no other lawyer she had known. He spoke deliberately, and even when she wept or became irrational, he stood quietly at attention, waiting for a return to sense.

"Bill, I'm glad the judge signed, but, forgive me, I don't understand why you wanted him to sign."

He lowered his briefcase to the polished floor. With his left hand, he pulled a white handkerchief from his back pocket and wiped his forehead. "It means that at least one judge feels that the children should not be returned to Connecticut until California has had a chance, in superior court, to review the case. Your husband was trying to 'have the bodies' removed from Snidely and returned to his custody. Now he's going to have to wait, at least until some time after October fourteenth, the date the case will be reviewed. It gives us some time to prepare."

"Oh. Did you tell me this before?"

"Yes. You're closing up fast on legal terminology, but that's what I'm for. Well—I can get on the freeway now, and you can go home. Stay off the streets tonight. It looks like the boys are going to have some fun."

>>>

Berkeley, Oct. 7.64

DEAR MR. PEACEMAN:

The parents of my students presented me with letters of support which made me sob and I attach herewith, for your use. I am allowed to see the children twice a week for one half hour, under the supervision of the probation officer. Tony says: "Why don't you come every day twice a week?" I've been having my court-ordered visits with Dr. McGorkie. He warns me that he sees lots of grown-up children whose parents fooled around with their lives as we're doing right now. You're a nice man.

Sincerely, Giershe

20

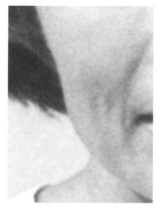

"Reeling and Writing,

of course,

to begin with,"

the Mock Turtle replied.

T
HERE SEEMED TO BE a conspiracy to exclude me from the proceedings; I wasn't to have any say and my fate was to be decided out of hand.
                                               —*Albert Camus*, The Stranger

After reading the "Testimonials from Parents," Giershe began to collect pills: codeine from Molly's medicine cabinet, sleeping pills from Elizabeth's medicine cabinet, Darvon and Valium from Jack's shaving kit. If she was invited to dinner at a friend's house, sometime during the evening she would excuse herself to go to the bathroom. She flushed the toilet and opened the cabinet above the washbasin as quietly as possible. Pill bottles were always on the top shelf. She read the labels carefully and took only one or two pills from a bottle. Inside her purse, she carried an Indian suede drawstring bag. She slipped the pills into the bag, pulled the string tight, put the bottle back on the top shelf, flushed the toilet again, and closed the cabinet door.

Ordinary folk consumed lots of pills, but Giershe was "quiet, unassuming, soft, kind, gentle, sensitive, warm, responsible, committed, intelligent, moral, honest, dedicated, perceptive, serene, devoted, loving, realistic, concerned, accepting, insightful, pleasant, optimistic, forward-looking, forthright, courageous, calm, graceful, good-humored, firm," and never took anything for pain except two Excedrins with a glass of water. And whiskey in milk, with Jack.

As Giershe's life spilled out in courtrooms, the psychiatrist's office, into Molly's diary, into Elizabeth's coffee cups, all over Jack's bed, or was caught and reconstructed in piles of white documents, her private collection of life-ending capsules and white discs grew until she had the nice round number of one hundred, almost all the colors of the rainbow represented. She didn't keep her pills in her purse. She transferred the contents after each theft to a second drawstring pouch which she kept hidden in secret places in her residence, sometimes underneath her underwear, or in a box marked "Winter Clothes." The pill pouch was difficult to hide and she often forgot where she had put it. It was also an embarrassment. She wished she had courage enough to plan a solemn walk into the river, like Virginia Woolf. She would have preferred a cyanide capsule hidden somewhere on her person. The act itself seemed neither heroic nor craven, was not a revenge or a sermon. She would leave behind no savage words and wished she could remove from the deed its implication of a statement left for survivors. What a bother it was to have to worry about those who remained alive! When she had nothing more to say or do, she would take the pills. She would not return to Connecticut to be placed in prison for kidnapping and she would not remain in California without Tony and Olivia, an admired teacher, thought to have once been married, with children, but that was long ago. She had to wait for her fate "to be decided out of hand," but the last act, almost a free willing of event, would belong to her.

>>>>

MOLLY GAVIN'S DIARY:
OCTOBER 12, 1964

> Giershe to dinner looking ready to explode. Learned that Peaceman's son was badly injured in a motorcycle accident.

OCTOBER 14, 1964

> Down to juvenile court in afternoon. Children brought from Snidely so that judge could question Olivia in chambers about incidents with her father. No one knows what was said. Tony escaped from outer room and ran into the courtroom with a candy bar in his hand, searching for his mother. He found her, gave her the candy and a kiss, and everyone softened at the sight. He then rampaged around the court and when someone came to take him away, he yelled: "Tell the judge I don't want to stay out there in that place! They're *mean* to me!" Painful. Did not see Olivia.

>>>>

On October 14, Giershe sat quietly in the courtroom. She sat in the front row next to Bill Peaceman, who had been at the hospital most of the night. She had all but given up trying to understand how her fate was being settled. She could have been invisible. The courtroom was a theater with rows of seats circling down to the judge's massive "bench," which wasn't a bench at all. He sat behind a barricade of heavy polished oak which extended from one side of the room to the opposite side, with neat piles of white paper placed in front of him. He was wearing a black robe. Giershe was seated six feet below his barricade and her neck hurt her if she stared upward at the little head, just visible, now and then, when he leaned forward.

Tony's assault on the court's tranquility came and went so fast. The kiss he left behind, wet and warm on her cheek, dried slowly, and left a puckery feeling. How odd it was not to know whether they were still in the building or had been returned to Snidely Cottage on the other side of the parking lot.

This was the second Hershey bar he'd given her. Apparently they gave them out freely, one per day, or perhaps attendants bribed him to behave, and when he wanted to give his mother something, candy was all he had of value. Mommy didn't like candy. She preferred drawings, but he had no paper, no crayons, no clothes of his own, no books, no place to keep tiny pebbles—an equal rain of rules falling on all the children. Boys were separated from girls, even though the boy was three (almost four) and the girl was his sister. No child could be allowed to wear his own clothes. Think how troublesome it might be to sort garments after laundering them! No child could have paper and pencils or crayons of his own. What about the other children not so fortunate? Could not the child share with others? But the others would take and destroy and might even use a pencil as weapon, or write on wall or floor. Books? Could a parent give her child books? Yes, if she was willing that such books be used by all. Fine, good idea, said the mother. Well no, perhaps that's not a good idea. The child might resent the others taking his books. There were lots of comic books and the children went to school every day. The school had books. Every child was required to take a two-hour nap after lunch? Yes, Tony and Olivia had resisted, but were beginning to settle down. Olivia said they used a hairbrush on her bottom? An exaggeration. A threat. The children must lie down on their beds. Play outside at nap time? But how could one child, or two, be allowed to play outside when the others were required to take a nap? Letters to the children censored? The letters were "screened" for inappropriate contents. No, they couldn't keep the letters. Where would they put them? The children complained about the breakfast cereal with too much sugar on top? Sugar was energy and the dietary specialist prepared identical breakfasts for all the children. They didn't *like* chocolate pudding? That's very strange. All children like chocolate pudding!

All right. Suppose a parent gives a child something he or she could wear, like a necklace, perhaps a locket with a picture of Mommy enclosed. Would the children be allowed to have these necklaces on their necks at all times? Well, not ordinarily, but since they are so young, yes, that would be allowed. So the next day Giershe looked for two sturdy lockets, with strong chains. Those she found in a thrift shop in Berkeley were not beautiful, but were heart-shaped, and inside she glued her face, cut from cheerful snapshots. She wrapped the lockets in tiny boxes, labeled one TONY, the other OLIVIA. Gifts were not allowed and on the following day, when she visited Snidely Cottage, she had to leave the boxes at the front desk until the probation officer arrived and stamped "B. Gough O.K." on each. She met the children outside in a little courtyard with a slatted wooden flooring. Olivia opened hers first. She placed it around her neck before opening the heart. She opened, and saw . . . Giershe. She solemnly closed it, opened, closed. "May I keep it and never take it off, even for a bath?" Miss Gough said yes. She would tell the attendants.

Tony was feverish. He sat beside Giershe, leaning heavily against her. He held his box in his lap. No one suggested he open it. "Mine's probably a knife or something you give boys. They won't let me keep it."

"Do you want a knife?" Giershe asked.

"No. I already have a knife. I want a locket like Olivia."

"Do you want me to open it for you, Tony?" Olivia reached for the box.

"NO! I can do it." He untied the blue ribbon and stuffed it in his jeans pocket. He took off the lid. His locket was larger than Olivia's and he stared at it. "Mommy, will they let me wear it, all the time?" He was very serious. Giershe nodded.

"They can't let one do something and not let the other do the same thing, can they, Miss Gough?"

"No, Olivia, Tony can wear his locket."

Tony slid down to the slatted floor with his box. He picked up the locket with shiny chain trailing after. As he tried to open it, he shifted to his most comfortable position, sitting on one bent leg, the other leg with foot on the ground and knee for a table. He opened the locket and saw Giershe smiling at him. "How did you get in there, Mommy?" Everyone laughed, as he had intended. He began to stand up.

"Tony, look out!" Olivia shouted as Tony stepped on her box. He dropped the locket, reached for it, and they all watched the locket disappear through the slats in the floor, the chain snaking after it. "Oh, poor Tony," Olivia said sadly.

"Oh, how awful! Perhaps we can get it, lift a board or something," Miss Gough said.

Tony climbed into Giershe's lap again, his hot head pressed against her chest, his arms around her. Giershe didn't believe in signs or omens, but found herself struggling with this minor catastrophe, pushing away heavy meaning in the accidental waywardness of objects.

"I'll get you another one. I can bring it next time I come."

"It was an accident," Tony said, tears dripping down his cheeks.

"I know, Tony, an accident," Giershe said.

"HOUSE WITH BARS, PLANE WITH BOMBS"
Tony, Oct. 1964

By October 26, it was apparent that David Kinnard was not going to agree to a compromise and his counsel in California was growing new feathers. David was represented in court by huge, flapping, vigorous, achieving, handsome Henry Hardy. Mr. Hardy crowded the courtroom with his energy, his determination to win for his client. He charged at Victory and seemed to believe that fighting a brilliant battle was worth nothing if one came in second. Truth could scatter before the assault, reputations pop like balloons on jagged glass, women could weep over lost babies—Henry kept on flapping, circling madly inside his own arena. He carried his theater with him wherever he went, in the lobby at recess, at lunch, and in the judge's chambers. He treated the judge indulgently, like a bumbling stagehand, and the judge was amused.

At recess one day, Giershe was standing with Bill Peaceman and Harry. The men were talking quietly. Henry Hardy broke from his cluster of admirers and on his way somewhere, fast, he bumped into Giershe, knocking her purse to the floor. "Oh, Mrs. Kinnard, I *am* sorry! Here, let me help you." He squatted down on the marble floor and as Giershe watched, he lifted her purse from the bottom, scattering lipstick, wallet, stray papers, comb, Kleenex. A prescription fell from her wallet and Henry helpfully stuffed it back. He muttered apologies as his big hand scooped items from around her feet. He held out the purse to her, letting it hang forlornly from the shoulder strap. It looked evil dangling there. He was gone before she had time to return it to her shoulder.

That same day, during a second recess, she heard his voice soar above the muted consultations: "An adulteress! That's what she is! A common adulteress!" She excused herself to go to the bathroom. In the metal cubicle, she looked in her purse for her Enovid prescription. She had seen him return it, but it was not there. Could she walk up to that bustling maniac and ask him to return her property? She could imagine him shouting out in the lobby: "A prescription? For WHAT? ENOVID! But my dear Mrs. Kinnard, what would *I* want with such a prescription? Surely you must have lost your ENOVID prescription somewhere else?"

In cross-examination, he early reduced her to childish confusion. Issues were black or white, answers had to be yes or no. And without Giershe's knowing quite how he staged the transformation, she was emerging as a perjuring, lawless, weak, unstable, possibly dangerous female who had the audacity to present herself otherwise and ask to be allowed to care for two children.

On November 1, Tony and Olivia had been in Snidely Cottage thirty-six days. They had not adjusted and, like all prisoners, thought only of getting out. Leaves were falling down over the fence into their bare play yard, and Olivia hugged Tony when she saw him there. She had begun to reassure him he would get out on his birthday, November fifteenth. She didn't ask Giershe to verify this prediction, and she helped Tony count the days. Did Olivia believe it? Giershe guessed she didn't, for she never spoke of a future away from her guards. When Giershe visited, Olivia kept her words and gestures wrapped under careful control until the half hour was gone. At the end of each visit she cracked, clung to her mother, screamed at the matron, and was carried off, struggling and sobbing against the white uniform.

Giershe dreamed each night of her visits to Snidely. The dream was not embellished, or cloudy, or crowded with a symbolic landscape. She saw the slatted verandah, the children in drab institutional clothes, Miss Gough so tidy in wrinkle-proof pantsuit, the eucalyptus trees bending in the breeze, Tony's soft brown skin, Olivia's clotted face peering over the matron's shoulder. She smelled Lysol. All day, every day, as she went from lawyer to court, to second lawyer, to school, to dinner with Molly and Harry, she thought of the children in Snidely. When she looked at Jack, his face faded into the sad little figures trying not to cry. When they made love, a part of her sat huddled in the corner of the room. She could sit apart and watch the bodies clutch, rub, contort, flush, subside into sleep, and then watch the dream come. The long drive through desolate land turning into freeway, the dying trees, the banks and gas stations filling the empty wastes, the cluster of county buildings, the linoleum floor in the lobby, the switchboard operator who plugged in and said "Mrs. Kinnard is here," Miss Gough with her clipboard, the walk through bare hallways, glimpses of listless older children in dark rooms, staring at TV. A little boy and girl walking slowly to the slatted wooden floor. They seemed to have forgotten how to run, or laugh, or tell silly jokes, or quarrel.

Dr. McGorkie pronounced Giershe fit, sane, with no mental aberration of any kind. She was not allowed to see his report, and she wondered why she had to pay for a psychiatric evaluation which she was not allowed to read. He had been paid to inspect the condition of her mind and she tidied her psychic house for him. She answered his questions calmly and thought of breaking his eardrum with a scream. He smiled at her. She smiled back.

"Tell me, Mrs. Kinnard, how do you feel about your husband?"

I hate him enough to kill him with a hatchet, slowly, first the hands . . . "Oh, we are caught in a fight for children we both love. I'm sure when it's settled we'll remember how much regard we have for each other."

"Mrs. Kinnard, if the court decision were to go against you, what would you do?"

Kill myself, but first I would try to kill the judge, and you. "Dr. McGorkie, I would have to somehow find a life for myself in my work, which I love and is most rewarding to me."

When the second fifty-minute session was over, the kind doctor put his arm around her and walked with her to the office door. She wanted to punch his fat stomach, hurt him with fists and knees, gouge an eye and throw it out the window. "Will you be wanting to talk with me again or is this all that's required of me?"

"This is the second visit and I'll not be needing to see you again. Good-bye, Mrs. Kinnard, and good luck!"

>>>>>>

MOLLY GAVIN'S DIARY:
NOVEMBER 14, 1964
> Verdict against Giershe. I drove her here in heavy rain. She became hysterical and violent.

>>>>>>

"Giershe, you're such a damn fool! Haven't you called enough judges and messed up the case with your lawless, insane behavior? Everything that has happened is your FAULT! I won't allow you to place a call to Kamilian from *my* house!" Harry's face was sunset red as he stood guard over the hall phone.

"Then I'll go call at the gas station! He has to realize what he's doing. He's killing me! He has to KNOW THAT!"

"Harry, let her call. What difference can it make now? I don't want her driving the car, she's in no condition." Molly was crying.

"My daughter is a maniac! All of this is her fault. In Connecticut, if she'd been able to control herself in court, none of this would have happened. She's not fit to have her children!"

"Oh Harry, how can you say that? She's *not* a maniac. Let her call. "

"GODDAMMIT! I want no more to do with *any* of it! The HELL WITH HER!" Harry slammed the door to his bedroom and Giershe moved quickly to the phone. Elizabeth stood nearby, massaging Giershe's shoulders. She winced and pulled away. She found Kamilian, Ed . . . Frank . . . 624-0844. She dialed. A woman answered.

"Yes, Kamilian residence."

"I'd like to speak to Judge Kamilian." Softly, whispering.

"I'm sorry, the judge has gone to bed. It's quite late. Perhaps in the morning. May I say who's calling?"

"Giershe Kinnard. We were in court today. Can you wake him? It's important. He must know, I want to tell him, he has to know what he's doing."

"It's unusual for someone to call the judge after hours. Are you sure—"

"I'm VERY SURE! It's my life he's wrecking. He has to be told."

"I can't wake him. It would do no good. He's not at liberty to hear testimony at this hour. I'm sorry, Mrs. Kinnard is it? There's nothing I can do. Good-bye."

Giershe dropped the receiver to the floor and ran through the house, brushing Molly aside roughly, dodging old Chinese pots, past the lovely cherrywood table, slipping on Oriental rugs, fumbling with the brass double lock on the front door. Elizabeth opened the door while Giershe was grabbing keys from her purse. She shot through the door, took the front steps in two leaps, and flung herself onto the gaping horsehair on the front seat of Jack's Ford. The engine roared and bellowed as she gunned the accelerator. She spun the car around in the middle of the street, narrowly missing Elizabeth. She drove towards the steepest hill in Berkeley, called Marin. You had to go fast to get your beast up to the first level and keep on going, faster, to achieve the second level, and coming down was the supreme challenge of skaters who had tried everything else. Kamilian lived on Oakcrest, up in the hills where all the good and prosperous people lived. A mile up into the fog, the homes larger and larger on the way, until a successful citizen could buy a mansion in the mist and look out over the descending order of mankind. She gripped the wheel, her foot pressing the accelerator to the floor. She could see a car following her, a Falcon shape, good Elizabeth guarding her sister, not condemning, loving the lioness as she loved her cats. Good! Good! A chase through the streets of their childhood, no fair stopping for stop signs, just gun it, shoot through quiet streets where families slept and children cried and mothers sleepwalked to their beds and shooed away the nightmares. Top of Marin Hill, through the stop sign, around the corner to right, then left, then right again, Falcon lights in rear, betcha good sister Elizabeth has never had such a ride! Screeching brakes at 1158 Oakcrest, next door to where Professor F. used to live. Not when he was lying naked next to his graduate students—that was farther down the hill—but where he had three children and lived next door to a judge whose son wanted to bomb troop transports headed for Vietnam and let his hair grow long. Lights out in the house.

Giershe tumbled out of her car and ran up the steps to the house. She stopped on the front porch. Bang on the door? Ring the doorbell? Throw rocks at the window? Suddenly she felt foolish. He was in there sleeping beside a nice wife, a small man without his robe, maybe even wearing pajamas, a tired man. Tired of human pain and mess, tired of documents and stipulations, weary of offspring. She sat down on the damp front steps, her Motion to Erase him wafting lazily into the still night fog. Her right big toe hurt and blood was oozing through her stocking. The blood was black in the light of the street lamp. Elizabeth climbed to her side and sat down.

"You feel any better?"

"Oh yeah, much better. Thanks for coming to my party. I sent out lots of invitations but I guess they were all busy."

"You want to come home with me?"

"No, I think I'll go to Jack's place. Maybe he's working there. I have to return his car, anyway."

"Good idea. I'll follow you over."

"You needn't. You've done enough. So much. All these weeks. You're a very dear lady. Isn't this a funny place to talk? Can't you just imagine the story in the *Berkeley Bulletin*? All caps. 'MAYOR'S SECRETARY ARRESTED FOR TRESPASSING WITH FELON SISTER ON JUDGE'S PROPERTY: JUDGE AND WIFE UNHARMED.' Are you going to work tomorrow?"

"The mayor has been very nice. I'll work in the morning and go to court in the afternoon. He understands."

"Elizabeth? How shall I live without them? How shall I *live*?"

Giershe hugged her knees and rocked back and forth on the stone step. Her hair was damp with fog. She shivered. She raised her hot face to the streetlight, her eyes shut tight, her lips pulled away from her teeth in a white grimace.

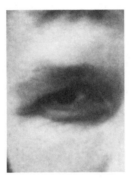

. . . when suddenly, thump!

thump! down she came

upon a heap of sticks

and dry leaves,

and the fall was over.

S

UPERIOR COURT OF THE STATE OF CALIFORNIA
IN AND FOR THE COUNTY OF ALAMEDA

MEMORANDUM OF DECISION

. . . Accordingly, this Court has given Mrs. Kinnard unlimited opportunity to present evidence of changed circumstances since February 1964, or of any significant matters prior to that time which were not presented to the Connecticut Court. There has *been no showing of any significant prior matter* which was not considered by that Court.

It is also clear that the Connecticut Court applied the same principle which California requires of preferential custodial rights to the mother in the case of very young children.

The evidence of changed circumstances is not such as to warrant this Court in modifying the Connecticut decree. It shows some factors favorable to Mrs. Kinnard, such as stable teaching employment in Berkeley, a seemingly pleasant and constructive environment for the children, and an apparent termination of certain conduct which weighed heavily against her in the February 1964 hearing in Connecticut. It also reveals negative factors, such as her *abduction of the children in August 1964.*

. . . Mrs. Kinnard has expressed concern that future orders of the Connecticut Court might reflect a punitive attitude toward her and thereby prejudice her legitimate interests as a mother. This Court is satisfied that the Connecticut Court has been and will continue to be mindful of her commendable desire to be with her children and of the *importance to these young children of receiving the loving care and nurture which only a devoted mother can provide.* If she can satisfy the Connecticut Court that she will abide by its orders, I have no doubt that her past behavior will not be permitted to jeopardize the paramount interest of making arrangements most beneficial to the children.

Dated: November 15, 1964

FRANK KAMILIAN
Judge of the Superior Court

>———>———>———>

On Tony's birthday, Giershe wept in the judge's chambers while Bill Peaceman patiently talked to her. Judge Kamilian was not there.

"Giershe, you can appeal. You don't have to sign the waiver, but if you don't sign, the children will have to stay in Snidely, and it may be many months before the appeal is heard. And thousands of dollars. This is your right, but you want to consider the children, and you have to begin to trust."

"Trust? How can I trust Connecticut? They have no intention of *ever* letting me see the children, or of dropping the criminal charges. Even if I were to return, they wouldn't let me have visitation privileges, and as soon as the children return, Connecticut will pay *no* attention to the judge's efforts. Even this judge says there's no change of circumstances, and he leaves me no possibility of changing my circumstances. I read his memorandum. I have a place for them to stay, a job, I'm respected here, and I've terminated that connection they so despise, and yet *even* Judge Kamilian says there are negatives. I abducted them twice against court orders, and *therefore* I'm not a fit mother—"

"He didn't say that. He said—"

"He did say that! Read it again. I'll never be able to care for them again. Connecticut will never agree to divided custody and will never allow them out of the state, and if I were to go back, *never* allow me to see them freely!"

"I admit that there seems to be an unnecessarily punitive element in the judge's memorandum, but perhaps he's responding to his sense of what's possible, and he can see no end to this mess unless you return to do battle in the state of original jurisdiction. I know this judge and I know he's a good man and feels you should have the children."

"Then why doesn't he claim California's right to decide?"

"He obviously doesn't feel he can." Bill's voice remained soothing.

"But he can! Judges can do anything!"

"Giershe, there's another consideration. Connecticut will never drop the criminal charges against you as long as the children are here. And you can't teach unless they're dropped. You'll also probably have to face those charges if you choose to appeal. You might even face extradition. I know it's unfair to you, but I am sure, and you have to believe this— You know I will not play tricks on you—you know that, don't you?"

He waited for her answer. Giershe gave herself over to fresh sobs at the thought of more courts, cross-examinations, money to be found, more of Harry's fury. He had asked a question. Did she believe he would play tricks. No. He was the only honest human being in the pileup.

"I know you do not play tricks! What are you sure about?"

"Thank you. I am sure, and I intend to continue my efforts for you and your children, that the judge will work with me and that we'll be able to get the children for you at least half-time, *if* you will do *now* what is painfully difficult for you to do. Sign the waiver and let the kids return to Connecticut." He sat quietly beside her. There was no impatience and he was acting as if they could talk forever in that still, book-lined room. The sobs ceased and she took the Kleenex he held out to her. He smiled sweetly, without urgency.

"Bill, what am I waiving?" Bill again explained the waiver, evenly, kindly.

"Okay. I'll sign. They *must* leave Snidely. Then may I leave?" He handed her a pen and told her where to sign.

"You can leave if you want to. I have about an hour's work to tie this up. I would rather you stayed in the building and then I'll go with you to Snidely to get the kids. The judge has agreed to let you be with them until plane time at ten P.M. this evening, as long as Henry Hardy is there to make sure nothing happens. You can go with the children to the airport and I think they need that. They'll be very confused and you can help them. Can you be a very courageous woman for a few hours more?"

"Did you know that Olivia told Tony he would get out on his birthday? Did someone tell her that?"

"I doubt it. The judge may have hoped, but I don't know. It's more likely that your Olivia wanted to cheer him up, and herself, and let the wish become prediction. She's a very wise little girl— Now don't start crying again. Just *believe* you're doing what is hardest for you right now, so that they'll have a home life again, until other arrangements are forced on Connecticut." Bill gathered up his papers and with his metal claw at the end of his metal arm, filed them in his briefcase. He snapped it shut and turned around so that Giershe could hold onto his good arm and walk with him out into the courtroom.

>>>>

The remainder of November 15, until the big plane lifted itself from the ground, passed with appalling speed and the silent, broken, kaleidoscopic quality of fine nightmare. Henry Hardy rode with Bill and Giershe to Snidely to gather up the children. They returned to Giershe's apartment for dinner and a birthday cake provided by Elizabeth, presents for Tony and Olivia. Tony talked and ran from person to person, chattered, giggled, and did somersaults on the floor. He leaned against Bill, and Bill said, "Hello, Tiger."

"Do you have a motor in your shoulder to make that work?" Tony asked. He touched Bill's metal fingers and Bill pulled up his suit sleeve to show the steel elbow joints.

"No, no motor. I went to school to learn how to make it move."

"Does it hurt?" Tony tried to climb into Bill's lap, carefully.

"Not now, no."

"Did you have it when you were little? Will I get one some day? Do you wear it to bed? Can you take it off? What happened to your real arm? Are you going on the airplane with me? Do you like my cake?" Eyes around the room twitched towards the boy and his questions. Tony pushed away from Bill. "Aunt Elizabeth, I want a piece of cake for that man. He likes my cake."

Olivia stayed quietly at Giershe's side. Henry Hardy, perhaps overcome by a sense of decency, left the family of grandparents, aunt, mother and children in Bill's temporary care for two hours. At eight P.M. all but Molly and Harry were swept up in three cars and drove together to the airport, Mr. Hardy following closely on Bill's tail, like a movie chase. But it wasn't a chase at all. Everyone was rational and well behaved. Elizabeth came along behind Hardy.

At the airport, Tony's face appeared over the shoulder of a stewardess. "Mommy! Hurry! You're going to miss the plane!" They disappeared into the crowd. Henry Hardy vanished. Elizabeth drove away in her car. Bill and Giershe sat down on an orange plastic bench and stared at each other. "Your wife—she must be a noble woman. Your hours are much too long." Giershe let her words die.

"She knows the Kinnard case. I seldom bring the office into the home, but she knows where I am and that I'll be home very late. I'm not much of a drinker and I don't suppose you are either, but there's a bar here. Would you like something for the road?"

"If you need it, but don't worry about me. I'm numb."

"Well, I'd like to be a bit numb. Come along." As he stood up, she saw pain flick in his blue eyes. She hitched her shoulder bag into place and picked up his briefcase. She followed his straight back into the dusk of the airport bar. They sat at a window table, and Bill placed his case on the seat before sitting down. They were silent while they waited for his scotch and soda and her Irish coffee. She studied his kind face. She considered him an unemotional man. He gave minimum force to his words and let others shout, cry, hate. In the candlelight, as he leaned forward over the table, she could see tiny lines in his tanned skin, and the left hand which lifted the water glass to his lips was older than his face. When the waitress brought the tray of drinks, Bill pulled his wallet from brown officer pants, flipped it open on the table, placed a ten on the tray, and stuffed the wallet in his back pocket. He shifted his shoulder wearily.

"Bill, how did you lose your arm?"

"Oh, that's a long story—one I don't think about much."

"Were you uncomfortable when Tony questioned you?"

"No. Kids ask questions, and under other circumstances, I think he would have listened to answers. Usually they're only curious about the mechanics. They think it's interesting to have a metal prong instead of a hand. But you're the first adult who's asked me since I left the hospital. Everyone seems to feel I'll just fall apart if it's mentioned."

"That's very American. In England, the attitude is different. I went sight-seeing with a friend who walked with those arm crutches. She'd say 'I'm a cripple' to the attendant . . . " Giershe was talking fast, protecting Bill, push-ing away the thought of the children flying away from her. He stared at her. She placed her hand over her mouth, and waited.

"The Korean war was over; it was September 1953. I was a career Army Air Force pilot. I was thirty and had no plans to leave the force. I was married and had two small children. The end of the war meant that I shifted from combat duty to the training of pilots. Good income and I was doing what I'd always wanted to do since I was a kid." Bill looked down into his drink and pushed the ice around in the glass with a green-tufted stirrer. "No one thought the truce would hold, and the government wanted more fighter pilots trained and ready to go to war. I returned to the states and my family joined me in San Antonio, Texas, not a bad place to live. I was assigned to train pilots, sometimes on a Sabre jet, sometimes older models. I liked teach-ing. It was eight to five with lots of variety. Not always in the air. But career Air Force people like a discipline that others find oppressive, and for the first time in my career I was the guy who had somehow to compel others into a lifestyle they thought was military, unreasonable—in peacetime."

Giershe tried to imagine this soft-spoken creature compelling others to do his bidding, forcing soft youth into discipline, opening his mouth to utter staccato commands. "But these kids, they were in the Air Force, weren't they? They had to do what they were told?"

"Yes, shape up or out. But they wanted the shape-up time extended, and resented the wartime pattern of training. They thought of themselves as civilians in training and I guess I thought I was training pilots for combat. Some of them fought us on hours of sleep before a flight, intake of alcohol, nutrition, exercise, all of which they thought they could monitor on their own without diminishing their efficiency. There was one guy in particular, a big, sullen fellow named Bradford. He thought he was in college. He liked to drink beer all night, or he'd sneak out to visit the girls in town and get back in bed just before roll call. He didn't fool anyone. He smelled like a brewery. He'd been warned, punished, and he still acted like we were all fathers restricting his liberty. He was very near the end of his training and I hoped we'd be rid of him within a few weeks."

Bill twisted his lean body, pulled his right shoulder up to his ear and let it drop down again. His left arm crossed in front of his face. While his fingers dug into shoulder muscles, he closed his eyes and let his head fall backward. The mechanical arm clanked once against the underside of the tabletop. Giershe waited. Bill tenderly lifted his right arm with his good hand and placed it on the table. The suit sleeve was unwrinkled and looked new.

"I don't like to wear this contraption. It hurts where it joins and after a day of wearing it, I'd like to leave it on the freeway. It's not necessary. It's just for show, for sympathy. Devices aren't yet the answer. So this Bradford guy was going up on his last training flight before licensing, and the same morning I was taking another fellow on his fourth flight lesson. Bradford had spent the night out, but no one called him on it. He was clearly under standards. We cleared the airfield first and were heading into a wind when he came up from behind and near as anyone can figure, must have closed his eyes and sat down on top of us." Bill filled his mouth with ice cubes.

"On top! My God!" Giershe shuddered.

"I don't remember past the impact, which was like dynamite exploding around us. Next thing I remember is the hospital and knowing I was missing an arm. I don't know how I knew that. I couldn't move anything—legs, or back, or head, or arms. They told me Bradford had sheared off our wing and my arm, then rammed himself into a hill and burst into flames."

"He died?"

"He died. My trainee landed safely, without my help, and was not injured. The next part of the story is more interesting, and I think you . . . I don't know . . ." Bill grinned.

"Go on, tell me what happened next."

"You find it strange that I smile?"

"Sort of. Yes, although sometimes I laugh and laugh at my own mess. It isn't hysteria. Something beyond the serious where our speck of existence is briefly comic. I try to hold on to it. It won't stay with me."

"Exactly. But I've had more time to think about that man lying on a hospital bed. Well, anyway, my rehabilitation began right away. The wound had to heal before I could be fitted for a prosthesis and my back was not working too well. I had to stay in hospitals for a year, and *everyone* marched in and out with his own plan for my psychic recovery. Good people, all of them. Trouble was, I refused to give up my idea of myself as career Air Force pilot. I would listen to their pep talks and then inform them that as soon as I got well, I intended to return to duty. They'd get embarrassed and the next time they visited they'd bring a priest, or a superior officer, or a different kind of therapist, or my wife. Someone to talk sense to me. I listened to all of them and asked for a secretary so I could dictate a letter to the Air Force command, asking permission to practice flying with one arm. I knew a plane could be fitted out with controls I could manipulate, and I knew I could convince them. Sooner or later. Meanwhile, I practiced writing with my left hand, exercised my back, got fitted for the arm, and learned to move it by body thrusts. *I* knew I'd be in the air again, but behind my back everyone thought I'd gone psycho. They were kind and sent all the letters I asked them to send, including one to President Eisenhower!"

"Great! I should have thought of that!"

"Towards the end of that year, my commanding officer came to see me. Very sad and glum. He said: 'Bill, it looks like you're going to be the only one-armed Air Force pilot in the United States services. The president has informed us.' And within six weeks I was back in San Antonio training pilots."

"And you had no problems?"

Bill looked sheepish. "Sure. I was more or less stuck with one kind of plane and some of the trainees weren't too keen to fly with me. I was an oddity—there goes one-armed Bill—but I persisted and was happy enough. Then one day—and I swear it just happened one day, without warning—I was flying by myself on a gorgeous day, testing a new gadget. I could see sixty miles. I was filled up with pleasure and very proud. Suddenly I heard myself say, 'Bill! You're an ass! Why don't you chuck this?' And I turned the plane around, landed it, and made application for retirement. I went home and told my wife—she cried she was so happy—and I phoned a few law schools. My alma mater had a good one and in a few weeks I was at the books. Two years of that, paid for by the U.S. government, and I went to work for Hart and Stanford. And here I am." Bill drank his ice water. His hand trembled when he placed it on the paper disc beneath his glass. He watched Giershe's face. She looked down at her hands, which were tearing a napkin into neat strips, then patterning them into squares within squares. She was a bit dizzy, and two tears oozed down her cheeks. Bill fished in his pocket for his last piece of Kleenex. He reached across the table and dabbed gently at her eyes. She sniffed and smiled at him.

"Bill Peaceman, I think you *planned* to tell me this story, but I won't accuse you of sticking my nose in a moral fable. It's your gift to me, better than money or magic potions, and I'll be saying thank you for a long time."

Bill smiled at her. "There may even come a time when you'll regard the legal profession as serving, occasionally, an almost useful function. The Law is human and helps people with their complicated lives, and it's better than managing a pizza parlor, or sitting on false glory as the only one-armed—"

"Career Air Force man—" Giershe chanted.

"In the world." Bill was running down; his face was haggard and the kind blue eyes stared at his empty glass, unblinking, remote. Giershe looked out over the candlelight at the smoke-haze, the couples at the bar, groping hands cupping loose buttocks, dyed hair on aging women, traveling to or from somewhere, waiting for the voice on the intercom, balancing between empty spaces.

"Bill, as my father says, I'm very selfish. I shouldn't have kept you so long. We have to drive to the courthouse to pick up his Rambler. And you have so many miles further, to San Jose. You could stay at my apartment and I could stay with my parents."

"No, no, I'm fine. Just tired. I may not look it but I'm glad we had this chance to talk. Now let's get on the road." He stood beside their table, formal, straight, once again the busy attorney, the retired Air Force pilot. He leaned forward to pick up his briefcase.

"Let me . . . please," Giershe whispered.

"Right. Thank you."

In comfortable silence, they drove back to the Alameda County Courthouse. Giershe was not thinking of what to do next, or what she would feel tomorrow, or even of who she might be, without children, job, or future. She felt a hope, a mysterious promise of a tougher task ahead for which she must be ready. She would create, from materials found in the wreckage, a new creature inside a human skin, add a little more flesh, and then wait for metamorphosis season to come round.

Bill drove into the courthouse parking lot. The headlights shone brightly on white paint lines which divided the absent thousands of cars which lived there during each workday. "Where did you park the Rambler?" Bill asked.

"Over there. Second lane from the entrance." Giershe stared out at two beige county cars. "I'm sure."

"Maybe you parked in the underground lot."

"No, I remember clearly that it was bright sun on last night's rain, the lock wouldn't lock, and the attendant walked over and helped me. Walked from that hutch at the entrance. I parked it right there."

"Right there, where there is no green Rambler?"

"Yep, no green Rambler. Not only is it not there, it doesn't seem to be anywhere. Fascinating development! Please hand me your magnifying glass. I'm sure it's here somewhere."

Bill cut the motor, hit the steering wheel with his good left fist, and began to laugh. Giershe had never heard him laugh. He slid down on the red vinyl seat, tangled his feet in the pedals, hooted and writhed in merriment. She sat quietly, waiting for him to become Bill again. He stopped, looked over at her.

"Oh, this case, it's not funny . . ."

And suddenly Giershe caught his infection, a worse case than his. Fits of giggles rippled up and down her spine, opened her sinuses, pushed salty tears through eye sockets.

"Giershe," he gasped, "did you leave the key in the car?"

"Oh no! I swear I didn't. I told you I locked it and anyway here it is, right here in my hand, ready to put into the ignition and drive away."

"Maybe your father, Mr. *Gavin*, came down here and drove it home."

"Could be—no—could not be. He gave me the *only* key and swore damnation for me if I lost it. Bill! What scoundrel would steal a car from a woman on the very day she has lost her children, from the *courthouse* parking lot? Who would do such a terrible deed?"

"I vote for Henry Hardy. Do you have another candidate?"

"Not even Henry Hardy. It's got to be someone worse, someone lurking out there with a Dastardly Deed list in his pocket."

Again they laughed and handed each other Kleenex from the glove compartment.

"Ahem, yes, I think I am again the competent officer of the court. I suggest we call your father."

"At this hour?"

"Just in case, and then call the police. I think I can get them to take the report on the phone, and then I'll drive you to your apartment, and maybe I'll be home in time for Christmas with the children."

"Fine. It's important in life to have goals, don't you think?"

22

"But I was thinking of a plan

To dye one's whiskers green,

And always use so large a fan

That they could not be seen."

O N THE DAY BEFORE CHRISTMAS, David Kinnard's offer to Giershe arrived by special-delivery airmail. She recognized the typescript, almost as distinctive as his tiny handwriting—the perfect margins, the Roman numerals for the month of the year, and his careful arrowing of corrections. The offer was tightly constructed, stingy, complicated, and no-exit. She felt she had to read it three times before she could sift her privileges from fifteen points. When she had extracted his gift to her—the shot glass of whey left from his pot of rich curd—she turned around to face the new year of 1965.

On New Year's Day, Giershe sat alone in her sunny apartment. She placed her typewriter on the door-top table which Jack had affixed to the wall to make it steady. It was the fourth time he'd provided this service. The same tabletop, four different walls in four dwellings. She inserted a clean piece of white paper, stared at it, and got up to tour the small room. Sliding doors opened out to a miniature garden, private and warm. She could sun-bathe nude if she wished, and the hummingbirds hummed past her ear on their way to pink four-o'clocks planted next to the doors. It would be nice to lie today in the sunshine. No, Jack had said to her last night:

"Okay. So you received David's generous offer. What in hell did you expect from that bastard? Now I want to know what you're going to *do!* Are you going to let him kill you? Are you?"

"No, but what . . . ?" She wanted Jack to put his arms around her. He was pacing the floor.

"Don't say 'What?' like the moron I know you're not. You have a good brain. Use it! *What* are you going to do?"

"I can't think when you pace around the room."

Jack sat on the desk chair. He had his car keys in his hand instead of in his pants pocket where they'd be if he planned to stay awhile. She stared at them. He put them in his shirt pocket, a sign that he wasn't going to wait too long for clarification.

"I'll try to convince one of the public schools to let me do a summer Headstart program with blacks, and I'll continue to look for a Montessori job here. I have to find something, anything, to bring in money." Giershe stared out the window at the fog drifting past a perfect half-moon. Jack went to the refrigerator, looked inside, and closed the door again.

"Answer the question. What are you going to do about regaining Olivia and Tony?"

She stood in front of him, blocking his exit from the kitchen. He gazed at her coldly, his neck pulled back from his shoulders, his blue shirt rippling in the breeze from the open sliding doors.

"I'm going to *concentrate* on getting them out here for the summer, or Christmas, and when they arrive I shall *vanish* with my precious cargo." She whispered the end of her speech and kept her eyes on his face. She waited, her knees trembling, her throat clogged, waited for any response from him. He raised his arms slowly, wrapped them around her, and pressed himself against her. They swayed together and she listened to his whisper:

"Dear Giershe, I couldn't say it for you. You had to decide. It's your life, your Big Event, and I can help but you're the actor and you're the one who'll have to play it out. Are you sure?"

"I'm sure. I'm just glad there's some time to get stronger." He pulled away from her and resumed his pacing.

"Have you thought about where you'll go?"

"I've checked out Tucson and I think I might like it there. It seems to be a good idea to leave California and it's not too far to the border. Few academics from the East go there, the heat is dry, and I think I'll be able to find a job and get my credential. There's a university."

"Christ! You *have* been stirring! You'll probably have to kick the Montessori habit. Too easy to trace you if you stay with it."

"That part hurts, but I can work with children in that way without using the name. I'll find something."

"Right you are. Why have you ruled out this huge state?"

"I haven't. I'm going to take a trip down the coast in the spring to see what it looks like. Except for Big Sur, I've scarcely an idea of what's down there. L.A. is out."

"You can't be sure of that. Who could ever find you in that mess? And it'd be a cinch for me to visit."

"You will visit?"

"Damn right! Christ! Imagine seeing you and the kids without gumshoes, phone taps, court snoops, Family Disservice folk, and NO DAVID! Let's go out for wonton and celebrate. Tomorrow I want you to sit at that typewriter and write down all the things you can think of that you'll need to do to get this thing planned, and while you're at it, you might make a few behavior resolutions for the new year. It's not going to be easy keeping your wits about you in all the divorce negotiations. You can't blow it, higher stakes this time. That fuckin' Cohen, what a waste of money!" Jack kissed her and let his hands wander over the skin beneath her shirt. "O-o-o-o," he groaned, "to have a happy Giershe again, laughing, tan, healthy, dispensing a magnanimity of sound all around."

Giershe typed *Behavior Resolutions for Giershe Kinnard 1965*, and immediately, like flies around ripening fruit, thoughts of her decay buzzed, crowded down to her fingers:

1. I shall not speak of Kinnard vs. Kinnard to attorneys or to Jack.
2. I shall not bow down to Grief.
3. I shall keep my temper.
4. I shall convey to Elizabeth, Harry, and Molly my deep gratitude for their help.
5. I shall help Berkeley Montessori find a new site.
6. I shall share my training with all seekers.
7. I shall look outward at community and world.
8. I shall tell no lies except to protect myself and Jack.
9. I shall not be jealous of Jack's time with Andrew, nor depend on him for interest and enjoyment.
10. I shall remind myself each day that I am a Mother, a Teacher, a Daughter, a Lover, and a decent human being.
11. If Gloom claims me, I shall withdraw from human company until I can greet others with a smile.
12. I shall support myself, drive my own car or walk, do my own washing, hem my own skirts, fix my own meals and eat them.
13. I shall not read legal documents of the past.
14. I shall call Olivia and Tony each Sunday evening and keep the conversation lively, loving, and short.
15. I shall take exercise—long walks or dance—once a day, until my body is again capable of expressing the delight of existing.
16. I shall learn to play my Autoharp.
17. I shall post this list and check each day's progress.

She yanked the list from her typewriter and looked around the room for a place to display it. Hanging on the front door was a small gold-framed mirror. She tacked the white sheet to the right of the mirror with four gold thumbtacks. She resolved further to look into that mirror several times a day to examine the face she took through the front door. Did the mouth pull down like Harry's? Did the eyes broadcast sorrow? Was it a hunted-animal face? Did the hair bounce and shine? Were the cheeks rosy from exercise, or blotched with inner disorder? Was the jaw set in hatred, or was it soft and supple like the jowls of an alert beagle? Was the neck smooth and flexible, or taut strings attached to a marionette head? She vowed to adjust the picture each day until she could walk outside wearing a mask of inner harmony. She would appear to be what she was not, until she made flesh out of thought.

She sat down again at her typewriter and rolled a new white sheet into place. She straightened her back and typed:

OPERATION POWDER

1. Invent a new name.
2. Apply for Social Security card under new name.
3. Acquire driver's license under new name.
4. Invent plausible employment history—résumé, uncheckable.
5. Explore employment opportunities in Tucson and southern Calif.
6. Think about acquiring false or borrowed college transcripts.
7. Disguises? Dye hair?
8. Invent family history—names of mother, father, residence, birthplace.
9. Acquire false birth certificate, or forged affidavit of birth.
10. Research missing-persons literature at library: Who searches? How do they conduct a search? What media are used? What mistakes made?
11. Maintain documented and publicized decoy intention to remain in Alameda County area: job contracts, public statements in speeches or panel discussions.
12. Reassure family I'll stay in area.
13. Press Conn. and Calif. attorneys for divorce settlement giving me children in Calif. at earliest possible date.
14. Get job and save every penny.
15. Talk with Jack about above plans and then destroy list.

She pushed back her chair and tried to stand up. Pain streaked down her spine and through her shoulders. Her right eye twitched, her throat ached, and there was a knife war in her head. She let herself sink down onto the sunny rug, her spine on the floor, arms outstretched, palms up. She opened her thighs to let the sun enter her. She tried to think of herself as a system of pipes, all the faucets open and gushing forth black liquid, draining, emptying. She slept.

>>——>

Early in 1965, the bills from good and bad attorneys were dispatched from Berkeley, San Jose, and New Haven. The totals were impressive and

Giershe realized, perhaps for the first time, that she had learned to lean up against Bill or Cohen without reckoning the cost of each minute of their time. She wondered how many years she would have to work at full salary before her present, not to mention future, legal debts would approach glorious zero. It occurred to her that perhaps one of the reasons there were so many missing persons was economic. If the debtor vanished, the bills would sit in a mailbox somewhere until the new tenant threw them into a garbage can. Would this hurt Bill or Cohen? She didn't want to think about that. With an almost voluptuous pleasure, she stopped opening bills.

By mid-January, she found herself in a battle with Time. She hid from it, danced around it, pleaded, "forgot" her watch when she left the house, put clocks in the closet, burned calendars, tried to sleep ten hours a night, and Time leaned against the fence, sucking straws. Time liked to turn around and amble back to 1964, 1963, 1962, 1960 (Tony's birth), 1958 (Olivia's birth), and especially enjoyed the company of a little girl who could roller-skate, ice-skate, walk on her hands, play an accordion, do a jackknife, tap-dance, do the splits, was a demon jacks player, could ride a horse bareback, converse with dogs, cats, horses and birds, and had never heard the word "vagina" or considered that her own uterus would ever be put to use. Ages eight and nine, that's where Time liked to stroll. Oh, what a time it was! An unending quest for grace in space! She was neither girl nor boy. The girls didn't want to pole-vault and the boys didn't care to choreograph Hungarian dances to a scratched 78 recording on a windup phonograph, but there was always a companion ready for the effort of the day; and if, as sometimes happened, the families in the neighborhood snatched away all accomplices, it was good to be alone for an afternoon and learn all the words to "Strawberry Roan," or "Methuselah Lived Ten Thousand Years Ago, There's Hardly Anything in the World He Did Not Know." Giershe told herself it was unhealthy, even somewhat crazy, to drift backward into a world where Commerce, Economics, Government, Church, Law, Marriage, Divorce, and Sex were irrelevant. She chided and scolded Time, commanded the slippery enemy to remain with her in the present, whereupon there was a rush in her head, a dizzy flight past her, and from far off in the distance came the wailing, circling questions. When would she see the children again? Would she *ever* hold them again? Was there anyone who could help her? Would the children prefer a life with David? Was there something about herself that was visibly insane, something seen by judges? Would she ever teach children again? Was Jack growing weary of loving a loser? Was Operation Powder a mirage? Was her existence an illusion? Had she invented Olivia and Tony? Was she one of Berkeley's deranged eccentrics, tolerated by the authorities because harmless and out of touch with reality? Was there a secret about herself which everyone knew but did not tell her? Perhaps the children were dead and all the litigation was a grieving mind's escape into metaphor.

Begging Time to stay with her, she crowded the hours with duties, errands, meetings with Montessori groups, appointments with realtors who might know of a possible site for a school, and jobs. She spent more hours than were necessary surveying black families in the ghetto for a market-research firm. And if Time had been in step with her all day, after dark, when all the children were asleep, all the daddies home from work, when it was twelve or one A.M. in Connecticut, Time died around her. It lay in state in her living room, its ghost filled the children's room, and the bed where she lay each night with Jack seemed weighted with binding sheets, white and coarse-grained. They were mourners at Time's funeral and swallowed whiskey in hot milk because they could hear no footsteps.

MOLLY GAVIN'S DIARY:
FEBRUARY 6, 1965

> Giershe stopped in with a plan. She talked with David and he *agrees* to send the children out here this summer if we put up a $3,000 bond. We consented, then began to worry. She might be tempted into trying to disappear with the children, with God knows what results! And my tooth collapsed—now I *am* a mess!

February was the month of Divorce Granted. Hammering out the details of a two-state divorce required almost as much lawyer time and Xeroxed documentation as the protracted hearing in Alameda County. Four lawyers went at the task almost full-time and the total owed climbed higher and higher, like an adding machine with defective wiring.

New Haven, Conn.
February 10, 1965

DEAR BILL:

> Our dear client has not had the courtesy to write me or telephone concerning her *private* negotiations with her husband. I haven't even studied the papers and am dictating this so that you

may have immediate access to the matter, because it is possible she hasn't even told you. After this case is over, *eventually*, I shall read *Alice in Wonderland* and believe it all to be true.

> Sincerely,
> Lewis Cohen

> New Haven, Conn.
> February 11, 1965
> AIRMAIL, SPECIAL

DEAR BILL:

I now find that "Alice" has a friend—you! Maybe I should go to Italy instead of Mr. Kinnard, and then both can play games quietly on the East and West Coasts. I'll take the children. My associate has aptly described the proposed agreement as an "illusory contract." He says, and I agree, that Giershe seems to be giving up almost everything and getting practically nothing in return. I trust you have presented the alternatives to her.

> Sincerely,
> Lewis Cohen

The AGREEMENT was stamped, notarized, dated, Xeroxed, and filed in both states, copies sent by registered mail to the parties, and thence Giershe was single, free, unencumbered, and tied with cords of steel to two identical stakes driven deep into the marble floors of courthouses in aforementioned states of California and Connecticut.

>>>—>

AGREEMENT

THIS AGREEMENT made and entered into on the 19th day of February, 1965, by and between DAVID KINNARD, hereinafter sometimes referred to as the HUSBAND, and GIERSHE KINNARD, hereinafter sometimes referred to as the WIFE:
WITNESSETH:
WHEREAS, there are two minor children . . .
WHEREAS, in consequence of disputes . . .
NOW, THEREFORE, . . .

CHAPTER TWENTY-TWO

FIRST: The parties hereto covenant . . .

SECOND: Except as otherwise provided . . .

THIRD: Husband shall not pay . . .

FOURTH: Husband shall have custody . . .

(a) During the summers, the children shall be sent to wife, and are to reside with wife until August 31st in the odd-numbered years . . .

(b) At Christmas in even-numbered years . . .

(c) Wife shall have full responsibility for the cost . . .

FIFTH: The parties further agree that:

(a) Neither shall do anything . . .

(b) Neither shall interfere with . . .

(c) Each shall at all times keep . . .

(d) Each parent shall take the children to church on Sunday and foster the children's religion . . .

SIXTH: Harry and Molly Gavin, parents of wife, have sent the sum of $ 3,000.00. In the event that Wife does not return . . .

SEVENTH: The parties understand and agree that . . .

(a) Any further litigation concerning the children is to be avoided . . . and allegations claimed to have been made by either child shall not be put forward as evidence . . .

IN WITNESS WHEREOF THE parties have hereunto set their respective hands and seals, the day and year first above written:

DAVID KINNARD

GIERSHE KINNARD

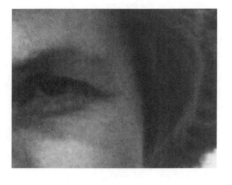

23 →

And Alice began

to remember that

she was a Pawn,

and that it would soon

be time for her to move.

"JACK, I MET A WOMAN named Shawna Flaherty in San Juan Bautista when I was down there to talk to the Montessori group."

"Yeah? Sounds like another Irish nut." Jack was sitting at his kitchen table staring at all the parts of a Sony recording system. Wires tangled around his feet. His reading glasses sat on the end of his nose. He banged them down on the table. "Fuckin' Japanese. I pay an arm and a leg for a system which is supposed to pick up whispers from every corner of the room and we got *nothing* today! I'd like to know what I'd do if I knew nothing about electronics. Oh God, I'm tired! Plug this into that socket over by the big lamp. Watch out! Watch the wires on the floor."

"She offered me her college transcripts." Giershe plugged in the cord and sat down on the floor to await further instructions.

"Hey, that's better. I'm getting some results. The fuckin' directions were wrong. How did you happen to be discussing college transcripts?"

"We weren't. Shawna and I went out to dinner after the lecture. We were talking Montessori and she broke in with 'Where are your children?' and I told her—briefly—and the next thing she said was 'You can use my transcripts if you want to.'"

"How old is she?"

"Young. In her twenties, I'd guess."

"That's not going to work."

"Well, I have a choice of Dianne's deceased mother's transcripts—too old—or Shawna's—too young—or my own somehow doctored to disguise the name."

"Why would someone go all the way through college and then give away her transcripts? Doesn't she need them for her own life?" Jack stood in front of his kitchen table sorting wires, two around his neck, one tucked into his belt, another under his right foot. Giershe laughed.

"You look very nice that way."

"Answer the question."

"I asked her, but she looked out of big blue eyes and changed the subject. I guess she's crazy. Lots of Montessorians are crazy. They don't calculate costs the way other people do."

"You might not need a transcript. You may have to forget about teaching. Now don't get SAD! Is this Shawna trustworthy, or don't you know?"

"I didn't trust her with anything. We only talked a few hours and mostly about nursery education. If I teach Headstart this summer, she wants to be my aide, without pay."

"Is she rich?"

"No, it's just that she has to put in time with a Montessori teacher in the classroom before she gets her diploma from England this summer. Jack, aren't you hungry? It's nine o'clock. Sherry on an empty stomach gives me a headache."

"Pull that plug and help me get all this shit into the boxes. There's cheese and crackers in the kitchen. Fix some for us and then later, after I've asked you a few more questions, we'll go out for wonton." Giershe staggered dramatically towards the refrigerator, clutching her stomach and groaning. "I don't think it's the sherry that's doing you in. Every time we talk about Operation Powder you piss and moan. Christ! I wish I had the opportunity to cut bait and run with a new identity and Andrew tucked 'neath my wing."

"So you say. I got my new Social Security card today in the mail, and tomorrow I'm going to apply for a driver's license under that name." She brought a plate of crackers and Camembert to Jack's desk. He stopped fiddling with wires. They stared at each other.

"Wait a minute! You *didn't* have Social Security send mail to your apartment address here?"

"I did not," she replied with precision. "I have a general delivery address under the new name." He hugged her and licked her face. She tried to hug back so fiercely he would hurt.

"You *are* thinking! You're getting strong! I love you! My love, are you going to introduce me to the new lady?"

"Her name is Cathy Heathcliff!" Jack pulled away from her.

"Giershe, now listen to me—"

"No, it's Lyndall Bennett. Okay?"

"Lyndall. Why Lyndall? Why not a name more like the one you have already? You don't want to look blank when someone speaks to you. Bennett is good. Nice and flat."

"Elizabeth and I used to change our names every time we plotted an escape from our parents. Lyndall was one of the names we fought over."

"Your childhood was filled with inconsequential trivia and fluff! No wonder you're so fucked! While I was wondering if I'd starve, you were choosing names for imagined exits from a secure home or running around tap-dancing or riding horses. You've had *no* preparation for the life you've led or are about to lead. I'm surprised you didn't write Social Security and tell them you needed a false name and identity—please send me a card." Jack put his hands on her bottom and squeezed. Giershe knew he was proud of her. He seldom scolded unless he knew she was feeling somewhat pleased with herself, and at such rare moments, he kept his hands on her, mixing touch with taunt, scowl with smile.

"I didn't choose my childhood or my years with David. They just happened to me. I began choosing— *Choosing*—what a funny-sounding word for the act of taking a direction. You have to puff out the ch-ch like a train going somewhere." She abruptly lost interest and pulled away from Jack.

"Come back here. My hands on you aren't going to drain your effort. There, that's better. Now, you were saying, when did you begin to choose?" His hands moved gently up and down her back and he pressed his lips to her neck.

"Jack! I can't think when you're so close. I have to be across the room."

Jack swayed their bodies towards the bed.

>>———>

Roma, Sunday

DEAR GIERSHE,

We are now settled in Roma. Our address is: viale Tor 33, Roma. The telephone number is 476313. If you want to phone, either do it person-to-person or write in advance saying when you'll be phoning—otherwise you might pay $12 for the privilege of exchanging mutual incomprehension with our Italian housekeeper. Also, if you phone, remember that our time is nine hours later than yours.

The splendid traveling bags with goodies enclosed were awaiting us in New York. I told the children you had made them. Both kiddies loved them and they looked very brave and venturesome, ready for anything, as they trudged up the gangplank with the gaily colored corduroy bags on their arms. The various objects in the bags have done yeoman's service in amusing them on shipboard and since.

David

>>———>

MOLLY GAVIN'S DIARY:
MARCH 28, 1965

Giershe's had an offer for summer Headstart with black children, and Berkeley Montessori is using one of her speeches for a printed brochure. It's long, but they want it. Ended the day with Harry most satisfactorily. We are wonderful!

CHAPTER TWENTY-THREE

Roma, 26.III. 1965

DEAR GIERSHE,

The apartment is extremely nice. The rooms are light and cheerful, with the typical Roman high ceilings and tile floors; the furnishing is pleasant, if undistinguished. There is a bedroom (for the children), a living room (which I use, in the evening, as a study, and, at night, as a bedroom), a kitchen (which has a table where we eat all our meals), and a dining room (which the house-keeper Gina uses as a bedroom). The bathroom has both tub and shower, inexhaustible hot water, and acres of green tile (as well as a washing machine). . . .

David

On April 18, at four A.M., Giershe rinsed her hair in Roux Chestnut Brown. Before looking into a mirror she combed out the tangles and tried to push stiff clumps into the loose style which should fluff around her face; she stared morosely at the brown stains on the wet towel. Her scalp itched and an unpleasant chemical odor clung to her skin. Her fingers were brown.

While waiting for her hair to dry, she opened the front door and stood beneath the yellow porch light; she stared at the rusted black Ford with its yellow-beige trunk lid. Her faithful mechanic was taking care of Andrew, and while she certainly didn't want him to case the coast of California with her (she had difficulty using her own brains when his were available), she would have liked him to kick the tires, test the oil, and kiss her good-bye. She turned off the porch light and closed the door silently. As she turned away from the door, a face appeared in the gilt-edged mirror. Frightened, she looked behind her. Seeing no one, she turned back to gaze at the reflection of hard white lines cutting deeply past her mouth, dark deep-set eyes ringed in black circles, and a thatch the color of compost hugging her head. She tried to poke fingers through the mass but the clumps of monochrome clown-wig hung together like spaniel ears. She ran upstairs to the bathroom and turned on the basin faucets full force, found the cider vinegar in the cabi-net, dumped half a bottle into the water. She hugged herself, murmuring, "I want my hair back, my shining hair. I want it back. Please. I don't need to change. Freak! Clown! Please let it rinse out. It says so on the bottle." She plunged her head into the rich familiar smell of vinegar. She rubbed until her scalp hurt and the water turned brown and cloudy. She cautiously rubbed hair between her fingers. A faint squeak. She combed hair down over her eyes, and yes, a little golden light in the brown. *Oh Jack, sneak away to say good-bye, send me on this first journey of* deliberate *lies with a recitation of the Boy Scout creed, help me hold on to what I want to become!*

It was five o'clock and she had to stop bleating and get going before the neighbors took their showers, kissed wives good-bye, and emerged from doors. She covered her head with a blue wool-challis scarf, tucked her turtleneck into her jeans, snapped her suitcase shut, and, halfway down the stairs, heard the front door open. Jack! She didn't want to see him, not now, looking so dumb-scared with freaky hair paling her crazy face.

"Giershe?" he whispered from the hallway.

"Go away! You shouldn't have left Andrew. I'm just about to leave."

"Giershe—what . . . ?"

"I *know* it's a mess!" She tried to push past him to the front door.

"I didn't say . . . But why did you do it? You don't need . . ."

"NO ONE ASKED FOR YOUR OPINION! Go away! I'll be late." Her voice shrilled in the hush of sleeping families.

"Sh-h-h-h." He backed up, away from her, as she kicked the suitcase towards the door.

"*Why* did you come? *I'm* doing this, not *you!* I've got to do it my way. Go. Go. I don't want to see you." She felt cold and her words came into her mouth like ice cubes, hurting her teeth. Jack's blue eyes turned gray. He opened the door.

"Good-bye, Giershe. Drive carefully. I'll see you when you get back." He let himself out onto the porch. She tried to follow, stumbling in her haste. She watched him run down the driveway, away from her. She tried to call him. "J-a-c-k!" A hoarse whisper. If only . . . his arms around her . . . the shurr-shurr of nylon jacket . . . so many times.

>>>>>

Giershe turned left, drove three blocks, left again onto the divided highway, and in five minutes the Ford joined the freeway stream of traffic going south to San Jose and beyond. Drive on, drive to adventure. Practice the parting, the empty bed. Imagine two hostages beside her. Memorize her employment history, invent realistic detail. Where was her husband? Her ex-husband was it? Vanished? Dead? Divorced? Lyndall Bennett, born in New York City? Oh, that must have been interesting. Yes, but she moved in childhood to California. She would be alert and trust to luck. Long-range plans had never worked out, and nothing in her future was likely to demand as much wit as cross-examination in a courtroom. Meanwhile, she was a wanderer searching for a place of plentiful shadow. She felt confident she would know at once when a refuge surrounded her. Probably near water with seabirds circling overhead. Simple, lazy folk, forgotten town, trees and flowers. No culture, no university. A movie theater and four gas stations. Somewhere.

She concentrated on glimpses of sea foaming on the shore, the fog hanging low on the horizon, the birds gathering far below, dancing forward as the water receded, dipping their beaks into wet sand. They fluttered up with the waves, and a lone surfer in black pushed out past a heaving swell, studying the power of water. She had never seen a surfer, had scarcely thought of a life so silly, but suddenly she loved that human being who tried so hard to understand an alien element. She would have to learn to live without Molly and Harry, Elizabeth, or gentle hands traveling over her skin. The skill would come gradually. She would grow accustomed to a phone which never rang, a mailbox with no letters, an address book filled with useless names. Facing front, with furtive glances over her shoulder, was a habit she could learn, like roller-skating on a rough sidewalk. Habit would cover her nakedness, replacing a skin she would leave behind. Already she felt new, eighteen years old and on her own, her feet conscious of gravity, again aware of nature's press on a body light with float and drift.

>>>——————>

CHARACTERS
Secretary
Personnel Director: BILL ANGLEMAN
Interviewee: LYNDALL BENNETT

SCENE: *Buenasombra, a town south of Santa Barbara, north of San Diego, the Pacific Ocean to the west, mountains to the east. Downtown office of Buenasombra School District, Personnel Department.*

Lyndall sits at a desk in the outer office. She stares at an application form. She is very calm, dressed in feminine white blouse with puffed sleeves, black-print gathered skirt, stockings, black Capezio sandals. Her hair is freshly washed, soft medium brown with golden highlights. The outer office is wood-paneled, with framed children's paintings in bright primary colors attractively displayed on two walls. A magnificent palm occupies one corner. Mr. Angleman's office door is closed. It is 9:30 A.M. Sun shines through the window behind the secretary's desk. There is no dust.

SECRETARY: Mrs. Bennett, if you've finished your application, Mr. Angleman can see you now. He has a board meeting at ten.

(She smiles warmly and opens the door to Mr. Angleman's office. She places the application on his desk, waits for Lyndall to enter, closes the door behind her. Bill Angleman stands up and puts out his hand to shake Lyndall's hand. He is alert, tall, about thirty-five, very handsome. His hair is sandy brown with fashionable sideburns; he is slim in tailored beige officer pants, dazzling white-and-blue-gingham long-sleeved shirt, blue raw-silk tie with silver tie clasp, and silver buckle on a narrow black belt which fits just so, setting off narrow hips atop fresh, eternal-press trouser legs. He points to a leather chair and reseats himself behind his desk. He places horn-rimmed glasses tentatively on his nose and smilingly inspects Lyndall's application. Lyndall sits down and gazes around the room. A fresh breeze blows gently through the open window; grass, purple petunias, and blue sky are visible from where she sits. Mr. Angleman's desk is tidy. In-box, out-box. An ivory figure of a Buddha. A large brass ashtray (clean). A white telephone with light flashing)

ANGLEMAN: *(He removes his glasses and places her application on the desk in front of him)* Well! Let me see, you've driven all the way from Berkeley? I'm from the San Francisco area and I don't think a day goes by that I don't miss the fog and the *energy* of that place. It is beautiful here, but it's a little too easy for my taste. But you didn't come all that distance to talk of my preferences. *(He glances at her application)* I wouldn't have thought you were into your thirties. Thirty-five. It's hard to believe. *(He stares at Lyndall, speculatively. She offers the appropriate feminine response, a delicate smile)* Well! Tell me something about yourself. You have two small children and you want to teach?

LYNDALL: Yes, I'm moving here for the health of my little girl, who has too many infections up north. I must work to support them. I have a background in . . .

ANGLEMAN: Montessori, I see. I used to be in private practice, in psychology, and I always promised myself I would find out more about the Method, but haven't taken the time. Let's see, B.A. from the University of Pennsylvania; my, you've traveled around. That makes for better teaching. And a Harlem kindergarten for a summer. Very interesting. How did you happen to choose Buenasombra?

LYNDALL: The name. What *is* a "good shadow"?

ANGLEMAN: I don't know how the town got its name, but idiomatically it means "good luck" and the first settlers probably also liked the trees. It's pronounced with the s sounding like z. I've been here five years and I still enjoy hearing the natives say the name, the lazy, sleepy sound. (*He melts his brown eyes and looks softly at Lyndall*)

LYNDALL: Yes. I need to work, and I plan to stay a long time. I've heard that you're searching for teachers to work in Buenasombra's ghetto. It's hard to believe this town *has* a ghetto.

ANGLEMAN: Oh my, yes! We keep it across the tracks—ha-ha—and most of our present teachers don't want to go there to teach. The work is challenging. Do you like challenge? (*Melted eyes again*)

LYNDALL: Yes, I do. I would consider myself very lucky to work with Spanish-speaking and black children. They need so much.

ANGLEMAN: I like your attitude. Let me tell you the district's needs. (*Lyndall listens, nods, waits*) Miss Bennett . . . Lyndall. I feel confident we shall meet again. (*He extends his hand to Lyndall and holds on to hers too long*)

Roma, 1.V.1965

DEAR GIERSHE:

. . . Both children have made fantastic progress in learning Italian. Of course, Olivia has the advantage of being able to read, so that the visual can reinforce the auditory, whereas Tony has to depend on his ears; also, Olivia gets two hours a week of Italian at school, but (for reasons which I don't fully understand) the kindergarten group gets no instruction in Italian. . . .

The bambini have seen far less of Italy than I should have liked—a combination of weekend bad weather and minor sicknesses. . . . To be sure, children view the world of European Culture through different eyes than those of an adult: for Olivia, the concept of "olden times" begins with Pericles and continues, without much differentiation, down to my childhood or even down to the period just before she was born. . . .

In general, Archaeology is usually more satisfactory than Art. To be sure, they needn't make the Grand Tour before they are five and seven . . .

"I can't read this letter! Don't ask me to make the effort!" Jack stuffed the letter in its envelope and threw it into his wastebasket.

"Don't throw it away. I want to save it. Who knows what use I might find for it some day?"

"It's no good for toilet paper. It's Corrasible Bond, nonabsorbent. I don't know why you read them, you know what he's trying to establish. A purity of purpose beyond criticism. He'll convince all the boobs easily. But his intention is not what stops me. It's the BOREDOM! David has always been boring. I've never been able to figure what the ladies see in him. He has a kind of oily good looks and he *concentrates* on the lady he wants. Is that it? You liked that, didn't you?" Jack scowled at her and didn't wait for an answer. "Yeah, you liked it for a while. Women are so fucked they don't know the difference between concentration and abuse. That's what they cry about and beg for—'Pay attention to me, you bastard!'—and then when you pay attention to their mewling selves, they think there's something wrong that you don't have anything better to do with your life. And that's where David wins. He's got all of Western Civilization, which he flashes as something fine to do, and yet he fixes his big gun on the little woman. She falls for the crap, he has his slave, or slaves. Christ! That stuff about 'olden times.' I'll bet Olivia has as much notion of Pericles as you do! Andrew at least knows that *everything* before his birth was olden times. He knows everything, doesn't he? He wouldn't change a diaper but he's an authority on visual and auditory learning? How the hell does he think the human race has learned language? Sure as hell not by reading! To be sure . . . to be sure. What an asshole! The whole world is an underground cemetery and we're all walking on top for a while. Maybe he'll get throat cancer!"

"Am I a slave now?" Giershe plucked the letter from the wastebasket and placed it in her purse.

"All but. No. One-tenth slave, one-tenth free, and the rest don't know. You don't seem to learn as fast as other people, although I'm also retarded. Our whole generation has been imbecilic. The war, Freud—it'll be a miracle if any one of us manages to pull the cord before he's smashed on the rocks below. But *you*, you're the only one of us who will somehow arrange to experience the fall and live through it. You seem dementedly determined to learn only from experience. You have a romantic attachment to original pain. At least *I* saw so much misery when I was a child that it seems wise to try to avoid it."

"And when did I first fall from the Path of Righteousness? she asked, with folded hands and adoring eyes. The glow widened and the wind ruffled his white beard. The Voice, when it sounded, seemed to come from above and behind him, and she bowed her head. . . . " Giershe folded her hands and tried to make her eyes look outward like the mother's photograph of an Air Force cadet who'd been called to his Reward. She crossed her hands over her chest and bowed her head. Jack grinned.

"Okay. That's enough. I guess I deserved that. But since you ask, just pick a date. *Why* did you go to Europe with him? Why didn't you stay in Europe when he returned? You had a good job and were having fun. Or in 1956, when you came on out to California to get away from him, why didn't you *stay* away? Why? I've always wanted to know, always. Can you answer me?"

His manner had become gentle, appealing, yearning for lost years. Giershe sat down on the floor beside his chair. She pulled his hands from his lap. There was a rough spot on his left hand and he liked to peel off the skin while talking.

"Pick a date—1956. All right, in that summer I *almost* didn't go back. And you're going to groan aplenty when I tell you the *profound* consideration which tipped the scale. I stared at myself in the mirror and concluded that no one would ever love a thirty-one-year-old woman, that it would be one-night things, that I would die of loneliness."

Jack gaped at her and yanked his hands from her grasp. She sat back on her heels and stared up at him as he began pacing the room.

"Women! I love them, they interest me, and every woman I've known has about as much ego as a gnat. They don't know where they're going or what to do with their lives. The more you love them, the less they believe it, and if you insist, for their own good, that they develop what potential they have, they think you want to get rid of them. They're all equipped with safety-through-failure devices which activate whenever they're threatened with self-determination. I refuse to believe they are *natural* slaves. They've been screwed up by US somehow. God, it's a lifework just to rehabilitate one female! Just look at you. You've no right to sell yourself short, to doubt your beauty and talent, and now, nine years later, I won't risk asking you whether anyone could love a forty-year-old woman because you'd give me the same shit. What difference does it make if some man loves you? Men have loved you plenty and what has it got you? Happiness? Direction? Security? Where would *I* be if I sat around worrying the question of whether anyone will love me, does love me, will continue to love me? I'd be packed away somewhere, to be sure." Jack stopped talking and stood in front of her. He gazed down at her, his eyes sunk back into his skull, his full lips closed in tired indifference.

Giershe stretched out on the floor to watch the hummingbird visiting the plumbago blossoms. The odor of dew on grass mingled with dry, sweet whiffs of carpet cleaner. The telephone, with cotton stuffed around its bell, buzzed. Probably Molly wanting to know why she hadn't called or visited in how long? Two days?

"Hello?"

"Is this Mrs. Lyndall Bennett?"

Blank.

"Oh—yes, yes, this is she."

"This is the Buenasombra School District Personnel Office. Mr. Angleman would like to speak with you. Hold on."

"Hello? Mrs. Bennett?"

"Yes! Hello, Mr. Angleman! It's good to hear from you."

"Yes. How are you? Back in God's country?" His voice was hearty and vigorous.

"Oh yes. I'm fine. It's a splendid day here."

"Mrs. Bennett, I'm afraid I have bad news for you. I've made a few calls on your application, and I can't seem to connect with anyone who can verify any of your employment history. I'm still trying to reach Dianne . . . what was her last name? The one from Harlem? I learned she's returned to San Francisco, but no one knows her forwarding address. We have other applicants and I'm afraid we're going to have to let you go inactive unless you can get better information to me as quickly as possible."

"Yes, I understand. The kindergarten in Connecticut, did you try them?"

"Yes—there's no listing under that name. Of course, I understand that private schools come and go pretty fast, but I suggest you do some checking and zip another résumé to me soon as you can. In the meantime, we'll close our activity. I'm sorry."

"No—no—don't be sorry, I understand. I'll do that right away, Mr. Angleman. Thank you for calling." The room was tipping.

"Good-bye Mrs. Bennett. Nice to have met you."

24

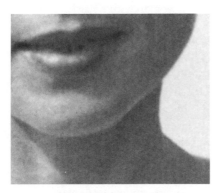

"I quite agree with you,"
said the Duchess, "and the
moral of that is—'Be what you
would seem to be,' or, if you'd
like it put more simply—
'Never imagine yourself not to be
otherwise than what it might
appear to others that what you
were or might have been was not
otherwise than what you had
been would have appeared to
them to be otherwise.'"

I N JUNE, GIERSHE KILLED Lyndall Bennett. It was an easy death. After all, the woman had existed for only a few hours in Buenasombra and for but a few minutes, faded and distant, in a telephone call, Bill Angleman on the lifeline. In her brief life, she had acquired a driver's license and a Social Security card, which were cast into a city garbage can in Berkeley. She would linger a while, filed in Washington, D.C., and Sacramento's Department of Motor Vehicles. The photo was blurred—"Oh, sorry"—a woman with a scarf around her hair. No fingerprints.

By June 15, Giershe had a new Social Security card in the name of Candida Lawrence. Jack thought she'd never remember to answer to "Candida," but that "Lawrence" was proud without being kooky, with an English dignity.

"I don't suppose you'd care to explain why, of all the names in the English language, you've chosen one which will cause everyone to wonder what fairy tale you popped out of?" Jack placed the blue-and-white card with red numbers to the right of his galleys and continued to read.

"I'm not going to talk to the back of your head, and anyway I have to meet Shawna at school. She's going to help me set up the environment. We *open* in two days. God, I'm so crazy-nervous." She tried to touch the floor with her knees together, unbent. She let her arms hang loose. Jack pushed his galleys aside.

"Okay, you have my full attention. Most of the women I know can touch the floor. I wonder why I can't. Do you want a sherry? Hey, you're not going down to Lincoln at night, are you?"

"It's hours till dark and Shawna is coiled for romance. I use her when I can get her and at eight-thirty she has a date."

"I'm ready for an explanation of 'Candida.'"

Giershe lay down on the floor and stared at Jack's tennis shoes.

"You could say that I like Candide, especially when he says things like 'WHAT A CHAIN OF TERRIBLE CALAMITIES!' He's such a simpleton, who continues to seek his happiness even after discovering there is a 'horrible deal of evil on the earth.' He plans to take care of his garden and that's the only plan I have. I don't expect to understand my outcast state, and I fear bitterness and cynicism more than death. The name will also serve to remind me to walk twice around the world before uttering a candid remark. Okay?"

Jack pushed himself from his desk. He stood up stiffly and groaned loud-ly. "'WHAT A CHAIN OF TERRIBLE CALAMITIES!' I like that. I must remember to use it." He placed his feet together near Giershe's bare toes, and bent forward slowly. His fingers stopped in the air, at least twelve inches from the tops of his shoes. He pushed, groaned, and gained an inch. He collapsed onto the floor beside her.

"Pretty soon the muscles will stretch and you'll have it." His sherry breath warmed a spot on her neck; his fingers dug beneath her bra until a hand covered one breast.

"It," he whispered, "what will I have when I have it?"

"Flexibility! Satisfaction!" The hand left her breast and unfastened the snap on her jeans. "Jack, stop! I told you I have to meet Shawna."

"It will only take five minoots." A joke. Giershe rolled away from him and stood up. She adjusted her bra and refastened her jeans.

"If it ever took only five minoots, I would feel just like a . . . cantaloupe. I'm becoming a *person*, following *your* curriculum, and this *person* is meeting Shawna in twenty minutes at Lincoln School." With arms akimbo, she scowled down at his mock-hurt eyes, his white teeth clamped together in pain.

"Oh cruel person, Giershe!" He rolled on the floor and clutched his fly. "What shall I do with my poor member! Oh—oh—cruel!"

Giershe laughed. It was all right. She had said no for a reason. Perhaps she could learn to say no for no reason. "Put it in a plastic Baggie in the freezer until tonight. Good idea?"

"Oh groan, groan, now she's getting uppity, cruel and uppity."

"You have five minutes before I go out the door. Is there anything you wish to *say*?" He looked very uncomfortable lying there on the floor, his hands slowly massaging the swelling in his pants. She slipped a pillow beneath his head.

"Oh thank you, kind lady. Yes, I want to know why 'Lawrence,' as if I didn't already know."

"You can't know, because I don't. I'll give you as many reasons as I can think of in five minutes. First, because he's so inconsistent. A misanthrope who wrote thousands of letters. A recluse who hated to be alone. A champion hater who wrote about love. Obsessed by sex and perhaps impotent. A wanderer who wanted roots. A pacifist who quarreled with *everyone*. Hated Christianity and wanted to be a messiah. Liberator of all women, prickly and contentious with those who loved him. He worshipped the sun and wrote about the darkest places, that void between two human beings—"

"Stop! I get the idea, but I don't understand why you want to wear his name. If you want a literary handle, Hawthorne wrote a nice little book about adultery. Why not—"

"I thought of that, but Lawrence makes me feel good, all that energy and fury, demented and wise, and anyway, 'Olivia Lawrence,' 'Tony Lawrence'—good names. I have to go. I'll see you tonight?" She bent down to kiss his forehead.

"Maybe, maybe not. Christ! Of course I'll see you tonight. I'll call you after dark to see if you got home safely."

>>>>>

At midnight, Giershe wrote:

SIMULATIONS FOR SUMMER 1965

1. Act *as if* July and August are all the time I will have with Olivia and Tony until summer 1966.
2. Teach Headstart class *as though* I am hoping for recommendations from the principal. In August, ask principal for letter of recommendation.
3. Consult with Berkeley Montessori about their new school site, *as though* I hope to become one of their teachers.
4. With Tony and Olivia, behave *as if* they will be returning to Centerville at end of summer. Do not lie to them. Avoid discussion.
5. Act *as if* I intend to fulfill verbal contract with S.F. group. Sign a contract if offered one. Urge a decision over summer.
6. Telephone Bill Peaceman and thank him for all he's done to make present arrangement possible. Tell him I intend to abide by it. Tell Cohen same.
7. Pretend with Jack that I'm not afraid. Don't let him know that leaving him seems impossible.
8. Borrow money from family. *Pretend* that Headstart funds had to go towards rent, utilities, lawyers' fees. Turn Headstart funds into cash. Make power of attorney for Elizabeth so she can cash final payment.
9. Impress Shawna with necessity of acquiring *as-if* demeanor.
10. Practice an attitude of sorrowful resignation, act *as if* I know what I'm about.

REMEMBER: It is true that sometimes the thought flashes through my brain: "Wasn't I out of my mind then, and wasn't I all that time somewhere in a madhouse and perhaps I'm there now."

— *F. Dostoyevsky*

At one A.M., she searched for a safe place to hide her list. At one-fifteen A.M., she tore it into tiny yellow jagged pieces and walked to a neighbor's garbage can. She lifted the lid carefully and poked the pieces to the bottom, beneath wet garbage.

>———>——>

At three-thirty on Wednesday afternoon, Giershe climbs the stairs in her apartment. She opens the door to the children's room. For seven months, the door has been closed, except now and then, when she thought she might try to remember their faces, or smell their absent bodies. She opens the windows. The yellow curtains flutter. A circle of ants around a dead moth on the windowsill. Two mattresses with yellow-and-orange madras covers lie on the floor. Olivia wants a canopied bed like other little girls. Tony wants what Olivia wants. Mattresses on the floor for children who make transcontinental, transoceanic trips between parents. Mattresses can be transported easily, on top of a '49 Ford when the mother moves across town, to another city, seeking employment or reduced rent. Shelves made of bricks and boards. Olivia helped sand and varnish. When was that? Not here. The children have never been in this room. They have slept in jail, in a room with twenty-five beds, and in Roma, on shipboard in berths, but not in this room. Margaritas in blue glass vases would help. But let them pick the flowers and choose the vases. Paper, pencils, crayons, paints, paper on the shelves. An easel in the corner, one of Olivia's "big design" paintings still clipped to its surface, curled, faded. Leave it there. Olivia likes to remember. Lego, Tinkertoys, flashlights. What does Tony like to do now? His music box, the one with the see-through top which Harry made for him, is dusty. Let him dust it. Will he play with it now? It was funny when he gave it back to Harry because Harry wouldn't let him remove the glass top and touch the mechanism. Forget the room, they will fill it with stuff from school, books from the library, rocks and shells from the beach. With quarrels and friends and deep night-breathing. Take a long hot bath. Wash hair. Put on something pretty for them. Put aside thoughts of school, be a mother.

>———>——>

Six-forty, California time. Giershe and Elizabeth stand inside the beige metal barrier marked No Admittance. Elizabeth puts her hand on Giershe's shoulder. "No sign of them yet." She looks worried. Does she know something she hasn't told her sister? "No one has come down the stairs yet. They'll probably bring them off last. Maybe they have to wait for the stewardess."

Wind and fog chill Giershe's cheeks and nose, and her orange cotton dress feels cold against her chest. Why hadn't she remembered to wear a sweater? A stewardess appears in the oval doorway. She turns her head and smiles into the interior of the plane. She holds out a hand to a small figure.

"I think I see them! Giershe, they're here! Olivia! Look this way! Where's Tony? There, dragging behind Olivia. Wait, Giershe. Dammit, we're not supposed to . . ." Giershe is walking through the swinging gate and is halfway to the stairway ramp. The stewardess, holding Olivia's hand, is letting her set her own cautious pace. Tony is stumbling over his own feet and clutching Olivia's skirt. Both children are lugging blue flight bags which, though small, seem to be pulling them down the stairs. Giershe stops ten feet away from the stewardess; the wind wraps orange cotton around her hips. She stares at Olivia—too thin, eyes too close together, clumps of curling brown hair covering her forehead, a sleazy gray-white turtleneck tucked partially into the elastic waistband of a brown something that looks like the stuff they put in Goodwill giveaway bins. And her knees, balls atop white knee socks. Only the feet look like Olivia. Dainty white socks in shiny black patent-leather shoes. Her Sunday shoes for the special trip in the airplane.

"Olivia! Sweetie! And Tony! Oh, you are here!" Elizabeth crouches at their feet and Giershe watches Olivia shift her body away from the stewardess and lean against Elizabeth's knees, the faintest smile, first to her aunt, then up towards the grinning stewardess.

"You are Mrs. Kinnard?"

"No, that's my sister. She's . . . Where is she? Giershe!" As Giershe walks towards the little group, Tony stares up at her. He gives no sign of recognition. He turns away and carefully places his satchel on the ground. He sits on it, his pudgy hands between his knees, one foot in high-top brown oxford tapping the ground. He is wearing gray trousers, a white shirt, and a blue suit jacket. His hair too short, scarcely a curl, the face round and solemn. What did she expect? That he would burst from the plane and run to her arms? That Olivia would shout "Mommy!" and come running down the ramp, golden brown hair swinging in the wind, eyebrows neat and arched above sherry eyes? That wearing a dress they loved would make her known to them? Instant Mommy off a hanger?

The stewardess smiles. "Good-bye, Olivia and Tony. You were good passengers." She walks back up the ramp, her heels clicking on metal stairs. The children ignore her. Giershe's knees are quivering. She puts a hand on Elizabeth's shoulder and lowers herself unsteadily.

"Hello, Olivia."

"Hello, Mommy. I'm glad to see you." She leans against Giershe's knee.

"What did you say? I can't hear you. A plane just took off."

Olivia puts her arms around Giershe. "I'M GLAD TO SEE YOU!" She giggles and hugs. Giershe pushes the bangs off her forehead and kisses her cheek.

"I'M GLAD TO SEE YOU TOO!" They laugh together, just being silly. Giershe looks over Olivia's head to see what Tony is doing. He's watching with interest, the foot still tapping.

"Hello, Mr. Tony, where's your tongue?"

Tony places the palm of one hand beneath his chin, his elbow on one knee. Something about the posture reminds her of David. What other pieces of David are locked inside his muscles? Genetic? Acquired?

"I left my tongue on the plane. We'll have to go back and get it."

"That's right, Mommy. He talked all the time, even when people were trying to sleep. And wouldn't stay in his seat. He wouldn't give me the window when it was *my* turn." Her eyes fill with tears.

"Come on, everybody. I'm parked in a ten-minute zone. Do you want me to carry your bag, Tony?" Tony stands up and hands his bag to Elizabeth. She holds out her hand to him. He puts his hands behind his back. "Okay, but follow me closely. I don't want to lose you in this crowd." Elizabeth moves quickly through the travelers, Tony walking fast behind her, Giershe and Olivia, hands together, treading on his heels.

"Gina *made* him hold her hand. He *hates* it! She was MEAN!"

"Are you hungry? Did you have supper on the plane?"

"We had supper, but I don't know if it was supper. We didn't like it. We drank all of the milk. They gave us straws. We've had a lot of straws. Mommy, you look pretty. Are we going to your house?"

"We sure are! But we have to cross a bridge first, and I think we'll stop somewhere for a hamburger. Elizabeth and I haven't eaten yet." Elizabeth unlocks the car door and places Tony's bag on the backseat.

"I get to ride in the front!" Olivia yells.

"No, me!" Tony pushes in front of her.

"I'll sit in back," Giershe says. Some things haven't changed.

"I think we can all get in front. Let your mother in first."

Giershe climbs in. Both children try to get into her lap. Olivia shoves with one shoulder, Tony slides into place and pinches Olivia's bottom with a fist trapped under her weight, perhaps accidentally. Olivia howls.

"Simmer down. You can take turns. Tony first in my lap because I haven't said hello to him yet and you right beside me." She puts her arm around Olivia. Tony faces front, his head pressed against his mother's chest. He picks up her right hand and kisses the fingers, slowly, deliberately. His head gives off a scent. Perfume? Hair goop? He always did know how to make love. Her hand grows warm and moist as he presses his lips down, then lifts, down again. They start across the bridge; Elizabeth points out the sights. Tony wraps Giershe's arm around his waist and squirms in her lap until his back is against the door and he can look up at her face.

"Mommy, where were you?" he asks.

"Where was I? When?"

"When you weren't there. Where were you?"

"Oh, you mean when you were away—in Italy. I was right here."

"No, not *that* time. You got on the plane but I couldn't find you. You were there but I couldn't *see* you." Giershe looks at Olivia for help.

"Oh Mommy, he means when they let us out, and we got on the plane and went to Father. He asks all the time, and we tell him ALL THE TIME, and he just doesn't want to listen."

"Oh—I understand. Let me see if *I* can remember. The judge let you out on your birthday and we had a birthday cake, and then we went to the airport, and you got on the plane and went to Father."

"*You* got on the plane *with* me. I remember." He is talking slowly, watching Giershe's face.

"I don't remember getting on the plane. I wanted to go with you, but I didn't have a ticket. You can't get on a plane without a ticket."

"You could ask Father for a ticket. He has money for tickets."

What tense is he in? Where has he lost himself? Tony squeezes her cheeks. She opens his hand and kisses the palm.

"Mommy! Did you go to my school to find me?" Faster now, insisting on an answer.

"What school, Tony?"

"The one in Italy. You remember? We had to get into a little bus and Gina made us stand still and wait. You could come to the school and see me?"

"Tony, Mommy didn't go to Italy. I *told* you that so many times!" Olivia is outraged, but there's an edge of tolerance in her tone, as though her brother is not responsible and one must go easy with him.

"Tony-baloney, do you know where you are now?"

"I'm here in your lap."

"Where were you yesterday?"

"Yesterday? I think I was on a ship." He looks puzzled.

"Good. And before that? Where were you?" Giershe holds her breath.

"Before that . . . I was still on the ship."

"Perfect. Where did you live before you got on the ship? No, wait—was I on the ship?"

"You didn't see me?"

"No. Was I there?"

"Olivia, was Mommy on the ship?"

"No, Tony. Just Father, and you, and me."

"I was not on the ship. Before you got on the ship, where did you live, my snuggly friend?" Tony traces her nose with his finger.

"I think . . . I think I remember. I lived way up in 'partment. And Gina lived there, too. But she took us away. 'Livia got a bad burn and I found a cane for her. She cried and cried and she had a BIG bandage and Father didn't come."

"They screamed at me to watch out for the hot water, but it was in Italian and . . ." Olivia starts to cry.

"Okay. That's enough remembering for now. Olivia, show me your leg." Olivia pulls her sock down below her ankle. A tear catches in the golden hair of her skinny shinbone. "I don't see any marks left at all. It looks like they took good care of you."

"They made me stay in bed FOR TWO WEEKS and I couldn't go home and they wouldn't even let me walk to the BATHROOM!"

"An' Gina had to carry her to the toilet and Gina STINKS. P.U."

Elizabeth laughs. "Tony, roll down your window and give the money to the attendant."

"Me! I get to do it! Tony's sitting in Mommy's lap so I get to give the money."

Giershe sinks back against the seat. *They have come home. They are here touching me, quarreling, exactly here, in this car. We can all stop remembering. How curious it is. Tony believes that his memory is mine, and mine is his, that memories overlap. Dear boy, I hope not.*

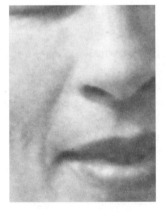

"With a name

like yours,

you might be

any shape almost."

THERE'S NOT MUCH that I remember about August. I know I didn't miss a day at school, but I can recall little that we did with the children. My hand trembled when I tried to demonstrate the Pink Tower. I couldn't place the centimeter cube atop the tower without its dancing off onto the rug, which made the children laugh, and my dry cheeks burned with shame. There was a little boy who was there every day. He sat at his table and stared at the electric clock on the wall. The minute hand clicked backwards, then forwards to the next minute mark. He was as skinny as Olivia, and he sat with bittersweet-chocolate arms resting on the white Formica tabletop. The top had golden flecks. His fingers were long and dry-brown; he exposed his pink palms as though someone had just said to him: "Let me see what you have in your hands!"

Each time the click sounded, his eyes opened wide and he said: "Theh it go agin. Theh it go agin!" Always twice, and a shiver in arms and shoulders. I tried to interest him in tabletop work. Towers, small blocks, number chains, puzzles. Two fingers would pick up a block and then set it down again. He lodged himself at his table all summer, and for me, he became metaphor. I couldn't stop thinking of his vigil, and often—in a car, in bed with Jack, while kissing the top of Tony's feverish head—I would see his frail figure in the space behind my eyes, shivering away the minutes I had remaining.

I studied Olivia and Tony as though they were foreign texts without footnotes. I didn't want to feel myself responsible for Olivia's malaise and reserve, or Tony's balkiness. I let Elizabeth, Harry, Molly, and Jack announce the sins of David—"leaving them with that woman," "hauling them all over Europe," "not being there when they needed him." Et cetera. They talked it up and I sat silent, knowing they couldn't cast off my shame at mucking up my life, and theirs. Had I not had The Plan, I believe I would have given the game to David that summer. Returned two children to sender in August, withdrawn from my job. Died, perhaps. Certainly I was not sustained by love of my offspring. When they talked of their life in Italy with Father, or their toys back home in Centerville, I wanted to stop their mouths and sandpaper the parts of their brains where these memories lived. I pretended interest and tried to change the subject. They must not know the hatred which fueled me.

Shawna and Tony began a love affair that summer. They teased, played tricks on each other, cuddled, and spent many hours in "discussions" which ranged from arguing about what Bigfoot was doing at that very moment to whether there was life on other planets and, if so, what kind of life, and when would it come to visit Earth? Shawna didn't distance herself from her love of Tony, as would any other young woman who presumably had a few other things on her mind. If Tony's demands on her were unreasonable ("But why *can't* I stay at your house tonight?"), she gave it to him straight: "Because I have another friend who is this night going to be with me. That's why."

"Then you could have *two* friends overnight."

"But if I have two friends overnight, then I have to divide myself between two friends, and there's only half of me for each one, and I can't decide whether to cut myself down the middle or at the waist, and it's a terrible mess, either way."

"Mess?" Tony looked scared.

"That's right. MESS!" Shawna hugged herself.

"Well, I've got a good idea. How about if I go to sleep with Mom *half* the night and then she wakes me up and takes me to your house and your *other* friend goes home? Does he have a home and a mom?" And so on.

Olivia and I liked to go to thrift shops to look for incredible bargains in clothes, toys, a pretty remnant, or to pass the time until dinner. Tony hated the smell of the shoppers and the garments ("They *stink* like Gina!"). One afternoon, while Olivia and I are absorbed in searching for a black anything for a thin child who thinks she looks "divine" in that color, Tony thinks up a trick. He's being pesky because Shawna is not with us, and I give him a dime and tell him to go next door and buy some peanuts. He returns with the peanuts and begins running up and down the aisles, ducking beneath the clothes, spilling peanuts on the shoppers' feet and plaguing Olivia.

"Tony," I say, "why don't you go outside and watch the people? We'll get through faster if you stop pestering us." He tugs at my shoulder purse. I know he likes to wear it and I let him take it with him. I watch him jiggity-jog towards the front of the store, one fat hand patting the bag. Peace. We find a black filmy blouse with tiny rosebuds embroidered around the neck. Olivia is very happy. We idle our way towards the cash register. Tony is fiddling with the doorstop. There's no purse in sight.

"Where's my purse? We want to pay and get out of here." He looks up, pretends to think, just like Shawna, with one finger pressed to his temple.

"Oh—it's sitting out in the traffic."

"Where?" I ask, going along with his joke.

"Out there." He points to the busy intersection—a stoplight, commuter traffic from all directions, cars honking, traffic cop blowing a whistle, pedestrians—and I catch sight of my purse in the middle of the crosswalk, legs stepping around it, people pausing, then moving forward again. I run from the store, unpaid-for black blouse in my hand, feeling a crazy glee at such a joke! Tony and Olivia tell each other the story of the purse in the crosswalk while I wait in line to pay. We are a family. We are enjoying. Then metaphor slugs me and I see my identity, tiny and inert, trapped in traffic. I press my purse hard against my stomach.

Tony again. Another day, in a pet shop. There is a talking mynah bird named Fred. He sits in a cage which hangs from the ceiling. There's a sign attached to his cage. Olivia reads it aloud for Tony:

"My name is Fred. I am a talking mynah bird. Mynah birds are native to India, Burma, and other parts of Asia. I eat plants, insects, and worms."

Tony walks around the outside of the cage and Fred turns on his perch, pecks a yellow foot, lifts a shiny black wing, and cocks his head at the little boy. Olivia has found a cage of gray tiger kittens and we stick our fingers through the holes. They nibble and lick.

"My name is Tony. I live here now but sometimes I live in Connecticut." We turn our heads to watch the bird.

"My name is Fred. What's your name?"

Tony presses his face against the cage. "I just told you. My name is Tony. Do you live here?"

"My name is Fred. I'm a mynah bird." Fred tries to peck Tony's nose.

"I *know* you're a mynah bird. I asked you if you live here."

"I'm a mynah bird. Birds can't talk." Customers are smiling benignly. Tony's voice gets louder.

"You can *too* talk! You have to listen! I'm four years old. How old are you?"

"Tony, mynah birds don't understand what you say. They just say any old thing," Olivia explains. Tony stares at Fred.

"Where do you live? Where do you live? Where do you live?" Fred asks.

"I *told* you I live here, and sometimes in Connecticut."

"May I have this dance? Birds can't talk." Fred lets out a sound like explosive laughter. Tony puts his fists on his hips and scowls at the bird. His audience respectfully waits. He times his act (always) and although he seems to be still ignorant of the nature of this bird's speech, something new comes to the dark eyes. A look of complicity? With Fred? With all of us? He slowly jigs around in a circle, a soft "Tum-te-tum-to-tum" marking the beat. He stands still and stares at Fred.

"Can birds talk?" he asks.

"Birds can't talk," Fred answers. Tony smiles. He puts his hands on his knees.

"Let me think. . . . What's your name?"

"My name is Fred. May I have this dance?" Fred squawks. Tony dances again. The customers laugh and clap their hands.

On the way home, Tony says: "I want to tell Father I talked to a mynah bird. Mommy, can I tell Father?"

"Of course. When he calls on Sunday. But you have to remember. I'll forget." I don't feel so happy anymore. I don't want to give David anything. Olivia tries to whisper something in my ear. "Say it out loud, honey. I can't hear you."

"When I talk to Father . . ." she begins softly.

"Yes?"

". . . he's a mynah bird." I take her hand in my lap. She leans her head against my shoulder.

>>>>>

Late at night, while waiting for Jack, I sometimes practiced being Candida. The scene was often a waiting room, perhaps a train station or a personnel office, a doctor's examining room, a place where I sat and awaited the calling of my name. The door opened. "Mrs. Lawrence? Candida Lawrence?" I would respond quickly, without fluster, and would leave my seat. "I am she. I am Candida Lawrence," and I would take steps to greet the caller. That's where the scene stopped, the required action having taken place. Sometimes I was Teacher and my pupils called me Candida or Mrs. Lawrence, or the principal ordered me to his office on the intercom.

Although I could type and take shorthand, spell and construct a sentence, I never visualized myself in an office. "That's just another of your notions you have to jettison," Jack scolded. "Teacher has a visibility you must avoid, even if you could risk having fingerprints sent to Sacramento or wherever they send them in Arizona. Private schools pay peanuts. Christ, there must be some office which would pay for your skills and not drive you crazy."

I didn't argue with him, nor did I tell him that when I wasn't thinking Teacher, I might be considering driving an ice-cream wagon, or selling vacuum cleaners door-to-door, or greeting tourists in Taos, or helping a lawyer research his documents (I knew a lot about that!), or garden work (about which I knew nothing), or anything at all (almost) as long as it was away from office machines, politics, and the "girls" who labored in the vineyards of men.

Jack was a planner and he wanted to help me think about my financial future. He wanted me to choose my site for resurrection after studying a government publication with graphs showing economic health, in decline or recovery. I assured him I'd been to the library, though I hadn't, and that books and pamphlets urged the Southwest for jobs, healthful climate, and everything else one might need for a new life. Sometimes I would look up at him at six in the morning, an hour before Tony and Olivia might awaken, and as he kissed me good-bye, I'd think: "Today I'll go to the library. Jack's right. It's practical. I'll ask Shawna to stay with the kids for a few hours. But what if someone sees me looking at a gorgeous volume of *Arizona Highways?* I can't check out the books because someone might inquire of the library staff what that felon Giershe Kinnard read in her last weeks in town. Maybe I could look in Molly's and Harry's books when they aren't home. Oh, surely it's not that important. I'll find a job. Someone will buy my services, me, Candida." And he'd say: "You're certainly thoughty this morning."

"Just sleepy. See you tonight."

My simulations of that summer required concentration on being, doing, saying, listening, the controlling of myself and my encounters with others, always with an awareness of an invisible audience whose responses were unknown, and perhaps did not exist. I was a life-size blown-glass figure cast in the shape of a woman, still attached to the artist's breath, hot, flexible, apparently transparent; but when one tried to see through to the other side, one saw distorted reflections of oneself. I could not assume that David was three thousand miles away, hatching Western Civilization for a summer collection of sweaty youth, or pursuing fresh ardors, or hunched over his typewriter, or putting his Centerville house in order. And after the end of Whitfield's summer session in early August, I began to imagine I saw him—scurrying around a corner, leaving a restaurant through the kitchen door, behind a hedge in front of my apartment, his face at the window of my bedroom (twenty feet above the ground)—and one night I felt compelled to wrench open the trunk of the car, sure that I would find him curled around the spare tire.

David's form—his odor and light—were easy enough to detect, but what about his agents, those people I would not recognize but who knew which woman to watch, suspicious actions to note, the conversations to remember and transmit, which post offices to guard, when to inspect the contents of a garbage can, and whose telephone to tap?

Behind my locked door, I studied deceit and began to understand its uses. Jack said: "Christ, you middle-class types! You're all so crippled—learning to lie at age forty!"

>>>>

On Tuesday, August 10, Shawna flew east, London her destination with a stopover in New York City. She was scheduled to return to the United States in three weeks and somehow find her way to Tucson no later than the end of August. I'm quite sure I did not discuss this or any other plan with her, and if I felt curiosity about her motivation or her acceptance of a not-quite-necessary and apparently unexamined role in Operation Powder, that natural urge to understand surfaced much later and has continued down to the present moment at my Olympia typewriter, as I try to order events.

Sometime before Shawna left town, I must have packed her car with boxes I intended to take on our journey, but I don't remember taking the boxes from the back of my closet where they joined less important possessions destined to remain behind. Each time I opened the closet door, I saw three stacked cartons with O.P. in black Magic Marker written on the sides facing outward. I can't recall carrying them downstairs, or putting them in my car for the journey to Shawna's bungalow.

I don't remember making the choices—this will go, that will stay—or finding a time to pack when Olivia and Tony would not be home. I know the principle of selection was need, present and future. Sentiment and nostalgia were routed.

The logistics of my departure from Berkeley took form in meetings between Shawna and Jack. Where? When? Who said what and then what happened? "But Jack, how did it get decided that I would drive Shawna's car to Tucson? Was it her idea?"

"Christ, I don't remember. Anyway, she's willing. You sure as hell can't drive your car, or mine, or Harry's. You can buy another car in Tucson. You know, that dame is a flibbertigibbet, as my mother used to say. Five minutes with her and I'm looking for an exit. What, pray tell, do you see in her?"

"Mystery, which she cultivates. Density, comedy. And we share a preference for the society of children. She has many devoted friends her own age but they all seem to have small children and she's constantly borrowing them. She'll say, 'My friend Ian,' and I never know whether the friend is her size or Tony's."

"I don't think I want to hear about it. I have to find the time somehow to drive her to the airport tomorrow night and then drive her car to San Jose and park it in my colleague Hank's garage. He's gone out of town. On Thursday evening, after your open house, I'll post myself somewhere near the freeway and watch to see that you and the kids get on your way to San Jose safely. You'll spend the night at Hank's."

"I'll put the Ford in the garage and Shawna's car in the driveway."

"Right. I'll see you at Hank's, after my union meeting."

"And Wednesday evening?"

"I have to spend the night with Andrew. Muriel's off with some creep. I'm going to put us both to bed at six o'clock and sleep twelve hours. My heart's been jumping around and my hands shake until I have to sit on them."

We had been whispering in my kitchen, and abruptly there was an end to words. While I stared into the ritual milk in the yellow enamel pan, Jack pressed his front to my back, his arms around my waist. The stove top blurred and I tried to swallow my lump. Jack didn't mind if I wept—he rather liked it, if there was a reason—but I was afraid to start, afraid I'd cry as long as arms were around me and there was a tongue to lap the tears.

>>>———>>>

Olivia and Tony gathered flowers, squabbling over which weed was "still pretty" and which flower would "stay open" in a hospital. Olivia insisted it was four o'clock all the time in hospitals, so they should pick four-o'clocks, a lot of them. I snipped off all the margarita blooms on the bush and knew they would stay open and pull sunlight into Molly's room. Tony clumped all of his weeds in his brown fist and asked: "Do they look pretty, Mommy? Do they?"

"Yes, Tony, they look pretty. Molly likes weeds and if you give her some, when she gets better she will look them up in a big book and tell you the names."

Olivia arranged her assortment in her hand—green nasturtium leaves at the back, then pink and white four-o'clocks, pale pink ivy geranium near her thumb. "I *know* she will like my bouquet," she said.

On the drive over to Molly and Harry's house, the children sat stiffly solemn, staring at their gifts.

"After Molly goes to the hospital, can we visit her?"

"No. They won't allow children under fourteen to visit," I answered, and then remembered that we would be crossing a border within forty-eight hours.

Harry opened the door as Tony was pushing the doorbell. "Stop that, Tony! Stop right now," he hissed. "Your grandmother is very ill and is sleeping!"

"But she wants to wake up now because I have a bouquet for her," Tony stated firmly. He looked into the old man's face for permission.

"You, Tony, why would she want to see *you?* No, you may not wake her."

Tony and Shawna had been practicing insults on each other, and this was a big one, but Tony seemed to have learned that it was good policy to exempt Harry from the good manners required of other people. He started for Molly's bedroom. Harry grabbed his arm. The bouquet spilled to the floor.

Whenever I felt angry at Harry, which was often, all the angers of the past seemed to catch fire inside me, as though banked under reason's ash and awaiting one match to ignite. On such occasions I either let the fires burn up everything in sight or escaped into comedy. I seemed to have no control over which way I would go. I stared at his red, crooked fingers pressed into Tony's plump flesh. I wanted to grab his blue-veined fragile arm and apply the same force. Would it crack and tear? Would I care? It looked like fire this time, but suddenly I felt a pressure in my left hand and Olivia's body leaning against my hip, and I could see Tony squatting down in front of his weeds, methodically arranging them, taking more care this time, ignoring the big feet below his elbow. He was calmly getting himself ready to do what he'd come to this house to do.

"Harry"—my voice sounded quite nice, soft and low, rather grown-up— "Olivia and I will take a peek into Molly's room. I can't take the children to the hospital and tomorrow night I have an open house and won't be able to visit. We won't stay if she's asleep." I moved past him with Olivia's hand in mine. "Come quietly when you're ready, Tony."

"Do what you want! You always have!" Harry would now go to the kitchen to sulk.

I turn the knob and push. The gasping rhythm of an electric humidifier in the corner, Molly's hoarse, irregular breath coming from an open mouth on a white pillow. Pink light, pink face, pink bed jacket, pink velvet cord tying back the long hair. How long it is! Molly doesn't appear for company with her hair down. A pink hearing aid lies quietly on the nightstand. Molly's left hand rests on top of a sheet which covers a body which seems much too slight. She had once been fat. When had she become so small? Have I not looked at her in thirty years? Her engagement ring, with diamond set in old filigree gold, has slipped over a blue-tinged knuckle, an inch away from its partner ring. I lean over the hand and by grasping the raised diamond between my thumb and forefinger, I succeed in narrowing the distance between engagement and marriage. This is all I can think to do. Her thumb moves into her palm and pulls the rings together, tucks them in neatly, but she doesn't open her eyes.

Olivia and Tony are next to me with feet pressed together and bouquets held close to their chests; their faces are reminiscent of Kennedy's two children, alert beside his casket, their energy folded inside. Molly's room is too small, too much furniture, too many pictures of people who have been dead for years. The bed, a cherrywood four-poster, pushes against the thought of movement, and is scarcely big enough for one tiny, sick woman, let alone man and wife. Is this where Molly and Harry are "wonderful"? In what manner does he come to her? Does he ask? Molly's underclothes are hanging on a hook just inside the open closet door. She wears a brassiere, a corset, a chemise, and garters for her support stockings, even when she gardens in jeans and a loose blouse. I didn't like to hug all that, like hugging a dress form, and would try to nuzzle my face in the soft skin of her arms which always smelled faintly of powder. The powder smell is in the room, mixed with the perfume she has worn all of my life. An iridescent blue-stoppered bottle which sits on her bureau contains this scent. I have often pulled out the stopper and dabbed some behind my ear. Is her perfume like her furniture polish—original, or if not, passed down from woman to woman? I know the recipe for the furniture polish which perfumes their house (equal parts mineral oil, turpentine, and vinegar) and I have a sudden need to learn the origin of the unchanging substance in the blue bottle.

"Molly? Molly?" I place my hand on her hand. It feels like dry leaf. She opens her eyes and quickly draws up a hand to cover the cold sore on her face. She tries to lift her head. I don't want her to try to move. Where's the ambulance, why isn't she in the hospital? Has everyone gone mad? What insane time schedule is being paced out in this museum? Why hasn't Elizabeth insisted or Harry demanded?

"G'she? Not at school?" Her voice is thick and deep.

"Molly, don't try to talk." She turns her head towards her hearing aid, and her right arm lifts from beneath the sheet. "NO, WE ARE STAYING ONLY TWO MINUTES." Tony places his bouquet on the sheet near the end of the bed. Olivia puts hers nearer Molly's struggling head.

"Oh dear . . . the children . . . mustn't catch . . . wicked illness."

"MOLLY, DON'T WORRY."

"Grandma Molly, I picked weeds for you. You like weeds?" Tony sets his bouquet closer to Olivia's.

"I hope you get well soon, Gramma." Olivia's voice is thin and anxious.

"Sweet . . . lovely . . . Thank you. You must not catch . . . outside now." Molly touches the flowers, but she is watching the children, who edge closer to her.

"Tony and Olivia, Molly is worried you'll catch her sickness and she won't rest until you leave. Don't bother Harry. Go out to the playhouse."

Olivia blows a kiss and Tony copies her. They tiptoe backwards out the door and I hear them running through the house and down the wooden back stairs. There is no place to sit down and I stand, feeling huge and healthy. Can she hear me? What is there to say? Five minutes ago I wanted the name and source of a delicate perfume, and now I want a life to continue. I want her to go on writing down the cleaning, the mockingbird's visit, the feeling terrible, the people who visit and stay too long, Harry's rages, and what plant got moved from where to where. If I cannot believe she will record my departure, how can I leave?

Molly covers her mouth with white Kleenex, but it hurts too much to cough. She lies now on her side and waits for the pain to pass. I fold a blue washcloth into a bowl of cool water on the nightstand, wring it tightly in my fists, and place it across her forehead. She holds it in place and smiles up at me. All love must move to action. There are no words. Her eyes close and she seems to sleep. I kiss her cheek, lightly, not daring to apply pressure against the soft skin. I want to go quickly. I don't want to be sucked into the vigil. I am selfish, haven't they said it often? Then let me be selfish and have something to show for it.

"Good-bye, Molly. Get well . . . please." I close the door behind me and go directly to Harry in the kitchen. "Harry! Why is she in that room? *Why* isn't she at the hospital?"

"In one hour she's going to the hospital. That's when she's supposed to go," he growls at me.

"But she is so sick! I don't understand why they haven't ordered her into the hospital long before now. What is the reason?"

"Yes! She is *so sick!* And Tony gave it to her! What could you have been thinking of when you brought him to her with that cough and fever? It's Tony's fault!" Harry is shouting and his face is so red I expect to see blood drip from his eyes. I know I can calm him easily. I must say yes, it's Tony's fault and because I let Tony come, it's my fault, I am selfish, I didn't think. That's what I shall do. I shall let Harry assign fault one more time. We shall have peace on this last day. I open my mouth.

"Yes, Harry, it is Tony's fault. Little Tony dragged himself over here to be with his grandmother, and he ran right to her and said, 'Here, Molly, have a little death! Lean down and I'll blow some on you,' and Molly said—"

"Shut up! SHUT UP!" Harry howls and starts across the kitchen towards me.

"Harry! Giershe! What a GHASTLY FAMILY!" Elizabeth is standing in the doorway. Her face is white beneath the makeup mask. "The ambulance is on its way, and I hope Molly's stuff is packed."

"Of course her stuff is packed." Harry sits on a chair and opens the *Berkeley Bulletin*. He reads the headlines.

"Good. You probably should ride in the ambulance with her and I'll follow in my car."

"Of *course* I'll ride in the ambulance with her. No probably about it." He continues to read.

"I'm leaving now. The kids and I will be home all evening. Can you call me when you get home—if there's news?" I squeeze past Elizabeth on my way out. She hugs me, and with her face turned away from Harry, her lips move without sound: "It . . . is . . . not . . . your . . . fault!" She pulls a finger across her throat. I don't know that I hurt until her acquittal verdict. I press her hand and hurry to find Tony and Olivia.

26

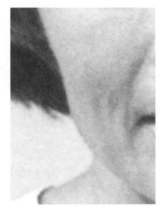

"And if I really am a Queen,"

she said as she sat down again,

"I shall be able to manage it

quite well in time."

THE ACT OF LOOKING BACK—a glance over my right shoulder as I walked down a city street, or turning around on the sidewalk and pretending to seek a late-arriving friend or a clock behind a storefront window, or, while driving, the continual shifting of my gaze from street to rearview mirror—became a habit as much a part of my nature as the sniffing of tree trunks and fire hydrants is for even the dullest of canines. On the freeway Thursday night, the rearview mirror told me nothing more revealing than that there were many cars on the road and all of them used lights to see where they were going. I tried switching lanes and checked to see if lights followed me. I watched motorists who passed me; one young man blinked his lights and held up his third finger because I was going too slow in the middle lane.

"Where are we going, Mommy?" Olivia asked.

Tony sat between us and tried to make his third finger separate and communicative.

"We're going to San Jose to spend the night."

"Are we going to sleep in a bed?"

"Of course you'll sleep in a bed. You can look through the apartment and choose whatever bed you like."

"I get the biggest!" Tony said.

"No, I do!" Olivia wailed.

"Maybe there's no biggest bed. Maybe they're all the same size."

"Can't you remember if there's a biggest bed?"

"No, Olivia, I've never been there before."

"Is Shawna waiting for us at the 'partment?"

"Tony, Shawna told us she was going to London to visit the queen. I wish you would try to remember things."

Ours was the only car to exit on Thirteenth Street, and perhaps for the first time in my life, I found an address by following directions in my head, having practiced several times, verbally, with Jack. I opened the front door, turned on all the lights, and while the children inspected beds, I exchanged my Jack-built Ford for Shawna's late-model Chevy and locked the garage door. I closed the front door behind me, set the chain lock, turned off the porch light, and let myself sink down onto the thick-pile beige carpet, my head feeling like the Grand Canyon stuffed with gigantic eyes.

Olivia and Tony jumped on all the beds and began quarreling over possession of the double bed in the master bedroom. The shrieking seemed the sweetest of sounds, but I didn't want the neighbors to be that much aware of our presence. I crawled across the carpet to Hank's bedroom. "Both of you—get your pajamas on and we'll either do eeny-meeny-miney-mo or the two of you can sleep in the same bed. How about that?"

"She snores!"

"I do not!"

"Okay. It's eeny-meeny time."

"She doesn't snore very much."

"I can watch and see that Tony doesn't fall off."

"Good, it's all settled. I'll just lie down here and wait for you to brush your teeth. Come on, get going." I stretched out on Hank's comforter and wondered if he had an alarm clock. I was ready to sleep for twenty-four hours.

"Mommy, where are you going to sleep? With us?" Olivia's question urged an affirmative.

"Oh my, that would be so nice—but Jack will be here later, after you're asleep, and I'll sleep with Jack in the other room."

Had I ever said that to them before? (Once—to Tony—I'd tried to explain—how many years ago?) Never, in three years, had Jack slept in my bed, under a roof which shaded the children, with their knowledge. Years of arriving at midnight, leaving at dawn, talking in whispers, stifling the sounds of pleasure, locking doors, putting on clothes to go take a pee, covering my nakedness sometime between predawn and seven A.M. Years of hiding a good fact from them, that their mother loved a man and liked to sleep next to him—no, not next to, *with*, joined together.

>———>———>———

In the morning, Jack departs before the children awaken. He takes a last look at Tony and Olivia. He says: "That's quite a handsome booty you've won!" I don't remember the good-byes we said, but they must have been swift and flat; the lump which formed in my throat after he closed the door was still there weeks later.

>———>———>———

Saturday, August 14, 1965: Kingman, Arizona, motel, 3:00 A.M. The children sleep, the blankets heaped on the floor at the foot of their bed, a sheet resting lightly on their small bodies. I experiment with the TV. I push all the buttons and wait, but nothing happens. I switch on the floor lamp and am able to see ON, OFF, and a dial with numbers. I push ON and wait. Nothing. It must be broken. I turn off the light and stare at the children. Dark heads, white sheet. Yellowish light from the parking lot. The box flickers and I watch people running through dark streets, shadows on rooftops, smashed glass, silent running. I turn the knob and hear:

". . . have sealed off twenty blocks. The strife called worst in Los Angeles history. . . . Fierce fighting again gripped the Negro section of South Los Angeles tonight. Officials called it the worst racial incident in the city's history. . . . There are reports that the National Guard may be called in to deal with the violence. . . . Just a minute . . . late report . . ." As each scene clicks into place, I see bodies huddled on rooftops, and uniformed men with guns held high, sprinting into crowds. I turn off the sound. One sense is enough to reassure me that no lawman in California will bother to seek a runaway woman accompanied by her two small children as long as the Watts colony is in rebellion. I push OFF and watch the newscaster grow smaller until he is a dot, then nothing.

I go to my bed, my double bed, four times, until Olivia and Tony finally stop drawing imaginary lines down the middle of their bed and threatening terrible retaliation if a toe or arm crosses over. Each time I lie down alone and close my eyes, Jack is beside me, but he isn't warm, has no smell, utters no groans, and when I move over to press close to him, there's no skin to touch and my stomach and knees develop spots of chill. It occurs to me that I am more kin to Jack than to the aliens asleep in the second double bed. I gave birth twice, but Jack gave life to me again and again, and as I feel the last of the blood-mix seeping, trickling, hot and wet, onto my cool thigh, I want to go to the bathroom and hold a tiny bottle down there, push out the last drop, cap the container tightly, and wear the essence like perfume, a dot behind each ear, until I can learn to live without.

The line down the children's bed now has several stray lumps crossing over. Olivia's leg appears to be resting on Tony's ankles and his face is pressed against her neck. Their hairs are mixed. I lift the sheet and insert myself between them. I become the line. Each child moves close to a side of me, warming, wrapping. My eyelids droop . . . the hot smell of children . . . sleep . . . sleep.

>>>

MOLLY GAVIN'S DIARY:
AUGUST 15, 1965
HOSPITAL

Today Elizabeth told us that Giershe and the children have disappeared, apparently to another country. Bitterness—our $3,000 and all we have invested in her. And down underneath, grief. But I am too sick to sort it out.

CHAPTER TWENTY-SIX

AUGUST 29, 1965
HOME

Goodmans stopped in and stayed too long. Had to listen to Harry's and Frank's analyses of Giershe's character. Sometime I must explain that I share *all* of those traits. She is a part of me. I will have to live with this grief.

AUGUST 31, 1965

Calls from Peaceman. He told Harry to call Henry Hardy. Both fear for the children. I am beginning to suffer *for* Giershe. *Why* didn't we try to get her back when there was still time? But did we have any choice?

" I call the Court of Domestic Relations

the Court of the Insoluble.

Every morning I pray that

I do as little harm

as possible."

Judge John F. Shea
New Haven, Connecticut

New York Times
May 1, 1979